Praise for Cat Bruno
The Pathway of the Chosen

THE GIRL FROM THE NORTH:

"A truly exceptional entertainment, *The Girl From The North* is author Cat Bruno's impressive debut novel and clearly documents her storytelling abilities for deftly created characters and unexpected plot twists. Very highly recommended."
— *Midwest Book Review*

"Cat Bruno has laid the foundations for a truly epic fantasy series with a vivid landscape and believable characters that you'll want to follow."
— Fantasy author EM Cooper

"*The Girl from the North* is a fantasy that you will get lost in. You will want to know what happens to Bronwen as she trains to be a healer, as she figures out who she is. You will be invested in her story. But not just her story, you will also fall for Conri. The High Lord of the Wolf Tribe, he is the key that can unlock Bronwen's memory."
— *Every Free Chance Book Review*

Pathway of the Chosen

The Girl from the North, Book One

Daughter of the Wolf, Book Two

DAUGHTER OF THE WOLF

CAT BRUNO

**PAINTED QUILL
PUBLISHING**

First trade printing January 2016

DAUGHTER OF THE WOLF

ISBN-13: 978-0692598276
ISBN-10: 0692598278

Book art by Simon Valev

Painted Quill Publishing
www.thingsfantastical.com
Contact Painted Quill: paintedquillpublishing@thingsfantastical.com

Author's Note:
This is a work of fiction. Names, characters, places, and incidents are either the products of the author's imagination or used fictitiously, and any resemblance to actual persons, living or dead, events, or locales is entirely coincidental.

Printed in the USA

For all those who continue to love and embrace fantasy, in text and in art. And for those in my own life who continue to love and embrace me, even when I'm often lost in this world of fantasy that I create.

1

Dirtied and travel-worn, the small party entered the city gates without incident; the guards were more concerned with the bag of coins that Sharron had handed them than with the dark mage who traveled with the group. To an outsider, they looked no different than many others who sought entrance to the King's City. Dressed in a fine riding suit, Caryss looked the part of a distinguished visitor, surrounded by her companions and sentinels, as was custom with any Northern lady. Despite her mud-covered clothing, her hair shone in the early morning light of the rising sun, crimson and burning.

Behind her blazing eyes lived an uncertainty masked by a silent anger. It had been nearly a moon since she last saw her foster mother, yet she thought little of the woman, and even less of the Academy. Her thoughts were often elsewhere and rarely fond ones. Yet they were her own, when little else seemed to be.

For the last moon, Caryss had neither seen nor heard from Conri, a small blessing, she thought. Yet still she could not mind-lock him from her memory, and the last encounter with him still stung, sickening her more than the babe had ever done, as if her hatred for him poisoned her. At times, she forgot that she was healer, having discarded her robes over a half-moon before. For hours at a time, Caryss rode, stroking the dagger at her waist, the images of her dead parents sharp and painful.

Her vows had become distant ones, nearly forgotten as they traveled, until the gates of the King's City had come into view.

When the King is healed, I will be free, she thought, *and I will find him.*

The morning sun was duller on the east and rimmed with fog, as thin white clouds threaded across the sky. Behind her, Caryss heard Sharron ask Aldric if all of the King's City was as gray as it appeared from a distance. Caryss did not hear his reply, for when she looked to the city, she was met with red-hued buildings, as if they had been painted in blood. Roads, too, were rivers of clay-colored mud, red and shining.

Only when she blinked did the King's City wash clean, stone and brick and wood once more.

*****

"My lady, I believe that is the palace ahead. If you look closely, you can see how it reflects both the gold of the sun and the blue of the sea, the colors of the royal family. Only members of the King's Guard are permitted to wear the blue and gold, so it becomes easy to recognize them as such."

Aldric's words cracked through the silence that had overtaken the group since they had entered the city, as they all glanced around with unhidden awe. None but Aldric had been to the King's City, and its size and splendor was like no other place in Cordisia with towering buildings and wide roads. After moons crossing through small towns and empty fields, the sounds and images of the crowded city seemed to overwhelm them, and they walked slowly, with heavy feet and wide eyes, having left their horses stabled outside the gates.

Sharron and Caryss had spent half their lives in Litusia, the small town that housed the Healer's Academy. While the Academy was home to many from all across Cordisia, the King's City was still nothing like it, and both women looked around them as if they had known not where they were. The two guards that accompanied them, Kurtis and Niko, walked a few steps ahead, while Aldric stayed behind, a dark hood pulled over his head.

It had been many moon years since he had visited Rexterra, yet Aldric knew there were many still who would recognize him. While he no longer kept wards on the others, he maintained a strong shield over himself, one that only the strongest of mages would be able to detect. Still, he walked with his head low, trying to blend in with all the people running about on the busy streets, heavy with various vendors on their way to the city square or to the piers. Around them voices thick with accents hurried on, and Aldric called out to Kurtis.

"Just ahead there will be a road on your left. Follow it until we reach the Lower Streets, which are near the piers."

As the last of his instructions left his lips, Aldric saw Caryss stumble, her boot catching on an uneven paving brick. Niko, who had stopped when Aldric spoke, reached for her, catching her before she could fall. The guard's hands were around her waist, and her jacket fell open, slipping off her shoulders. Aldric's gaze shifted to her mid-section, which she had kept hidden as they traveled. For a moment, he was surprised to notice how rounded her stomach had become, until he remembered that she was several moons with child. She talked little of the babe, yet he realized her condition was quickly becoming more evident. Before they had departed from Tretoria, Aldric and Willem had agreed that it would be best if word of the babe was not shared, yet as he once again looked at her, he realized their folly.

Already our plans must change, he thought, shaking his head.

With words just above a whisper, Caryss said, "Thank you Niko. I must do a better job of watching where I am stepping with all these people about."

8

Her words, much like she herself, were distant ones, and Aldric stepped toward her. For the last moon, she had insisted that they call her Caryss, although she offered little explanation for the change. Once, he heard Sharron asking if she would be Bronwen once again after her Healer Journey, yet Caryss had answered that she would never again be so named, telling the other Northern woman that she only recently remembered her Eirrannian name. When Aldric would have questioned her further, she had looked at him with stony, gray-green eyes, and he had said nothing.

His hands tight beside him, Aldric watched as she adjusted her jacket, pulling at it until it was again covering her stomach. Her boots were edged with mud, as was the bottom of her long skirt. He knew that beneath the skirt she wore fitted leggings, as did Sharron, as they had been riding for the last moon. Looking at her, he could not remember when last they had bathed.

Clearing his throat, he said, "Caryss, we must get out of these clothes before we make our way to the palace. There are several inns near the piers and we should have no problem finding rooms there."

Slowly, as if his words were not ones that she understood, she replied, "Of course. Is there coin still?"

Surprised by her question, Aldric stuttered, "Willem gave us plenty, and we have spent little."

For much of the trip, Caryss had not been herself, and Aldric had hoped that once they had arrived in the King's City, the woman who he had first met at the Academy would return. So far, he observed, she had not.

Looking tired and pale, Caryss simply nodded and followed her guards. Behind her, Aldric stared, then continued on, keeping his gaze on her.

Soon, they reached the outer edge of the piers, an area that ran several blocks around where the sea bordered Rexterra. Although they could not yet see the Eastern Sea where it met with the Lisania River, the smells of fish and salt surrounded them, telling them they were near. It was morning still, and although clouds still covered much of the sky, a light glow trickled through, yellowing the faded wood and brown brick. There were few places that Aldric liked more than the piers in the King's City, and, for a moment, he closed his eyes, thinking back on a time when Leorra still lived.

Loud, insistent squawking from a gull pulled him from the memory, and Aldric opened his eyes, noticing the crowded streets with people rushing about, as often was the case here. In the Lower Streets, all were welcome, he thought, recognizing some from across the Eastern Sea and others from beyond the Three Seas. Voices sung and words were shouted in languages that even Aldric did not know. He watched as Caryss struggled to keep pace with the guards.

Even though the Academy had been home to many, Aldric knew that Caryss had never before been among so many who were from so far. There were those with darker skin than even his beloved Leorra, some with the light hair and light eyes of the far north, and others still with nut-colored skin and angled eyes, having come far from the east. Near the piers, he knew, many were not Cordisian-born, and the appearance of two Northern women, a dark mage, and two Arvumian guards would cause no alarm. There was safety here, unlike the palace.

Ahead of him, Caryss walked, her head hanging to her chest as she eyed the uneven pavers. Without warning, she stopped, though they were still a distance from the inn. With little regard to the crowd around her, Caryss hunched forward, bent in half, and vomited. They had eaten nothing since arriving in the King's City, which now seemed a blessing. Beside him, she heaved, her body trembling and her breath coming in gasps.

Before he could reach for her, Sharron neared, wrapping an arm around Caryss's waist.

After a moment, her back arched and trembling, Caryss stood, wiping at her mouth with the back of her sleeve, and stepped out of Sharron's embrace. Her hands still shook as she reached into a pouch attached to her riding pants. Drawing out a small, amber-colored bottle, she uncorked it and lifted it to her nose, closing her eyes as the scent of peppermint filled the dank, salty air.

When she opened her eyes, they were wet and shining.

"Take this," Sharron offered, giving Caryss a large flask.

After several sips, Caryss sighed, "Does it always smell so, Aldric? I will never eat fish again I think."

With a quick snort, he answered, "One gets used to it, I suppose."

A look of disbelief across her pale face, Caryss muttered, "I will not be one of them. I had expected much of the King's City, but already I find myself missing the Academy."

The two guards had not realized that Caryss had stopped, and Aldric looked about for them, which was made difficult in such a crowd. When he could not find them, he hurried back to the women.

"Niko and Kurtis must not have seen us stop. Are you able to continue?"

"Not just yet. I feel as if I am on a boat and these bricks beneath my feet are swaying." With a wave of her hand toward an area with several wooden benches, she added, "Let me sit for some time. The pavers here seem to be shifting beneath me."

Aldric did not like leaving them, yet Caryss looked wan and frail, more so than usual. With a nod, he hurried off, glancing back as Sharron and Caryss made their way to a small courtyard. He knew that none in the

King's City had learned of their arrival, yet still he worried. Despite the decades-long truce between mage and Tribe, there was still no real peace between the two. And, even now, the Lightkeepers kept watch.

They were all well-trained as he himself, perhaps even more so, Aldric admitted. Without a strong ward over Caryss, a Lightkeeper could well sense the babe. He hurried then, running through the uneven streets, dodging between vendors and stalls, brushing up against several shopkeepers as he made his way to the high piers.

As he rounded a bend, he spotted the guards, deep in conversation. Niko was gesturing wildly with his thick arms, and Aldric rushed toward them across the wide street.

"Are you not being paid to keep watch?" he scolded as he neared, keeping his words low, despite the anger behind them.

With reddened cheeks, Niko mumbled, "We had thought to find you near the inns."

The men, brothers he had found out as they had traveled, were only just out of boyhood although they had the size of men twice their age. Willem had paid them well, Aldric knew, and his temper flared again at the thought.

"You would not have had to find us had you not wandered off. Now come with me."

Uncertain about how much longer the guards would be needed, Aldric said little else as they made their way back. The less they knew, the better for all, Willem had told him.

Back at the courtyard, both women were seated on a faded bench. Steps away, he watched Caryss sip from the flask, a healthy flush across her cheeks. He called out to her as a woman neared the bench.

"Heyo!" he cried.

The woman was dressed in a long, tiered skirt that hung to her feet, and, even from behind, he could tell that she was an Islander. Her dark skin looked polished and smooth under the soft sun. Beneath a brown leather vest she wore a loose-fitting, white tunic that hung to her elbows. Her wrists displayed gold bracelets stacked to the edges of her sleeves. When the woman lifted her hands, jeweled rings encircled her long fingers.

Bracelets slid down her arm as the woman reached for Caryss, chiming as if in song.

Again he called out, in warning this time, yet Caryss did not seem to hear him.

Jumping toward them, Aldric watched as the woman fell back, her brown and gold arms bent and flailing at her sides. Before he could offer aid, the woman dove to the ground, her gold bracelets clanging as her head thumped off the bricks.

When he neared, the woman's skirt was over her knees and one of her sandals had been flung under the bench. Aldric quickly kneeled beside her and lifted her head, cradling it between his scarred and thin hands. The fingers of his right hand lay near the edge of her cropped hair, and, soon, they grew sticky with blood.

"Caryss," he hissed, rocking the woman's head and staring at her closed eyes, "She is bleeding from the fall."

He said nothing further as both healers rushed to him, kneeling at his sides. The guards, having also seen what had happened, stood behind the woman until she was surrounded.

As Caryss pressed her fingers against the woman's long neck, he asked in hushed words, "What did she say to you?"

Ignoring his question, she stated, "Her life pulse is strong. She will wake soon."

He watched as her hands moved from the woman's neck to the back of her head, where she pressed squares of white linen. He knew that she was trying to stop the bleeding and said nothing else. Instead, Aldric stood, circling his hands. Humming softly, he hurriedly warded the women before placing a heavy ward on himself as well. None would be able to see them or hear them, but he could not keep the ward for long.

"You must hurry before the ward falls," he informed Caryss, who only nodded.

When she turned the woman's head to the side and lifted the bloodied fabric, Aldric gasped as a large gash, nearly the size of his finger, appeared.

"How long do I have?" Caryss asked as she covered the wound.

"I will hold it until you are finished if I must. What is it that you plan to do?"

Caryss gently moved the woman's head toward Sharron's hands. Reaching into a pouch, she explained, "If she is to live, I must stitch her. I know not where to go, so I suppose I will have to do so here."

"What if she wakes?"

Looking up at him, eyes late gray now, she answered, "Keep the ward strong. I will do the rest."

Her words were sharp and her gaze serious, and Aldric did not reply, although he did still wonder what had caused Caryss to push the woman from her.

The Islander was not a small woman, full-hipped and full-breasted, yet Caryss had thrown her as if she was a child's doll, with little effort. Another gift from the High Lord, he thought. He would question her later, Aldric decided, turning his attention back to the ward, weaving the swirling air around him tighter. Despite the raised voices of the crowd, Aldric could still hear air hissing around him, as if he was snake caller from the Far East. Once the ward was wrapped noose-like around them, he looked to his feet, where Caryss knelt, the sleeping woman still unmoving.

The woman's head lay in Sharron's steady hands, while Caryss hurriedly moved a long silver needle along the woman's hairline. When she finished, Aldric counted eight finely stitched crosses, but the Islander no longer bled.

Sitting back on her heels, Caryss wiped her hands on her dark pants, then again reached into a pouch, pulling out an amber-colored bottle. With the lid removed, she placed the bottle beneath the woman's nose as a strong scent of spice emerged.

"Hold the ward a bit longer, Aldric," Caryss called. "She will wake soon and will not thank me, I think."

As if she had heard the healer's words, the woman's eyes flittered open, blinking heavily until they finally rested on Caryss. Although unfocused, the woman gazed suspiciously at Caryss, letting her nearly black eyes, thickly lashed and outlined in thick kohl, trace the Northerner's own light eyes. Then the woman's gaze traveled to Caryss's belt, where several pouches hung.

After a moment, the woman sat up, slowly and with Sharron's assistance.

Pointing, she whispered in heavily accented words, "What is it that you carry there?"

Looking away, Caryss mumbled, "Ointments and the like. A few tools that I need when I heal."

With a wave or her jeweled and sparkling fingers, the Islander laughed, "Child, I do not mean to ask what is in your bags. You carry something far more important, do you not?"

Caryss, uneasy and quiet, looked to Sharron who shook her head, in warning no doubt.

Before either woman could speak, Aldric warned them, "Tell her nothing. You have done enough."

But the Islander was quicker than he, and, before he could move, she had reached for Caryss, grabbing her hand. "Who are you, child and why have you come to the King's City? Your kind are not well-loved here."

Again Caryss looked to him, afraid to look at the newly awake woman.

"And who would you be, mother, to ask so much?" he answered angrily, directing his question to the dark-skinned woman,

"Mother, is it, my friend?" she half-sung, sitting up further, although she still held Caryss's arm. "Have we met before for you to address me so?"

13

"It matters naught to you who I am." Aldric hissed, his words harsh as his hands whirred to steady the warding.

Dark, oval eyes watched him, laughter at their edges. Around her, the others quieted, as if she was a fabled siren of the sea. She stood then, gracefully, as if she was emerging from the sea, not from a cracked and soiled street. Slowly, she balanced herself, finally letting go of Caryss. Her height was impressive, taller than Caryss and nearly even with Aldric. Around her wrists, her bracelets danced, twirling and spinning as gold flecks of sunlight dotted her arms. About her long, thin neck was a colorful scarf, with vibrant blues and purples, reds and yellows, clean and sparkling, shockingly so in the dust and dirt of the piers. Her pale ivory dress hung to her ankles, fitted tightly across her large breasts and snug again over her wide hips.

"Have you never seen an Islander before, my child?" the woman called, looking to Caryss, whose cheeks burned red.

The woman was not smiling, but her eyes were kind and her lips curved, Aldric noticed. He would have interrupted, but Caryss shook her head, raising a hand to him and quietly replied, "Only in books."

With another laugh that carried across the bricks, the woman teased, "Do I look as if I have come from the pages?"

There was a long pause before Caryss answered, but her words, when she finally did, quieted them all.

"You look as if I should have remembered you."

None spoke, until Caryss called, pointing to the woman's thick leather braid tied about her waist, "Your pouches are of a kind with mine. Are you a healer as well?"

"Enough of this, Bronwen," Aldric hissed, using a name that had not been spoken in over a moon.

He stepped toward her, even as the ward began to shake around them.

"Let the girl be, as she is in no danger here. As you should well know, mage. Child, my name is Nahla, and I have been in the King's City for several moon years, although I am not healer-trained as you have been. But I have some skill in the art, as many of my people do, a gift from the Great Mother, it is said."

"What brings you to the city of kings?" the woman asked.

Aldric could take no more and moved until he stood between the two women. "She is tired and road-weary, and knows not what she asks, nor who you be."

"Who I am? I have already told you who I am. Nothing more or less than she."

His words grew sharper yet, as he warned, "Do not seek to fool me, not here, not in this spot. For I know more than you could guess."

More gently than he had expected, Nahla told him, "No doubt you know more. Or you would have not addressed me so. Now let us forget this discussion, for I do not think it is one that we should have here, with so many others around. Let me invite you all back to my home, which is but a few blocks from here."

"We will not follow you anywhere!" Aldric screamed, pushing Caryss further away.

"My dark brother, I think you should follow me," Nahla called to him, stepping near. "If not for your sake, then for the sake of the child you travel with. And, again, if not for her sake, then for the sake of her own child. You are far from home and know not what the King's City holds. It is not for me to question why I stumbled upon this one's path, nor why she has stumbled upon mine. I seek no answers from the Great Mother of us all, but I trust her all the same."

Looking up at him with soft brown eyes that seemed to hide nothing, Nahla chimed, "But, I have heard her, and I will listen."

"Now follow me, Bronwen, if you are so named," the woman whispered, smiling and shining, as if her Great Mother had truly touched her, draping her in rays of light.

*****

Despite Aldric's warnings, the group followed the woman from the central piers, edging the streets until they neared an unfamiliar area, even for Aldric, who still complained. Caryss had stopped listening after he threatened to drop the ward, as if she had known that he would not be able to shield them much longer.

When they had finally arrived at Nahla's bottom-floor home, the mage was pale and shaking, and Caryss nearly apologized. Yet, there was something about the woman that stopped the words. Instead, she reached for Aldric, holding his trembling hands between her own as they waited for Nahla to unlock the brightly painted door.

Into his ear, she whispered, "She will not harm us, Aldric."

His eyes blazed in reply, but he said nothing as they entered.

The space was no bigger than Caryss's room had been at the Academy, yet cluttered and cramped with trinkets large and small. Niko and Kurtis stood by the door, while Aldric trailed Caryss as she crossed the room toward a large bed, which took up nearly half of the room.

Nahla gestured for Caryss to sit on the bed, which she did after moving aside several large and colorful pillows. Sharron took a seat in the room's only chair, and Aldric stood near the edge of the bed, his face still drawn with fatigue.

When Caryss looked up to see where Nahla had gone, she realized the woman had taken to the floor. Yet, still she appeared to the healer as if she was a queen atop a throne of woven blankets and jewel-like cushions. The room itself was warmly decorated, with tapestries hanging from the walls and potted plants stationed throughout.

It was the tapestries that caught Caryss's eye with images of the Southern Cove Islands stitched and painted across them. A few showed rolling waves and clear skies, much like the beaches of Tretoria. But the ones that most intrigued her were the ones that featured the Islanders themselves, often in embrace. After a moment, Aldric's warnings finally rang true, and a blush colored her face as understanding slowly surfaced.

Nahla, who had been watching her, called out, "Am I not a healer of sorts, my child? All who come to me are in need, and some are broken. Many are sick. I do what I can for them, and they leave better off than when they entered."

Aldric shook his head, as if unable to contain the words that spilled forth from his pursed lips, "She will speak in riddles all day if you let her. You have seen who she is, now let us be gone from here."

It was clear that he addressed Caryss, and to her they all turned. Yet, she sat silently, with her chin in her hands and her eyes still on the nearest canvas. The man woven there stared back at her, as if he might speak.

Unlike the others, he stood alone, in front of an open field, high grasses behind him and a fiery orange sun overhead. Dressed all in black, and larger than any man Caryss had ever seen, he was imposing and intense, with thick, braided hair hanging down his back and over his shoulders. In his hands, he held a thick, leather whip, although there were no animals to be seen. At his hip hung a curved sword, which shined nearly white, as if made of pearls. The wide, arched blade lay exposed and intimidating, and Caryss doubted that she would even be able to lift such a sword. Across his back another sword was sheathed, although she could see little of it as the man faced the room.

Even though the whip fell to his feet, unmoving, and the sword lay untouched, he still appeared ready to strike, as if preparing for battle. His eyes, dark and guarded, hinted nothing, yet the man smiled. She could not tell which to believe.

"Do I know this man, Nahla?"

Her words cracked like ice across the silence of the placid room.

"How would you know him?" answered Nahla, and although her words had been spoken clearly, still they rang with jest.

16

"I have never left Cordisia, at least as far I remember. Yet, I recognize that man, as if I have met him."

Shaking her head, Caryss continued to stare at the wall hanging, then added, "No, that's not quite right. I have not met him. Yet, I believe I will. Yes, that is it. I feel as if I need to meet that man. Who is he, Nahla?"

As Caryss spoke, she crossed the room, as if wrapped in a mage-spell. Her words held certainty, but madness as well. Stepping in front of Nahla until she was near the wall, Caryss finally paused. The Islander watched, as if in judgment. She half-expected the man to emerge from the threaded jail, yet even her touch could not bring him forth.

Behind her, Nahla sighed and rose. "Oh child!" she breathed, "You are a strange one. You know nothing of my people and my homeland and nothing of the Great Mother who watches over us. Yet you want to meet that one? Not many of my own people would make such a claim."

Her warm words tickling the back of Caryss's neck, Nahla added, "However, I find myself believing you."

To Aldric, she called, "I am surprised that it was not you who claimed recognition, mage. Long ago, I learned not to judge what appears and mistake it for what is. Here before me sits barely a grown woman who shines with light, yet burns with darkness. And, you, brother, are nothing but dark, yet your heart grows lighter because of her."

Aldric said nothing, as he half-begged Caryss to do, and Nahla continued, "Let me tell you of my people, since you know so little of us. We are an ancient tribe, older than any from Cordisia could claim. We have long lived in seclusion, guarded on all sides by sea and sand. But even though few have ever attacked us, we have long warred with one another, and brother has killed brother in order to rule. While the Great Mother weeps at death among kin, she only intervenes when her vows have been broken."

"Is it not so with most gods?" Caryss asked, letting her eyes fall upon Nahla and thinking of what Kennet once told her of the Tribe.

Nodding, the woman murmured, "Perhaps it is so. But our vows are strong ones, and few break them once given. You have been invited into my home, which is a blessing among my people. Once inside, your secrets become my own, as the Great Mother has willed it, and so do I swear."

Bowing her head slightly, Nahla placed the fingertips of her right hand on her lips, before moving them up to the center of her forehead, then crossing over to her heart. She ended by placing her open palm against her womb. Beside her, Aldric quivered.

In a voice laced with song, Nahla continued, "I come from a long line of weavers, talented women, and a few men, that could spin nearly anything into an object of beauty." With a wave of her hand, she told them,

"All of the tapestries here were done by my blood-kin and carried with me when I came to Rexterra. Except for that one."

Her bracelets clanging as if bells, Nahla walked toward the wall where the man watched them. With fingers skilled at caressing, she traced his cheek.

"I should send him back to the islands," she purred, her gold-rimmed fingers moving toward his neck.

Caryss watched as the woman let her hand linger there, on the man's thick neck, wondering what the woman had planned.

"In the last few moons, he has made me lose coin. Many are frightened of him, and, now, when I have business to manage, I take him down. My mother's mother called him Otieno, for he carried the night with him, it was said."

Half-chanting, Nahla continued, "He would travel from village to village, as a *diauxie*, a medicine man of sorts, but not healer-trained as you are. You do not have his kind in Cordisia I have learned. For a small price or token or meal, he might mend you. But not of injury or illness. *Diauxie* are sought when all else has failed. When death is near."

With another wave, she explained more. "But, that is not all that he was, for he was once born from a line of kings. For many moon years, he trained as a warrior, and became named *Sefusana*, Prince of Swords. Few dared to challenge him, and most feared him. While we have far fewer people in the Cove than here, and only a small army, he was named commander, and answered only to the King. Then, he disappeared, with none to see him off and all wondering why he denounced his kin-right."

"From kingsman to beggar for this man," Caryss murmured.

With a nod, Nahla told her, "Aye, he chose to walk a different path. A darker path, some say. The one he still walks. He wanders the islands, and even though he is never without sword, it is said he no longer wields them. It is said, too, that he has lost his taste for blood. But my mother's mother has told me different, and swears that he hungers still, or did so when she last saw him."

"You said that few seek him out. How is it that your kin was with him?" Aldric asked, unable to conceal the doubt in his words.

Her hands fells from the tapestry as she twirled to face the mage. In a voice no longer etched in song, she told him, "Several moons ago, he allowed my mother to weave his image, which is what you see here. After she had completed it, he insisted that it be sent here, to me, even though we had never met."

"A charming story," Aldric mumbled.

"What reason do would I have to lie?" Nahla cried.

18

Caryss hurried to intervene, reaching for Aldric as she drew him away from Nahla. Into his ear, she whispered, "Trust me, please. We need this man, Aldric. *She* needs him."

Knowing that she did not need to explain more, she called to Nahla, "Once I am free to leave the King's City, I will find him."

"Child," Nahla gushed, softer now, but with a warning all the same. "You do not seek him. He finds you. And even that comes with a price."

To Aldric, she asked, "Dark brother, who is this child you have brought me?"

Not expecting an answer, Nahla walked to where Caryss stood and without hesitating, wrapped her arms around the girl, hugging her as a mother might a child. Then, she leaned down and whispered into the girl's ear, low enough that no one else could hear. After Caryss nodded, Nahla stepped around her, and gently removed the tapestry from the wall. She quickly rolled it up and then tightened it with a piece of leather that had been tied at her wrist.

Handing it to Caryss, she said aloud, "I have done my part it seems. I am but a step on the long path you walk, Bronwen, but I will help when I can. You need only send word or find me. The Great Mother wills it so. "

Caryss gently kissed Nahla on the cheek. "May your Great Mother bless you as she has done me by crossing our paths."

After a few moments, Caryss departed, clenching the tapestry in her hand as the others followed her. The smells bothered her less now and the reddish haze faded, the distant city no longer blurred. While she had been with Nahla, Caryss felt free, more so than she had in moons.

As if the gods no longer watched her.

2

After the group departed from Nahla's, Aldric secured rooms at a nearby inn, unassuming, yet clean. Few would notice them there, he had told Caryss.

It was nearly evening when they departed, having spent hours in the washrooms. Nearly all of their clothing had been replaced, although Caryss still dressed as a wealthy Eirrannian. She had pleaded with Aldric to let her wear another riding suit, but he had insisted that she don one of the dresses that Willem's housekeep Chien had readied.

The gown was long, falling to her feet and covering her Tretorian sandals, which surprised her, for Chien was much smaller than she. The material was fine, soft and smooth as it draped over her body, although the color was not one she would have chosen. It was dark, not quite midnight, but near enough. Only now, under the rays of the setting sun, did Caryss notice that the gown was more blue than black.

As she admired the delicate threadwork, Aldric approached.

"What was it that Nahla whispered to you?" he asked as they walked.

Distracted by thoughts of Litusia, she absently told him, "Nahla blessed the babe, and although her words were her own, I understood. And she told me that when I was ready to find Otieno that I should return to the piers, and she will see that we get to the Southern Cove Islands."

"Caryss, really, is that wise?" Aldric asked, trying to keep the disapproval from his voice.

"Perhaps not," she mused. "But when I finish here, doing the work of others, then for once I will allow myself a choice. I have had much time to think, Aldric, and I wonder when my life was ever my own. Even as a child, I must have been watched. For how else would he have found me? I was but an Eirrannian girl, nothing special and with no powers or mage-skill. I am a gift, little more than that."

"A gift?" Aldric stuttered beside her.

"Are there not tales from the North of sacrifices to appease the gods?"

"In generations long dead, Caryss," he hurriedly replied.

A half-smile crossed her face as she answered, "And yet still there is peace between Eirrannia and Tribe. Such peace is never without cost, Aldric."

"Who would offer such a gift?"

"I know not," she said, "But the child did not seem surprised when Conri arrived."

He reached for her then, grabbing her arm and whispering through clenched teeth, "What child do you speak of?"

In a voice she hardly knew as he own, she explained, "Myself. I have recalled much of late, although most times I do not even who I was or who I must become. The Academy was my home, but what if I should have never been there? Who is Caryss? I only know Bronwen, yet I feel less like her each day."

Aldric pulled her toward him, strongly, more than she would have thought him capable of, and held her by the shoulders. With his light eyes clear and sparkling, he said to her, "You might not have chosen this path, but you are here now and must walk it fully and freely. To hear you speak so makes me want to turn back. You have a skill that very few have. Learned or god-touched, it matters not; you are a talented healer. How dare you seek to waste it?"

Never before had Aldric addressed her so, and Caryss was startled by his words, and shaken by his hands on her.

"I am no longer Bronwen, that girl who spent half her life as healer."

"Then be Caryss. Find her path," he pleaded, loosening his grip.

"Coming from you Aldric, I find those words to mean little."

He shrugged, dropping his hands from her. "Do you think I have learned nothing? I will not let you become like me. I will not have you destroyed as I once was."

She pushed her blazing hair from her face and walked away, unsure of where she was heading, but unwilling to face the look of disappointment in Aldric's eyes. Caryss knew that for the last moon she had been withdrawn and snappish, speaking little with Aldric and Sharron. And, as their concern grew, she attempted to avoid them as much as she could. Whether it was the babe developing inside of her or the knowledge that her returned memory had given her, Caryss knew not. But she felt uncertain and less like herself each day. Her life at the Academy was over a moon gone, yet at times it felt as if she had never been there at all. Since Conri's last visit, much had changed, and with her returned memory of her parents' death, her past had started unraveling.

"I will be neither Bronwen nor Caryss if I do not heal the King, Aldric," she mumbled, to none but herself.

3

Much like any other morning of late, Crispin had been up before dawn and seated at his large desk, examining reports concerning the state of the nation's coffers. It was a job that he liked little, yet one that was necessary as the King's health worsened. His brother was little help, although, mercifully, he was occupied at the northern border, investigating a recent death among his troops stationed there.

Recently, Delwin and he had argued often, especially since their father had become bed-ridden and unable to communicate. To keep the peace between them, Crispin had taken to trying to avoid his brother, which was difficult to do when they both occupied the palace, despite its size. With his father's condition worsening, Crispin feared what would happen if the King died, knowing that Delwin had still not accepted that the right of rule should go to the elder brother. Out of desperation, Crispin had sent word to the Healer's Academy on the other side of Cordisia, seeking help.

Crispin closed the ledger that he had been trying to make sense of and pushed his chair away from the paper-strewn desk. Rising, he paced about the room, unease settling onto him. Crispin rolled his neck to and fro, stretching his back and shoulders and closing his gold-rimmed eyes in a moment of escape.

Rubbing at his forehead with ink-stained fingers, the prince sighed, "The coffers must wait."

After grabbing a large robe from a hook near the door, he raced from the room. As he walked the silent hallways, Crispin realized that it was nearly time for his evening meal and his stomach rumbled in hunger. Yet he walked past the kitchens and toward a vacant wing of the palace, one he often used when he sought privacy. Few knew the Grand Palace as he did, not even Delwin. As children, Crispin and his cousin Willem had explored all corners of the palace and beyond; a game that Delwin had never enjoyed.

This evening, he chose to exit through a back courtyard, one filled with raised garden beds filled with sweet-smelling herbs. The courtyard was used mainly by kitchen staff, and, at this hour, he knew that none would be there. Once free from the palace, he headed toward the Lower Streets, slipping the oversized robe atop his clothing and lifting the hood until his head was fully covered. The sun had not yet set, although it hung low on the horizon spreading a dusky orange glow across the bricks and stones.

As he walked, briskly and with his head down, Crispin's thoughts cleared. The night felt damp and the multi-colored cobblestones beneath his boots were smooth and slippery as he hurried along. With each step, he thought less of the crown's coffers and more of the woman. Her hands, despite the thin, delicate fingers, were strong. Her hair was as pale as snow, hanging loosely down her back and falling in soft waves. Her eyes were green, yet of a shade he could not describe, although often they seemed to be as dark as pine. Her skin, which she kept covered when he would visit, was speckled and streaked, he knew, the markings of a cross-breed. Still, Crispin thought her beautiful, yet he told none of her existence.

Each time he visited, Crispin was awe-struck by the woman, so unlike anyone else. Unlike Nicoline even. Once, during his first visit to her, she had explained that she came from the North, but was not Eirrannian. Her mother's people, she told him, were ancient ones, and while she did not know her father, she believed that he was Rexterran. Moon years before, she had come to find him, although she never had. Instead, she stayed in the King's City, rarely leaving the Lower Streets. Cross-breeds were rare, even near the piers, and she kept herself well-masked.

If he wanted to see her, Crispin had to travel to the Lower Streets, and, tonight, he had need of her and quickened his pace.

Nightfall approached, and the air turned thicker, stained with amber and red. The scents of the piers wafted on the wind as it ruffled his hood. Again, his stomach rumbled, and he remembered how he had eaten nothing since a light meal before the sun had fully risen. Realizing that he had coin in the pocket of the well-worn robe, Crispin slowed his pace and looked about, hoping to find a fishmonger or food vendor.

A group of people around a large cart caught Crispin's eye, and he wandered over to the crowd, inhaling the scent of battered and fried fish as he neared. Taking his place in line, he waited, as any other would, listening to the conversations of his people around him. When he raised his head to see how much longer he would have to wait, Crispin noticed a woman standing between two large men.

Her hair, fire-streaked, fell across pale cheeks, and her gown was a costly one. Eirrannian-born, he knew, and wealthy as well. Of late he had been too distracted to recall all that his aides told him, although he remembered something of a visiting Northern statesman. Perhaps the woman was his daughter, he wondered.

Crispin was just steps from the woman now and, with his hood still drawn, stepped closer.

"Are you kin to Seinn MacAllister?" he asked, mentioning the Eirrannian official.

When the woman looked at him, he noticed how eyes shifted shades, from gray to green. He had but a moment to look at them before her guards stepped forward.

Her hair, polished like copper, shined more vividly than the setting sun and fluttered as she backed away from him.

Following, he called, "My lady, might I have a moment of your time?"

As he asked, Crispin watched a dark-robed man approach, wearing a heavy fabric, despite the mild weather. Into the woman's ear, he whispered. He was no guardsman, yet he spoke to her with purpose and intimacy.

The prince knew that he should leave, yet something kept him there, rooted to the stoned street, as if his legs had hardened into stone or marble.

When she spoke, Crispin shivered, his body covered in prickled flesh.

"Sir, I am new to the city and do not believe it possible that we could have been acquainted previously. I'm sorry to rush off, but we have somewhere we must be."

Unaccustomed to being dismissed, Crispin addressed the man.

"It is admirable and right how you protect your lady, yet you have nothing to fear from me. Might I just have a moment of her time?"

For a moment, the two men looked at each other, and even though they both were hooded still, their eyes met. Recognition crossed the eyes of both, and they stood unmoving and unspeaking once again, the silence seeping across the stones.

It was the woman who finally intervened. "We must depart at once."

When neither moved, she looked toward the prince with curious and clear eyes, yet he knew that she did not recognize him.

The dark-robed man whispered, "We have somehow stumbled upon what it is that we seek. How strange this all seems."

Noticing her puzzled expression, Crispin asked her, "It is me who brings you to Rexterra, my lady?"

"I do not know you any more now than I did moments ago," she answered, reaching for the mage.

Crispin nearly laughed at her response, appreciating her ability to speak her mind, a trait that few had when in the presence of the King's Heir.

"Follow me," he told them both.

Pulling at the mage, the woman began to object, but he shook his head and motioned for her to follow. Crispin knew not what their presence meant, nor did he recall the mage's name. Yet he knew enough to want to keep them close.

*****

Caryss walked alongside Aldric, steps behind the disguised man, and hoarsely asked who the man was.

Without slowing his step or turning to face her, Aldric replied, "That man is the next in line to be King of Rexterra."

Stumbling, Caryss reached out and braced herself on Aldric, stunned at his words. Shaking her head softly, she tried to respond, but, after several attempts, she gave up and followed along. The girl had not been wrong, she realized. So far, the trip was far easier than Caryss had imagined it to be.

But with that ease came more worry.

*****

4

By the time that the group reached the palace, the sun had fully set, and mage lights reflected off the neatly cobbled streets. On the way, Aldric had explained why they had come. When Caryss handed him the letter that Willem had sent, the prince hurriedly read it, then tore it into pieces, which he threw into a large iron-covered drain. She had not read the letter's contents herself, but the prince asked little else of them.

The darkened sky masked their entrance as they followed Crispin past an unlocked metal gate.

"Is it so easy then to enter the palace? Surely a first-year in the mage-guild could offer better protection than an old, iron gate," Caryss stated.

"Oh, I'm sure that one could. Yet, sometimes simple is best, and really, no one but me comes to this side of the palace. Few even know of this gate's existence," the King's Heir interjected.

Her cheeks flared red, as if he had scolded her, and Caryss said nothing more. Instead, she stared at her feet, the straps of her sandals muddying as they walked through a large garden. The prince resembled Willem only slightly, Caryss thought, watching him as he led them through the courtyard. Crispin was of a smaller build than his cousin, although he too wore his hair cropped short. She thought often of Willem, remembering his promises of freedom, ones that she dared not accept.

Moments later, she asked, "Why did you not send word to Willem of the King's health?"

They were near an exterior wall of the palace when he paused. Graying stone covered by sprawling ivy revealed an unkempt section of the Grand Palace. The others were still steps behind them as he looked at her, his gold-rimmed eyes examining her. His eyes were akin to Willem's, and she did not look away.

"My cousin has risked much for me and has lost more. It has been half a lifetime since he left here, but still my brother does not forget. He lives because Delwin does not know where to find him. The risk was too great to contact him directly and the message too important. I did what I thought best."

After a moment, Caryss, unsatisfied, prodded further. "Does merely speaking against the King or his sons warrant exile in Rexterra?"

With a laugh, he answered, "Is that the story he tells? That his exile came from a disagreement with my father?"

Shaking her head, she swiftly added, "He talks little of his time here, and when last he did, we both had much wine between us. But I do recall him mentioning a fight with your brother."

The others were now close enough to hear their exchange, and, without looking behind her, Caryss knew what Aldric's expression would be. He had warned her to talk little of her past and to trust no one, not even the prince.

Crispin still watched her, paying little heed to the others, as he told her, "It was more than just a quarrel between kin. Willem had a choice: exile or imprisonment. The choice seemed an easy one. Other than that, I will say no more. Healer, perhaps you have been too long sheltered at the Academy, but you are in the King's City now. My city. Do not forget your place."

The prince turned away from her then. Caryss raised her hand, but before she could reach for Crispin, Aldric slapped her hand away, and muttered low enough that only she could hear, "Leave it be!"

Caryss nodded, holding her stinging hand to her chest.

In front of them, Crispin shoved the ivy aside and placed his hands against the wall and held them there. Moments later, a door appeared, where there once was none. The group followed him inside, although Caryss noticed looks of surprise on the guards' faces.

Slowly, the group continued through a nearly dark hallway, and, when Aldric would have called a mage-light to guide them, Crispin shook his head. Soon after, Crispin stopped abruptly and pushed open a wooden door, entering it, and gesturing for the others to follow. When they were all in the room, he slammed the door closed, leaving the room in total darkness. Before Aldric could summon a mage-light, Crispin had a large orb pulsing in his hands, which he then set on a small, round table, the light spreading a soft, moon-like glow over the room.

Caryss stood near the back corner of the room, listening with her head down as Crispin addressed them.

"You must first understand that I am the only one who knows why you have come and it must remain so. When I sought a healer, I had not thought I requested a dark mage, however, and, even with my cousin's words, I know not what he is doing here."

Her throat burned with words, yet Caryss waited, still listening.

"My father is near death, despite both healer and mage at his bedside. If he had died in battle, or of just cause, I would find either possible. But his illness is not a just one, nor is it one the healers recognize. That is why you are here. For a moon year or more, I have suspected that his illness is being caused by something. Or perhaps someone."

He cleared his throat before he continued, "Few know of the King's true condition, and it must remain so, as I stated in my letter. If word spreads of his frail health, I will know that is has come from one of you. Just as if his health worsens, you will be responsible. Be so warned."

Finally, Caryss could no longer stay silent. "I am healer-trained and have vows, Prince Crispin. I need not be reminded of them by you."

"You are young and cannot be long in Master robes," he retorted.

With anger edging her words, Caryss told him, "I am no Master yet."

"The king is dying and the Academy, one that would not exist without the support of Rexterra, sends a student?" Crispin roared, his eyes erupting as if aflame.

Before she could answer, Aldric called, "You know nothing of her, prince. She is more healer than those who have worn the robes for half their lives."

"You look as if you are here to see the city, as any moneyed Northern girl would do. This is the King we speak of!"

Walking toward him, she laughed, "Was that not your request, my lord? You did not want any to know that you had sought a healer, and now you complain that I do not look the part?"

He said nothing.

Stopping just in front of him, Caryss gazed up, noticing still how his eyes burned, red and gold, as if the heat of the sun lived there.

Without looking away, she said to him, "Within the moon year, I will wear my Master robes. For half my life I have studied the healing arts and for half of that, I worked in the clinic, where I have saved more than I can count from death. With me is Sharron, another senior healer, as well as Aldric, who you seem to already know as a mage. Sharron, as I do, has vows that we hold sacred, and neither of us will seek to further harm the King. Aldric once was mage, well, still is I suppose, but he has sworn his services to me and offers no threat to you or the King. The two at the door are hired men, hired by your cousin I should mention, to see us here safely, as they have done."

"What are you keeping from me?"

His words had been sharp, as if he still did not believe her.

Yet, calmly, Caryss answered, "Tell me of your father. All that you can remember. When he first grew ill, what symptoms he showed, what improvements he has made."

Crispin seemed as if he would argue further, for she had not heeded his question. Yet, after a moment, he explained, "I do not believe his illness to be a natural one, yet the mages can find no source for it, nor can the healers. He sleeps nearly all day, and when he is not sleeping, he shakes and mumbles. He can communicate in a way, but few can make sense of it. If you seek to question him, I shall be there to aid you in understanding what he says. He eats little, and only then it must be mashed and fed to him, and barely resembles the man he once was."

With a long sign, he added, "I am not sure how much you know of my people, but we are not prone to illness or sickness. Our lives are usually blessedly long, which only makes my father's health more difficult to understand."

"I would like to see your father as soon as possible."

For another long moment Crispin was silent, as if he might not allow it. Then he simply nodded. "As it is, I think your arrival was timed well. If any ask, you have not come as healer. Rather, you will see him as uncle, kin from Eirrannia to visit. Is that understood?"

Trying to fight the smile that curved her lips, Caryss nodded. She did not tell him that she knew little of the North.

*****

After a meandering walk through the back hallways of the palace, the group turned onto a mage-lit hall, one that had thick, textured silver paper glued smoothly to the walls and lush, wine-colored carpeting beneath their feet. The room that Crispin had led them to first was nothing like where they found themselves now, and Caryss reached a hand out to touch the swirling pattern on the walls around her. She let her hand trail against the wall as she followed a quick-stepping Crispin.

The mage-lights, encased in sconces along the walls, cast a gentle haze across the hall, and the silver paper reflected it back, creating a shimmer of light over the long corridor. Caryss continued to follow, as did the others, hurrying after the prince, who had not glanced back at them.

As she watched him, he turned sharply and ascended a narrow set of stairs, serving stairs, she thought, having heard of such. When they reached the top, Crispin paused, still without turning to them and instructed them to wait.

While he was gone, Aldric approached Caryss, and looking about nervously, whispered, "I must remind you once again to trust none, not even the prince. We are no longer at the Academy, and little here is what it seems. The palace itself is like its own country with its own set of laws and its own factions and divided loyalties. Do what you can for the King, then let us be gone."

Knowing that the warning was fair, she nodded, and, as Crispin had yet to return, asked, "He seems troubled, does he not? Or has he always been this way?"

Breathing sharply and looking around, he quietly told her, "His father is near death, which for a man of his line and his age is a rare thing.

29

And he has not yet mentioned his brother, who contests his reign, I have heard. He is troubled indeed, but it is not for you to fix, Caryss."

Shivering at his words, she looked down the hall, listening as footsteps neared. For a moment, the hallway stilled.

The walls shifted, and the patterned paper that covered them seemed as if it rippled, sending shards of light throughout the hall and across the silent faces that waited for Crispin's return. Suddenly, it was as if she looked at him, at herself, at Aldric, Sharron, and the guards, from a different angle, as if she was not quite there with them, but watching them from a distance.

Crispin, his boots heavy and laced high, walked toward the group, tall and broad, like most of the royal line, yet he was no longer alone. Behind him walked a boy, not yet into manhood, with a face that was not quite childlike. The boy's face was serious and controlled, and his eyes held captured sea and sky. Even though he was lanky and thin, he still showed signs of his father: his eyes were rimmed in gold. Eyes that expressed nothing one moment, and, then, a moment later, Caryss could read the boy's story written in the gold and blue that swirled there.

As she continued to stare at the boy, he looked past his father and his fierce eyes, sheltering his story once more, locked with hers. In size, he was a boy, but his sky eyes were older than most, Caryss thought.

Breathlessly, with a hand to her chest, she asked, "What is your name, child?"

When he did not answer, she looked toward Crispin. The prince's brow was creased and his mouth turned down as he stared back at her. Quickly, she glanced back at the boy, only steps behind his father, and when their eyes met, he gently nodded to her, but still did not speak.

"What did you say about a child?" Crispin demanded, looking behind him then back at Caryss.

"I asked your son his name," she explained, not understanding the prince's anger.

"My sons are not permitted in this area, and the hallway is now empty. Describe the boy that you saw."

Pointing, she told him, "He stands just behind you. The one with the blue eyes and fair hair."

Turning quickly around, Crispin searched, and, moments later, replied, "My sons all have dark hair."

Not giving up, Caryss exclaimed, "Does no one else see the boy? Child, speak up! What is your name?"

When she looked again to him, the boy's image shook and wavered, solid one moment and misty the next. Dropping her head, Caryss closed her eyes. A moment later, she raised her head, glancing at the boy once more. He stood quietly, close enough to touch his father's back, yet his hands remained at the sides of his loosely-fitted pants. Across his face was a half-smile, as if he could not contain his glee at fooling all but her.

Inspecting him again, Caryss suddenly realized that he was not dressed in the manner the Rexterrans favored. In place of the snug pants and high boots that Crispin wore, the boy's pants were thick, simple linen, hanging loosely from him. On his feet, he wore low boots of hardened leather, not as supple or as fine as the Rexterran boots, nor as costly. His tunic was also loosely fitting, as if it was too large, woven with a wide thread, a subtle pattern of stripes running from side to side. Crispin's tunic, in contrast, was plain, yet finely made, tightly woven with an expensive fabric. The boy looked a pauper next to the King's Heir.

Caryss turned away from the boy then, and looked to the mage, pleading, "Aldric, do you not see the boy, the one with the dirty boots and oversized tunic?"

"I see no boy, Caryss. You are overtired, I imagine. Perhaps we should delay your meeting with the King," he gently told her.

"So you believe that I am imagining the child?" she asked, stepping toward where the lanky boy stood.

With steady hands, she reached up and tried to hold the boy's face, as a mother might. Her hands went through him until they touched, a loud clap echoing around her, proving her folly. Again she tried, and, again, her hands glided through the air as if the boy had never been there at all. Yet, he lingered still, fading, but present. When she lifted her gray-green eyes, his own ones watched her, the shadow of his smile hovering on his sun-touched face.

He wants me to see him.

Addressing him, and doing little to hide her annoyance, Caryss scolded, "So you are like the girl then, is that it? What games the two of you play! I will warn you as I have her: do not dabble here long! When you time-walk, you risk becoming trapped. Take heed and rush off."

She followed him as he glided further down the hall and whispered, "He is not ready to meet you, but do not despair. Walk the path you find yourself on, and it will lead where it should. Hone your craft. Master the sword. Ready yourself."

Once Caryss had spoken the words, she knew them to be true, even if why she had said them made little sense. She knew with certainty that the boy was Crispin's son, and understood that the boy was not in Rexterra, which meant that Crispin had not seen the boy in many moon years, for her description of him had not caused any reaction from the King's Heir.

When full comprehension finally came, she again looked to the boy, who was now nearly invisible. He bowed to her, shimmering and fluid, and with more grace than Caryss had ever before witnessed. His eyes, bluer than any she had seen, brighter than sea and sky, were ancient ones, yet thickly lashed with youth. He would become a fine man, she thought, and smiled, with a fondness that caused her to ache.

How the gods play with me, she thought, shaking her head and sighing loudly, the noise jarring her out of the daze that had fallen over her as she spoke with the boy.

Behind her, raised voices brought her back.

"What is this about, mage? Is the healer a half-wit?"

"She is tired, prince. We have hurried to get here, and the travel has taken a toll on all of us. The girl is as talented a healer as the Academy has to offer. Willem would not have sent her had it not been so."

Caryss paused, trying to find the words to explain what she had seen. And then she knew. Just as Crispin was not ready to meet the boy, she knew, too, that the boy was not ready for his father to see him. Not yet.

It is not my story to tell.

Turning back to the prince, she said, "Forgive me, sir, Aldric is right. I have had little sleep, and perhaps dozed off while we waited. But I would still see the King."

She let her eyes meet his, and she saw that he did not believe her. Finally, he gestured for the group to follow him, and, within moments, they were outside his father's door, which appeared no different than the other doors that had lined the long hallway.

"There are still guards inside. Say nothing until the men leave the room," he whispered before placing his hand on the center of the metallic door.

After resting his hand on the door, Crispin stepped back and waited for the door to swing open, which it did, slowly, revealing a large, dimly lit room. Caryss could see little else, but trailed Crispin as he entered. She kept her head down, unsure why she did so, but she could sense a large amount of mage-work throughout the room, and the idea of so much power made her uneasy, especially as she had seen so little of it at the Academy. Without looking up, she tugged at her dress, knowing that it fit snugly across her midsection.

Crispin was speaking to the men still inside the room, four in total, positioned at each corner of the large, carved bed frame. What he said, she could not hear, but the men departed, although she knew they would not go far.

When the door was once again closed, she raised her eyes, letting them quickly scan the room, before resting them on the man lying asleep on the massive bed, dark wood shaped into spiraling turrets. He was draped in a finely woven blanket, covering him entirely, except for a pale, spotted face that was thin and drawn, eyes closed and mouth slightly open. The king looked ill, yet he did not appear any worse than many men of his age that she had treated at the clinic.

Her voice low, she asked, "Can you tell me of your father's pain and what seems to worsen it? Also, I will need to know what the other healers have done for him, as well as what they have suspected him of having. And what medicines he has been given and takes now."

Shaking his head, Crispin answered, "I will have the Palace Master prepare a list. You need to understand that as far as any healer can say, my father's illness is not treatable, and, had it been, they would have healed him by now. Truth be told, there might be little that you can do, but I had to try."

With no further interruptions, Crispin hurriedly explained how, over the last few moon years, his father would spend hours in bed, unable to speak. But, often, he would recover enough to emerge, ruling once again. At other times, he would have moments when he seemed well-healed, weak, but sound. Yet, those moments were few of late, and his father had rarely left his room over the last few moons.

As Crispin talked, Caryss watched the sleeping man, noticing the rash that covered much of his body. With one hand on her healer's belt, and the other on the King's blanket, she asked, "Might I examine the King?"

The prince moved toward the bed and gently uncovered the King. "Father, there is a healer here who wishes to look over you."

The king did not respond, nor did it seem as if he had heard his son's words. Yet, Crispin stepped back, allowing Sharron to take his place across from Caryss.

Rubbing her hands together to warm them before she laid them on him, Caryss bent forward, placing her fingertips against Herrin's neck. Next, she placed them on his wrists, feeling for his life pulse.

Turning to Sharron, she stated, "Rapid beating, much too fast for a man at rest as he has been." Just before she lifted her fingers, Caryss hesitated, pushing them against the man's thin skin once more.

"His life pulse has slowed now and barely beats. His hands are cold, as well, although his chest is warm. Blood movement must be checked. No fever or signs of infection, although his skin is irritated, and there are numerous areas of mottling."

As she worked further down his body, Caryss continued to call out observations to Sharron, who had at some point taken a thick pad out of her own healer's pouch and was writing down what Caryss was saying. The other four men in the room did nothing to interfere, nor did they speak. After she had finished examining the King's body, Caryss addressed Crispin.

"I must try to wake your father. First, I will try to rouse him as if he were only sleeping. But if that does not work, then I will try to do so by other means."

"Other means?"

"Yes," she distractedly told him, "I have a few mixtures that I have brought with me, and I believe that I should be able to wake him for a bit with one of them. It is very important that I speak with him."

"Are you mage-trained as well then?"

Without looking in the King's Heir's direction, she answered, "No, I have no talent in that area, but I have long been interested in the herb garden at the Academy, as well as investigating those used in other parts of the world. I do not believe there are many who could rival my knowledge of herb lore."

When he did not argue, she slipped her fingers into a pouch and drew out a darkly colored bottle. The glass itself was clear, but the liquid inside was a dense, deep purple, nearly black.

"Before I open this bottle, I will try a few more times to wake your father. But, if I am not able to do so, I will need to have him drink a few drops of this mixture. Is he able to swallow?"

"What does the bottle contain?" Crispin asked.

Holding up the small bottle, Caryss explained, "Mostly it is peppermint, grown at the Academy. However, the dark color you see is a result of a combination of two things. The kola nut and a coco leaf, although there is a bit of licorice in there as well. All four work together as a stimulant, and, in your father's case, should increase his life pulse enough to wake him. His heart beats too slowly, although, it often jumps and speeds up as well. If I am to help him, then I will need to try to regulate both his life pulse and his beating heart. The herbs themselves are harmless when used as I will use them. The kola nut and the leaves I must get from the Southern Cove Islands. Not many know how to use them effectively, so I understand your concern. I should add that there is a touch of hemlock as well."

She looked back at him then, knowing that even he would know how deadly hemlock could be, and asked, "Do you know the Healer's Oath, my lord? I seek to do no harm here."

"If my cousin had not sent you, then much would be different. For now, you can proceed."

His words were enough, and Caryss set the bottle on her lap, returning her attention to the King, softly calling his name and rubbing his shoulders, then gently moving her hands about his chest in a circular motion. A few times, Herrin stirred, yet his eyes remained closed, and Caryss shook her head.

Toward Sharron she said, "He sleeps as if he has been sipping poppy milk or lavender tea. What more would you try?"

Across from her, the other woman answered evenly, "If you had time, you could wait until the effects of the herbs wore off, but as we have little to waste, I think we must see what the tonic will do. He should have woken by now."

Had Caryss been watching, she would have seen surprise cross Crispin's face as Sharron spoke. For she was as Northern as Caryss herself, although her dark hair and eyes did not make it seem so. The room quieted as Caryss uncorked the bottle, the scent of peppermint filling the air. Behind the crisp smell of the mint was a bitter stench, strong and energizing. Deftly, she placed a dropper into the bottle, filling the clear tube with the dark liquid. When she moved nearer to the King, Crispin walked toward the edge of the bed and a hand grabbed him above his wrist. Hesitating, he looked up to find the Sharron holding him tightly.

Quietly, she scolded him, "Let her work. We have traveled over a moon to be at the King's bedside. Do no stop her now."

Caryss looked up as Sharron spoke, noticing how she held onto the prince. Sharron, of a similar height to Caryss, wore her hair tied tightly at her neck, in a healer's knot, the dark strands pulled away from her pale face. Her cheeks were flushed, as they often were, and her full lips red. Sharron was often quiet, yet Caryss was growing fond of the woman, who she had not known well before they departed the Academy. Like most Eirrannians, Sharron had a touch of mage-sight, although she spoke of it rarely.

Trusting Sharron to prevent Crispin from interfering, Caryss refocused on the King, telling him, "I am a healer from Tretoria, newly arrived from the Academy and I am here to see you well. In a moment, I am going to give you a few drops of a tonic that will rouse you."

She knew that Herrin would not yet hear her words, but still she said them, as she had done many times at the clinic. Once she had finished, she nodded toward Sharron, who placed her hands beneath the King's head.

With smooth and steady fingers, Caryss opened the King's mouth, holding it ajar. Then, with her other hand, she dribbled the nearly black liquid onto his tongue, rubbing at his cheeks until he swallowed.

"It should not be long," she told the others.

As she held the King's chin in her hands, she felt his jaw tighten. When his lips twitched, she hurriedly sat him up with Sharron's help. With several pillows behind him, the King leaned back, his body trembling and his legs shaking. When his eyes flared open, Caryss smiled gently.

"King Herrin, my name is Caryss and I am healer-trained. Can you hear me?"

Her words were spoken in Common, and, after a moment, the King shook his head.

35

"Good. I have given you something to keep you awake for a bit, and I need to ask you a few questions. Do your best to answer."

Much to her surprise, the King smiled, his skin, nearly translucent, wrinkling at his eyes and lips.

"You are often asleep, my lord. Do you ask your healers for it to be so?"

When the King answered, his words were strained and hoarse, spoken slowly and with difficulty, as if his lips had turned to stone. "I ask them to ease the pain."

Before she could ask another question, Crispin called out, "Father, this is the first time in a half-moon that you have spoken!"

Herrin's golden eyes were dull and yellow, but he turned to where Crispin stood and said to him, "I am not yet dead."

Silence followed his words, a rebuke, Caryss thought, with interest. As she reached for Herrin's wrist to again feel for his life pulse, he turned toward her, grabbing her fingers with his own. He had little strength and she could have pulled away had she wanted to, but Caryss waited, letting him embrace her.

After a moment, he grunted, "You look too young to be a healer."

With her free hand, she reached for his neck, and told him, "I have trained for twelve moon years at the Academy, King Herrin."

His life pulse was stronger now, beating with some regularity.

"So you were but a child when you arrived," he mumbled.

As she was folding down the blanket that covered him, he asked, "Are you from Eirrannia?"

Caryss nodded, gently pulling her hand from his and moving it to his stomach, where she pressed and rolled her fingers, feeling for displacement or swelling.

He struggled to speak as she did so, but managed to squawk, "You are kin to Derry then."

Laying her ear next to his chest, she listened to his breathing, and answered, "I know not whom I am kin to and was an orphan when I arrived at the Academy."

He continued to talk as she examined him, and Caryss let him, hoping to keep him awake for as long as possible.

"Eirrannia is a strange land and her people stranger yet. Many fear them, especially here in Rexterra," he explained, his words still edged and course. "I blame the mages, you see, for they have long told tale of how the North breeds monsters and rebels."

Before she could stop herself, Caryss laughed, "Am I a monster, then, King Herrin?"

His smile was bright, lighting up a face covered in rash and scars.

36

Still smiling, she called to Sharron, "Have a listen here."

To the King, she instructed, "Lie silent for a moment and breathe as deeply as you can."

After a few moments, Caryss said to him, holding out her hand, "Reach for my hand, King Herrin, and grab my fingers as strongly as you can."

He did as she asked, although his grip was weak and his fingers chilled.

"Are you always so cold?"

"You know little, child!" he cried, squeezing her hand harder.

When he did not release her hand, Crispin jumped forward, exclaiming, "Father, you need not hurt the girl! She knows little of our ways."

Looking up at the prince, she watched as he glanced at her, noticing the confusion on her face.

"Do they teach you nothing of Rexterra at the Academy?" he asked her, the clouds separating in his eyes.

With a shrug, she gazed back at the King, noticing his eyes were less cloudy now and brimming with specks of gold and orange.

"They teach us of your plants and healing practices. Little more than that do we need."

After the King released her hand, she pushed the long sleeve on his tunic up, examining the red rash that laced up and down his arm. Pressing her fingers into his mottled skin, she grimaced, unsure what would cause the reaction.

"Does your skin itch?" she asked.

"Nearly enough to drive me mad," he answered, his words half-whispered now as he began to fade.

"Is that why you ask for the poppy milk so often?"

Wanly nodding, he answered, "The poppy milk dulls it all."

"And makes you sleep overmuch!" she chided him.

With a sudden burst of energy, he told her, "I am still your king, girl!"

Caryss bit at the inside of her lip to prevent herself from laughing, but she knew that Crispin watched her, and knew, too, that he had seen her smile. She cared little.

Pulling his sleeve back down over his icy skin, she asked, "Sir, can you walk?"

"I have not been able to do so in many moons."

"Yes, but have you tried much? If your body grows accustomed to being carried about, your legs will lose their strength and ability to hold your weight. Regardless of how weak that you feel, you should not stop trying to manage on your own. Who has advised you to stay abed?"

"I cannot recall who first suggested it, but most likely it was one of the Masters," he said, looking to where Crispin stood.

Waving off the prince before he could reply, she told him, "My lord, they are wrong. It will take a few moons for your legs to regain the strength that they have lost, but it can be done."

Then she looked back at the prince and said, "Lord Crispin, why was your father told to stay abed? Why was he not permitted to attempt to walk about the palace on his own?"

Crispin cleared his throat with a slight cough. "He is King here, Caryss, and for those of our kind, weakness is not accepted. If he would have fallen, and there were others around to witness such, well, nothing good would have come from the incident. Mayhap it is difficult for one like you to understand, but there can be no hint of any loss of power. Or the vultures would strike."

"But surely word has spread of his sickness? How do you explain his lack of public appearances and such?"

Firmly and quickly, he answered, "The King can be ill, but he cannot be weak. He can suffer an injury, from which he must recover, but he cannot be permanently damaged. For now, the word is that he has been sick, but recovering."

"I see," was all that she replied, although her tone suggested she did not fully agree.

Standing up, she walked to the edge of the bed, placing the bottle back in her pouch as she did so. When she was near the King's feet, she pushed the blanket from him again, reaching for his pale and scaly legs.

"There are some movements that your father will have to practice many times a day, ones that will serve to strengthen his legs," she told Crispin, showing him as she did so. "I will visit several times a day to make sure he is doing so."

Sharron neared her, taking the King's legs and moving them as if the King were a babe.

Backing away from the bed, Caryss told Crispin, "There is much that I cannot explain here, but there is much I can yet try. I will need access to the King at all times."

"Yes, of course," he stated, "I shall spread word that a niece of my Uncle Derry has arrived, and we will find rooms for you near the King."

"How will you explain my visits? For they will be often."

"You are kin, and I have asked you to read to the King while he sleeps."

Crispin's face had not revealed the lie, nor had his voice changed. In truth, she had nearly believed him.

38

Beside the King's bed again, she leaned down to him and whispered, "Soon, the tonic that I gave you will wear off and you will grow tired once more. My lord, we must get you off the poppy milk, but I fear it will be a long process, moons even. You must not allow the Masters to give you so much, and even then, only when you can bear no more."

Herrin nodded at her, his eyes heavy with sleep.

From across the room, Crispin called, "Can you not give him the tonic every few hours to counteract the poppy milk?"

Pulling the blankets up to the King's chin, Caryss answered, "It is not meant to be given so often. Once a day would even be too much, and, soon, it would lose it effectiveness, as did the poppy milk. We must have patience, Prince Crispin, for this will be no easy task."

When the King's eyes began to close, Caryss pressed her lips to his forehead.

To Sharron, she said, "His hands and feet are as cold as ice, yet his head burns."

"I noticed that as well," Sharron agreed, her words still edged with a Northern lilt.

The soft sounds of the King's breathing filled the room as Caryss gathered her things. Behind her, Aldric stood, still quiet, much to her surprise.

When she was finished, Crispin said to her, "I will need some time to find you rooms. Until I do, let me show you to our dining areas. Caryss, you will be noticed, but, if I know my cousin at all, then I know he has warned you of the ways of the King's City. Remember the story we have agreed on: you are kin to Derry, Willem's father. Nothing more."

He looked away from her then, and toward Aldric. To the mage, he said, "Keep yourself well-guarded. You will not be met with any welcome, from what I recall."

"I am a hired mercenary. Nothing more," Aldric replied, staring back at the prince.

Sighing, Crispin turned to leave, adding, "If you heal my father, Caryss, I will owe you a great debt. If you are not the healer who you claim to be, then you will not ever leave the King's City. None of you will. Nor will any of you survive. Do not give me cause to regret, for there is more to me than I have shown."

Her forest-dyed eyes met his sun-kissed ones, and, for a moment, her gaze was his gaze, and he saw through her eyes. He saw the boy.

*****

Caryss remained at the side of the King until a man dressed in the colors of the King's Heir arrived, wearing a silver vest over a soft tunic of a deep blue. They followed him, past the guards, who, Caryss now noticed, were wearing gold vests over black tunics. The man led them down the same hallway they had traveled earlier, but then he turned and took several steps toward a dimly lit area. Around them were several doors, and the unnamed guard pointed at them.

With a heavy accent, he said, "My Lord Prince has had readied a few rooms for you."

As he was talking, a woman dressed in the same colors, with the same plush vest over a fitted dress, exited one of the rooms. Seeing the group staring at her, she nearly dropped the pile of towels that lay folded neatly in her hands.

Caryss noticed the serving girl staring at her; she was young, just entering womanhood. Her hair, dark and wavy, was tied at the side, hanging nearly to her waist. The girl reminded Caryss of the Academy and of the clinic where girls just as this one carried nearly identical linens. With a sign, Caryss forced her thoughts away from that past and looked from girl to guard.

Nodding toward the woman, the guard told her, "Leesa will see to your needs. The small door there on the right leads to her room, and she will serve you well. Leesa," he called, "Show them to their rooms, and have the kitchen send some food."

"Yes, sir," she mumbled, the blue scarf covering the top of her hair bobbing up and down in reply.

Once they were all settled, each in their own rooms, with Caryss in between Niko and Kurtis, and Aldric and Sharron across from her, Caryss lay on the bed, relieved to find it soft and full, unlike the beds at the inn. Closing her eyes and sinking deeper into the silky blanket that covered the bed, Caryss turned on her side, thinking of little else, and, soon, she was sleeping, the fatigue of carrying the babe taking its toll on her body.

*****

5

"Explain to me again how you let them escape."

The words were spoken with a quiet calm, yet were as deadly as a viper's hiss.

"My Lord, I did not let them escape. They just disappeared. And when we discovered that they were gone, no trail remained. We looked all day and found nothing. Not even a feather."

"Not even a feather!"

He was laughing now, although both knew there was no humor in it.

"Conall, you disappoint me. Are you not a Wolf? Does your blood not run hot for a taste of Crow?"

"Of course it does Conri!" Conall fumed, nearing his brother, "Just as hot at yours. My eyes redden and my teeth sharpen! But I am telling you, there were other forces at work here, ones that we could not see or hear. We had the men shackled, and they should never have been able to fly free. Yet, it seems that is what happened. You tell me what that means!"

"Their wrists were bound. Is that what you are telling me?"

"Yes," Conall told him.

"Crows cannot fly without use of their hands. How many men were with you?" the High Lord asked.

"Twelve," Conall answered, just steps from his brother.

"And did you pick all twelve?"

"I did not. Lazaro put together the hunting party, but I knew all of the men."

Running pale fingers through dark hair, Conri barked, "Not well enough, it seems. One of your men, under your command but picked by the hand of another, must have unshackled the Crows. I will leave it to you to find me that man."

Conri's eyes were black when Conall looked up, and he stepped back, waiting to be dismissed.

"You will find me this man, Conall. Do not let me see you until you do."

Conall nodded, knowing any other words would only further anger his brother. He watched as Conri walked away, fearing what would happen if he did not find the traitor among his men. For the last few moons, the High Lord had been distant and detached, more so than usual, quick to strike and quick to anger. There was much on his mind, more than just the difficulties with the Crows, Conall knew.

Something had changed in his brother. Something was missing.

*****

A gentle tapping at her door woke Caryss. Slowly, she sat up leaning against the wall, without rising. On the morrow they would retrieve their belongings from the inn, yet no one else knew that they were in the palace.

Again the knock came.

She knew that Niko and Kurtis were not outside her doors, although Aldric had placed a heavy ward at its entrance. For a long moment, she did nothing. But the knocking was persistent, and, finally, she rose.

When Caryss reached the door, the haze of sleep had lifted, and she hesitated, uncertain who would seek her at such an hour. Suddenly, she turned, rushing back to a small table beside the bed. There, she found her healer's bags and reached for the largest one. With stiff, sleep-swollen fingers, she untied the laces of the pouch and pulled the dagger free. Walking back to the door, she tucked the blade into the sleeves of her long underdress.

Slowly, Caryss turned the handle of the door, squeezing the hilt of the dagger with her other hand. As the door opened toward her, she looked up and relaxed her grip.

"Has something happened to the King?"

"You really should not be answering your door in the middle of the night, Caryss."

"Well, then, perhaps you should not be knocking on it in the middle of the night, my lord."

Ignoring her retort, he added, "One of your men should be with you at all times. Despite how it might appear."

Stepping back from the door, Caryss asked, "Is the palace so unsafe? My men are on either side of me."

She did not mention the ward.

"I once believed my father to be the most well-guarded man in all of Cordisia, yet he is now half-dead."

The prince's words trailed, until they were but a whisper.

Caryss said nothing, but looked across the room at him as he entered, pushing the door closed behind him.

"You do not object to my being here, do you?"

Still dressed as he had been earlier in the evening, but without the large robe he had been wearing when they first met, Crispin nervously looked around. Caryss was near to answer him, but realized he had not expected a refusal, so, again, she said nothing. A silence spread across the room like a cloud of smoke. Several times the prince opened his mouth as if to speak, yet each time he closed it again, as if uncertain. Caryss waited, until the quietness of the room became too much for her to bear.

"Why have you come?" she asked, the words harsher than she had intended.

Clasping his hands together to stop them from flittering about, Crispin said, "The king sleeps."

As he spoke, Caryss realized that she wore nothing but a light underdress, one that had grown snug over the last moon. With a slight blush spreading over her cheeks, she stepped back from him.

The room was dark, although dull light from the orbs outside offered specks and streaks of gold. From where he stood near the window, Crispin appeared lined and dotted in silver, as if kissed by stars. As she stared, he never looked back; instead he glanced out the window, as if searching.

Finally, he dropped his head and half-pleading, called, "Tell me about the boy."

So he knows, she thought, remembering the boy's bright eyes, bluer than any that she had ever seen, as if he had been born of water.

"Truly, you could not see him?" she asked.

Without turning to face her, he said, "I saw nothing. How old did he appear? Why would you think him my son?"

Before he moved, Caryss reached for a small blanket, wrapping it around herself, the dagger tucked against her body.

"Perhaps ten or twelve moon years. He still had the look of a child about him, yet he was tall and thin."

"And he told you he was my son?"

It was then that Crispin crossed the room, his eyes focused once again.

Shaking her head, she answered, "He said nothing to me, but knew that I could see him. The boy seemed surprised that I could, I think."

Even in the dim light, Caryss could see disbelief on the prince's face.

"I will ask again if you are mage-trained, healer."

"I am no mage, Prince Crispin," she sighed. "Nor can I recall any mage-sight. But I know what I saw, and I know the boy noticed me as well. The skill here is not any of my own. It is your son who is so gifted."

"You have not told me why you think him my son!" Crispin roared.

Looking around and expecting to hear another knock on her door, she slowly answered, "He resembles you, even though his eyes are nothing like yours. Nor his hair, truly. There is an air about him that feels thick with the blood of kings."

"What madness this is!" he shouted at her, striding toward where she stood and grabbing at her arms where they held the blanket.

His hands were strong, holding her nearly immobile as he hissed through clenched teeth, "You say you are no mage, yet you woke my father as if he was not near death. You say you are no mage, yet you tell me that you have seen my son. A boy who few know exists. You say you are no mage, yet you stand before me without fear or weapon."

With eyes flaming gold and orange, he demanded she answer. "Who are you to know so much?"

For a moment, she thought of pushing him from her, knowing with little doubt that she would be able to do so, as she had once done to Pietro. Instead, she looked up at him, her gray-green eyes dull next to his blazing ones. Even with his blood hot and his eyes afire, Caryss did not fear the prince. Her weapon, unseen and unborn, was more than even she could explain.

Her gaze and voice steady, she explained again. "I am a healer, no more than that, prince. But you came here to ask what I saw, and so I will tell you. I saw the boy, your son, and although he told me naught, I recognized him for what he is."

"And what is that?" Crispin fumed.

Only then did she hesitate. The boy's path was his own, one that he had long walked alone.

Into the silence, she cried, "A future king."

His hands fell from her so quickly that Caryss stumbled backward, landing on the thickly feathered bed with a soft thump.

"I heard you offer him a warning. What risk is he taking?"

The prince's words were hoarse and low, as if he had not meant to say them.

Caryss, seated on the edge of the bed, told him, "I have heard it named time-walking. It is not unrelated to mage-sight, yet it is a skill that few can master. I told the boy to take heed to not be trapped."

"Time-walking causes one to travel to the past, is that not so?" he asked.

"I suppose that is the case. I know so little of it all."

Before he could speak again, Caryss, with a rising voice, asked, "But the boy does exist, Lord Crispin?"

The room stilled, and neither moved. Caryss, with her hair falling long and wavy against the blanket and her eyes more green than gray under the glimmer of the pulsing orbs outside, stared at the prince. He did not trust her, she knew, although she blamed him little for it, especially after all that Willem had told her of life in the King's City. And then she remembered what else Willem had told her. About Crispin's two sons, and their Rexterran-born mother. The boys were much younger than the one that she had seen. And, even in the darkness of the hallway, Caryss had noticed the boy's light hair and blue eyes, which were nothing like Crispin's. Except the gold that rimmed them.

Into the silence, she rasped, "He is light-haired, as if he spends much of his day playing in the fields under a bright sun, and his eyes are not Rexterran. On the edges of those eyes were rings of gold. The same ring of gold that greets me when I look upon you."

"Jarek," the prince whispered, walking away from her.

On the other side of the room now, he called to her, "His mother named him Jarek. I have not seen him since he was a babe."

Drawing a long breath, Crispin continued, "Few know that the boy lives. And it must remain that way."

Caryss nodded, but it was not enough.

Crispin again rushed to her, and, when near enough, he hissed, "I will say no more of him until you have sworn it to be so."

Before she knew what she did, she grabbed the prince's hand and placed it between her own. When he turned, their eyes met, gold and green and gray. Neither moved.

"*A mi onoiur, a mi mohour's onoiur, san la sliahs fairann, ghaellam,*" Caryss whispered, watching him. "On my honor, on my mother's honor, with the mountains watching, I promise. In Eirrannia, we call it the Woman's Vow."

With a laugh that was not a pleasant one, Crispin answered, "You seek to reassure me with words of the North?"

Dropping his hand, she shrugged, "I seek to reassure you with my word. The boy knows it to be so already."

"He is a boy, no more, and one untrained. His life is a simple one, and he knows little of who would harm him."

As she spoke of the boy, of Jarek, Caryss knew that there was much to him that his father did not know, that there was power in him, just as with her own child. Yet, she told him little more.

"Where is the boy?" she asked instead.

"When last I knew he was in Planusia."

His reply had come quickly and had surprised her, thinking he would lie.

"He is Nicoline's son."

Jumping up from the bed, Crispin backed away from her, his eyes dark with anger.

"What do you know of her?" he cried accusingly.

Still seated, she raised her hands to him, the dagger beneath her leg, tucked behind the blanket. With a calmness she did not feel, Caryss told him, "Willem feared we would not be able to seek a meeting with you. He told me to use her name to beg for an audience, but only with members of your own guard."

"My cousin has become a fool in his exile!"

Shaking her head, Caryss answered, "I have known Willem half of my life, yet I knew nothing of him, of who he is, until a few moons ago. Even then, he only told me what he believed was necessary. Your cousin has done nothing to earn your wrath, Crispin."

While the prince thought on her words, Caryss added, "He never mentioned the boy."

Between them hung a silence, one that spoke of mistrust and doubt, yet in it too was a desire to believe, Caryss knew.

Finally, Crispin seemed to temper his fire. "I can have a letter to my cousin in less than a quarter-moon. What would he say of you if I inquired, Caryss?"

His threat was a light one, and she hastily replied, "He will not know me as Caryss. While I was at the Academy, I was known as Bronwen, a name that my foster mother gave to me."

The prince was ready to interrupt, questions written across his sun-darkened face, but she again raised her hands to him.

"As a child, I was brought to the Academy with grave injuries. My parents, it was believed, had died while I had survived some accident or attack. None knew who brought me into Tretoria, but I was found by some Tretorian Guards and brought to the Academy. When my injuries healed, which did not take long for they were more serious in look than in truth, I was asked of my past. I remembered nothing and had nowhere to go. So the Academy became my home, and I became one of its best students."

"And now?" he asked.

With a laugh, she said, "I am here, and others are not. I may be of the North, even though I remember little of it, but I am as well-trained as any."

"Yet you are no longer named Bronwen. Why?"

A fading smile across her face, Caryss explained, "I was never Bronwen, Prince Crispin. I am a healer, true, but I bore a name of my own before that one was given to me. It was only in the last few moons that I learned of that name. It is the one I use now."

With her words came memory. And, soon, her eyes were wet and her throat thick. Caryss could feel the prince studying her. Her hands fell back to her lap, long and pale, like tapered candles. She did not look up at him, swallowing hard as she struggled for control.

"Have you ever found yourself lost, Crispin?" she asked, her voice a whisper.

After a moment, he told her, "My life has been set since my birth, and I have little choice but to follow. It is near impossible to get lost on such a path."

"And Nicoline? Was she not of your choosing?"

Sighing heavily, he stated, "You see what came of that, Caryss. A son I will never know. I suppose it was then that I learned, as my father had wanted it, that my life is not my own choosing, but what is best for Rexterra."

His eyes, lighter now, still watched her. "How did the dark mage find you?"

He would tell her no more of himself, she knew then.

"Aldric seemed necessary," she lied.

"How so?"

"No other Healer Journey has started here, prince. Even knowing as little as I do of Rexterra, I was not fool enough to believe that two simple-minded guards would be enough to keep me safe."

Doing little to hide his mocking, Crispin told her, "Only one from the Academy would believe a dark mage the key to safety."

"He has sworn an oath to me."

With a bitter laugh, Crispin said, "Oaths mean nothing to one such as him, girl. They must teach you nothing of the world at the Academy."

"I have reason to believe that he will never break that vow."

"You must tread carefully and trust few, Caryss."

Smiling broadly and matching his mockery, she answered, "Now you sound like your cousin."

"He is a wise man," the prince shrugged, "And I owe him much. So much that I will never be able to repay him. But, if he has sent you here, and cares about you the way I suspect he does, then I must do all that I can to keep you safe."

In a move that seemed to surprise them both, Crispin dropped onto the bed next to her, rubbing at his cheek with ink-stained fingers. Caryss stiffened, feeling the prince's thick leg next to her own. His pants clung to him tightly, wrapping muscle in taut cotton while she was still draped in the blanket. A few times she had caught Crispin watching her, while she spoke, and she half-expected him to ask her about the babe.

"When did you last hear from Willem?" she asked in haste, suddenly worried that the prince already knew of the girl.

His fingers, tipped in black, fell to his lap. "It has been several moons I believe."

Several moons. He does not know of the babe then.

Beneath her leg, Caryss could feel the dagger, unsheathed, the blade cool against her bare skin.

"Tell me of Nicoline," she asked him, pulling at the blanket.

When he hesitated, Caryss worried that she had asked too much, having known the prince for less than a day. Yet, with the orb-light's glow in the otherwise dark room, she felt as if she had known him longer and

47

wondered if it was because of Willem. Not for the first time, she thought of his promise to take her to Eirrannia.

She was still thinking of Willem when Crispin muttered, "I met Nicoline by chance, you know. We had been out riding, Willem and I. We were younger then, and although we both had some responsibilities, we had a certain amount of freedom. Much more than I have now or will ever have again. Ofttimes, we would leave in the morning and ride for hours. On the day we met Nicoline, we had gone farther north than ever before. To Shantora, a coastal town across the Planusian border. It was long past midday when we arrived. I was not even twenty moon years at the time, but I thought I knew much. But I soon realized that we would not be able to make it back to the King's City before nightfall."

His cheeks puckered with a smile. "Once I knew that we would be gone for the night, we found the nearest inn. None knew us there. And we had coin to spend. And ale to drink."

Realizing that he had talked of Nicoline in many moon years, Caryss listened, trying to learn more of his son.

"Before long, Willem and I were quite drunk. And somehow ended up in the Eastern Sea. Fully clothed. When it came time to make our way back to the inn, we had no coin and dripped with salt and sea."

Crispin's hair was cropped short, his eyebrows dark. His lashes, when Caryss glanced at him, were long and shining black, rimming eyes that glowed gold. His face was long and square, his chin strong, his cheeks high. Her own cheeks burned as she examined him, but the prince did not notice. He was younger than Willem, by several moon years, she knew, but there was still a resemblance between the cousins, even though Willem had Northern blood in him, while Crispin's lineage was all Rexterran.

As she watched him, he continued, "There was a clothier, a small shop I believe, and we hurried to it, although it was nearly dark. We had hoped to sell or trade our clothing for coin, for even as salt-stained as it was, it was Rexterran still. But the shop was closed."

With his eyes on the wall across from them, Crispin laughed, caught in the gleeful memories of his youth, before the feud with his brother embittered him.

"Willem had the ease of the North in him, despite having been raised in the King's City. Before I could object, he was stripping off his boots. With rolled-up pants, and a bare chest, he banged on the doors of the clothier, yelling for the shopkeeper. As it turned out, his plan worked, and, soon, we were ushered inside. Willem explained our need and offered up his boots for sale. We only needed enough coin for a night at the inn and lodging for our horses. His boots, hells, even our tunics, were worth more than anything he had in his store. But we were drunk, covered in sea

48

and sand, making a mess of his store as I recall. It was there that Nicoline found us."

Finally, Caryss interjected, "Why not explain who you were? Surely you would have been given a room or clothing?"

When he looked at her, it was as if her words made little sense to him, and his smile dropped, his jaw clenched.

"You are a healer and must have no thought of how it is to be always watched. We had ridden far enough that few knew us. Yes, I could have proclaimed myself as King's Heir, but, rarely, did I get to be anything but. There comes a certain peace when none know you, and neither Willem nor I desired betraying that."

Her words came fast, before she could think of their impact. "I lived in that same peace, or thought I did, for most of my life."

"And now?" he asked, his eyes upon her, his face grave and drawn.
I should have said nothing.

Silence covered the room again, until Caryss finally explained, "A few moons ago I would spend my evenings in my rooms alone or at the Healer's Clinic. Now, I am alone in a room with the next king of Rexterra. One's path is often not what we once thought it might be."

Her words were hot, although she had spoken them more in reflection than in accusation. His eyes still watched her, and Caryss's face reddened, her hands wet and warm in her lap. Unable to return his gaze, she looked away, although her life pulse raced, as if she were no better than swooning girls.

"Nicoline is Planusian," he told her, "And at the time, was an acolyte serving in the Temple of the Moon, I later learned. She had followed us into the shop, although she was there for reasons of her own. It was naught but chance that the owner had unlocked his door. When I first noticed her, she was just inside the doorway, dressed simply, in a poorly fitting robe of cotton dyed a pale blue. It hung just past her knees, as if she had outgrown it the moon year before, and on her feet were sandals like one would wear to bed. Her hair, hanging loosely, fell near to her waist, the color of sun-whitened silk. But it was her eyes that I will never forget. So blue that I thought she had been born of the sea, like the myths of old, a tailed and scaled fish-girl come to lure me from land. Willem knew that I was enchanted before I had time to even call out to her."

"It was she who spoke first, and, in a voice that sang of field and farm, asked if we needed aid, having heard the earlier exchange between Willem and the tailor. She did not know who I was, Caryss, yet offered us clothing for nothing in return. She gave us coin too, all that she had, which was just enough to buy boarding for the horses."

"What clothing did she offer?" Caryss asked.

"Rough-spun robes and pants made at the temple. Once a moon, the acolytes would travel to nearby cities offering food and clothing to those who were in need. We took what was offered. And invited her to join us."

Caryss noticed a slight upturn to the prince's smooth lips. His hands, too, were smooth, as if he had not touched weapon in moon years.

"A few moons later, I asked her why she had joined us, yet she would say little more than she was fulfilling her duties as an acolyte and making certain that we were well."

"So you think that she knew who you were?" Caryss interjected.

His smile disappeared as Crispin shook his head. "That first night? No. Later, in the King's City, she discovered who we were. But that first night, she knew me as a horse trader. She drank no ale, although Willem and I continued to do so. And, before long, I was professing my love for her."

Caryss laughed then, although she knew that she should not. "How much of that was the ale talking, Crispin?"

As if he was unused to being teased, Crispin huffed, "As we rode home, I thought of nothing else but her, and for moons after."

Biting at her lip to quell the words on her tongue, Caryss said nothing.

"I was young, but no fool, and I did not need Willem to remind me, as he did often, that my father would never approve of Nicoline. To my father, she was nothing but a plaything for me, which he tolerated. It was not until moon years later that he forbid me from seeing her further."

The prince's story, as often happens with memory, was not linear, she realized. His thoughts had become scattered, although she knew enough to make sense of them.

"My father told me that I could keep her as a toy, to get my passions out, as men of my line have done for many generations. I was reminded that there are women we marry and women we take to bed, and, ofttimes, the two are not the same. I know not what you have learned of my kin, but we are an old line, older than most in Cordisia, and in our blood runs the blood of gods. So it has been, and so it must be. Cordisia was gifted to us to rule when our line was cast out from the skies, forced to live among the mortals. As King's Heir, I must be both Rexterran and god-born, as must my recognized heirs."

Beside her, Crispin was serious and grave, as if he believed the words that he half-growled. Caryss cared little for talk of gods and men, even less so the last few moons, and she nearly told him so. Nor did she think he to be very god-like, seated beside her on a narrow cot. Others, Rexterrans perhaps, might fear him, worship him even, but, to her, Crispin was no more than a man with gold-kissed eyes. And another man claiming allegiance to a god unknown, she thought, believing it to be madness.

But he was next in line to be king, and, across the hall, his father lay dying. It would not serve her well to make an enemy of the next Rexterran king. Still, she fought to stay silent. For Jarek, she remained so.

"The next morning, we departed with aching heads and rough-spun clothing. Nicoline had been given her own room, as often is the case for anyone from the Temple of the Moon. When we rode out, she was nowhere to be found. Moons later, I saw her once again."

"In the King's City?" asked Caryss.

With a quick nod, Crispin told her, "She was there with others from Planusia, from the temple. I was, well, I was no longer the horse trader whom she had met."

"Was she terribly angry that you had hidden who you were?"

"It mattered little to her who I was."

"What happened next?" she asked him as he rose from the bed, walking again to the curtained window.

Pushing aside the heavy, draping fabric, he stared into the darkness, flecks of orb-light sprinkling over him, coloring his dark tunic with bits of silver. For a moment, he glowed, as a god might.

When he next spoke, it was of Nicoline.

"I convinced her to stay in the King's City even though she could no longer be an acolyte. For a moon year and a half, she stayed, living in a house near the piers that Willem had arranged for her. My father suspected as much, but he did not intervene. Not until later. After Delwin got involved."

The prince's hands were tightly clenched against the wooden frame of the window. His next words, deep and edged, cut across the room.

"Delwin and I had begun to argue more then, and he no longer accepted without complaint that I would be King's Heir. He began following me, or had others do so, and, soon, knew of Nicoline and where to find her."

Caryss remembered most of what Willem had told her of what had come next, but, without interrupting, she allowed Crispin to continue.

"Once Delwin knew of her, everything changed. Nicoline had told me of her life before the temple, of her mother, although she knew not who her own father had been. Did Willem tell you of her, Caryss? Of her past?"

For a moment, she hesitated, uncertain how much to admit.

"I know little of her and knew nothing of your son."

Half-truths, Caryss was learning, helped one to survive in the King's City.

She did not know if he heard the lie on her lips. "Before she entered the temple, she lived with her mother, who had once been a brothel worker. It was there that Nicoline was born and her father unknown," his words trailed off.

"And Delwin learned of that?"

"He told my father of it all," Crispin hissed, shaking his head as if he could change the past.

When the prince pulled back from the window, Caryss nearly gasped. Moments before, he had been rimmed in the soft silver light of the orbs, yet now, just steps from her, Crispin burned bright. Red and flaming, etched with fire.

When he spoke, the words no louder than a whisper, her skin burned, until she feared it would blister. His breath was fire hot, his eyes edged with flame.

"Delwin knew Nicoline was with child before I did."

In the center of the room, where the prince was now standing, the air grew warm and smoky, a cloud of gray rising from his feet.

"My father tried to have her killed. Before the boy was even born, he had her house, the one that Willem had purchased, burned to the ground. When that did not work, his men tried to drown her," Crispin choked, emotion thickening his words.

With a hand to her mouth to block the smoke, Caryss watched the prince as he closed his eyes, hands tight at his sides. For how long she could not tell, he said nothing, standing as still as a courtyard statue. Slowly, the smoke cleared. When she dropped her hand, her eyes stayed on Crispin. His own eyes, when he opened them, stared back at her, gold-rimmed, but flameless.

"Both my father and brother had learned much about Nicoline. But not enough. You have seen the boy, Caryss, and know there is more in him than the blood of Cordisian gods. It was the same with Nicoline, although she begged me to say nothing of it. Had I told my father of her skill, he might have relented and let me marry her. Or he might have tried to kill her sooner. I had played the game and lost. He made me choose."

"Choose between what?"

"The throne and my son," he cried.

Later, he whispered, "I am King's Heir still, and my son knows nothing of me."

"Your son knows you, my lord!" she exclaimed, jumping up from the bed, "He has mastered the skill of time-walking so that he might know you."

"Why were you able to see the boy if I could not?" he pleaded to her, stepping back as the air once again warmed around him.

Time slowed.

Crispin, moments before blazing and bright, dulled to a faded shade of white, and Caryss fell back onto the cot. With shaking hands, she felt for the dagger, discovering it under the blanket that had fallen from her when she had risen in haste. Tightening her fingers around its worn hilt, she brought it toward her until the blade was hidden once again beneath her leg.

In a voice that she did not recognize as her own, Caryss said to him, "I am with child, Prince Crispin. And the babe is a god-touched, although no kin to yours."

Had Aldric been in the room, he would have stopped her from speaking, and, she knew, he would have been right to do so.

When Crispin looked at her, she bit her lip until the bitter taste of blood seared her tongue, forcing her to confess no more.

"Does Willem know?" Crispin finally asked.

"Yes, but not many else do," she answered softly.

"Did he advise you to tell no one, including me?"

Her only answer was a quick nod.

"You should have listened," the prince fumed.

When she said nothing, he asked, "What was he thinking to send you here?"

Again, she said nothing, recognizing her error.

"He has become a fool since I last saw him!" Crispin hissed, striding back to the window.

With a sigh that deepened as she breathed, Caryss explained, "I am here to heal your father, naught has changed. I am a healer, prince, with oaths and training. The babe does nothing to change that."

Her words, she sensed, mattered little. And when Crispin faced her again, Caryss was not surprised to see the fury on his face.

"As king, one of my first acts will be to see to the instruction offered at the Academy," he told her, with disdain. "You have been here less than a day and already you admit to me that you are with child. And not just any child, but one with the blood of gods in his veins! This is not Litusia! I just told you of how I cannot even trust my own brother, and, within minutes, you tell me what few know. You will not last long in the King's City, Caryss."

Before she could reply, Crispin had crossed the room, stopping in front of where she sat. "You have the body of a woman grown, but the mind of a child," he yelled. "Was I not clear when I requested a healer come in secrecy? Was I not clear when I warned that none could know your purpose here?"

"Tell me of whom you've encountered and spoken with since being here, Caryss," he demanded, drops of warm spittle falling onto her bared legs, uncovered by the too-small robe.

53

"If you seek to scare me, my lord, you should not waste your time," she told him, more calmly than she felt.

Faster than she thought possible, he grabbed her, his hands pulling at the loose sleeves of her underdress as he yanked her up to face him. In her hand, she gripped the dagger, letting her arm fall just behind her hip, knowing he could not see what was hidden there.

"Who have you told about the King?" he hissed, his breath hot and wet against her forehead.

Spitting words at him, with a defiance that was unfeigned, Caryss answered, "I am not the fool you think I am, prince. None know that I am here, and only a whore that I helped at the piers knows I am a healer."

Without releasing her, he said, "My cousin sent you into a pit of snakes that will curl about your legs and climb up your body until they wrap themselves about your neck. They will squeeze the light out of you, Caryss, and they will kill you, laughing as they do so. You should not be here. You are not fit to live among the snakes and rats."

Feeling his hands relax, she stumbled away from him, nearly tripping over the edge of the cot. With her back to the window, she looked to him, realizing she had misjudged him, and, she could admit, now feared him. He was right, she now knew, the King's City was nothing like Litusia.

"If I leave, your father will not live." she called to him, letting her eyes fall upon his. *Let him know my words for truth.*

"If you stay, I fear that I will be unable to keep you safe. If any find out about the babe, you would become little more than food for the vultures."

"You make little sense, Crispin. I am a healer! Few would even think to threaten one such as me."

"Aye, you're a healer. A beautiful, quick-witted one. But, you are a fool nonetheless. You trust too soon. And ones whom you should not. Have you thought that I might be lying to you, Caryss? That I didn't see the boy because he did not want me to? That he does not want me to see him because he knows that if I do, he will soon be dead?"

When he stepped closer to her, she pressed her back into the window, all color fading from her face.

"You would not kill your own son," she gasped.

Again his hands were on her, pinning her to the window. Behind her eyes, the room began to darken, tinged in red.

"Over ten moon years ago, I chose the throne over him. If I must do so again, I will."

Shaking her head, Caryss gazed at him. She did not believe his words, yet questioned why he had spoken so.

54

"You sent for a healer," she mumbled, trying to make sense of what no longer did.

"If my father dies now, I will have a fight ahead that I am not yet prepared for. Nearly all is a game in the King's City. All! And all you have brought is a fallen mage, a woman, and two guards who were bought. You have lost before the game has even begun," he railed at her.

"You know nothing of me, prince," she hissed, anger burning hot as the babe finally woke.

The prince was so near to her that she could feel his life pulse as it thumped against his tunic, his chest against her own. She could have pushed him from her, Caryss knew, feeling the strength of the babe growing, yet she did not.

"Tell me of the babe's father, Caryss," he whispered, the words suddenly soft and sweet against her ear.

Caryss paused, then turned her face until his lips were near her own. With a half-smile across her face, she told him, "I will tell you nothing more."

Her words were so close as to be a kiss, yet neither moved.

Finally, the prince pulled his head back, slightly, and asked, "Who is he? If the babe is god-touched, she will have both friend and foe. I might be able to help."

Feeling as if her legs were near to collapsing beneath her, Caryss struggled to stand. The prince's words, his last ones, only added to her unease.

I will not tell him of Conri, she vowed.

"How do I know which you are?" she breathed.

Laughing now, the prince's eyes were light and glimmering, as if nothing had changed. "You are learning, girl," he told her, stepping back.

"How fares my cousin?" he added, from across the room.

Hesitatingly, Caryss replied, "He is the same as when you last asked, I would guess."

As if she had said too much, Crispin clapped his hands together, the sound clanging around the room until Caryss thought that Aldric and Sharron would wake. No knock came.

With a suddenly throbbing life pulse and a cool air around her, Caryss asked him, "What have you done to the ward?"

His smile bright, his teeth straight and white, Crispin teased, "The student continues to learn."

"What have you done to the ward?" she screamed, now knowing that none could hear.

"It has been strengthened. You need not worry."

"What is it that you want from me, prince?" she asked, her voice low, as if her screams had left her throat raw.

55

"Is the babe Willem's?"

When she did not answer, he said, "Why would he send you here alone like a bone to the dogs?"

Again, Caryss did not answer.

"Did he truly think you would be safe here? That his child would be safe? He has been gone for over ten moon years, but Delwin hates him still and would see him dead. I had thought him to know better. He has forgotten the ways of Rexterra."

"You speak of him as if he did not sacrifice his own life for yours!" she scolded.

"Is that how he tells it?"

"You are here, and he is not. That is story enough."

The prince's laugh was harsh when it next came. "How well you play your role as healer. Tell me who you really are, Caryss," he said to her, roughly.

It was her turn to cross the room in long strides, closing on him with the dagger still clutched in her pale fingers, the black blade shining and sharp against her hand.

When Caryss was within reach of him, she cried, "For half of my life, I have trained as a healer. You will find few who know as much as I do. I play no role, other than the one I have since I first entered the gates of the Academy. I am a healer, no more. I have little interest in these games you speak of, and less in what you think of me. I am here to do as I must, as my oaths bind me. I am here to heal the King. Nothing more."

"Sent here by a man who was too afraid to come himself!" Crispin retorted angrily.

"Your memory is faulty, prince, and you forget that you are the reason he can't return. I thought Willem to be more than cousin to you, and, now, you speak as if he is more enemy than kin."

"I had thought so, too, but he makes me doubt his good sense by sending you here, as if in sacrifice."

Caryss let him believe the lie, having realized that it was safer for Crispin to believe the babe to be Willem's than the daughter of a Tribesman.

"Did Willem think none would know the babe as god-touched? Blood is blood, and the babe will have enough to be fire-kissed."

"I know not what Willem thought," she huffed, growing increasingly weary of the prince's questions.

"If the babe is born in the King's City, will you keep it hidden? Was that the plan?"

"Write to your cousin and ask," she curtly told him.

Watching as his eyes brightened, Caryss stepped back, now able to recognize the streaking of his power as the flames in his eyes flashed.

56

"It will not be long before my brother learns of you, despite my efforts. As a healer, you would be offered protection. As the mother of a traitor's son, you will get none. As the man who brought you here, I will have to answer for that. No good can come of you being here, Caryss."

"No good? Is the King being healed not what you sought?"

His eyes, gold and orange, scanned her. Standing in the thin dress, Caryss shivered under his gaze. Suddenly fearing that he would see the dagger, she backed away from him, keeping her hand behind her. His next words made her stop.

"What I seek is the throne."

"Then why send for me?"

"I need my father to remind the people of Rexterra that I am his chosen heir. He needs to be well enough to do so, and, these last few moons, he has not been."

Her mouth falling open, Caryss exclaimed, "How easily you admit to being the snake you warned me of, Crispin."

"My father took my son from me. I will not have him take the throne as well!" he roared.

In less than a day, Caryss had come to understand that in the King's City, power reigned and deceit rewarded.

As if her own gray-green eyes were aflame, she looked at him, her life pulse flittering. Her back straight like a Northern pine and her eyes as clear as the rivers of Eirrannia, Caryss cried, "Your son is better off without you."

By the time he reached her, Caryss saw him through a haze of red. Her hands steadied as she shifted the dagger.

When his hands reached for her, she raised her own, striking at him with the dagger's hilt. The blade, black and sparkling, was gripped taut in her hand.

Blood dripped from Crispin's cheek, just below his eye, where the dagger's handle had sliced open his skin. Looking down at her fingers, she saw that she, too, was bleeding.

Wiping the dagger on her tunic, she calmly stated, "If I had used the blade, you would be dead."

As Crispin reached to feel the wound, Caryss walked to the cot, squeezing by as he stood stunned and silent. Once more she wiped blood from the dagger before sliding it into the sheath that lay on the cot. Throwing the dagger onto the small side table, Caryss examined her fingers, quickly realizing that only the middle two had been cut, and neither was as bad as it could have been.

From a pouch that lay near the thrown dagger, she gathered bleached cloth, wrapping it tightly around the middles of her fingers. They burned, but she paid little heed to the pain, reaching for another pouch.

Without turning toward the prince, she commanded, "Sit on the bed."

She thought he might argue, but was surprised when he said nothing. Stumbling, with a hand still to his cheek, he fell onto the cot.

"I have misjudged you," he whispered to her as she sat beside him.

"No. You have not," she answered, grabbing another white linen from the pouch and holding it to his cheek.

Little else did she say, but for the next hour, Caryss cleaned and stitched his wound, carefully and with a steadier hand than she had thought possible. She kept her stitches tight and used a fine thread, hoping that the King's Heir would have little scar to remember what she had done.

"I will heal your father, Crispin, for that was the task I was given. Other than that, I will do and say nothing, as I want no part of your fight."

He nodded, the tiny, black crosses beneath his eye marring an otherwise handsome face.

With her hands in her lap, she sighed, "I suppose I should apologize for striking you."

With a weakened shrug, he told her, "If you had not struck me, I would have struck you. You have learned fast the ways of the palace."

Caryss pulled a small, amber-colored flask from the pouch. She placed it into Crispin's hand, closing his fingers around it. "If the pain is too much, place a few drops on your tongue."

His smile widened until he was laughing and asked, "Am I to trust what you give me? What poison hides in the bottle?"

Shaking her head, she answered, "There is no poison. Hand it to me and I will show you."

After the prince had given her the bottle, she pulled the topper off and placed the end of her small finger into the deep brown liquid. While he watched, she placed her finger onto her tongue, as she had instructed him to do. After he nodded, she placed the cork back onto the bottle, and set it on the cot between them. When Crispin did not reach for it, she said nothing. A small bowl of a creamy salve sat near the flask, and, silently, she dipped her fingers into it.

With fading orb-light surrounding them, Caryss looked to the prince, his eyes softly calm.

I will not survive here, she thought, watching him and remembering his words.

The left side of his tunic, near his shoulder, was speckled with blood, as red as the streaks of blood that lay across the bottom of her dress. With the same fingers, wrapped and throbbing, that she had used to stitch him, Caryss again reached for his cheek, letting her fingertips gently rub the lavender-smelling paste over the row of crosses.

A sweet smell of flower and mint filled the room, and her hand lingered on his face.

Her chest rising as she breathed deeply, Caryss traced a path from eye to lip. Neither spoke. The glow in his eyes told her much, and Caryss leaned into him, dropping her hand as her lips found his.

A slow burn filled her, and no words were spoken. Another game, she thought, but did not say.

Later, as the prince slept angled next to her, Caryss slowly reached for her healer's belt. After a few moments spent searching, she pulled another flask from a pouch, a rose-colored one, smaller than the others. When the topper was removed, cherry laurel and apple scented the room.

Slowly, so not to wake the prince, Caryss filled a glass dropper with a greenish liquid. Pressing her body into his back, she leaned near to his face, watching as he slept. With his eyes closed, his fires extinguished, he seemed at peace, as mortal as those he sought to rule.

Earlier, the prince had boasted of his god-blood, yet, beside her, in slumber, he was as any other man would be.

Her hands, healer's hands, pale, Northern hands, did not shake or tremble as she brought the dropper to his half-open mouth. When the glass was clear, free of the laurel and geranium tonic, Caryss placed her fingers on Crispin's neck. With each beat of his life pulse, her fingers twitched.

Rolling away from his, Caryss stood, unclothed. The prince did not move, as she knew he would not. With little light to guide her, Caryss dressed, gathering her clothing from where it lay across an ornate chair. Making little noise, she filled her pouches with the dagger and flasks. Lastly, she sat back on the edge of the bed to lace up her sandals, one of the few things that remained of her time in Tretoria. Before she rose, she once again felt for Crispin's life pulse as the soft sounds of his sleep filled the room.

Dressed and ready, she hurried from the room.

*****

6

"Wake up!" she begged, shaking his shoulders.

The sun had long set, and a purple haze fell over the room. The night was cool and skin prickles spread atop her skin.

When he hadn't responded, she slapped him across the face, and the clang of the strike echoed off the walls of his small bedroom. Clutching a worn, faded shawl that had nearly fallen from her shoulders in one hand, the woman raised her other hand. Even though it trembled, she brought it to the boy's cheek again, slapping him with enough force to redden his skin. This time, he shuddered, reaching his skinny fingers to rub where her hand had just been.

"Did I not tell you to leave him be?" she sighed, watching as he opened his sea-lit eyes.

The boy nodded as he hurriedly sat up, leaned against the wall, and cried, "The most wonderful thing happened, mother!"

As her face paled, Jarek noticed the darkness outside the window across from his bed, and, when he spoke again, his words were hoarse and his stomach grumbled loudly, "I did not mean to be gone so long."

"Tell me what happened," Nicoline told her son, shaking her head as she sat down next to him.

"A woman saw me! As I walked down the hall of the palace, she noticed me and asked who I was."

She gasped, her mouth suddenly dry and her chest heavy. At the edges of her eyes, sky-blue and shining, hung tears.

"Mama," he stuttered, "The woman has a daughter like me, one that can time-walk. And I never told her my name."

Nicoline said nothing.

"Please don't cry, mama," he pleaded, wrapping a long, lanky arm around her.

Since he was a small boy, Jarek had told her that he could visit other places while he slept, and, after nearly a moon year, she had finally understood that he was not just dreaming. He could tell her of places where he had never gone and of his father, who he not seen since he was still at the breast. As he got older, he grew stronger in his skill, able to travel farther distances and with less time needed to recover. Still, she feared for his safety, and had often begged him to stop, afraid of what would happen if he was discovered in the palace. But he was a curious child, different than his most, and he longed to know his father. When Jarek had been old enough to realize that he was unlike the other Planusian boys, she had told him of his father.

Nicoline had never known her own, and she had long vowed that her son would not be able to say the same. Since then, nearly all of his time-walking had been to Rexterra.

"Jarek, you must tell me what happened," she said, explaining again the dangers of being seen.

With a voice still sweet with youth, he told her, "It was not father who saw me; he never does. It was a woman with hair the color of fire! She saw me as soon as I walked toward her, even though I had not called out to her. But, I could hear all that she said as if I was really there with them."

With a deep crease in her forehead, Nicoline asked, "Her hair was not dark?"

"No. It was red, but not the color of blood."

Distractedly, Nicoline mumbled, "It was not Lillia then."

"She did not tell me her name, but she seemed to know who I was."

"What did she say to you, Jarek?"

Smiling, as if he did not sense any danger, he answered, "She told me to become strong, and that I must learn how to fight. And she told me that father was not ready for me, but he would send for me when he could."

"Was there aught else that she said to you?" she asked, the words coming in short bursts.

Looking serious now, Jarek pushed his straw-colored hair, long and wavy, from his face, and told her, "She yelled at me, mama. And told me that I must not time-walk so often or where I could be found by those mage-trained."

Liking the unknown woman already, Nicoline laughed and said, "She is right, Jarek. You must stop. It is not yet time for you to be in the King's City, and you are but a child."

"Mama, can I learn to use a sword?" Jarek begged, jumping up onto his knees.

"Silly boy," she joked, swatting at him. "What need do you have of a sword when you have air and sky as weapon?"

"I must be able to use a sword as well, as they do in Rexterra, if I am to return there someday. You have told me that some skies will never answer, mama, as much as I may call."

Nicoline looked at the boy, still nearly half her size, and shook her head. His mage-skill was sharp, stronger than her own, she often thought. He would spend hours in the fields, far from anyone, and, even though she could not see what it was that he did, Nicoline could feel the clouds shift and knew who had commanded them to do so. Jarek, she knew, rarely acted on impulse. His actions were often well-considered ones, even though his time-walking carried great risk. Until now, he had not been seen.

"We will compromise. You must tell me when you are going to spirit-walk, and will only do so with my permission from now on. If you can promise me that, then I will find you one who will teach you the ways of the sword."

Jarek jumped from the be with a whoop, before rushing back to hug her, pulling his lanky arms tight against her thread-bare shawl.

"I will not disappoint you, mama. I will be a warrior like Cordisia has never seen before. I will open the skies above on my enemies and knock them to the ground with my sword," he vowed, waving his arms about as if he held both sword and lightning.

As he danced and played, Nicoline thought on their past. For nearly eleven moon years, he had been her son only. The two of them lived alone on the large farmstead, allowing them the freedom and space to explore and expand their Elemental skill. None suspected that they were anything but a widowed mother and her beloved son. Yet if Jarek had his way, all would one day know him as the rightful heir to the Rexterran throne. A boy's dream, she thought.

Nearing midnight, he fell asleep. Seated at a small desk in the main room of the farmhouse, Nicoline reached for parchment and ink. With no one else around, she began to write, calling in a favor that was long overdue.

*****

7

For the last few moons, Pietro found himself as the most senior healer at the Academy. Word soon spread that he would be named as the new Master Apprentice, or so Master Torino had informed him. Pietro himself could only wait, although he often thought of his Healer Journey and where it might take him.

Over the last moon, Pietro had spent more time with the Masters and less at the Gull House. He rarely saw Talia, or her cousin Louissia, and only occasionally saw Kennet, who spent even more time alone in the library since Bronwen had departed. Tonight, though, he decided to forgo his studies, and hurried to an inn near the Litusian piers. The sky had already darkened by the time that he arrived, and he quickly entered, letting the heavy, whitened wood slam closed behind him. He had replaced his robes with a simple tunic overtop fitted trousers. For the next few hours, he would no longer be healer.

A leather-covered stool near the end of the long sandstone bar stood empty, and he rushed toward it and ordered an ale from a heavily bearded Tretorian. Watching as the man poured the honey-colored ale into a stout mug, he noticed a woman sitting alone at a small table near the main door. Dark hair fell across her face as she stared at her mug. Her bodice, Pietro saw, fit snugly and was dyed a blue so deep as to be black. Her lips and cheeks were flushed red, the kiss of the ale, he knew.

Grabbing his mug, he hopped off the stool, walking slowly to where the woman sat.

"Might I join you, my lady?" he asked, with only the hint of a smile on his face.

When she glanced up at him, her eyes a stormy gray, Pietro's lips parted further, his teeth gleaming and straight.

In the low, husky voice of one used to long days at sea, she called to him, "Yes, but I will need another ale."

With a nod, Pietro returned to the bar, motioning to the innkeeper to send him two drinks. As he waited, he thought on what to say. Soon, with two foaming mugs, he returned.

"My name is Alonzo," he told her as he swiftly sat down, presenting her with the mug as if in tribute.

"And I am Neena," she answered, without smiling, and looked at him from the corners of her eyes.

"What brings you to Litusia?"

Shaking her head as the bitter ale dripped from her lips, the woman told him, "I am a cook aboard a merchant ship out of the King's City."

After another sip, she said, "You are far from home, are you not?"

He glanced at her again, understanding that she was not like the girls he had often dallied with at the inns. She was older than he, perhaps by as many as ten moon years. Lines creased her brow and edged her gray-black eyes. He would not be surprised if she was not a cook at all, for she had the look of a warrior about her.

"I have been at the Healer's Academy for nearly half my life," he finally explained.

"You are Rexterran, are you not?"

Shrugging as he downed much of the ale, he told her, "I was once."

After a moment, he added, "How fares Rexterra?"

While he would not have guessed the woman to be Rexterran, that she recognized him to be suggested she knew the city well.

"I have been gone from Rexterra for over a moon, and news is slow to reach us while at sea. The king lives last I knew, although he must not be well, as few see him. The city itself is much the same, although you might not recognize it for all the building that the King's Heir has done."

Warmed by the drink and more relaxed than he had been in a moon, Pietro teased, "I hear something else in your words. And your hair is far too lovely to be Rexterran."

Her slate-colored eyes looked at him, questioning and unsure, as if she was unused to such scrutiny. He knew then with certainty that she was more than what she pretended. For a moment, he considered whether she was Tribe. Her skin, even rose-tinted from the ale, was not as pale as the Tribesman's, nor were her eyes as dark. Yet there was something to her that was unlike all else in the tavern.

Before he could speak on it, she stated, "I was born east of here, in a land where women are kings and fighters and men are little more than breeding stags."

Having never heard of such a place, he inquired why she had left.

Neena only answered once her mug had been drained. "I believed that I was in love with a Rexterran man and followed him to the King's City. You seem to know enough about the ways of men to know what happened next."

"Aye," he agreed, but pushed for more information on where she had been born. "I have never heard of this land that you speak of, where women rule as kings. How far east must one travel to reach it?"

"Another ale and the tale is yours," she laughed, the sound deep and throaty.

When two more pints were in front of them, Neena told him of Sythia, of the women she called kin, and how they had warned her that she would not be allowed to return if she followed the Cordisian man. But she did not head those warnings and had remained, even after the man married another.

"Do you miss your homeland?" he asked, thinking of his near return to his own.

"I was once a sure shot with bow and arrow," she sighed, her eyes looking past him. "Yet have not had one in my hands for nearly seven moon years. I would return if I could, but Queen Makeena will not welcome me, I fear."

Thinking on his brothers, Pietro inquired if she thought to find a place among the many mercenary groups throughout Cordisia. As both woman and foreign-born, she would not be able to join the Royal Army, but skilled fighters were needed always. And the mercenary groups paid well, he had heard.

Shaking her head, Neena explained, "I have a daughter. Her presence is tolerated aboard the ship. Elsewhere, it would not be, I think."

Understanding more of her plight, Pietro pushed her mug toward her, while reaching for his own. Once they were empty, he leaned back, rubbing at his hair.

"My name is not Alonzo," he told her, his words fast and pitched.

When she smiled, he laughed in return.

"I *am* healer-trained," he explained.

"I did not doubt you were, although you do not seem old or ugly enough to be so."

His life pulse had quickened and his hands warmed.

"I will be visiting the King's City soon," he slurred, yet his vision was clear. "Mayhap we could meet for another drink."

Pushing her thick hair from her face, Neena gazed back at him, her eyes wrapped in mist. She was as unlike Louissia and Talia as any could be. She was untamed and strange, yet Pietro wanted little more than to wrap his fingers through her hair. Her lips, long and wide, parted, and his eyes grew fire-touched.

"Come with me," he begged.

Her nod, slight and silent, caused him to shake as he rose. Dropping coin on the table, he reached for her hand. As his fingers burned, hers, rough and cool, joined his as they hurried from the tavern.

I will see her again, he thought, blinded with reddened lust.

*****

Once outside of her room, she leaned against the wall, trembling. She did not think her legs would carry her across the hallway, but she noticed the King's door remained unguarded and hurried to Aldric's room. As she suspected, his door opened for her, although her ears buzzed and her skin prickled as she rushed inside. The ward had been a strong one.

Standing over his bed, she quietly cried, "Wake up!"

Her fingertips, stained yellow, pushed on his chest until his eyes opened.

"We must leave at once," she hissed.

Jumping up, mostly unclothed, Aldric ran for the door and closed it. "Did the girl visit you again?"

As he searched for his clothing, she told him that it was the King's Heir who had visited her.

With an unlaced tunic and pants slipping from his thin waist, Aldric called, "Are you in danger or has he harmed you?"

There was too little time to tell him what had occurred.

"I will explain later. Please, Aldric, just do as I ask," she begged.

The mage watched her, yet said nothing, and, after a moment, rushed to grab his boots. Pulling the scuffed and scratched leather onto his bare feet, Aldric neared her, stumbling.

"What of the King?" he asked, reaching for the door.

In a whisper, she cried, "I do this for him! I will not have my vow broken."

She reached for him, locking her fingers into his, and told him, "I mean to take him from here."

Beneath her hand, his lanky fingers stiffened, as if he finally understood her plan.

"Without any knowing, I presume."

When Caryss nodded, her hair fell across her face, covering her gray gaze. If Aldric could have seen her eyes, he would have seen fear there.

"And we cannot wait until the sun rises? What of Crispin?"

Aldric was fully dresses now and standing by the door, with one hand raised, as if to undo the ward.

When she answered, Caryss realized the truth of her words, as if she now sensed her path changing. Her words cracked, as if lightning, shards of white sparkling the darkened room.

"I must trust no one, not even the prince. If he cares for his father, he will come to understand what it is that I must do."

"This is madness," Aldric mumbled, pressing his hand against the door.

Before the door opened, she told him, "We must get Sharron and then the King. His door is unwatched, but heavily warded. If you cannot unbind it, then I know not what to do next."

"The ward can be undone. But what of Niko and Kurtis?"

"They were bought with coin. It was unwise to trust them as we did."

As she spoke, Caryss looked up at his slate-blue eyes, and saw surprise there.

"If you leave them, they will be questioned and killed," he told her, with little emotion.

For the first time since she had entered his room, Caryss hesitated.

Without looking to him she said, "What happens after we leave here is of little concern to me."

She knew not what he thought as the mage watched her, but when he opened the door, she inspected the empty hall before rushing to Sharron's room. Without turning, Caryss realized that Aldric was several doors down, outside the King's room. Just steps inside Sharron's room, Caryss nearly screamed, covering her gaping mouth with the back of her hand.

"I knew that you would come."

Her hand fell as she pushed the door closed.

"You half-scared me to death, Sharron. I had not thought you'd be awake," Caryss whimpered, holding a hand to her chest as if she could not breathe.

Sitting on her bed, the other healer was fully clothed in a pale riding suit, her long skirt twirling around finely made, supple boots. Her hair, faded lighter by their moons spent in travel, was braided, hanging across her shoulder. Sharron looked as if she had long been ready, and Caryss envied the woman's ease.

Rising from the bed, Sharron murmured, "What of Crispin? I heard him enter your room."

Leaning into the door as her legs began to tremble anew, Caryss gasped at Sharron's admission.

Finally, she mouthed, "He will not wake, but we must hurry nonetheless."

When the other healer was beside her, Caryss embraced her and whispered, "You could have warned me not to come here at all."

"For others, that might be how it works, but, for me, the sight has never been so easily tamed," Sharron softly explained.

When they opened the door, a low humming throbbed through the still-empty hallway.

*****

Placing his hands onto the center of the door, Aldric watched as his fingers, scarred and misshapen from moon years as a mercenary, pulsed, rising and falling as if drumming. The ward was strong, much stronger than he had imagined. For a moment he wondered who had bound it, thinking of his brother as he remembered how gifted he had once been. The Mage-Guild was well practiced in ward-work, yet Aldric knew that few could design a ward as complex as the one guarding the King's door. And even fewer could dismantle it.

Closing his eyes, he let the pulsing fill his fingertips like a swift-moving river. As if riding the waves, he weaved and swayed, his hands never straying from the door. The current was fast, pulling at him until he dropped to his knees. Around him, Aldric discovered the flow, riding it, faster and faster until he sensed it settling.

Rising again, he fought to control the stream, just long enough to create a break in the current. With one hand on the door, his other hand pulled free, waving as if it was not his own, dancing with the air.

Again he rode the wave as it spiraled down, dropping him again to his knees.

When next he stood, Aldric's breathing was shallow and loud. With both hands on the door, he pulled at the ward, twisting it, remaking it until it answered to none but him.

In words as old as earth, he sang, calling for the ward to fall. Around him, the hallway blackened and his head fell, heavy, against the door, slamming into it until he saw nothing but darkness.

*****

"Help me get him into the room," Caryss cried, although her words were no more than a whisper.

Both women had arms under the mage, dragging him into Herron's room, while the King slept, croaking snores echoing through the room.

Across Aldric's forehead was a large cut, blood falling into his eye and down his cheek. His life pulse beat strong, and the gash was not a deep one, and the women dropped him near the edge of the bed as they hurried toward the King.

After quickly removing the blankets that lay atop the King, Caryss realized that he was unclothed. Working together, the women had him dressed swiftly in a simple sleeping robe and loose sandals. In one corner hung an ornately embroidered jacket, yet it would easily mark him as king.

When they had finished, Sharron asked, "How will we move him?"

"I had not thought on that," Caryss confessed, staring at the still-sleeping king.

Aldric, awake now and holding a hand to his head, mumbled, "There was a cart in the garden that we passed through earlier. If we can get him there, it will do."

His words were hoarse, as if he had not spoken in moons, but his solution was a good one, and both women nodded, pulling the King until he, too, was in a seated position.

"Can you walk?" Sharron called back to the mage.

Waving a blood-soaked hand, Aldric stated, "Think not of me and see to the King."

Out of one of her pouches, Caryss pulled a small flask. Uncorking it sent a strong smell of fennel and cacao into the room. Just before she was about to drop the dark liquid into the King's mouth, she paused.

"Perhaps it would be best if he did not yet wake," she said to Sharron, who agreed as she slipped her arms beneath the King's shoulders.

Herrin had once been a large man, and even in Litusia did they hear tales of his robust appetite. Yet his illness had stripped him of that, and, now, he was smaller than both women, little more than skin-covered bones. While Sharron grabbed his upper half, Caryss moved to the bottom of the bed, turning his legs until Herrin appeared to be awake, seated on the edge.

"King Herrin," Caryss half-sung, rubbing at his legs.

"King Herrin," she called again as Sharron struggled to lift him.

Aside from some grumbling, the King said nothing, and his eyes remained closed.

"He is heavy with poppy milk," Sharron informed her, although Caryss, too, had known such was the case.

Aldric stood behind them, but when Caryss looked to him, he was pale, more so than usual, and still he seemed to sway, as if he was aboard a ship. The undoing of the warding had taken a heavy toll on him, she knew, as her own life pulse quickened.

With little choice, she told Sharron, "Until we reach the cart in the courtyard, we will have to drag him, for even in his state, he is too heavy for either of us to carry. We will leave the way we came since few know of that passage."

"Aldric is too weak to ward us, I fear," Sharron whispered.

Dropping the King's feet to the floor, Caryss said, "Then we must hurry. And hope none are awake at this hour."

As Caryss and Sharron shifted, each one gripping the King's upper back and arm, Aldric croaked, "I will do what I can."

With a slip of cotton pressed to his head, the mage led the way from the room, into the dimly lit hall as the healers dragged the King along the lushly carpeted floor which softened their steps. The path seemed much longer now, ten times as much as when last they walked it, and Caryss breathed heavy and her pulse beat hard against her tunic as they made their way to the exit.

A faint humming followed them, and she knew that Aldric had somehow warded them, her skin prickling at the thought.

When they reached the door, Sharron softly said, "I will fetch the cart," and hurried off.

No one spoke, even once she returned.

With one final tug, the King was half-thrown into the waiting cart, exposed and gaunt in his dressing gown under a fully-mooned sky. The cart was not large, and the King's legs hung over the edge, but Caryss nearly wept when they rushed off, undetected, into the quiet night, the throbbing of the ward now gone as Aldric's strength left him completely.

At some point, Aldric had placed his torn and graying coat over the King, draping him with it, and again they hurried on, the sky beginning to lighten. Soon, she worried, the King's disappearance would be noted, and she forced herself to run faster, pushing the cart as she did so.

When the wheels of the gardening cart first found paver, Caryss stumbled, and Sharron took over. The outlying Lower Streets were dim, small orb-lights hanging from rusty poles. Jogging beside the cart, she noticed dirt and mud clinging to the edges of it and falling from its wheels.

None would think him to be their king, she thought, nearly laughing as she ran.

*****

8

Her job here was done, she knew, looking at the King once more.

Soon, it would be time to leave Rexterra, and, with each step away from the palace, Caryss had felt the noose of snakes about her neck loosening. The Lower Streets all seemed the same to her, even though they had long ago been designed in a neat grid. Slowing her step, she looked around, as if lost in a never-ending maze.

"I have lost my way," she called to Aldric, who had slowed as well. Soon, all three stopped, the moon overhead silver and rounded, casting her watchful eye upon them.

With a snort that was akin to a laugh, Aldric told her, "You are not a child of the city, Caryss. Follow me."

He continued on for several blocks before turning down a narrow street that led them away from the docks. The bricks became uneven, causing the cart to rattle and shake and the King to nearly tumble from it. Sharron lunged forward once as Herrin lurched, reaching for him and pushing him back into the cart.

"Tread carefully," Aldric hissed in warning, before turning back to guide.

She said nothing in reply, finally recognizing where they were. Just ahead was Nahla's door, and they paused just above the steps leading down to it. Sharron nodded at her, and Caryss nearly leaped down, half-falling into the brightly-painted door, banging her fist on it until her knuckles reddened.

Finally, the sound of a chain being unhooked on the other side could be heard, and Caryss dropped her hand to her side and waited.

When the door opened Nahla stood, wearing only a copper-colored skirt. Even her jewelry had been removed.

Caryss knew not what to say and was only able to mumble, "I need your help, Nahla."

Nahla's deep brown eyes scanned her and then looked past her, toward the others. When her gaze reached the King, she slowly shook her head.

"Do any know that you are here?" she whispered with words edged in disapproval.

"None know," Caryss promised.

"Were you followed?"

"No. We escaped without any notice, but we have little time," Caryss answered, knowing that Nahla recognized the King.

"Child, I had not thought to see you again, but I am not surprised that I was wrong." Her words were softer now, and Caryss felt her eyes fill with tears, yet she fought to keep them unshed, ill at ease with such emotion.

"Come in, and make haste with it," the woman scolded when she hesitated.

Aldric helped Sharron maneuver the cart down the steps, and, although it was loud, none were around to hear. When they were all inside, and the door closed, Nahla asked why they had come, yet she made no mention of the King.

"I need a ship," Caryss explained. "We will not be able to leave through the gates. If we did manage to get the King through unnoticed, we would not be far gone before they tracked us down."

"Which tells me that none know that you seek to leave Rexterra. Or that you have the King with you."

Caryss's cheeks burned red, but she stated, "The palace no longer seemed safe. For any of us."

Nahla nodded. "You feared for the babe. You are wiser than when last I saw you, even though it was but days ago."

Why does everyone think me a fool? Her thoughts were sharp, yet Caryss bit the words, tasting their bitterness on her tongue.

"Where do you wish to go?" the Islander asked.

Caryss looked around the room, noticing that nothing had changed since last they were there. Aldric was seated on Nahla's only chair, and Sharron tended to his head. Strips of cotton rimmed his forehead, but the bleeding had ceased. His hood would cover much of it, Caryss thought. He was still weak with fatigue, yet she knew that he listened.

"To the Southern Cove Islands," she finally confessed.

From across the room, Aldric cried, "What of Eirrannia?"

It was not unexpected, and Caryss stuttered, "Despite what some think, I am no fool. Crispin will look to the north first to find us. Eirrannia will wait for the girl."

Ignoring the argument between mage and healer, Nahla chimed, "You seek the *diauxie.*"

They were all standing now, in a half-circle, although the King was dozing in the cart near the door. Nahla walked over to Herrin, removed Aldric's coat, and tucked a thick, plush cream-colored blanket around him. When she finished, she ran her thumbs across his closed lids, whispering, as if in prayer.

"Why has he not woken?" Nahla questioned, her hands hovering near the King's face.

Sharron, as if she did not fully trust the woman, stepped to the King, laying her own hand over him, as if she sought to protect him.

It was she who told Nahla, "His body has become dependent on poppy milk. Without it, he would likely not survive, yet, with it, he is as you see him now."

"A drugged king is an easy one to control," Nahla mused, cradling her hands against her chest, which was now covered in a nearly translucent scarf.

To Caryss, she asked, "Do all healers from the North collect broken men as you do?"

Her words, spoken in clear Common with the ringing lilt of the Islands, silenced the room. Not even Aldric responded.

"I know, child, I know," Nahla finally interjected. "Your heart is a pure one, and your intentions good ones. But I fear that you do not understand men, especially the *diauxie*. He is not one who simply follows."

Raising her hands, as if they were a shield, Caryss told her, "It is not me whom he must follow."

With a laugh that was as pretty as a song, Nahla called to Aldric, "And you warned her that I would be the one speaking in riddle."

Growing annoyed, and with little time for jesting, Caryss stammered, "I will find him, and he will come to Cordisia with me. If you will not help me, be quick with your refusal so we can be gone."

Nahla stopped laughing then, and her words became etched in stone, "None make demands of a *diauxie*, girl! With a look from him, you would be unable to move, as if you had become a marble statue. With a whisper from his lips, you would cry tears of blood. With a touch, you would burn as if aflame, your skin hot as if melting."

"Will you offer us aid or not?" Caryss asked, her words nearly empty, as if she grew weary of such warnings.

Sighing deeply, Nahla said, "There is a man leaving for the Cove when the sun rises. As it is, I happened to see him earlier today and know this to be true. With the right amount of coin, he will offer you passage and say nothing of it. Unlike others, he prefers to sleep aboard his boat and will be there now. I will go now to speak with him while you wait here."

"Aldric, give her the coin," Caryss instructed.

As the mage handed her a bag heavy with silver, a gift from Willem, Caryss watched. Her eyes flashed white as she stared, and the room seemed to waver. There, just before her, stood Nahla still, but in place of the coin, she now held a dark-eyed, light-skinned babe with shining hair.

Before Nahla could leave, Caryss cried out to her, "He did not tell me of you. Or of your son."

73

Gasping, her large white teeth almost in a scowl, Nahla hissed, "You are surely mad. I have no son, and no child has been born from my hips."

Caryss looked to Aldric, who gently shook his head at her, as if to beg her to say no more.

Yet, she could not stop. Not now, not once she saw what would come of her meeting Nahla. Like most things, she knew once again, their meeting was more than just chance.

"I have seen you cradle him, at your breast. You will have a son."

Walking, as if in a daze, the few steps to where Nahla stood, Caryss gripped her shoulders when she neared, and pleaded, "We met because we walk a similar path. Half a day ago, those paths crossed. Your son and my daughter will be kin. And kin to the darkness."

"My path is my own, as it has always been. I will walk no other," Nahla sharply replied, moving her fingers rapidly from heart to womb in what Caryss recognized as a protection spell.

She knew that she had not been wrong, yet Caryss asked the mage, "Will it be this way until the babe is born?"

With eyes full of questions, he told her, "As she grows, so will her power. You must learn to control it."

"Perhaps the *diauxie* will be able to teach me how," she sighed in response.

Nahla said no more as she strolled from the room, her long, layered skirt swaying as she moved. When the door was once again closed, Aldric moved until he stood in front of it, his hands clenched at his sides. An ashen hue colored his skin. Not fully recovered, he had said little since the palace. Still, Caryss knew that he would further weaken himself if she required it.

He watched her until she asked, "What is it?"

"Are you so certain that she can be trusted?"

"What choice do we have? If she betrays me, then she will have to answer for it. And not just to me."

Aldric looked up, wide-eyed, but understanding, and stated, "Conri."

"Do not speak his name to me," she hissed, backing away from him.

As if he was the mage he once was, Aldric boomed, "He is the babe's father, Caryss! Even if you have not seen him in a few moons, he will come once the girl is born. You must ready yourself."

"Do you think I forget?" she cried.

In a softer voice, she told him, "Let him come. He will see that I am Bronwen no more."

Those words were the last that she spoke before Nahla returned. Both Aldric and Sharron stayed silent as well. The king slept, unbothered by all that surrounded him, unaware of what would come.

*****

9

As he walked, his thick, leather boots crushed low-lying, lush ferns beneath black-toed tips. Atop the ferns lay fallen Poinciana blossoms, as orange as a setting sun. Had his eyes not been skyward, he would have noticed how the vivid flowers carpeted the ground, leading him from forest to sea.

Overhead, a painted gray sky hung low. Around him, the air was wet, clinging to his skin and beading across his face and arms. His hair fell long and loose down his back, braided and reddened with clay.

He traveled alone, as he always had, swinging a scimitar in front of him, the curved blade clearing a path out of the high grass. Trees stood, scattered to either side of him, but their trunks looked thin and vulnerable compared to him. The sleeves of his tunic had been torn free, exposing large, well-muscled arms and shining brown skin.

At his waist hung two more swords, neither curved. On his left hip, he carried a narrow blade with a thin handle, the tip both fine and sharp. Tied at his other side was a broadsword, sheathed in dirtied leather and nearly forgettable in its plainness. However, it was the sword that lay across his broad back that most noticed.

The sword was vast, strapped tightly against a faded and tight tunic. Hanging from the frayed, plaited edges of his hair to the middle of his legs, the sword was long and, wider than his hand, thick and unsheathed. The blade itself did not shimmer or shine, but the steel was clean and sharpened. The hilt was made of well-worn leather, softened by moon years of use, but unadorned.

Few could lift it, not that he would even let them try.

None of his other swords had been named, but the Greatsword had been a gift to him, forged by a blacksmith from across the Three Seas, and had come to him bearing a name. Otieno dared not change it after hearing the story of the goddess of war for whom she was named.

Enyo.

A huntress who, along with her brother, roamed lands far to the east. While her brother was stronger and more skilled, her bloodlust was unmatched. Or so the blacksmith had told him, many moon years before. While the man's gods were not his own, Otieno had listened, and, at the tale's conclusion, did not change the sword's name. None but he knew it, although some called her by her other name.

Bloodlust.

Reaching up, Otieno traced the blade with scarred fingers, smiling in memory. Dropping his hand back to his side, he let the falling water wash the blood from his fingers. In mist and rain, he continued on, the scimitar slicing through the high, wet grass once again. Even as hours passed, the blood remained. For the *diauxie* could see that his hands would always be stained red.

*****

By the time that Nahla returned, the sky had lightened and the sun hid just below the horizon. King Herrin still slept, and each time Caryss felt his life pulse it was steady but slow. She knew that the poppy milk that he had been given at the palace would soon wear off, and he would wake, yet knew not how he would fare. She and Sharron had discussed their options, and both agreed that they would have to wean him from the milk slowly.

Caryss, jumping from the King's side, rushed to her and begged her to tell them what had occurred.

Dropping the much lighter coin purse onto a small table near the door, Nahla told her, "As soon as you are ready, you should hurry to the docks. The man is named Hestor, and while his ship is smaller than many others, he has made the journey to the Cove hundreds of times. He has business further south, but has agreed to drop you at Bautista, the main port on the southeastern edge of Francolla, the largest of the islands. With fair weather, you should arrive within a quarter moon, or, at most, a half-moon. Hestor has long been a client of mine, and, while he does not know who you are, or whom you travel with, he will be discreet. For a fair price, I have bought you passage and meals. Aside from Hestor, there will only be three others aboard, two men who have long been in his employ and a woman who cooks for them. She is an Islander who might offer you some assistance once you make port."

When Nahla noticed Caryss ready to speak, she shook her head and raised a gold-rimmed arm.

"After you pass those doors," Nahla said, pointing behind her, "I would advise you to trust no one. Name the King as your ill father who seeks warmer lands. It is not so far off and has been known to happen often. Keep the dark mage hidden as well, for my people have long known how to spot dark magic. Keep to yourselves, even once you arrive."

Aldric began to question the woman, but she ignored him, taking a seat among the pillows on her large bed and watching as they gathered what little they had. Most of their belongings were still at the first inn, yet they had no time to retrieve them, nor did any think it wise. Caryss suspected that Aldric had more coin than he had given to Nahla, enough, even, to replace all of their belongings.

Once more Caryss asked about the *diauxie*.

"He is known to have a fondness for Francolla, which is why I instructed Hestor to take you there," Nahla stated, unmoving from the bed. Caryss knew that her mage-sight, although true, had unnerved the Islander.

From across the room, Caryss called to her "I owe you much, more than I will ever be able to repay."

The room grew hushed until Aldric stated, "We must go, while the King still sleeps."

Before she reached for the door, Caryss paused and turned back to Nahla. She could not leave without once more telling Nahla of the babe.

"Nahla," she began, "I know not where the mage-sight came from. Nor do I know how it will come to be, but I was not wrong. You will bear a son. A son of the Tribe. Both kin and friend to my daughter."

Silence followed as Nahla said nothing, but her soft eyes told Caryss much.

In the Islander's light brown eyes, oval and lined in kohl, Caryss saw acceptance.

She knows I speak the truth.

*****

Surrounded by the Vollaxo and Lisania Rivers, which emptied into the Three Seas, the King's City had been a center for trade and commerce for hundreds of moon years, which had funded its growth and development. The piers wrapped around the city, but the docks in the northeast corridor were the most used. While the group would have preferred to depart from the lesser-used southern docks, they had little choice and hurried past newer moorings fitted with iron and rope.

As they neared the older docks, paint-chipped and rusted quays greeted them. Searching for Hestor's ship proved simple enough for there were few that had southern-styling. Along a group of slips near the end of the piers, many of which looked as old as the King's City itself, they came upon the small, multiple-sailed boat. But what set it apart was its sun-yellow mainsail, and they had hurried to it as glowed in the faded, early morning sky.

Caryss eyed an intricately knotted rope holding the boat to the pier and a ladder hanging from its side. With a look to Aldric, she asked, "How will we get the King aboard?"

"There must be a ramp about."

The mage stepped in front of her and grabbed the hanging ladder as it swayed. Sharron, just behind them, pushed the King. His cart, muddy and creaking, had not fared well across the bricked roads and would not last much longer.

"Go on ahead. I will wait with the King," she told Sharron.

When last Caryss was on a boat, moon years before while at the Academy, she had quickly grown ill, vomiting until her stomach heaved and nothing remained. Looking at the boat brought a new fear into her.

Her mouth suddenly dry, Caryss called up to Sharron, "Have you any ginger root?"

The other healer was in the center of the swaying ladder, but managed to cry, "I used the last of it before we reached Rexterra."

Remembering the bit of coin she had in a pouch at her waist, Caryss pointed to the central square and addressed Aldric, who stood atop the boat, "I am going to hurry back. I won't survive the journey well without ginger."

The king still slept, so she left him in the cart and ran back, following an orb-lit path until she was near the area where food stands nearly outnumbered ships. Caryss glanced around, noticing all varieties of fish, most she did not recognize, as well as breads and cheeses, fruit and vegetables. The smells were overpowering, and her stomach churned, forcing her to raise a hand to her mouth. Finally, near a wooden stall laden with fresh-caught fish, she spotted a large pile of ginger root, clumped together and uncut.

Reaching into a small pouch at the edge of her belt, Caryss grabbed several coins and crossed to the stall. As she neared, she noticed a woman grinding dried peppermint leaves, sending a sweet scent into the air and masking the fishy odor that seemed to be everywhere. She watched as the woman took the crumbled mint and mixed it into a thick, pale paste. For a moment, Caryss smiled, recognizing what the woman did, having often done the same for many moon years.

In Common, she asked, "How much for five bundles of the ginger?"

Without looking up, a voice croaked, "Twenty pence."

Caryss looked at her coins and grabbed the two smallest, setting them within an arm's reach of the woman.

"Have you ever thought to add sage to the tincture? In combination with the mint, it relieves even the worst head pains, especially ones brought about by bad nerves."

The white-haired woman's grinding stopped, and she glanced at Caryss with eyes that matched the dull waters beneath the docks. As if she had never seen a Northerner, she scanned Caryss from head to feet, before settling on her belt, and the many pouches that hung from it. Nervous under the woman's scrutiny, Caryss moved nearer to the booth, reaching for the ginger until she held five large bundles. Before she could leave, the woman addressed her.

"Sage, you say. I will have to try that. What brings you to the King's City, healer?"

Stuttering, Caryss replied, "My father is ill, and I am trying to find a cure for him."

With a cackling laugh, the vendor told her, "The King's City will only make him worse. Our streets are crowded and our air is heavy with coal and soot. I have never left, so I know more than others. You must not be well-trained if you cannot see the danger that surrounds you."

"I am taking him from here. To warmer lands," Caryss explained, backing away. With a forced smile, Caryss thanked the woman and ran off, clutching at the knotty stalks of ginger as she fled.

When she neared the boat, she noticed Aldric pushing the King up a wooden ramp, and she caught up to them quickly, breathing heavy. Her life pulse throbbed unevenly against her shirt as she looked about nervously.

"I hope to never return here, Aldric," she muttered, as they both now stood on the hull. Between them lay the King, still covered by Nahla's blanket.

Before Aldric could reply, a man approached. He was not what she had expected, and Caryss haltingly asked, "Are you Hestor?"

With a wide smile missing a few teeth, the man bowed deeply and joked, "The one and only. You must be Nahla's girl. When she said that I'd know you by your hair, she did not lie!"

His tone was warm and his smile genuine, and Caryss laughed.

"You are as bright as a sun rising over still waters, my lady."

"I hope your skill as a captain is as fine as your charm, sir," Caryss teased, enjoying the man's glee.

"They are rivals, I am told," he answered, before waving his arms wide. "May you enjoy my castle while you are aboard. We will depart shortly."

"We must leave at once, captain," Aldric interjected.

Caryss glared at the mage, although he seemed not to notice.

Within moments, though, the ramp was raised, and the smaller of the crewmen had climbed down the ladder. Next, he untied the four thick ropes that still held the ship onto the dock. When all four were untied, he walked to the end of the boat and pushed it, before jumping into the water. A few strokes later, he was climbing up the ladder. Caryss watched as he and the other man grabbed long wooden beams and pushed the boat even further from the pier. As the ship distanced itself from the dock, Caryss closed her eyes and let out the breath that she did not know that she had been holding. The king was still dozing and she stepped close enough so that she could kneel beside him. Grabbing his hand, she brought it to her lips and gently kissed it.

Into the lightening sky and with the wind blowing her long coppery hair against her reddened cheeks, Caryss whispered, "Keep us safe, daughter."

Unseen, the captain watched. With his back to a guardrail and his hand on the tiller, Hestor looked across the hull to where she knelt. Shaking his head into the crisp breeze, he wondered who the girl was, especially since King Herrin had no daughters.

*****

Through a window across the room, the morning sun slanted and shined onto the bed, casting a yellow haze onto the sleeping man. His eye was blackened and a thick streak of crosses lined his upper cheek. As he rolled to his side, Crispin paused, reaching swollen fingers to rub at the sides of his forehead. After lifting his head for a moment, it fell hard against a pillow.

Groaning, his fingers dabbed at the slice under his eye. He had not thought the healer would strike him and had not seen the shining weapon until it had been too late. Thinking of the girl, he wondered if she was awake, for the hour was late and the sun high, yet he felt as if he had had too many ales. Behind him lay the girl, pressed against the wall. Before turning to her, Crispin readied himself and tried to find words to explain why he had spoken so harshly. Half a life spent at the Academy had not prepared her for life in Rexterra, nor anywhere else, he thought.

If I had used the blade, you would be dead, she had told him.

Crispin knew that she had not been wrong. He had recognized the flash of the dark-bladed dagger and could feel the power humming through it as she struck. How she had come to have the blade was as mysterious to him as the girl was herself. Drawing a deep breath, he again lifted his head while swinging his legs until his bare toes struck the floor.

He was going to have quite a bit to explain, especially the injury to his face. Even now, his cheek pulsed, reminding him of his folly. With his clothes scattered across her room, Crispin rose to retrieve them. Once dressed, he crossed the room. For a moment, he hesitated, wondering if the healer would regret what had happened between them.

As if he was boy of fifteen and not a man grown, Crispin reached for her, his fingers slightly trembling. Pulling back the blankets, Crispin laughed gruffly.

*****

10

As Otieno neared the shoreline, the air swirled stronger around him, sending his braids across his face and shoulders. His snakelike hair curved and slapped at him, but the man paid them little notice as he slowly edged the water, leaving long boot markings in a trail behind him. The sun was high and bright and the sky nearly cloudless. The wind was unusual, a Northern wind, not the warm, moist air that usually circled the Southern Cove Islands, causing a shiver to rip through his body.

Looking over his shoulder, Otieno checked to see if he was being followed, but only noticed a string of fishing boats bobbing in the water and children at play in the surf. When he neared the children, a small boy ran toward him, kicking up foam as he ran through the bubbling sea.

After a day of rain, the sun had remerged, lightening the sky. Otieno's step seemed lighter too as he slowed it, watching the bare-chested child approach. Skin reddened by sun and surf, the boy glistened, stopping just steps in front of the *diauxie*. Noticing the boy's light brown eyes upon him, Otieno's lips opened, exposing straight teeth stained brown from chewing cacao leaves.

"Have you ever seen the dance of swords?"

The boy's wide eyes stared at the *diauxie*, moving from the small scimitar held by Otieno to the broadsword and rapier tethered at his belt. The boy trembled, as if overcome with chills, and said nothing, yet his eyes told Otieno much. Taking several steps back, Otieno bowed, his braided hair falling thick over his face. When he lifted the curved scimitar, sparks of light spread across the sand, beckoning the others to watch. Soon, Otieno was surrounded by sea-soaked children.

With their gazes upon him, he began to dance, just as he did each morning and evening with none around as witness.

The scimitar, with its womanly hook, moved through the salty air as if it swayed to the sounds of the sea. Above him, the sword circled. When he brought it near his waist, Otieno spun, flipping the scimitar from hand to hand, fast and smooth. Not once did he falter, even as his spinning intensified.

Next, he reached for the rapier, parrying with the scimitar as he pulled the thinly bladed sword from its scabbard. When he lunged forward, the children gasped, scrambling back from him, their eyes filled with fright and mirth.

Placing the scimitar in an etched leather scabbard hanging from his belt, Otieno held the delicate rapier as if was a ray of light. Sun streaks cut across his dark clothing when he moved. Again he jabbed, thrusting the sword into an invisible foe. Red-stained leather wrapped around the hilt of the rapier, part warning and part reminder. Where hilt met blade hung a thin metal chain, and, from the chain, hung an ivory figurine carved into the shape of a large-eared, tusked and wrinkled animal. As Otieno swung the blade, the small figure moved as well, spinning and twirling.

In a slow sweep, he sliced through the air, left to right, down and back up, fast and concise. The sword hummed, and, as he continued slicing downward with it, the air stilled around him. The tip of the sword led the strike and Otieno's feet did not move. This was the gentleman's sword, graceful and silent.

Just as quickly as he brought the blade down, it rose, crossing his body until he swung a backhanded stroke, opening up the throat of his imagined enemy.

The rapier was soon replaced with the broadsword, and the *diauxie* exchanged turns and parries for two-handed hacks and swings. There was no mercy with the broadsword, for it was the warrior's blade. The fight was over quickly and without style, forgettable, but deadly nonetheless.

The boy who had first approached tugged at Otieno's tunic as he sheathed all of the blades. "What of the Greatsword? Will you dance with it as well, *aba*?"

The boy, no more than seven moon years, stood just to Otieno's knee, and suddenly seemed to be without fear.

"Not while the sun shines, child," Otieno told him.

"Is it a moon blade, then?" the boy asked, unaware that the *diauxie* was readying to leave.

After a moment, and with the boy's fingers still pulling at his shirt, Otieno answered, "It is not of the moon or the sun, but is nearly as old. It comes from a place where the mountains reach for the stars and are covered in snow year-round. Where the rivers run cold and brisk for nearly the full moon year. Where the people are pale-skinned like ice. She is no dancer, that sword."

When the boy opened his mouth to speak again, a tall girl with thickly curled hair and flashing eyes grabbed him and pulled him back toward the others.

With his hand still in hers, she called to Otieno, "My brother talks too much, *aba*. He is always telling tales and asking questions even when mama tells him hush."

Otieno, pausing, told them, "It is never wrong to seek answers to what we don't know. Never stop asking. There are more powerful weapons than those that I use. A sword is not the only path to victory. Finding your path and walking it as fearlessly as you can is the mark of a true warrior."

Breaking free from his sister's grip, the boy ran toward Otieno. He stumbled through the sand, nearly falling, but he reached Otieno quickly and reached up to again tug on him.

"*Aba!*" the boy cried until Otieno slowed. "I live near here, and mama always cooks more than we need. Would you join us for the midday meal?"

The boy was a determined one, and Otieno slowly nodded, nearly admitting to him that he had not eaten well in a quarter-moon. "Lead the way and I shall follow, as long as your sister here approves."

His words were light, and even the girl laughed, "Mama always does make too much food."

As they walked, Otieno asked, "What is your name?"

"Davon. And my sister is Laila."

Otieno had traveled far in the last quarter moon, and the chance to enjoy a full meal had been too tempting. The boy was a likeable one, but it was the girl whom he could not take his eyes from. She reminded him of another girl, one he tried often to forget. A girl who haunted him still. A girl whose blood still stained his hands.

*****

It was nearing midday when he slammed the door behind him. Rubbing at a throbbing cheek, he paused, wondering if he should retrieve the salve that she had left with him. The bitter taste of mint remained sharp on his tongue, souring his mouth. Heading toward his father's room, Crispin decided that it would be unwise to further trust anything from the woman.

Once he reached his father's door, Crispin abruptly stopped. The door was still unwatched, despite his instructions the previous night that the guards return within in the hour.

With shaking hands, he pushed at the door.

The ward was gone, and the door fell open as if it was no longer made of wood and steel. Around him, the room blurred red and murky. Staggering to the bed, Crispin reached for the down-filled blanket. Yet, before his vision cleared, Crispin knew what he would find.

Collapsing onto the bed, he sat, trying to decide what to do next. When he remembered the others who had accompanied the healer, he jumped up and rushed back down the hall. Flinging open the dark mage's door, Crispin searched the room.

"Hells," he screamed, quieting only when he heard footsteps nearing.

Hurriedly opening the door of the other healer, the prince closed his eyes. She too was gone. The sound of heavy boots increased, pounding and drumming. For a moment, he thought of running, knowing who came. Before he could, his brother's voice roared.

"Crispin!" his brother shouted, "Where is father?"

It was not long before Delwin was beside him, several of his men trailing behind.

"What in the hells happened to your face?"

With moon years of practice, Crispin lied, "I was struck at the docks last night and spent the rest of the night being tended to."

His brother's eyes were edged in gold fury. "When will you learn to keep away from the filth of the Lower Streets?"

Crispin said nothing as Delwin continued, "You should find your wife and let her know that you are safe. She was quite worried about you when we visited her this morning. My men spent hours searching for you."

"I'm a man grown, Delwin, and need not permission to do as I wish," Crispin wearily replied.

"So be it," Delwin waved. "We have more pressing matters. What of father? Where has he gone?"

It was then that Crispin knew that his brother had been informed that the King's Heir was the last to be seen with him.

"I was with him last night. Before I went to the docks."

"And you have not seen him since?" Delwin pressed, his voice growing deep.

"Not since last night. Have you checked the courtyard? Perhaps father woke and was taken outside. He has asked to do so often in the past."

"My men have already been there," his brother said, pushing by him and back into their father's room.

As he followed, Crispin thought of the previous night, trying to remember what had occurred. His thoughts were slow, addled by the tonic no doubt. He had visited his father before knocking on Caryss's door and had dismissed the guards soon after, not wanting the King's Guardsmen to see him with the healer. He wondered if she had assumed as much and had seized the chance to gain access to the King with none around. Yet, he realized, she still would have had to get through the heavily warded door.

"Delwin, send men to the gates!" he cried, thinking of the dark mage who traveled with her.

"You think it is so urgent then? He could not have gotten far in his condition, Crispin," Delwin told him, as if in scolding.

Distractedly, Crispin answered, "He must have had help. You said that your men have searched for him without luck. I know not where he has gone either. That merits some urgency, Delwin. Meet me near my rooms at the next bell."

Appearing more concerned now, Delwin hurried off, back down the hall. Once he and his men were gone from sight, Crispin ran back to Caryss's room.

As he pulled blankets from the bed and kicked over a small side table, Crispin turned to find the door being opened.

"Where is she?" he screamed at the two men staring at him.

Both men paled until the shorter one stuttered, in stilted Common, "We have not seen her since last night. Nor can we find Sharron or Aldric."

"You have not seen her since last night?" he asked, more quietly as he walked toward them.

"Aye," the both nodded, in unison.

"What of her clothing and bags?"

The two men looked at one another.

When neither answered, Crispin warned, "You both must realize how this looks. She comes here with little and leaves abruptly under the moon's watch. Do you not think that you both will stand accused if anything is amiss?"

He watched their sun-darkened skin yellow, and added, "For your safety and because I do not think you were involved in her disappearance, I will take you to my own private quarters. Once there, you must tell me all that you know, or I will not be able to protect you."

"We know nothing about her, my lord," one of them told confessed. "We were hired to see her here safely. For most of our journey she was withdrawn and quiet. It was not until we came upon the whore that she showed much interest in anything around her."

The taller man, who had stayed silent mostly, reached for his sword, a thick broadsword that hung heavy at his belt.

His sight burning red, Crispin growled, "Keep your hands from your weapons and come with me."

Once the man's hand released the hilt, both followed as Crispin fled. Just outside his office, he hesitated until his hands felt the soft pulsing of his warded door. Sighing, he waited for the ward to release as his fingers warmed.

When all three were in the room, he closed the door and turned back to the men.

"Tell me all that you can about the healer."

The taller of the two now spoke. "Like Niko said, Caryss was quiet much of the time. We were hired to escort her here safely, which is what we did. Truth be told, we thought we would soon be dismissed. When we woke here today and could not find the others, I assumed that we were no longer needed. We are owed coin, though, and need to find the mage before we depart. Once paid, we will return to Arvumia."

Shaking his head forcefully, Crispin said, "I will see that you are paid. Now what of this whore? Was she known to Caryss?"

"It did not seem so. I know not how they met, but Caryss tended to an injury the woman had."

"Tended to her how?" Crispin demanded, losing patience.

With a twitch to his shoulders, the man answered, "She was lying on the ground, and Caryss was stitching a gash on the back of her head, I believe. The mage kept them warded, and we kept them safe."

Two of his guards now stood just outside the door. Crossing the room, he opened the door again and called the men in.

With his men behind him, Crispin fumed, "She is a healer! I would expect her to do nothing else. Tell me what else you know of this woman."

"Caryss followed the woman to her rooms," the smaller man cried, as if to free his brother from the prince's interrogation.

"And what of it?" Crispin asked.

Neither answered.

"Now is not the time to grow silent," he told them, the threat unhidden.

"Forgive us, my lord, but we have our orders."

"She is not returning!" he screamed at them. "You have two choices. Answer my queries or you will become well acquainted with the inside of a Rexterran jail cell!"

Again, the men looked to one another. The younger one nodded.

"What more would you like to know, Prince Crispin?"

"Tell me everything that has happened since you first arrived in the King's City."

For more than an hour, the men told him of their movements over the last day, including time spent with the Islander. The woman was like many others who came to the King's City, and while it surprised him that the healer would visit her so eagerly, it also reinforced his belief that Caryss was unfit for life in the King's City, especially life at the palace. The smaller guard remembered Caryss asking the woman about her homeland. Crispin pressed the men further, until he decided that, soon, he himself would need to visit the Islander, for she had been one of the few in Rexterra to speak with Caryss.

*****

The wooden box sat between her crossed legs, and she took a long breath before opening the lid. Nahla traced her fingers over the red-orange leaves of a lush flower that had been carved and dyed atop the box. It had

87

been a gift from her mother many moon years before, and there was little that she prized more, having brought it with her to Rexterra. Around her, the slanted rays of the midday sun entered through the small windows of her bottom-floor dwelling.

Gently, her long fingers pushed open the lid. Nahla rested her chin against her chest, softly rocking herself back and forth as she eyed the box's contents.

With a soft moan, she reached into the box, pulling out a silver coin. Streaks of sunlight struck the coin, sending glimmering lines across her bare arms. Her fingers flipped and twirled the coin before setting it on the floor beside her. One by one, she removed coins from the box and piled them neatly beside her.

"Thirty!" she sang, as she laid the last one down near her.

Since shortly after arriving in the King's City, Nahla had saved every copper that she could. And, for the last few moon years, her services had been in high demand, and she had been able to increase her stash of coins rapidly, especially since she had never moved out of the cramped bottom-floor room. Staring at the pile of silver coins, she nearly wept.

She had long dreamed of having her own inn, and, now, with the five coins, given to her by the mage, she could again meet with Horace, who had moons before asked her if she was ready to buy his building. It was on the edges of the Lower Streets, but he had kept it well-maintained, as she should know, having spent many nights there. When Aldric had handed her the bag of coins, she knew that it was more than necessary to book passage aboard Hector's boat. Yet the mage insisted that she keep it, although they both knew that his act was not one of generosity, but one of necessity.

Even without the coin, she would have said nothing of the girl, but had not admitted as much to the mage.

A loud knocking jolted her from her thoughts, and Nahla hurriedly threw the coins back into the box. As she hurriedly rose, her skirt tangled around her foot, hurling her back to the floor. Gathering the coins again, Nahla listened as the pounding grew more insistent. When the silver was once again in the box, she tucked it into a small hole hidden behind a tapestry.

When she opened the door, despite expecting to be visited, Nahla struggled to keep her face free from expression. Clenching a well-worn brass knob, she looked up at the man who stood just steps from her.

"Prince Crispin," she said, bowing her head slightly.

For a moment, they stared upon one another. She noticed a large, stitched gash across the side of his face and wondered how he had come to have such a fresh injury.

Without taking his sparkling-gold eyes from her, the prince called to someone behind him, "Is this the whore?"

Stepping forward were the two men who had been hired as guards for Caryss.

Before they could answer, she laughed, "Few call me whore in my own home."

"Will you permit us to enter?" he curtly asked, waving the men away.

"Have I much choice, my lord? You may enter, and your men as well. But not those two," she answered, pointing at Caryss's guards as her words hardened.

The prince watched her. Nahla stared back. Finally, he motioned to his men.

"Tonnio, have the rest of the men wait here. You will enter with me," he ordered.

When the man nodded brusquely, Nahla stepped back, finally releasing her hand from the knob. Behind her, the door remained open, and, moments later, the prince entered. Nahla watched as he scanned her room, and noticed that his cheeks did not redden as he looked upon the tapestries. His guard kept his eyes on her and his hand on the sword, much as she expected.

After he had completed his check of her room, the prince asked, "Why did you deny entrance to the Arvumian men?"

Her words accented but clear, she told him, "When last they were here, they were with a Northern girl. She was an unusual woman, my prince, and I would just as soon not welcome her back."

Crispin stood within an arm's reach of her, and she watched his eyes darken as she mentioned the healer.

"What do you know about the girl?"

Nahla had expected his words as well and replied, "She is a healer, my lord, as I'm sure you well know."

"I have no time for games," he hissed. "Answer me true or my men will drag you through the streets and throw you into a cell."

"Why ask what you already know?" Nahla hummed at him, unfazed by his threats.

"Once more, tell me what you know of her."

With an exaggerated sigh, she stated, "My lord, you came here under a full sun in the middle of the day. The Lower Streets are filled, as are the piers. You traveled freely and under no guise, with five of your own men in full uniform trailing behind you. Your men stand outside my door, and have been seen by hundreds already. Word has surely already spread that you visit Nahla the whore. If you had wanted to imprison me, you would have done it already and without so many to witness it."

"I am King's Heir, and answer to none," he fumed.

Crossing to stand just in front of her, he yelled, "I could burn the streets behind me as I walked and none would dare stop me. I could have my men drag you into the market square and slice your pretty neck from ear to ear and, still, none would stop me."

His words crashed around her, forceful and loud, but Nahla stood in the storm, unmoving and unafraid. She watched as his guard drew his sword, but looked back at Crispin in time to see him wave the man off.

When he reached for her, Nahla did not waver. She licked her lips as he grabbed her shoulders. Laughing, she threw her head back, exposing her long, sleek neck for him.

"Why take me to the piers, my lord? Have your man slit my throat now," she purred.

Their eyes locked, and Nahla noticed how specks of gold swirled at the edges of the prince's. His cheeks were flush with anger and his lips looked swollen and red. Many a morning, her own looked similar.

I misjudged the girl.

Bold with the knowledge of the girl's actions, Nahla retorted, "You are not here to kill me. Release me and I will tell you all that I know."

Her words, half-whispered and edged with the winds of the Cove, lingered.

Finally, the prince dropped his hands and stepped back.

"When I first came upon the girl, she was vomiting near the piers. As I was kneeling beside her, a passing street cart came loose and struck me."

Pointing to the area behind her head where black crosses, much like his, could still be seen, she continued, "I felt something hit hard against my neck, and only remember waking up later with the healer standing over me. She had tended to me, with the help of the other healer, and I begged them to come here so that I might offer some token of gratitude. She would have declined, but I could not see clearly, much less walk back to my room safely after what had happened."

Nahla paused to see if she should continue, and when the prince nodded, she went on, "It was clear to me that she was new to the King's City, yet I found it odd that she traveled with the mage and guards. Soon, I learned why."

"What do you mean?"

It was then that she paused to let him think she was too nervous to speak more. Finally, she sighed, "Well, the babe of course."

When his face paled and his eyes caught flame, Nahla realized that Caryss had not told him of the babe. For a moment, her thoughts scattered as she sought an explanation for what she had said. Yet, she knew that it was too late.

"I advised her against telling anyone of the babe," she told him.

The prince said nothing, and he seemed to forget that she was there.

"There are many women like her, my lord, who find themselves with child but without husband. I feared it was why she was forced to leave her training."

"When was the last time that you saw her?" he asked, trying to recover, although he could not hide his surprise from her.

"I only saw her the once, and that was a few days ago," she lied.

"You have not seen her or the mage since?" he asked.

"I have not."

"Her guards told me that she inquired about your homeland, as if she might travel there?"

It was then that Nahla worried. The guards knew too much, even though their knowledge of Common was slight.

Weaving truth together with lie, she told him how Caryss had been interested in the tapestries. She further explained how she had teased the girl about what they illustrated.

"It is not unusual for a young women to want to learn what it is that I can teach, Prince Crispin."

As if he no longer cared what it was that she knew, he turned from her.

"Please, my lord, tell me what you know of her. Is she not healer-trained?" Nahla called.

"I will tell you nothing," he cried, nearing the door.

"You are lucky that I am allowing you to live," he continued. "If I find that you have lied to me, it will no longer be so."

They left then, and she rushed across the room, to lock the door. Her fingers shook and her gold cuffs rattled as she reached for the chain. After three attempts, the chain finally slid into place, and Nahla fell to the floor. With her back leaning on the door, she closed her eyes and prayed to the Great Mother, whimpering in chant.

Later, once she recovered, Nahla reclaimed the box and stared at the silver once again.

Thirty silver pieces were enough to start over, she knew. Just as she knew that if her lies were discovered, the prince would have her jailed or worse.

I must go, she thought, looking around the room.

First, she dressed, pulling on a long, crimson skirt and cream tunic. On the inside of the skirt hung a large pouch, invisible to any onlooker, and Nahla hurriedly dumped the coins into it. Tying a braided belt around her waist, she moved across the room, gathering scattered copper into a small pouch, which she then hung from the belt. With another glance around the room, she eyed all that she had collected in her time in the King's City. She could do little now, having had no time to prepare for the hasty departure.

And so she reached for the chain once again, unlocking her door and striding from the room.

Even as her heart pounded and her palms grew slick with worry, Nahla walked slowly to the piers, letting the glow of the sun warm her prickled skin. Heading toward the piers, it soon became clear that she was being followed. Two silver-vested men watched her when she paused at a fish vendor. Leaning against his cart, she eyed the men, unsurprised that the prince had ordered his men to follow her.

"I'll take the small one," she said, pointing, to the dark-haired woman behind the cart.

After handing the woman a copper, Nahla waited as the woman wrapped up her purchase.

Stopping again at a bread cart, Nahla noticed the men several steps behind her. Acting as if she had not seen them, she continued on, making her way back to her rooms.

Throwing herself on the bed, Nahla again looked around the room, as if searching for an escape. She gazed at the empty place on the wall where the tapestry of the *diauxie* once hung. It was the healer's fascination with Otieno and her insistence upon finding him that caused Nahla to believe that she was indeed god-touched. For none other would seek the man.

A daughter whose father would, no doubt, care about her safety, she suddenly realized. And that man, Nahla knew, was a son of a god.

Her magic was small, but she had learned all that her mother's mother had taught her. And even though she did not often use it, Nahla had not forgotten what the earth magic could do. With little time, and the guardsmen outside her door again, Nahla walked to a large-leaved plant, propped in the corner of her room. Its ferny leaves brushed against the pale walls, standing nearly as tall as she. Few even noticed the plant, despite its size, and none had ever commented on it. Yet, she had nurtured it since arriving, tending to it as her grandmother had instructed.

The plant was heavy and the metal pot was difficult to grasp, so she dragged it to the center of the room, leaving a trail of dirt and fallen leaves across the floor. Once it was in the middle, between her bed and the door, she sat down, with her legs on either side, straddling the pot. Her wide sleeves hung freely down her arms, so Nahla paused to roll them up to her elbows before reaching into the pot.

Gently humming the song her grandmother had taught her many moon years before, Nahla grabbed two handfuls of the still-moist soil and sprinkled the dirt across the floor, in between her legs. With her long fingers, she drew circles in the dirt, weaving them together, then erasing them with her other hand and repeated the pattern. Her nails were nearly black with mud and the edges of her skirt soon followed, but on she hummed, a strange smile gentle across her high-cheeked face.

"Great Mother, help your daughter in her time of need," she sang.

"Great Mother, shine your light so that I may walk in your shadows," she whispered.

"Great Mother, mother of all, mother of light, mother of dark, mother of all in between, walk with me through the high grass, fly with me across the clear sky, swim with me over the great rivers, and lift me above the soaring mountains."

From a pouch that hung on her belt, Nahla drew a small dagger, and held it in her unscarred, steady hand.

As she slowly glided the blade across the palm of her other hand, she called, "Great Mother, my blood is your blood, and it flows for you. Taste it and know my heart."

Thick drops of blood fell onto the dirt, red mixing with black and brown, staining the white tiles. Nahla leaned her head back and let the blood fall, praying that the Great Mother would hear her call.

*****

"My guards have spoken with the guards at the gate. None have seen anyone matching father's description last night or at all today. Nor did they notice anything unusual. The palace has been well-searched, although my men were told to make no mention of who or what they were looking for. Crispin, I believe it is time to involve the Mage-guild."

"We do not need the mages. Not yet," he told his brother. "If we were to summon them here, then the palace would be abuzz with word of father's disappearance. Let us wait until evening at least. I am on my way to meet with father's guards, and then I will find Master Young, who had taken over father's care. Perhaps he will have some idea of what could have happened."

Nodding briskly, Delwin stated, "I heard that you left the palace this afternoon. Had you word about father?"

Realizing that nearly all would be remembered, Crispin explained, "I went to the piers. There are women there who heal in ways that the masters cannot. While father has been ill, there are still those who would take his money, and there was talk that the King had been spotted in the

Lower Streets over the last few moons. But I am convinced now that it was all folly and poor use of my time to chase after such nonsense."

Half-cackling, Delwin laughed, "You thought father was with a whore? He could not even walk let alone much else. You are overly fond of the Lower Streets, Crispin, as that gash across your cheek shows."

"I will see you at the evening meal," replied hastily, not wanting to listen to another lecture from his brother.

He left his brother standing outside his office, and set off to find Tonnio. For half the day, Crispin had searched for the healer, despite having little to go on. Her hired guards had been of some help, yet the Islander had told him little, although he suspected there was much she had not said. Two of his men were tasked with following her, and, soon, he hoped to learn more.

The Arvumian men whom Caryss had traveled with were being kept in his own rooms, under the watch of his men and unpermitted to leave. They seemed to know little, and their Common was poor, but he had erred much in the last few days and was no longer willing to trust any. He had not yet told his brother of the men or of the healer. Yet, that, too, would soon have to change.

It was his father's men who worried him the most, for the King's Watch had seen him with Caryss. They believed her to be kin, and he had not told them aught else, but Delwin would no such kin existed. He only hoped to find the healer before his brother learned of her.

Unless he could convince his uncle, the lone Eirrannian in the Grand Palace, to recall a fire-haired cousin. With the thought ringing loudly in his head, Crispin rushed to find Derry. And when that was finished, it was long past time that he sent word to Willem.

*****

11

After half a day spent aboard the ship, Caryss was thankful that she had ample amounts of ginger. Aldric had shown no ill effects from the tilting and bouncing, but both healers had fallen ill almost immediately after they had left the dock. The king slept often, and they alternated tending to him, including making sure he consumed enough liquid and mashed food. He was much like a babe, the women had joked, and still heavily dependent on the poppy milk.

Every few hours, Sharron would grind up the roots of the ginger and mix it with water, and the two of them would sip it slowly. While it helped and they were able to walk about the cabin of the boat, Caryss looked forward to landfall, which the captain had assured her would be in another two days. The weather had been fair and a strong wind kept the boat sailing at a steady speed, much to her relief.

With little to do, her thoughts were often troubled as she reflected on the last few moons. When she had first left the Academy over a moon before, she had done so as a true Master Apprentice and wanted little more than to heal the King and complete her Healer's Journey. Ever since Conri, ever since the night of the babe's creation, nearly all had changed.

Yet, she was a healer still and had done what she must to save the King, which had meant taking him from the King's City.

As she walked across the wide planks of the boat's stern, she thought about Prince Crispin, wondering what he must have thought when he first awakened. Placing her hands on the railing of the ship, Caryss looked across the blue water, clearer than any she had seen before. The sun was falling behind the horizon just to her left as streaks of orange and red reached across the gently rolling waves and toward her, pointing at her, as if in accusation.

If she could not save the King, her gamble would have been for naught, and her life and the child's would be in danger, she knew.

Caryss gripped the railing tighter as the dark thoughts swirled.

After a few minutes, a presence at her side caused her to pull her eyes from the sea. "What will happen if the King dies?" she asked Aldric, who now stood just to her side.

As if he sensed her mood, he stated, "He was half-dead when you first arrived in the King's City. You played no part in his illness."

"But I could have stayed and tried to heal him there," Caryss sighed, wondering if she could have trusted Crispin to keep them safe.

"You were fighting against the tide, one that you could not see. How many healers do you think have worked on him? And not just healer, but mage too. None have helped, Caryss. The King was no more than blood and bones. You at least are trying to give him life."

For a moment, they were both silent. Her hair was loose, blowing across her face, as if to shield it. Sharron had cropped the mage's hair short hours before, which caused him to look more stern than usual. Most would fear the dark mage, with reason, she supposed, yet Caryss never had, even when they first met at the Academy.

Whispering against the wind, she told him, "I poisoned Prince Crispin."

She watched as Aldric closed his eyes. His own hands gripped tightly at the ship's railing, his knuckles white and tense.

"We will have an army at our backs when his death is discovered," he finally groaned.

With a snort that she had meant as laughter, Caryss explained, "He is not dead. I am better skilled than that, Aldric. I used the same tincture on him as I have done many others at the clinic, one which causes heavy sedation, yet few after-effects. He will have woken after half a day's sleep."

"What is this tincture?"

"A mixture of Aconite and Chloroform. It causes a deep sleep."

"Aconite? I have heard the name before," Aldric stated, turning toward her.

"There is another name for it. In the North, it is called Wolf's Bane."

"Caryss," he warned, his voice nearly a growl now.

She said nothing to him, but her face glowed and her teeth shined under the orange glow of the setting sun as she smiled.

"You play a dangerous game. With men much more powerful than you," he warned. "Conri will not be able to protect you from a Rexterran army, Caryss. Nor will a babe at the breast. What will you do when the forces of Rexterra rise up against the woman who stole their king?"

"We will fight them. With fire and sky. Earth and water."

Her words were still whispers. Yet she knew that he had heard.

"When have you held a sword in your hand? When have you drawn a blade and blood from an enemy?" he questioned her, loudly.

"The night we left the palace I nearly killed Crispin," Caryss calmly told him, enjoying watching his cheeks pale and his eyes widen.

"You just said the tincture was safe," the mage stuttered.

"Aldric," she half-sung, "You asked when last I lifted a blade. And I answered. Before I put him to sleep, the prince and I argued. If I had not struck him, he would have struck me. I had little choice but to draw the dagger."

White-faced and hoarse, Aldric croaked, "What dagger, Caryss?"

Her laughter sounded half-mad, even to her own ears when it followed.

"The only dagger I have."

Her head tilted back as she laughed, until Aldric grabbed her, pulling at her shoulders until his eyes found hers.

"Fear not, Aldric. The blade never touched him."

Confusion darkening his eyes, he asked, "Where did this occur?"

Caryss shrugged her shoulders, "In my room."

Aldric's fingers trembled where they held onto her. He was thin, but still had strength in him and her arms began to ache. She struggled to tear herself free from his grasp, but he would not allow it.

Finally, he half-threw her from him and asked, "Do I want to know more?"

"Crispin came to my room hours after we all last parted. I was asleep, yet heard his knocking and rose. He offered a warning of sorts, or perhaps a lesson in courtly behavior, and then grew angry when I did not seem to heed his words. He thought me a fool, Aldric, as if I was little more than a country girl on her first visit to the city."

"He was not so far off," she head the mage grumble.

Interrupting him before he too lectured her, Caryss added, "He told me that I would not long survive the King's City, which seemed more than just idle words. He left me with little choice but to flee, and I knew that I could not have done so had he woken."

"It sounds as if you think he wanted you to take the King?"

Nodding in agreement, Caryss stated, "He was testing me. If he is not the one who ordered the poisoning of the King, then of course he would want his father safely away from the palace."

With his back now to the boat's railing, Aldric sighed, rubbing grayish fingers across his newly clipped hair.

"Even if he had wanted his father to be safe, he will not be able to long protect you. Prince Delwin controls the army and will have men after us once he learns of what has happened."

"We must find the Prince of Swords. And then we must get to the North, where we will find shelter and aid, if necessary," she told him.

As if he was beginning to understand, Aldric said, "And the *diauxie* will help get us there safely."

For a moment, Caryss felt as if Bronwen stood at the railing. Tears filled her eyes and the fading sun blurred into a fiery haze. *I will not cry; I am Rexaria.*

She turned to Aldric and wrapped her arm around him in a tight embrace. He stood unmoving until finally, awkwardly, he placed his arms around her. For a moment, they stayed that way, as a salty breeze, sea-scented and warm, whipped their clothes and threw Caryss's hair across the mage's face.

"Did you tell the prince about the babe?" the mage asked quietly as she released him, tying her hair into a healer's knot.

Caryss shook her head and Aldric sighed again, as if with relief.

Her hair tight against her neck and her eyes wide and green, Caryss told him, "She will be queen, Aldric. She will be like none other, like none that Cordisia has seen." She gave him no time to respond as she begged, "Promise me that you will never leave her side."

In the dusky light of the setting sun, she could feel heat coming from him, as if his body was tinder and his words flame.

"Just as I have sworn vows to you, I will swear them to the girl. I will teach her the ways of the mages, both dark and light, so she will not fear either. I will follow when it comes times for her to lead, even into the darkness, if that is what she asks."

With tears on her cheeks, Caryss could only listen.

"Caryss, I will die for her, so that she may live."

"As would I," Caryss sobbed as Aldric reached for her.

*****

"Who are you?"

The image flickered, but she answered still, "I bring word of Caryss."

"What would you know of the girl?" he roared as flames erupted from his hands, casting streaks of red across the floor.

"My lord, you misunderstand. She is like kin to me," Nahla pleaded, on her knees, her hands mud-covered and raised.

"Kin? That you even know her name surprises me," he growled.

For a moment, it seemed as if the man was real, and Nahla scurried backward, leaving trails of mud across the floor.

"A few days past we met in the King's City. She was in need of aid, and I her only friend," she hurriedly explained.

The flames lessened and then faded, as if he believed her. The man, pale and dark-haired, but edged in silvery shadows, steadied, yet his words sounded distant, echoing as if thunder.

"Tell me what happened," he demanded.

She could see little of him as the shadowed halo darkened. Knowing he was her only chance at safety, Nahla squeezed her hand into a fist until blood fell again onto the floor. Hastily mixing the dripping blood with the dirt, she silently begged the Great Mother for more time.

When the man's face steadied, she cried, "She has the King with her, although his sons did not permit her to take him. She feared for her safety, and for the safety of the babe and escaped the palace at nightfall. I helped them find passage to my homeland in the Southern Cove Islands. Hours later, I was visited by the King's Heir, who sought the healer and his father. Even now, his men wait outside my door."

"Why did you call me here?" the man snarled, showing his teeth, as if in threat.

His eyes yellowed as he spoke, yet Nahla refused to cower this time.

"I do not have long," she yelled, letting her chestnut eyes meet his.

"There is more. Much more," she added, more quietly, thinking of the men outside her door. "But my magic is slight and already my fingers are burning. Please come to me as quickly as you can. My home is in the tenth block of the Lower Streets, near the piers. Ask for Nahla."

Long fingers reached for her, as if they could tear more words from her throat. While no fire burned there, his hands were hot like embers. Nahla knew that he could not touch her, yet still her skin seemed to blister and burn where his fingers neared.

"Why would I help you?" the man asked, although she had to strain to hear his question.

She had no time to think. No time to wonder if the healer had been crazed.

"Caryss told me that I will bear a son of the Wolf."

When the man's hands dropped, a chill came across her. Falling back from her knees, Nahla whimpered, fear coming despite her attempts to fight it.

Suddenly, the man nodded. But he was more than shadow now, dark and opaque.

When she blinked, he was gone, yet still she cried, "Hurry!"

*****

"Conall!" he screamed, racing across the shining ebony floor.

His reception room was without warding, and those who entered had reason, or suffered for disturbing him without one. When the woman had first appeared, Conri had thought her to be from the kitchens, yet soon he knew his own error.

Streaked by dusky sunlight, she had called him with blood. But it was the not summoning that had surprised him most.

It was the name that she uttered, one that he had not heard in over ten moon years. Much had changed, he realized, screaming for his brother again.

She remembered more now, more than he had ever allowed. Had he been stronger the night the babe was created, he would have never allowed the mind-lock to weaken. Now, he could no longer make her forget.

Behind his eyes, a red haze formed, clouding his vision and again stirring the fire at his fingers. A noise startled him and he turned to find Conall hurrying into the room.

Smoke, gray and swirling, circled the High Lord as he extinguished the flames.

"Where have you been?" he demanded.

A rare blush across his long face, Conall answered, "Tending to the *Epidii.*"

"I had a visitor," Conri explained, running his smoldering fingers through long, dark hair. "A woman from the King's City. She claims to have seen the girl."

Conall's gray eyes widened as he asked, "Mage-trained? How was she able to find you?"

"She was not in the flesh. Her magic tasted ancient and unfamiliar. And of blood."

Conri watched as understanding spread across his brother's face. Conall had always been well-learned, knowing more than even Conri could claim.

"She uses earth-magic, brother. What news did she bring?"

"The girl departed from the King's City in haste. Has word spread that the King's health has improved? She was there but a few days."

"There has been no news of the sort," Conall told him. "My men would have reported it already, if it were the case. Who was the woman? How can you be sure that she is to be trusted?"

Conri hesitated. "I tasted blood on her words."

"The old gods offer aid, but it comes with a price. It was the woman's blood you tasted."

"I knew as much," the High Lord stated, nearing his brother. "She made mention of the babe as well. Find this woman and bring her to me. I must know what has happened in Rexterra to change what the girl had planned. If this Islander knows so much, she must not be permitted to talk of the girl with others."

"Aye," Conall agreed. After a moment, he asked, "When last did you see her?'

It was clear of whom he spoke.

"A moon or so ago," Conri sighed, although there was much in his voice that Conall could not make sense of.

"It has been too long. You should go to her," his brother told him.

Quieter now, the High Lord stated, "She will not want to see me. Not now."

"How can you be so certain?" Conall questioned him.

Conri did not answer for a long while. Red rays of sunlight fell around him, staining his dark clothing until it shined crimson. He knew Conall suspected that something was amiss, and, finally, in a voice rimmed in fire and smoldering with flame, the High Lord explained, "The Islander called her Caryss. It seems she has remembered."

He did not need to look at Conall to know what the Tribesman thought.

"Is there more? If not, I will depart at once."

Conri's sleek face betrayed little now, as his face was again mask-like and cold, his eyes dusky and controlled. "See that the woman is not hurt, and get her to me as quickly as you can."

"As you wish, High Lord," Conall replied, before bowing and rushing from the room.

Conri watched as his second-in-command raced across an open field toward the stables. Conall traveled much, more so than any other Tribesman, nearly all of it at Conri's bidding. Yet there was none else he trusted as much, and only a few knew of the girl. The High Lord wanted to make certain that it would remain so, or he would have insisted long ago that the girl come to the Tribelands.

The shaky peace that had long existed among the Tribes threatened to break and already the Crows had knowledge of Caryss. None would harm her, he knew, not until the babe was born, for doing so now would draw the attention of Nox, which none wanted. For now, Conri figured, Caryss was safe.

Or so he had believed, until the Islander had appeared.

Slamming his hand against the glass until it shattered into hundreds of sun-dyed shards, Conri fled the room, cursing his father.

*****

"Why did you dismiss the Kings Guard last evening?"

He had expected the question. Ever since he realized that Delwin had learned the identities of the men who had guarded their father's door, Crispin had readied himself for it. Even though the guards had been dismissed before Caryss had stepped into the room, others had seen the fire-haired girl and would likely have not forgotten.

After a brief visit to Lillia, who had not seemed to believe the story of his injury, Crispin had gone to his office. With none around, he thought long on what he would say to his brother.

Well-practiced and with even words, Crispin told him, "A few moons ago, I sent word to the Healer's Academy that we were in need of a new Master. One that could, with luck, find what ailed father. I kept my mission hidden from all, including you."

"We have had an army of healers and mages for him," his brother interrupted, slamming the thick, wooden door behind him as he entered.

"Let me finish," Crispin huffed, holding up a hand. "The healer who the Academy sent was on her Healer's Journey and arrived in the King's City several days ago. I had planned on telling you as soon as I met with her. Until I realized that she was Eirrannian, that is. I knew that you would not let her anywhere near father, even though she has been trained as well as any other once you learned of her homeland."

When Delwin would have again interrupted, Crispin stopped him by standing up. Rising in haste, the chair fell hard to the floor, blowing paper and letters across the room. With a bang, the chair crashed against a shelf of books behind the large desk.

"You know that my words are true!" he yelled, letting his anger ripple across the room before Delwin could strike first.

His face aflame, red and bloated, in sharp contrast to his neatly pressed commander's jacket, Delwin stepped toward Crispin until both brothers stared at one another across the desk. For a moment, neither moved.

"I will admit that I should have informed you of my plan," Crispin later confessed. "At the time, it seemed wisest to keep the news that father was in need of a healer quiet."

"Who is this woman?" Delwin demanded.

Swallowing hard, Crispin told him, "She came well recommended by the Master Council. I did not know she was Eirrannian until her arrival."

"Did she see father?"

His brother's words were clipped and tight, as if he had to force them out.

Forcing himself to nod, Crispin answered, "For an hour perhaps. I was in the room at all times. She was young, but skilled, and had father awake within moments."

He watched Delwin, trying to interpret his reaction to the news that the King had woken, even for a short time. But his brother had spent half his life with the Royal Army and betrayed little.

Trying to match him, Crispin continued, "Father even spoke a little, answering her queries about his health. She would have done more but had left her tools at an inn near the Lower Streets."

Without much effort, Crispin weaved lie and truth together to form a story that he hoped his brother would believe, a story that would allow

Caryss enough time to travel far from the King's City. Hours earlier he had decided that it must be so. For now, the King was safest gone from the city, but Crispin had to make it seem as if he had no part in his disappearance. To that end, he would make Caryss the enemy, without hinting to where she might have gone.

"The girl did not know the city well," he went on, "So I offered to go to the inn to retrieve her belongings if she would stay with father. Which meant that she would be alone with him, aside from another healer that had traveled with her. Another woman, I must add. With two trained healers at his side, I saw no need to call the Kings Guard back."

With his voice low, Delwin growled, "What are you telling me? Did this Northern bitch do something to father? And what of your eye? Were you attacked in the Lower Streets when you sought her things? Are you such a fool to be set up so easily?"

By now, his brother fumed, although still he revealed little.

Crispin's words spilled free, as if they were truth, which, he thought, some were. "As for me, I do not think myself overly foolish, Delwin. She came bearing papers from the Academy, and I observed her skills myself. If it was she who has taken him from the palace, I do not think that she will harm him. She is a healer and will honor her oath."

"You speak as if you know this Northerner. You have long been a fool where Eirrannia was concerned. A fault of our cousin's, I would say. You played into her act," Delwin screamed.

Before Crispin could distance himself, Delwin had reached for him, grabbing at his tunic. Spittle hung at the corners of his mouth, wetting Crispin's face as his brother yelled, "What treason is this?"

Pushing hard at his brother's hand, Crispin struggled to free himself. Once free, his tunic torn down the middle, Crispin stepped back, yet his hands burned with rage.

"Would you have had me tell all of Rexterra that the King was near death?" he cried.

When his brother said nothing, Crispin continued, bitter and unforgiving.

"I will tell you what would have happened. Instability. Rebellion. We would have war on our hands. Our hold on the throne has never been weaker, as you well know. There are many who have long waited for a reason to strike, and the King's death would give them one."

Delwin, wiping at his face with the back of his well-fitted sleeve, said nothing.

"You know, just as I, how the leaders of the People's Crown seek to stir an uprising. And that is only one of many enemies who would see Rexterra crownless. We might not agree on much, brother, but neither of us wants to see the throne taken from our family."

Dropping his arm, Delwin asked, "How do you know this healer is not in the employ of the People's Crown? Is it not their way to work in such a manner?"

The People's Crown, Crispin knew, was a small, but growing, group originating in the Lower Streets that had grown displeased with the monarchy. Over the last few moon years, rumblings reached the palace of the organization, although they were not seen as much of a threat. Delwin had long feared the group would try to strike, just as he feared Eirrannia would and others to the east. To him, Rexterra owned all of Cordisia, and any talk of it not being so was near enough to cause war. For moon years, the King and Crispin both had advised Delwin to worry less, yet, for now, the People's Crown was an easy target. One that Crispin would need to use.

His plan had been a complicated one, he knew, yet he would not let his brother take the throne so easily.

"This girl was no more than a healer. I checked with the gate-guards, and, according to their records, she arrived just before making herself known at the palace."

"Did you not say that she took rooms in the Lower Streets?"

Delwin was far too quick, Crispin mused.

"Only briefly was she there. Not long enough to encounter any from the People's Crown."

"Why would she take father if she had nothing to gain?"

With a long sigh, Crispin told him, in truth, "She believed he was being poisoned. She said as much before I hurried to get her belongings. Perhaps she wanted him far gone from here. She is healer-trained, Delwin, and seemed to only have concern for his health."

"What folly! This woman has put him in harm's way by taking him from here, yet you seem unworried."

The accusation in Delwin's words was clear, yet Crispin refused to further enrage him. Instead, he told him, "Where could one such as she go? She came with nothing, as a healer who had spent half her life on the other side of Cordisia. She has, at most, a day's ride on us and has little knowledge of Rexterra or the lands beyond. Our men will find her by the morrow, I would guess."

"You think she is making her way back to the Academy?"

Crispin was certain that as soon as Delwin exited his office he would have a battalion of Royal Army readied. In truth, Caryss could be only a half-day ahead of them, and, Crispin knew, there was a good chance that she was taking the King back to Tretoria. But it was a risk that he had to take, hoping that the woman who had struck him would not be so foolish to take the King where all would suspect.

While his brother and his men followed that trail, he himself would not stop searching, thinking back to the woman near the piers. She knew more than she had told him, the prince realized, and, after Delwin's departure from the city, Crispin decided to revisit her. Time would give him answers, Crispin thought, yet did not say.

"It seems most likely. Within a quarter-moon, the King should be safely back."

"And if she is not at the Academy, then what, Crispin?" Delwin asked, arching an eyebrow as if convinced his brother had not been completely forthcoming.

"If she is not found in a timely manner, then I will leave the search to you."

"Even if it takes me to Eirrannia?"

Crispin hesitated, understanding what it was his brother threatened.

"The Royal Army is yours to command," Crispin told him, his words plain and steel-like.

With a nod, Delwin left, hurrying off without closing Crispin's door.

As the prince walked to it, he thought of the healer. A moon was not nearly long enough for her to escaped beyond his brother's reach. But it was all that he could give her, he thought, slamming the door closed behind him.

*****

A dark haze stained her eyes until she saw nothing but obsidian shadows. Her knees ached until she could support herself no longer, and her head fell to the floor. There, forehead pressed into dirt and blood, she stayed, as if in supplication.

Nahla did not know how long she slept. When the darkness lifted and her vision cleared, she rolled to her side, rubbing at her eyes with tingling fingers. Dim orb-light filtered through her curtained windows, telling her the hour was late. A sharp burn pierced her hand, and she drew it to her chest, cradling the sliced palm. Her hands, like most of her, were mud-covered, her skirt dirtied and her tunic blackened. With a moan, Nahla pushed against the tiles with her uninjured hand until she was standing on wobbly legs. Bent in half, she hobbled to the bed.

The Great Mother had answered her call. But the toll had been a heavy one, and she ached as she had never done so before. With shaking fingers, she reached for a tinder box, lighting three tall candles next to her bed. In the soft glow, she examined herself.

Dried blood covered the slice across her hand, but it was not as deep as she had feared. An oval-shaped mirror lay next to her and she reached for it, half-smiling as her dirt-smeared face reflected back. Her cheeks were dotted with mud and a clump of dirt clung to the side of her forehead.

Nahla pulled the tunic, stained with blood, over her head, then used it to wipe at her face. Her eyes, lined more than when last she looked, stared from the mirror, scanning the room. In the center sat the large fern, and, around it, dirt had spilled and smudged. Streaks of blood stained the floor, crimson and jagged.

Her steps were slow as she rose, but her legs soon steadied. Across the room, Nahla found a straw-edged broom, and she carried it to the mess. With dirty hands, she swept, slowly for her arms felt heavy and bruised.

Until a pounding at her door caused her to jump.

Putting a hand to her bare chest where her life pulse fluttered fast, Nahla waited, uncertain as to who would come at such an hour. She knew the prince's men hovered close, and knew, too, that had they wanted admittance, they would not be knocking.

Grabbing a faded blanket from her bed, Nahla crossed the room. With a silent prayer to the Great Mother, she slowly turned the handle.

Leaning against the door, Nahla stared at the man. Mist circled him, as if he had come from the sea.

"Praise be the Great Mother," she whispered, moving aside to let him enter.

His words were sharp and lilting when he spoke. Deep and as old as the sea, his words echoed through the room.

"Is she so named? The one who aided you in finding my brother?"

Swallowing hard as she backed away, Nahla told the man, "She has many names, yet is nameless. So we address her as she is. The mother of us all."

Across from her, the man smirked, his pale face surrounded by graying hair.

"I have not been to the Southern Cove for many moon years, yet when you speak, it is as if I am there once again. Your kind are fond of such answers, I recall."

"And what answers are those?" Nahla asked, with a hint of defiance.

"Ones that make the asker more confused rather than less," the man laughed, a strange sound that seemed out of place in her small room.

Glancing at the door behind him, Nahla hastily said, "What of the guards? Are they no longer watching me?"

With a wave of his hand, the man told her, "You need not worry about them. Tell me of the girl. When did you last see her?"

It was near sunrise, Nahla knew, which meant that Caryss had been gone nearly a day, which she told him.

"Where has she gone?" he demanded of her.

Instead of answering him, Nahla asked, "Are you the babe's father?"

She recognized the man to be Tribe, yet she feared him less than she should, Nahla mused.

"I am father to none. The babe you refer to will be my niece, if all comes to be. It was my brother who sent me, for he is the father, as well as my lord." Stepping toward her, he asked, "Where is the girl?"

"She is no longer here," Nahla sighed, knowing that she should fear the man but too weakened to care overmuch.

"I can see that. Where has she gone?"

The man was just steps from her, and Nahla gazed at him fully. He was tall and lithe, muscled tightly underneath his light brown tunic. His hair was a light shade of brown, yet edged in gray, although his skin was unlined and smooth. When her eyes reached his, she drew in her breath.

Yellow eyes stared back at her.

"Did you not hear my question?" he called to her.

Stumbling for words, Nahla mumbled, "I will not see her harmed."

Again he laughed, his light eyes shining.

"The girl is kin to me. Why would I harm her?"

"Give me your word," Nahla pleaded, "Promise that she will not be harmed. There are others who seek to find her as well."

"What others?" he demanded, sweeping upon her with speed and force.

She hesitated. His face, eyes now rimmed with black, lashes long and thick, was so close to her own that she could feel the warm hiss of his breath.

With a stutter back, she told him, "The Rexterran Prince. He and a few of his men visited me, searching for Caryss and asking what I knew about her and when last I saw her. Just as you have. It is his men outside my door."

Snorting, he replied, "The prince visited you here? In the Lower Streets? Do you think I'm a half-wit?"

"I know nothing of you, not even your name. I only know that I speak the truth. Caryss is being hunted. But, after what she has done, it is no surprise."

Nahla's words were sharp. A slight tremble rocked her body, yet she would not step back from him.

"I tire of these games," he told her, stepping back. "You called for help, and now I have come. What trouble is the girl in?"

As he waited for Nahla to answer, the man walked toward the edge of her bed, running his fingers along the large, lined blanket. She knew not why he did so, yet she called to him, "When the girl came to me, she was not alone. Under the mask of night, she knocked on my door. With her were the dark mage and the other Northern girl. But that was not all. In an old garden cart sat the Rexterran king, drowsy and weak."

The man looked at her again, dropping his hand from the blanket.

"Herrin was with her? Are you telling me that she has taken him from the palace?"

Nodding, she replied, "I'm telling you that she has taken him from Cordisia."

"And his sons knew none of this?"

To his credit, Nahla noticed, the man's face betrayed nothing.

"When Prince Crispin visited, he questioned me about her. It seemed as if he knew none of what she had planned. But, aye, he knows now that the King is gone."

"How did he know to seek you?"

"When Caryss first came here, she had two guards with her. When next I saw her, they were not with her. It must have been them who told the prince of me," Nahla explained.

With a quick nod, the man asked, "Why would she want to take the King?"

For the first time since the man had entered her room, Nahla smiled, "Have you met Caryss? I only knew her briefly, yet understood that she is unlike most. I think she wants to see him well and believed that she would not be able to heal him in the King's City."

"And she came to you for aid," he stated, starting to make sense of her words.

They had been long talking, and outside her rooms, the skies lightened.

"My lord, I am not safe here. Nor are you, I fear."

With another wave of his long-nailed hands, he smirked, "I have little to worry about here. But perhaps you are right. We have little time."

Nahla nearly wept with relief, but before she could react, he was speaking again.

"What of these guards? Is there much that they could tell?"

"They have been with her since just outside Tretoria, I believe," Nahla answered.

Before he looked away from her, Nahla noticed how little yellow remained in his eyes.

"You know where the girl has gone."

With a nod, Nahla told him, "You will too if you promise to take me from here."

"What did you tell the prince when he came?"

"Just enough. But he knows not where she has gone."

Before he could ask more, Nahla added, "She sails for the Cove. Once there, she hoped to find a man my people call the Prince of Swords."

"Why would she do that?" he asked, doubt edging his words and darkening his eyes further.

"He is unmatched in battle, but, more, he is an unusual sort. We call his kind *diauxie*. Not only is he well trained with the blade, but he is a type of healer as well. I think the girl feels a kinship with him."

The man sighed, unsettling Nahla as it made him seem more human. And less like he was, which she still could not understand.

"My brother will want to know where she has gone. And all else you can recall. For now, it seems as if Caryss should be safe and well away from the King's City."

His eyes, finally fading, met hers, and he said, "Gather what you need, but you must be able to carry it. First, we will visit the palace. Then, we find my brother."

The man moved to the door, waiting as she scanned the room trying to decide what to take with her, although she still did not know where they were going. There was much that she wanted to pack, including the tapestries that her mother and mother's mother had made for her, yet they were too big to carry.

Before gathering a few items, Nahla dressed. On her feet, she tied the only boots she owned, lacing them under the long-flowing skirt. A clean tunic replaced the one that she had used to wipe the blood and dirt from her face. Her hands were still stained, so she hurriedly scrubbed at them while the man watched, a slight curved smile across his face. Once clean, she wrapped a scarf around the injured palm.

With no choice, Nahla walked to where the coin was hidden. Grabbing the coin and another pouch, which contained a dagger, she crossed the room, tying the two pouches to the belt at her waist.

"Hold my hand, until I tell you it is no longer necessary," he stated as they exited through her door.

She nodded, unable to speak, and did as he requested. His hand was warmer than she would have guessed, much like any other man's would be. The sky was red-edged as the sun rose. Walking away from the Lower Streets, they passed stalls and carts, voices raised in barter and greeting. Yet, none seemed to notice them.

Suddenly, she understood.

Whispering, she cried, "They cannot see us."

He rushed on, and she thought he would not respond, but, then, he added, "A simple magic, but a difficult one to maintain for long. We must hurry."

The man said no more, and neither did Nahla. She focused on keeping up with his long strides, as he bounded toward the palace and out of the Lower Streets. His hair flowed behind him, just to his shoulders, and his legs were long and lean. In the foggy orange of the morning, his shirt looked like soft fur, and his light boots like hooves. Above his head appeared pointed ears, triangular and twitching, as if they listened.

As her own legs ran hard and fast, she wondered what she would see if she were not trailing behind him. If, instead of his high cheekbones and sharp nose, she would find a tan and cream muzzle. If, instead of his full red lips, she would find jagged teeth.

It was then that she remembered the healer's words.

Squeezing at his hand tighter, she asked, "What is your name?"

"I have many, yet am nameless," he told her.

Just behind him, Nahla could not see his face, yet could hear laughter in his words.

Before she could object, he added, "Most call me Conall."

With his name silent on her lips, Nahla understood. She knew Caryss had not been wrong.

*****

12

The rider had found him at the clinic, and, by the way the man's clothing was wet and dirtied, Willem knew that he had traveled with little delay from Rexterra. When he had handed Willem the letter, the pain of exile flared strong. The orange seal of his cousin, a flame-tipped sword, greeted him as he flipped the letter over.

Not looking at the man, Willem told him, "There are a few inns just down the street. Take this for your troubles."

The man nodded, reached for the bag of coin and hurriedly departed.

Rushing to the rear of the clinic, Willem found an unused room, dropping the curtain behind him. He ripped open the letter, breaking the seal, hardened wax falling to the floor around him.

By now, he easily recognized his cousin's script.

Cousin,

I will keep my remarks brief. A few moons ago, I requested aid from the Academy. I had hoped to keep you as far from this as possible, especially since my brother's hatred for you has not lessened. However, through no act of my own, you were made aware of the request. Father had grown worse. And his own healers did little but supply him with poppy milk. Excuse the mess of these words, but much has occurred. The Northern girl arrived in haste and brought hope. Yet, this girl has done something we will soon all regret. She has taken father. With no word to me, or any other, she departed under the cover of night. I was last to be seen with her, and she, in order to escape I now realize, fed me something to cause a great sleep to come over me. When I next woke, at midday, she was gone, as were the two others. Her guards remained.

My brother has sent men to find her, to the Academy, as that seems where she might have gone, although, in truth, I do not know where the girl is. He has given me a moon to find her before he sends nearly all of his men to Eirrannia, for if she is not at the Academy, she must be there. I do not need to tell you what that means.

We must find her. You must send me word in haste as to where you think she has gone.

It had been unsigned and without names, yet there was little doubt as to what the letter meant. Willem stared at it, reading it thrice over before striding from the room.

As he rushed toward the library, a full midday sun shining high, he struggled to make sense of what she had done. Bronwen was as true a healer as any he had known, and he could not imagine that she would break her oath.

Unless the babe was in danger.

When he reached the library doors, taller than any in Rexterra even, Willem threw them open as if they were little more than the curtains that the clinic used. He bounded up the stairs, remembering where Kennet kept his office.

Without knocking, he entered.

Behind a desk strewn with paper and ink, Kennet sat, his metal-rimmed spectacles nearly falling off his face. When he saw who had come, the librarian dropped the quill from his black-tinged fingers.

"Have you had any word from Bronwen?" Willem demanded, pulling the door closed behind him.

With a stutter, Kennet told him, "She promised to send word from the King's City, yet I have heard little."

"Kennet, if you are lying, I will see that you are banned from the Academy. I will ask one more time. Has Bronwen contacted you?"

The thin man stood up from behind his desk and slammed his hands down, sending papers spilling over the sides. His face was red with rage, and he opened his mouth to speak.

"I have heard nothing!" he called out, surprising them both.

The two men looked at one another for a long moment.

"Has something happened to her, Master Ammon?" Kennet whispered, his voice cracking with strain.

Willem shook his head from side to side and, rubbing at his forehead, explained, "She arrived in the King's City a few days ago, without incident. She even met with the King. However, it seems that she is no longer at the palace. And my cousin does not know where she has gone."

"Is my uncle still with her? And Sharron?"

"I believe they both are," Willem sighed, regret bitter on his tongue over how little he could help Bronwen.

"Is the King healed so soon, then?" Kennet asked.

Without looking at him, Willem answered, "I do not think so."

"It does not seem like Bronwen to abandon the King before trying all that she could to improve his health."

The boy had failed as a healer, yet he was brighter than most and had been sent to Master Tywinne as an assistant. Soon, Willem knew,

Kennet knew more than even the aged master. He was not without usefulness.

"Can you give your word that what I next say will go no further than these walls?"

Kennet's face whitened, but he nodded.

After a moment, Willem stated, "Bronwen has left the King's City, as I mentioned. And without word to any as to her plans. But, more, she did not leave alone. She kidnapped the King."

Kennet's hands reached for his face as a loud gasp escaped his mouth. When he would have spoken, Willem lifted a hand.

"I do not believe that she means to harm the king, and there must be some explanation for what she has done. But, Kennet, this changes everything for her."

Through tight lips, Kennet muttered, "But what if the King wished to go with her? Then it is not kidnapping."

Nodding, Willem said, "I thought the same. She would not act so rashly if not for the King's health. Still, she must be found. Before the Royal Army is set upon them."

"Would it really come to that?" Kennet cried.

"She has kidnapped King Herrin! Willingly or not, he is gone, and his sons do not know where he is. Her crime is punishable by death, Kennet!"

"There is no crime if he went willingly," the librarian mumbled again.

"To his son, it will not matter whose choice it was to leave," Willem told him, knowing his words to be true.

Pale and green-hued, the boy stared at him. "What would you have me do?" he finally muttered.

"I must find her," he mumbled, unable to think of anything else. "If you have any news of her, you must send it on to me so that I can track her myself."

"Where do you think she has gone?" Kennet muttered, still appearing sickly.

In response to Kennet's question, Willem asked his own. "Where would be your guess?"

With wide eyes and a gaping mouth, Kennet half-croaked, "The only place where she might find safety."

The North called, and Willem could do nothing but answer.

*****

"Tell me more of the woman you loved. Tell me of her magic."

113

He looked away from her as his shoulders tightened, high and bony beneath a fading tunic. They were still at sea, still days from reaching the Southern Cove Islands, and Caryss was becoming impatient, unable to sit quietly as the ship sailed. Eager to find Otieno, and ready to head north, she had developed a strong distaste for sailing, and all aboard knew it.

Realizing that she needed a distraction, Aldric replied, "They call it earth magic, and few are as strong at it as Leorra was. She could draw rain from a clear sky, just as she could turn a soft wind into a ferocious gale. I watched once as she planted a small seed into the ground. Next, she brought rain upon it, gently, streams of water dripping from the sky. When she raised her arms and exhaled, the gray clouds vanished, replaced by a bright and clear sky. But what she did next proved to me that her power was well beyond any that I had acquired."

He sighed, keeping his eyes toward the sea, as they stood at the railing, the spot where Caryss could often be found.

"Their magic requires more than mine. What I have is more of a gift, one that as a mage I have learned to use and to improve. But, the Island gods did not give their magic freely. Those blessed with it must work at it just as they must be willing to sacrifice a part of themselves to strengthen their talent. That is why some call it blood magic. What it easier to give than one's blood?"

"That is what interests me most," she told him, "To receive their magic, they must regularly give of themselves. It tempers the power and balances the scale, do you not think?"

After a long moment, he said, "I suppose that is true. I had not thought of like that, but from what I know of earth magic, your words hold weight. Leorra was never one to live excessively. She ate when hungry, slept when tired, and moved as if the wind was at her back, never following the same path."

"In Cordisia, we have all sorts of magic, yet no one to control it. Unless you count the Tribe among those who sit on the other side of the scale."

Aldric nodded at her words, then added, "Without the dark, the light cannot be seen. Just as with sacrifice comes reward. Perhaps in the end it is all about balance."

"That is what we will have to teach her, Aldric. She must always seek to temper the dark with the light."

He did not need to ask whom Caryss referred to, for it was clear the way her eyes grew misty and forehead creased that she meant her daughter. The girl born of light, but made in darkness, who forever would face a battle that few could understand. Caryss was growing wise, having time to think on concepts often left to the sages and learned men.

"On the morrow we will be within sight of the Cove. You should rest now, Caryss, as we will have much to do."

The words were spoken kindly, but they were still a dismissal, and Caryss turned to leave. When she was gone from sight, Aldric closed his eyes. The air hummed around him in song, sweet and warm, and, for a moment, he believed that Leorra had sent it, welcoming him to her homeland.

*****

"The wards will be strong here. Stay close to me."

She simply nodded, following quietly behind as he briskly walked down thickly carpeted hallway. They had arrived at the palace with little difficulty and had even entered the main doors behind several armed and gold-vested men, which Nahla quickly realized were members of the Royal Army. None noticed them, yet she clung to the man's hand as if at any moment someone would.

"Do you know where her guards are being kept?"

"No. I only know that I saw one of them with Prince Crispin," she whispered.

"Did it appear as if he was heavily guarded himself? Or in shackles?"

She paused for a moment in thought before again softly replying, "A man stood along side him, but he was not shackled."

"Which makes me think that they are not yet jailed. We do not have time to search this whole place."

The uncertainty in his voice surprised her, and she stumbled, falling into his back. He slowed until she had regained her footing, and then continued, more slowly this time.

Into the silence, Nahla murmured, "Would not Crispin have wanted to keep the men near him?"

"If they have not been imprisoned, yes, he would want them kept close, out of his brother's reach. We will start in his quarters first."

After a few more steps, he told her, "I am going to drop the veil, which means that all will see you. I shall remain guarded. When we encounter a serving woman, you will need to ask her where Prince Crispin's rooms are. Let her know nothing of you."

Before she could reply, she heard clanging, and looked over the man's shoulder to see a capped woman carrying a large, silver tray, that bobbled as she walked. The plate slid across the tray, crashing into a large metal goblet, the sound traveling to where Nahla stood.

Without delay, Nahla rushed toward her, reaching up for the tray. As she steadied it, Nahla smiled up to the dark-haired girl, whose white apron was already stained across her midsection. The girl, no more than twelve, looked at her with relief, then her eyes widened as orb light shined on Nahla.

Sensing her fear, Nahla said, in Common, "Child, I am a guest of Prince Crispin's and only just arrived from the Southern Cove. Your palace has turned me about, and I can't seem to find my way back to his rooms. Would you be kind enough to show me the way?"

In halting Common, the girl answered, "Are your rooms near the Heir's quarters, my lady?"

With a half-smile, Nahla lovingly told the girl, "Yes, that is just the name for it."

The girl nodded and walked back to where she had just come from, then looked over to see if Nahla followed. When she noticed that she did, the girl continued, although her steps were slow and controlled as she held the tray out in front of her. Behind Nahla trailed the man, yet the girl never sensed that they were not alone. And so the three walked on, from one finely decorated hallway to another. Large framed paintings of noblemen and noblewomen stared down at the group, but they encountered no one else until they reached an entryway where the girl hesitated.

When the girl stopped, Nahla looked past her shoulder and noticed a door that was guarded on each side by two large, silver-vested men.

"Thank you child. I can find my way from here."

Knowing when she heard a dismissal, the girl offered a small bow and fled. When she was gone from sight, Nahla turned toward the man, surprised that she had been able to see him while the girl had not. His eyes were scanning the hallway, ending on where the two guards still stood.

"We will search that room first," he whispered out of the darkness, as if the walls talked to her and not a man.

When she started to walk forward, he reached for her arm and grabbed her fingers, murmuring, "Distract them. I will do the rest."

As soon as she could, Nahla pulled her hand away, then rolled her shoulders back and held her head high, walking toward the men as if she had known them for moon years and as if she was welcome in the palace. When her footsteps were heard, both men looked down the hall and watched as she approached. Neither reached for sword.

With a smile as wide as she could make it and eyes slightly downcast, she approached. For nearly her whole time spent in the King's City, Nahla had played many roles, from lover to friend to mother to foe, and many more beyond. Here, she would simply play another one, she mused. She would do as she must, for a girl that she hardly knew. Yet, the Great Mother had willed it so, and Nahla acquiesced, glancing up at the men through half-opened eyes as she glided toward them, hips swaying as she walked.

When she was within arm's reach of the guardsmen, Nahla's lips curved, and she asked, "Sirs, I seem to be in need of some assistance. I am to bring a gift to Prince Crispin, and yet have not been able to find him. The gift is most urgent, and I must find him at once."

Bowing his head to her slightly, the shorter guard replied, "Leave the gift with us, lady, and we will see that he gets it."

Laughing, she chimed, "Well, you see, the gift is me. I would wait with you, but, alas, I do not think it would suit the prince to have me seen so openly."

Both men fought to hide the smiles from their faces, and, again, it was the shorter one who spoke, as he told her, "We have not seen Prince Crispin all morning. You would do better to wait elsewhere."

Nahla looked to where the dark one stood. He was nearly beside the taller guard, whose eyes were on her. Again, his presence was not noticed, although she could see him clearly.

What a strange magic, she thought, before looking back toward the man who had just addressed her. She knew that it was time, and did not look to the man for approval. Instead, she acted.

"Perhaps I should leave you with a taste of his gift, my lord," she hummed, stepping into the man.

Before he could withdraw, her hands were on his waist, brushing against the hilt of a sheathed sword, pulling him close. His cheeks reddened, blotchy and hot against her own cheek. Then, she tilted her long neck back and stood tall, letting her lips reach for his.

She knew what would happen next, to the other guard. His death was nearly silent, until he fell to the floor.

The man pulled away from her faster than she would have thought he could, but, still, it was too late. The Tribesman was faster, slicing the man from the bottom of his right ear to his left, a clean cut opening his throat, just as the he had done with the first. Another kiss of sorts, she thought.

Both deaths had been quick, a small mercy. Yet, when Nahla looked to the floor where the man she had kissed lay, she fell onto the wall, overcome by fast-flowing blood that made his silver vest look black. She did not think that she could move, and leaned her cheek against the wall, closing her eyes to the scene before her.

Just as her eyes closed though, a hand grabbed her, pulling her into the room. He looked as if nothing had occurred; both hands and clothing were blood-free.

Into her ear, he whispered, "Are these the men who were with Caryss?"

Their eyes were on her, unwarded as she was, and Nahla saw recognition. Days before, she was the one standing in accusation. Her pity for the men vanished.

With a nod, Nahla stepped back, until Conall stood between the Arvumians and her.

"What is your name?" he asked, pointing to the man who stood slightly in front.

Stuttering, the man replied, "Niko, sir."

"Niko, why were there guards outside your door?"

"The prince feared for our safety," he gasped, fear whitening his face.

Conall laughed, and the sound was not unpleasant, Nahla thought.

"I doubt the prince had any real concern for either of you. What did you tell him of the girl?"

When neither man spoke, the Tribesman told them, "I will have my answers. If you would like to make it difficult, then so be it."

Before either man could reply, he crossed the room, stopping just before Niko and grabbing his tunic with two, long-fingered hands.

With his eyes on the guard's, he asked, "What does Crispin know of the girl?"

The guard hesitated, looking over to where Nahla stood, and she saw hatred for her mixed with his fear. Still, he was silent. Nahla knew what would happen next, yet did nothing to stop it.

While his eyes were still on hers, she smiled, and hoped it was the last thing that he would see. Her smile did not fade when Conall pulled a curved sword from its scabbard. The blade was thick and silver, shining and clean. It looked like most swords, which surprised her, for he was not like most men.

But the Tribesman had no real need of the sword at all, Nahla suspected. Faster than her eyes could follow, he swung, dropping the blade to just below his left hip before slicing it upward, across the guard's stomach. With no armor to repel the blow, the sword slashed through the tunic.

The guard reached for his stomach, but collapsed to his knees instead, gargling until his body fell forward, head crashing to the floor. Around him, the carpet darkened, and the bitter smell of blood and bile filled the room.

Covering her mouth with the back of her hand, Nahla stepped back again, away from the pooling blood that came like a wave near her boots. The man had deserved his death, she thought, remembering that the Great Mother always punished cowards. Yet, still, she felt as if she might retch as the taint of death filled the room.

118

The remaining guard, Kurtis, scrambled away from Conall, until his back was against a window on the far side of the room. His face was without color, his hands shaking as he held them up for the Tribesman to see.

"I have no sword," he stuttered in Common.

Blood dripped from Conall's sword as he neared the man, a shining, crimson trail following the Tribesman as he crossed the room.

Stepping slowly toward the man, he called, "What does the prince know of the girl?"

Thick words, garbled and mad-touched came from the pale man's blue-tinted lips, "That she took the King."

"How did he know of the Islander?" Conall smoothly asked, nearly on top of the guard.

"He made us take him to her," Kurtis hissed.

Wiping the sword clean across the man's pants, Conall asked, "But how did he know of her?"

With a cough, the guard stammered, "We had no choice but to tell him."

"One always has a choice, young man," Conall lectured, his words crisp and deliberate. "I had a choice as well and you still live, while your kin lies dead."

The Tribesman's words caused prickles to spread over Nahla's body, as if she had taken a sudden chill. He spoke with a calm that left the guard half-mad with fright, she saw.

Suddenly she recalled the prince's visit and cried out, "Does he know of the *diauxie*?"

The guard's silence was answer enough. If the King's Heir did not know yet that Caryss traveled to the Southern Cove Islands, he soon would. She was but days ahead of him.

"Kill him."

Her words were spoken softly, yet her ears rang with them, a sharp, hissing sound that banged and pounded.

"Kill him," she moaned, backing away further until she fell against the door. Beneath her feet, the carpet, once gold laced with green leaves, told of what had occurred, now stained red with blood and brown with shit and bile.

When Conall moved, a rush of cool air sent another chill across her body. Nahla opened her eyes to watch as Conall fell upon the helpless guard, who had just enough time to cry out. As she gazed across the room, she saw the man clutching at his midsection, wrapping his arms around his body as if to shield himself from what was about to come. It wasn't enough as the curved blade struck him at the back of his neck and continued until the guard's head rolled from his body.

119

Half-open eyes looked up at her until the room blackened. Scratching at the door, she searched through the dark haze for the handle. Nahla's knees buckled as she collapsed to the floor.

Hands reached for her, drawing her up. As the Tribesman carried her from the room, she let her eyes fall on the dead guards, who just days before had been in her rooms. Much had changed in the few days since she had first met Caryss, and Nahla sensed that more would change as well. More bodies would fall at the Northern girl's feet.

She clutched at him as he raced down the hallway. With words more breath than whisper, she asked, "Who are you?"

When they neared a corner staircase, he rushed down it, her head heavy on his shoulder. At the bottom of the staircase, he followed a row of mage-lights until streaks of sun could be seen shining through thickly paned windows. He pushed at a wide door with his a blood-splattered hand until they were in a lush courtyard, sun pouring upon them, golden and warm.

Still she shivered.

He set her down then, and the two sprinted between neatly trimmed hedges until an iron gate appeared. Breathing hard, she followed him through, emerging on the other side of the palace grounds.

He led her away from the palace, yet in the opposite direction of the Lower Streets.

The further they walked from the palace, the more confused she became. Yet Nahla asked no questions. Soon, they were near the eastern edge of the city limits, far from the southern area, where the piers were. Scents of sea and sand greeted them as the Tribesman hurried along, still clutching at her hand.

Perhaps we will sail to the Cove, she thought, staring upon the Eastern Sea.

Their boots left deep imprints in the sand as they rushed on, yet Nahla saw no sails.

Unable to keep silent any longer, she asked, "Where are we going?"

Her breathing was labored as she hurried to keep pace with the Tribesman.

He slowed then. Mounds of sand and high sea grass offered cover, although she had seen no one since they had neared the beach. Large crags, black and sharp, lined the coast, making it impossible for ships to dock here, she knew. Again, Nahla asked where he had taken her.

And still Conall did not answer. Instead, his yellow eyes scanned the coastline.

Conall did not look to her as he continued searching. She wondered if he had forgotten she had followed, for his face was strained and his sharp eyes appeared pained.

Finally, he mumbled, "I have not had to stay veiled for so long before, nor have I had to veil another. I must rest for now, until the *epidiuus* arrives."

With some grace left in him, the Tribesman collapsed. Lying on his back, he stared toward the sky.

"The *epidiuus*?" she breathed.

"He will carry us home," the man whispered, low and hoarse, words swallowed by air and tide.

As if sensing her confusion, he added, "I must tell my brother of what has occurred."

"The babe's father," Nahla uttered.

Beside her, the man said nothing, breathing slowly, his eyes half-open. Thinking again on what Caryss had said, Nahla looked upon him, with new eyes.

Under a clear sky and a warm sun, the Great Mother showed her the way. She reached for Conall's hand, as a woman might a man.

Let it be so.

*****

"You know what she has done?"

"Yes. Although I do not know why. It does not seem like something that she would do."

"Which girl? Bronwen or Caryss? Bronwen was naught but a healer, devoted to the healing arts and little else. I know little of Caryss."

The words were spoken without accusation, and Willem had not lied. Even her name had come as a surprise to him. Yet he noticed that it had not been the same for the High Lord.

The two men were seated on rattan chairs with cushions the color of a clear Litusian sky. After speaking with Kennet, Willem had decided to contact Conri, but before he could do so, the High Lord had arrived at his door. Under normal circumstances, he would have been concerned about such a coincidental arrival, but given the nature of the trouble that Caryss faced, Willem thought little more of it. Although he could admit that having the Tribesman so near unsettled him.

"She is not safe," Willem explained, keeping his voice clear. "My cousin has asked for a quarter moon to find the King. But, after that, he will not be able to stall his brother any longer. Even now Delwin searches for her. And, if I know Delwin at all, he will use the situation to his advantage and will send the whole of his army after her. Word will spread that he has saved the King, while Crispin did little. In truth, Crispin might be accused of aiding her. If the King does not recover and is unable to speak on Caryss's behalf, her life will be forfeit."

Toward the end, his words were high and taut with emotion. It would do little good to try to convince the High Lord that Bronwen was safe.

"That is why I am here," Conri stated. "I have learned where she has gone. And I need you to find her for me."

"I had hoped to do just that," Willem replied.

Conri looked beyond him, his gaze distant and unreadable. He was dressed in black leather, yet it was soft and supple, unlike armor. Despite the warm Tretorian breeze, Conri wore a tightly weaved cape across his back, which he had pulled over his head, sheltering him from the bright midday sun.

"Where are your loyalties, Willem? With the Rexterrans or with Caryss?" Conri called.

Without pause, Willem answered, "Must it be one or the other? I want her safe. I want the King's health restored so that Crispin will rightfully sit the throne. And I care little what happens to Delwin."

"If, after the quarter moon expires, Caryss has not been found, what will you do? The Rexterran Army will hunt her, and your cousin, as you have admitted, will be able to do nothing to stop it."

His words had sharpened, and Willem struggled to find an answer. He had not thought of what would happen if he could not find her.

When the silence lengthened, Conri again asked, "Which side are you on?"

With as steady of a voice as he could manage, Willem told him, "I will do what I must to protect her from Delwin's men."

"You will raise weapon against your kin?"

"I have done so before and have this life to prove it," he sighed, waving his hand about.

Paying little heed to his reply, Conri further questioned, "What if it is not Delwin that is the threat? Crispin is heir and will sacrifice much for the throne. Including a woman who means little to him."

"I will not draw my sword against Crispin," Willem cried.

His eyes darkened, yet his voice remained clear and calm as Conri stood. "I will not tell you where she is."

"Will you kill me then?" Willem asked, trembling hands reaching for his wine goblet.

The High Lord waited to answer, hovering across from Willem. With burning hands, Willem watched him, knowing that even his flames could do nothing to one such as Conri.

Finally, Conri shrugged and the air around them cooled.

"Caryss has few allies, and I would be a fool to kill off the ones that she does have."

His words were clipped, as if he had been reluctant to admit them. When Conri stared at him, his eyes light, his dark hair shining under the high sun, Willem recognized the look on the man's face. As if he had seen it before.

"There is something I must show you," he told the Tribesman.

When Conri objected, Willem pleaded that he needed but a few more moments. For a long moment, Conri did not move, but, then, in two long strides, he was beside Willem, silence striking a barrier between them as they walked. Despite the moon years that the two men had been acquainted, Willem had never shown Conri the painting, as if it had been his secret. His fingers trembled slightly as they neared the room.

Stepping back, Willem let Conri enter. On one side, the curtains were open, allowing yellow rays to shine and streak across the room. On the far side, the mural glowed, as if bathed in starlight. Willem watched as the High Lord of the Wolf Tribe stepped close to the wall, raising his hand toward the mural and pulling it back just before he touched it.

Conri's eyes moved across the painting.

Without turning around, he mumbled, "She visited you."

"Only once, but it was enough," Willem told him.

"She risks too much, yet I have never known another who could time-walk as easily as she does."

"There is much that she will do that others cannot," Willem stated, without any uncertainty in his words.

"Will you be ally to her, Willem?" the High Lord demanded, although he still had not turned from the painting.

For many moments, Willem could not reply. Finally, his voice low, his throat burning, he said, "Forgive me, High Lord, but she is like the daughter that I will never have."

"What of your Rexterran kin?" Conri half-growled.

"I will draw sword against them if I must."

The words, new ones, were true, Willem now knew.

With a nod, Conri then turned to face him. "She is the only daughter that I will ever have. The Wolves will answer to her, the Crows will fly from her, and the Bears will hide from her. Cordisia will be hers when she is ready."

The Tribesman's eyes were dark now, as dark as wine.

"She will need ally and army to take the throne," Conri warned.

Willem did not need to ask what throne the High Lord meant. There was only one in the whole of Cordisia that was so heavily coveted.

"Your kinsmen exiled you," the High Lord continued. "Yet, she will see you returned to your homeland, in full glory. Teach her the ways of the King's City. Teach her what I cannot."

"You suggest war will come to Cordisia," Willem stammered, stepping toward Conri.

As they both looked upon the painted girl, the High Lord stated, "War has already come."

Nothing else was said, but Willem understand Conri's earlier questions. Lines were being drawn, and it was time to choose a side. For nearly all of his life, Willem had sided with Crispin. Exile had been his reward. When war came, it would not be the one he had thought.

It would not be between brothers. Nor would it be among the Tribe. None would be safe, if Conri guessed right. It was, as the High Lord suggested, the time to choose ally and friend.

Now, Willem had done so.

13

"His shaking worsens."

"As we thought it might. I had not wanted to keep him dependent on the poppy milk, but we have little choice. Sharron, his body is too weak to fight the withdrawal."

Both women were seated to either side of the King, and Caryss held Herrin's speckled hand in her own. His skin was nearly translucent, yet a splotchy red rash dotted the tops and ran up his arms. Cupped between her long fingers, Herrin's hand trembled, as did the rest of his body. They were days gone from the King's City, yet still the King slept overmuch.

He would occasionally rouse as Sharron fed him, but he said little. Even then, his words were difficult to understand. The day before, Caryss had cut his poppy milk by half, yet, by midday, the King thrashed and shook, so much so that both healers feared he would hurt himself. Since then, each time his poppy milk was given, it had been infused with distilled lavender and chamomile. Now, the poppy milk was being decreased in smaller doses, a long, slow process. Caryss had admitted that she had not thought his dependency to be so extreme.

"We will need to send for more dried poppy heads, which will not be easy I fear. I am not as familiar with the growing season of the Cove or what flowers and plants are native. Perhaps the *diauxie* will be of some aid."

Sharron looked up at the mention of the shaman, as men of his nature were known in the North. For the last few days, little mention of the man came from Caryss, and Sharron wondered if doubts began to grow regarding her decision to head south instead of north.

"You have not spoken of the man of late," Sharron mentioned as gently as she could.

Across the sleeping king, Caryss shrugged, and then continued her gentle massaging of the King's legs.

"Do you recognize the word *fennidi*?" Sharron asked, joining Caryss as they stretched and moved the King's body to keep it from further weakening.

Caryss's memory had opened in many places, and she was much more at ease speaking the tongue of their homeland. Often, the two would speak in Eirrannian, and, even as unpracticed as she was, Caryss was improving quickly. Yet there was much about the North that Caryss did not recall.

"The *fennidi* are much like the man you seek, I believe. Not only do they train in hunting and fighting, they have an ability similar to mage-sight. They call themselves truth seers, yet their skills are not like those found in the mage-guild. I have only seen a few, and know little about them, as they tend to choose to isolate themselves, even from Eirrannians."

Her face showing interest, Caryss said, "I know nothing of them. Do they live near the Tribelands?"

Sharron laughed, a sound rare and light, and told her, "Much like this Otieno, they are usually only found if they wish it. I have heard tales that they live in the Faelan Mountains and around Edan Lake."

"That's in the center of Eirrannia, is it not?"

As she asked, Caryss continued stretching the King's legs, lifting one then the other, as if he was walking. Each time, his eyes remained closed and sounds of sleep came from him.

Sharron reached to help and nodded.

"Should they not be easy to find then, these *fennidi*?"

"There are not many of their kind, and they have long made their homes among tree and river. I have never heard of any seeking them out," Sharron explained, thinking on her childhood and the tales of the elusive wood sprites.

"What strange men exist in this world," Caryss sighed, stroking the King's hand gently. "I would learn more of them though."

Sharron told her all that she remembered of them. They were an old people, unlike both Tribe and human. With skin the color of summer leaves and shining silver hair, none could mistake a *fennidi* for aught else. Having only seen a few, Sharron recalled that they were no taller than children. Yet, they were known for their deadly skills, having long ago learned to use plant and mountain as none else could. As such, none bothered them, for fear of becoming trapped in spell or struck with the tip of a poisoned arrow.

When she finished, Caryss asked, "Can we find them?"

With another laugh, Sharron told her, "We have already done much I would have once thought impossible. You still wish to head north soon?"

"Even more so now. The girl must learn all of Eirrannia if she seeks to rule one day."

Any further conversation was interrupted when Aldric rushed into the small room, crowding the small space. His face was flushed and he was smiling, catching both women by surprise, as he was often straight-faced and serious.

"We approach Francolla. Hestor says that we will make landfall on the hour," he told them.

While Caryss gripped King Herrin's frail hand, Sharron watched. For the last few moons, she had been troubled. Yet, with each day gone from the King's City, Caryss seemed to shift, a lightness returning to her, as if her path was once again her own.

126

*****

"How can this be?" he screamed, before turning to face the three men who stood behind him, dressed in the silver and blue of the Heir's Guard.

All three looked away from his gold-flamed eyes. None spoke and silence spread across the room, mingling with the smell of blood.

"Four men are dead!" Crispin roared, his face reddening and his hands pointing at the two bodies lying dead on the floor.

The other two, his own men, had been removed, although streams of red stained the hallway where they once stood. Several of his guards were flanking the halls now, tasked with questioning the palace staff and instructed to remove all traces of the dead men before his brother heard what had occurred.

His words harsh and heavy, he again demanded, "Find out who has done this."

It had not taken much to realize that Caryss's guards had been targeted. It was their deaths that had been sought, and his men had only been in the way, the prince knew.

Only one other knew of the foreign guards.

"What of the whore?" the prince hissed to the remaining men.

"The Islander, my lord?" the nearest man to him asked, his words even, marking him as well-trained.

"Yes. Raoll and three of his men were working shifts to watch her. Take enough men to bring her back here without incident."

A curt nod was dismissal and agreement, and the man hurried off.

From the moment that he had met the woman, Crispin suspected that she was hiding much from him. His fingers were nearly aflame, and it took more power than he thought he had to control the fire that wanted to burst free from them. Behind his eyes burned a red haze, which colored the room orange and reminded Crispin of all that had occurred since Caryss had entered his life.

Not for the first time, he wondered who the girl was, before striding from the room, his remaining guards following.

*****

14

He was not as she expected him to be, although still her legs wobbled. Standing before her was a man looking much like any other, his back against a wall of windows. Behind the Tribesman, a falling sun cast faded red streaks across gray clouds.

Since arriving in Cordisia, Nahla had never traveled outside of the Rexterran borders. Now, just in front of her was the High Lord, in a room larger than any she had seen. So far Eirrannia was much like a dream, painted in vibrant hues of grass and tree.

The *epidiuus*, as if come from a dream too, had carried them to Eirrannia. Nearly a full day had been spent in travel, yet the animal had not wavered, and only required a few hours rest somewhere in the center of Cordisia. Nahla could make little sense of all that was happening and had ceased trying soon after the creature took to the air. Once, Conall noticed her shock and teased her before explaining how the Tribe often used the *epidii* for long travel. She had told him that few would believe her and most would think she was mad if she talked of her ride atop a glowing animal.

As she mused, the High Lord called to her. His words sounded as if he had swallowed sand and salt, sea and sky. Quietly, he roared.

"Tell me of this man that Caryss seeks."

With only a slight tremor in her voice, Nahla explained, "His name is Otieno, although few know him as such. He is what my people call a *diauxie*, although he is not like any other medicine man I have known. There are stories about him that take the elders a whole day to sing, and I cannot tell you if they are truth or lie. He is not a healer like the girl is, but many seek him when they are ill."

"I thought him to be a warrior of some sort," the High Lord stated, although still he did not look to her.

"Oh, to be sure, he is more skilled than most with a sword," Nahla told him, growing more at ease. "He has been called the Prince of Swords, even. Yet, moon years ago, he set about on a different path, or so I have heard. He travels alone, crossing the islands of my homeland, by foot or by boat, with the wind as his guide. The Great Mother has called to him, as she does with us all, and he follows her way."

"Why would Caryss wish to meet him? What can one such as he, half-mad and wandering, do for her?"

Without hesitation, Nahla told him, "He will help build her army."

Across the room, the man shook his head, sending his dark hair over his face. Nahla knew little of him and could not recall Caryss mentioning him by name, although there was little doubt that he was the babe's father. There was a coldness to him, despite the fiery glow that rained upon him.

"Has she told you what she has planned? You knew her but a few days."

Nahla could hear accusation in his words, and told him, "The girl shared much with me. Too much, perhaps, but she thinks of me as kin."

With a laugh that was not as pleasant as his brother's, Conri said, "She is much a fool of late.

"The *diauxie* is a swordsman like few before him, my lord," she disagreed. "Will the child not need to be protected?"

"It is my duty to protect my child!" he howled, turning toward her so quickly that Nahla scurried backward.

Pressed against the wall, Nahla breathed, "Caryss disagrees."

The High Lord quieted then, as if her words had been weapon, and Nahla continued, "She did not come here. She did not call for you. She came to me, and I did what I could to help her escape the King's City."

His words exploded around her, as if thunder, shaking the room so much that she thought the tall windows would shatter. "She forgets her place!"

Before Nahla moved, Conall came rushing into the room, glancing between her and his brother with concern clear on his face.

"What is going on here?" he called.

When it was clear that his brother was not going to answer, Nahla softly, calmly, said, "Your brother does not understand the ways of women. I am trying to teach him."

The gentle roll of Nahla's laughter spread throughout the room, and both men looked at her, trying to determine if her words were meant in jest.

Under their watch, she added, "I know little of what occurred before Caryss came to the King's City. However, she refused to talk about you, my lord, even when I asked. Her love for the babe is clear though, and I think all she does is for the child."

"Brother, the girl has remembered," Conall interrupted, raising a hand, as if to calm the High Lord's fury. "You told me as much. She needs time to understand all that has occurred, now and moon years ago. It must not be too much a surprise that she wants little to do with you or Tribe."

"In her rebellion, she acts in folly, endangering herself and the babe," the High Lord cried, cutting off his brother's explanation.

To that, Nahla said, "You have misjudged her, as I did at first. The girl has the blood of gods in her, and the Great Mother will watch over her. Caryss knows the path that she walks, for it is now one of her own choosing."

He was steps from her now and hissed, "She will not long survive it by making enemies by the day."

"Those enemies will need to find her first," Nahla countered, wondering when she had become the healer's defender.

"Would they not first search for her in Eirrannia?" she pressed.

With only traces of thunder behind his words, the High Lord asked, "What would you have me do?"

There was much that she did not know, Nahla could admit. But she had long known the ways of men and women, and she told him with ease, "She will come to you in time if you let her decide when that will be."

"She will have many enemies, and few to defend her," he argued, although his eyes no longer appeared as dark as night.

"The girl is not the fool you think she is. The *diauxie*, if she can convince him to join her, is a man like no other and will keep her safe."

"He is but one man. Here, she has Tribe as kin and ally."

Nodding, Nahla told him, "I know little of your ways. But I know the ways of women. The girl seeks to walk her own way, and you must let her try."

"You advise me to do nothing?" he hissed in disbelief.

Sighing, Nahla replied, "I advise you to wait. Let her come to you when she is ready."

Conall interrupted before the High Lord could answer. "Conri, for now, she is safe. Neither Crow nor crown knows where she has gone. If you wish, I will find her, and give her warning of what she faces."

His words seemed to satisfy Conri, who brusquely nodded, "For now, she can remain there. Make ready to travel, Conall. The woman will stay here."

The High Lord walked across the room until he stood just before his brother. Nahla watched, listening to their exchange with unfeigned interest.

"You must convince her to return the King, Conall. It is not the time to challenge Rexterra."

She listened as Conall agreed, and then watched as the High Lord strode from the room.

After a moment, she warned Conall, "You will be chasing a ghost who chases another ghost. Do not expect the hunt to be an easy one."

Conall looked to her and heatedly replied, a big-toothed smile over his face, "A wolf never fears the hunt."

Without replying, Nahla looked upon him, at his fearlessness, and she found herself hoping that their son would share it. The thought surprised her, and she bowed her head, silently thanking the Great Mother.

"Before you depart, will you walk me to my room, Conall?" she asked, the words heavy with unspoken meaning.

It would be as Caryss had claimed, Nahla knew. Her own son would be Tribe, too.

Neither spoke as they headed toward the room that had been prepared for her. Her booted footfalls loudly echoed, each step leading her closer to what the girl had seen.

Once at her room, Nahla entered and Conall followed. As she closed the door behind them, she saw knowledge in his eyes. But, more, she saw desire.

And, stronger than all, she saw power.

The power of gods, his and her own. When she reached for him, Nahla thought she heard lightning strike the sea.

*****

After giving the King his sweetened poppy milk, Caryss and Sharron moved him to the pushcart. The boat had been fastened to a medium-sized dock, and Aldric was already standing on the thick planks of a well-maintained pier. Caryss nodded toward him and walked across the boat to where a large ramp was angled, big enough to accommodate the cart, which Sharron pushed a few steps behind her.

When they were all standing on the wobbling pier, Hestor joined them as his deckhands unloaded several wooden crates.

As she struggled to regain her balance after nearly a quarter-moon at sea, Caryss thanked the captain, "My gratitude for getting us here so quickly and safely."

Throughout the voyage, he had been pleasant and respectful, as Nahla had promised. With luck, he would be gone from the King's City long enough that none would think to question him.

His skin, sun-darkened and wrinkled, crinkled when he smiled.

"A strong wind was at our back, lady. The sea agrees with you."

Even Aldric laughed at the captain's words.

"Without the ginger root, I would not have been able to get out of bed!" she exclaimed, trying to maintain her balance.

Hestor let his eyes meet hers and with a suddenly deeper voice, he said, "The islands are a wonderful place, my lady, but there is danger still. I do not know what it is that you seek to do here, but trust few. Find what it is that you need and be gone. I myself am staying just a night. Is there any other assistance that I can offer?"

"I do not know how long I will be here," she told him truthfully. "There are a few supplies that my father will need. Is there a market near?"

131

By the way the corners of his mouth rose, Caryss knew that Hestor had not believed Herrin to be her father, although he had never questioned her further. Yet, still, she worried anew about what his knowledge would mean and if Crispin's men learned of him or Nahla.

Seeing the fear in her eyes, Hestor stepped close to her and placed a loosely-draped arm around her waist. "My men and I have long days ahead of us as we sail south, to lands that few from Cordisia visit. We will not see Rexterra for many moons I think."

Hestor is a good man, she thought, but still noticed the large pouch of coins hanging heavy from his braided belt.

Caryss quickly embraced him. Into his ear, she whispered, "May the wind always be at your back and the sun on your face."

When she released him, her eyes were clear and a wide smile covered her face. He bowed to her, and nodded before walking back to his ship. She watched him for a moment, remembering how her foster mother Sheva would often remind her that a small kindness was more valuable than a small coin. She had not thought on her foster mother in quarter-moons, she suddenly realized.

Knowing that sending word to Sheva would only bring trouble, Caryss squeezed her eyes closed to prevent tears from falling.

Her voice low, her eyes downcast, Caryss told the others, "Hestor said there is a market nearby. Let us go there."

The sky above was bright and blue, and the midday heat was strong, much stronger than the Tretorian sun that Caryss knew well. Her clothing, thick riding pants and a cropped jacket over a loose-fitting tunic, was ill-suited for the islands and stuck to her skin as she walked. Aldric was dressed as he always was, well-worn boots and a dark, tattered tunic. Only Sharron appeared ready for the warmth as she wore a simple dress made of cotton and linen.

Aldric must have noticed her discomfort, and, as he walked beside her, said, "It oft times takes half a day for your body to adjust to being ashore."

With a snort, she told him, "I had thought that I long ago adapted to a warm clime, but the heat here is nothing like it was in Litusia. I have never so much longed for my healer's robe."

"There is no harm in wearing it now, Caryss."

After a moment of thought, she said, "It seems strange to wear it again, I think, after having gone without for the last few moons. Should I wear it to meet Otieno?"

"It will matter little what you wear if we cannot find him," Aldric answered, his tone curt.

He thought her a touch maddened, Caryss mused, and had not ever liked the idea of searching for the man.

"I will find him. I have never doubted that, Aldric. Why would I travel so far and risk so much if I believed that it would all be for naught?"

"And when you do find him?"

Pulling her hair into a healer's knot at the base of her neck, she told him, "I will convince him to return to Cordisia with us. He is a mercenary like you once were, is he not?"

"Caryss," Aldric warned, "If you think to simply buy him with coin, then this journey will have truly been for naught. What does gold mean to one such as him? Did you not listen to anything that Nahla said? He once walked astride with the King here, but heard a different calling. His path is his own, and coin is nearly useless to him. You must find another way."

Pausing next to him, Caryss looked at him, her jaw tight. "Then I will find another way."

Aldric stopped as well. Again, his words offered warning.

"Caryss, he is not Crispin, nor Willem, nor any other man who might see your smile and fall to his knees."

She said nothing and walked on. When he was beside her again, she told the mage, "He is a man still, like any other."

From the corner of her eye, she could see him shaking his head, and knew her answer was not one that he liked or approved.

"Have you forgotten yourself? With this new name, have you forgotten the woman you were moons ago?"

His question stung, as he knew it would, for Caryss noticed how his eyes shined.

Sharron was just ahead, and, although she heard their exchange, said nothing as she pushed the King onward down a wide, sandy path. As they neared the market, a crowd of Islanders shared the road. Caryss watched as the women carried empty baskets on their hips. Long braids of rope were attached to the baskets, allowing the women to drape them across their bodies and keep their hands free.

Without glancing away from a woman with a basket that had been dyed green and blue, Caryss asked, "Would you have had me remain a fool, Aldric?"

The mage's cheeks flushed red, but still she pressed on. "A few moons ago, I knew nothing of my past, not even my name. I knew nothing of my parents' deaths. I knew little of men and mage-skill and even less of the politics of the throne. If I am to remain free, then I have no choice but to learn as much as I can now."

Walking in stride with her, he said, "Aye, learn what you must. But do not become what you are not, Caryss."

"I no longer know who I am or who I should be."

133

Aldric grabbed her, with no concern as to how it appeared to the others around them, who were much more in number as they neared the edge of the village.

"Look at me!" he hissed.

When she refused, the mage placed a hand underneath her chin and jerked it upward, forcing Caryss to watch him as he addressed her. His hands, scarred and rough, scratched her cheeks, but he would not let her go.

"You have played the insolent child for long enough," he scolded. "Any more time spent troubled and bitter will keep you such forever. You have made your choice, and now must remember your vows. Yet, if you must fight, do it cleanly. Teach the girl your ways, Caryss. Not his."

"My ways will not keep her alive," she whispered through clenched teeth, her eyes still on him.

With ease, she threw his hand from her face, turned, and hurried off, jogging past Sharron until a cluster of buildings appeared.

Sun-faded and light-colored, the buildings were similar in hue to the ones in Litusia, but they were long and low, spreading out to either side of the road. Near the center was a large inn, and Caryss nodded toward it as Aldric caught up with her.

"I have grown hungry. Let us see if there are rooms available ahead. We can find the market later."

Within moments, the group was inside, including the King, whose forehead was damp with sweat. He had woken under the hot sun, and Sharron had gently explained to him where they were. Yet, even awake, he showed signs of the poppy milk dependency and his thoughts were not clear. Traveling in the cart had not been kind to him either, she knew.

To their right was a large room filled with round tables and wooden stools. The room was empty except for two women dressed in brightly-patterned tunics, deeply cut and hanging to their feet. Long braids hung heavy down their backs, and one woman was heavy with child.

Both women stared at them, and Caryss hesitated, uncertain if they knew Common. As she glanced at Aldric for assistance, one of the women called out.

"Why do you transport the man so? You would not bring me a dead man, *leseda*."

The woman's words were in lilting Common, and Caryss paled, knowing not what to say.

"He is not dead," she finally told them. "But he has been ill, and we have come to bring him to a warmer clime that might make him fare better."

"Keva," the other woman chided, "Do not scare the girl. Your eyes are as sharp as ever, and even I can see the way the old man's chest lifts and fall."

Toward that woman, whose dress was dyed red with swirls of yellow ferns dotting it, Caryss asked, "Do you have any rooms available?"

"You are Cordisian? Have you coin to pay?"

It was the other woman who answered.

Nodding toward them both, she said, "We are, and, yes, we have coin."

The kind woman with the pleasant voice stood up, and Caryss asked, "How soon until the babe arrives?"

"In the next moon or so," the woman told her, although the words were strained.

"Have you any other children?"

A pained look crossed the woman's face as she replied, "If the Great Mother wills it, this will be my first. Two others have not survived birth."

With understanding dawning, Caryss told the woman, "For over ten moon years, I have trained as a healer. If you wish it, I could examine you. Perhaps after I put my father to bed."

The others were quiet around them, although Caryss could feel Aldric watching her. Had he not told her to remember her time at the Academy, she thought, without taking her eyes from the woman.

"A healer? I have heard the word. Let me show you to your rooms, and then we will talk further."

Nothing more was said, and the trio followed both women, sisters, Caryss assumed, away from the serving room. Soon, the women stopped, opening several, nut-colored wooden doors.

The woman named Keva said, "You will not find cleaner rooms in all of Francolla."

As Caryss looked about the room, she could not disagree. The first was small, but tidy, with two cots in the center. Across the back window hung curtains the color of the Francollan sun. Like nearly all in the Islands, the room was bright and vivid, and even the blanket across the cot seemed painted like a sunset.

Staring at the swirling floral patterns, Caryss asked, "Are most Islanders so welcoming?"

With a laugh, Keva told her, "You will find most to be cheerful and willing to help. It is our way, as shown to us by the Great Mother. Our own mother used to remind us to smile through our tears, a common phrase here in Francolla."

It was hard not to feel at ease with the sisters, and Caryss found herself smiling in return. Sharron had taken the King to a room, with Aldric following, and the two were lifting Herrin onto the small bed. Neither woman showed signs of recognizing the King, although they did ask once again about him.

"Does he always sleep so much? It is midday."

"The trip was long, but we are hopeful that he will recover soon. There is a market nearby, is there not?"

"Oh yes, just down the street. But if you are hungry, Asha can see that you are well-fed."

Not wanting to admit how hungry she was, Caryss told them, "Once we are settled, something to eat will be most welcome."

The sisters recognized the dismissal and walked down the hallway and back into the large entry. Once out of sight, Caryss entered the room where Aldric and Sharron now stood.

With a look to the King, she asked, "Did he rouse at all?"

"A bit. His skin is dull and puffy. He needs water and food soon," Sharron told her, lifting a light blanket from Herrin's legs to reveal puffy knees.

"He will be fine here for a bit."

With that, they rejoined the sisters, seating themselves at a large, round table in the empty inn.

Keva, swollen with child, leaned against a polished mahogany counter, while Asha busied herself in a nearby kitchen.

Caryss watched the woman rub at her belly and looked at her own, rounded, yet still disguised by a large tunic. Pulling at her shirt, Caryss glanced toward Aldric.

"How long do you think we can stay?"

With a shrug, he told her, "Perhaps a quarter-moon."

He did not need to tell her that he feared Nahla would betray them. Nor did he speak of the Arvumian guards, who had been left in the King's City. In their haste, their departure had not been well-planned, she knew.

His words, clipped and short, were still warning, Caryss understood.

Keva was near enough that when Caryss addressed her, she did not need to raise her voice.

"Is there aught you can tell me of the *diauxie*?"

Caryss watched as Keva's face stiffened, as if she had not expected to hear the name spoken by a Cordisian. For a moment, Caryss thought she would not answer. Even Aldric looked upon her with disapproval.

Setting a plate in front of her, the woman finally explained, "They are unlike most Islanders. The Great Mother speaks to them in voices only they can hear."

With a nod to show that she understood, Caryss told her, "I have been told that some are like healers or near enough."

"There are a few here in Hallava, and they are not difficult to find. If you have coin, they will tend to your father. When you are ready, I will take you to them."

There was hesitancy in her words, as if Keva wanted to say more, but could not.

"What of the Prince of Swords?" Caryss inquired, just as Asha entered, carrying a tray laden with sliced meats and halved citrus.

Neither sister spoke and silence spread over the room like dusk, dark and foggy.

Into the haze, Caryss asked, "Do you know the man called Otieno?"

Asha hurriedly placed the tray onto the table and looked at her sister with sharp and slitted eyes.

Keva gasped, "Do not speak his name, *leseda*!"

When Caryss recalled that Nahla had spoken the man's name, she waved her hand at the women, telling them, "I was sent to find him."

From near the counter, Keva cried, "Light one, the man you name is not *diauxie*. Moon years ago, he gave up the privilege to call himself such. He is more outlaw than healer. There are many others who could help your father."

"No," she told them, keeping anger from her words, "It is he that I need."

Both Keva and Asha looked upon her oddly, as if in disbelief.

As way of explanation, she told them, "I will not seek your help, nor will I bring him here, if you so wish. But there is none other that I seek. Your Great Mother has willed it so."

Keva's mouth opened into a gasp and she cried, "What does a *leseda* know of the Great Mother? Our gods are not yours."

With a calmness that she was no longer feeling, Caryss answered, "The Great Mother is mother to us all. It matters naught what we name her. Under her watch, I have healed her children and birthed her babes. Do not tell me that I do not know her. I have served her for half my life!"

Asha put a hand on her sister's arm, "Let her be. She speaks some truth."

"I seek no quarrel," Caryss exclaimed, "I only seek this man."

"He is not so easily found, nor will he be inclined to help a Cordisian," Asha told her as she set the tray in the center of the table.

The women, who had earlier been so welcoming, now stood as if Caryss was more foe than friend.

Half-pleading, she told them, "I seek to do no harm. And I thank you for your food and aid. Let us not talk on him anymore then."

As a show of peace, she invited them to sit, although both declined. In silence, she and Sharron ate. When the sisters had returned to the desk,

Aldric reached for a small fork. There was much he wanted to say, she knew.

When they had finished, Caryss rose, while Sharron squeezed what juices she could from the fruit into a small mug, to bring to the King.

Nearing the sisters, Caryss called, "You are nearing your final moon. Did the other two make it as long?"

She was close enough to see that Keva's eyes were wet as she mumbled, "Neither survived birth."

"May I feel for the babe?" Caryss asked.

After a moment, Keva nodded, and Caryss reached her pale hands onto the woman's rounded abdomen, still covered by a flowing dress. Gently moving her fingers in large circles, Caryss worked them from just below Keva's full breasts to the bottom of her rounded stomach. Then, she reached for her wrist and placed her fingers there, feeling for her life pulse. Her fingers lingered there, tapping then resting.

Stepping back, Caryss told her, "I would like to do a more thorough examination. Will you follow me to my room?"

Keva looked to her sister, who nodded.

Turning back to the others, Caryss asked, "Sharron, will you see to father while I check on Keva and the babe?"

Sharron wiped her hands across her long skirt and asked, "Have you any soup stock or broth?"

While Sharron and Asha hurried off to the kitchen, Caryss followed Keva back down the hallway until they reached the rooms. Caryss looked in on the sleeping king, then found Keva already seated in the other room.

Even though she no longer wore her healer's robe, Caryss still had her pouches tied at her waist. She did not know if she would have need of them, but unloosened the strings of the largest one as she neared the bed.

"Before I came here, I was in training at a healer's academy in western Cordisia," she began. "Half my life I have been there, and, for several moon years I worked in a clinic that offered aid and healing to all. I do not know if you have anything similar here, but I have more training than most because of my time there. I have lost count of how many babes I have helped birth. Can you tell me what occurred with the two that did not survive?"

It was clear what Caryss spoke of, but Keva did not answer at first.

"Lie back, with your feet flat for a moment," Caryss instructed into the woman's silence.

When Keva had done so, Caryss told her, "The more I know of the past births, the more I will be able to help you now."

She kept her words soft, just above a whisper and waited for a response. When there was none, Caryss leaned closer to Keva, and explained, "First, I will listen for both your life pulse and the babe's. Then I will feel for how the babe is positioned. You will feel my hands prodding and pushing across your stomach, but have no fear, for what I do will not cause injury."

Keva nodded, although Caryss noticed that her chest heaved, as if her breath grew heavy.

Placing her ear to the woman's rounded abdomen, Caryss listened, counting to herself in tune with the rise and fall. Several times she moved, listening and counting again.

Once complete, she lifted her head and said, "The babe has a steady pulse, with no interruptions of note. Does it move much?"

The question was simple enough that Keva finally answered.

"In the morning, after I have eaten, I feel turns and kicks. But little else through the day."

"There is not much room left, and I am not surprised that is all you feel. Do not concern yourself overmuch."

Her hands were again on Keva, although this time Caryss had pushed the woman's dress high. Her long fingers kneaded the woman as she felt for the babe.

After a few moments, Caryss looked to Keva and explained, "The babe is a big one, and, by now, should have its head low. However, it is not the case." Taking Keva's hands, she said, "Feel here," and moved the woman's fingers to her midsection, just to the right of her navel.

"The babe's head is high and its feet low."

With a slight nod, Keva murmured, "It was so with the others as well."

It was the first that the woman spoke of the two who had died, and Caryss stood silent, hoping to hear more. The hot, island sun filtered through the curtained windows, causing Keva's skin to nearly glow, light brown except for stripes of pale pink and white that stretched over her belly.

"Who assisted in the births?" Caryss asked.

"Asha was here, as well as a female *diauxie*."

"I know it must be difficult to speak of, but can you tell me of the births?"

She trembled when she spoke, and tears dotted her cheeks, but Keva told her, "With the first, it was nearly two full days from when my waters came. When the babe still had not come, the *diauxie* thought there was not room, and cut to make some. By then, it was too late, and the babe never drew breath. For the next, over a moon year later, I was cut again, early on, yet, she, too did not draw breath. I remember little from that time, *leseda*, and nearly did not live myself, for I grew too weak with blood loss. I only know what Asha has told me, that the babe was born misshapen."

It was not unknown for such to happen, Caryss knew, and she reached for Keva's hand, telling her, "There was nothing to be done, then."

Nodding, the woman asked, "What of this one?"

"Will you allow me examine you further? To see if you have opened for birth?"

Keva again nodded, unable to speak, and Caryss pulled a small wooden stool to the end of the cot. Before she began, Caryss removed a small bottle from the largest pouch that hung from her belt. The bottle itself was clear, but the liquid inside was copper, and when Caryss removed the topper, a strong scent, bitter and tart, filled the room. Caryss poured a small amount of the liquid onto her hands and rubbed them together.

"Put your knees up, Asha, and try to relax. I will be as quick as I can."

As promised, Caryss did not take long to examine the woman. When she was finished, her brow was furrowed. Again, she poured the strong-smelling liquid over her hands, unspeaking as she did so.

With no warning, she suddenly said, "The babe must come soon, even though your body has not readied for its arrival. There are ways that I can change that, though, if you would let me."

There was confusion written across Keva's face, and, as way of further explanation, Caryss told her, "If you wait any longer, I fear your babe will not survive the birth, just as the others."

"My husband is still at sea and will not return for at least a quarter-moon," Keva cried.

"The babe is, at most, a moon early. But it is not small and will not suffer for the early coming."

From the doorway came a voice, low and sharp, "Why have none of the *diauxie* suggested what you do?"

Caryss did not turn, but she knew that Asha had joined them. From her words, it was clear that the older sister doubted what Caryss had opined.

"How can we know that what you say is wise? You wear no dress or chains to mark you as a healer," Asha called, striding into the room.

Capping the bottle closed, Caryss sighed and stood.

"I wear my skills tied to my waist. I show them with these fingers long trained to stitch and mend. I had not thought to come here to the Cove with my ailing father and find a woman near birth. But I am a healer, and Keva has dire need for my skills. You should decide within the next few days. If a time comes when you can no longer feel the babe move, you must find me as soon as you can. On the morn, I will set out to find the man whose name you will not hear. I do not know how long or how far I will need to go, but your island is not so large that I would not be able to return here if you have need."

Caryss walked toward the door, but before she could leave, Asha called, "You will find him two villages over, a quarter of a day's walk at most. I heard talk this morning as I served breakfast. He was not named, but it was him."

Dropping her head, Caryss nearly wept. *He is so close.*

After a moment, she told both women, "I will leave at once. On the morrow, I will return. Take the day to think on this, and, if it is your wish, your babe will be in your arms before I next depart."

Her words were not untrue ones, Caryss knew. If the babe was to live, it must come early. And her time on the island was not long.

I am healer still, Caryss knew, walking from the room to where Sharron sat next to the King.

But, more, I am Rexaria.

*****

"She appeared in good health when you last saw her?"

"I could tell that she was with child, and, as with many women, she was overly bothered by the smells of the piers. But she was hale enough."

Conri's eyes held a purple haze. Watching him, Nahla could see his concern for the healer, despite the troubled history that Conall had mentioned. Caryss, in truth, had spoken little of the babe, but Nahla did not say such to the High Lord.

He paused, rubbing his slender fingers against his cheek, and said, "Did she seem weaker or more tired than one would? What of food? Did she require much?"

"My lord, I was not with her long enough to see her eat. She seemed healthy enough, more so than most even. She did not complain, nor did she seem to suffer. You worry overmuch."

"Children born of the Tribe are not as others. As you might soon see."

It was only the two of them seated on a bench made of stone in a large courtyard. Nahla had found the tree-lined spot hours before and had not left, enjoying the Northern sun. The Tribesman had come upon her as she dozed, but when he had neared, a chill had come, wakening her.

Keeping her eyes from him, she said, "Conall has told you then."

"There is nothing he keeps from me."

She would have laughed, but Conri was not like his brother, and there was little ease about him. Instead, she asked, "Did he seek your permission?"

141

As if bored by the conversation, Conri rose and stepped away from her. Conall had warned her not to anger the High Lord, advising her to avoid him as much as she could. Yet, Nahla had not been able to do so. Covering a smile with the back of her hand, she thought of her mother who had often scolded her for stubbornness.

When he still had not answered, nor departed, Nahla told him, "Fear not. The Great Mother will see that I am well."

With a laugh that rustled the leaves of the large oak hanging overhead, Conri asked, "Is there anything the Great Mother cannot do?"

"What is gone is gone. She is unable to give breath to the breathless or life to the lifeless," Nahla sighed, rubbing at her closely shorn hair.

"Your god is a wise god then," the High Lord remarked evenly, so much so that Nahla knew not if he spoke in jest or not.

Nahla was intrigued by Conri, yet she still could not decide what to think of him. Most feared him, she knew, just as she understood why it would be so. Yet, it was Conall who had killed, not the High Lord, not that she had witnessed. Over the last day, she had observed him do little but pace across his vast home. Few approached him, even though many Tribesmen lived near. It was not unusual for a dozen or more to be in the High Lord's home, yet he paid them little heed. He was, Nahla thought, quite isolated.

He left her with her thoughts, then, striding away as if in a rush. He was sleek, thin and lithe, his hair the only indulgence as it hung to his shoulders, shining and ebony. Conall, while kin, seemed softer, gentler even.

Until she recalled what he had done at the palace. Her thoughts turned then to the son Caryss had mentioned.

What will come of a child born of wolf and sun?

The stones beneath her grew cold, and Nahla dropped to her knees, dirt and grass under and around her. Eirrannian dirt.

The Great Mother reaches far, she thought, letting her forehead fall.

*****

The sun was high and bright, and a strong gale swirled around the two men as they stood looking out across the rolling sea, orange and red streaks rippling through the water where the sun struck it. The thinner man was pale, and had his head dropped low, while the thick-shouldered man stared straight, as if the sea had answers.

"Where do you think she has gone?"

"If she has not gone to the Tribelands, there seems only one place that would offer her safety," the taller man answered.

Willem, his hands clenched at his sides, turned on his heel. For several moments, he had forgotten that Kennet stood near. His question was one that he had thought long on since the High Lord had visited, yet no answers had come.

Except for one.

"Would she be so predictable? Your uncle would advise against it, no doubt."

When he nodded, Kennet's glasses slid down his large nose. "You think she has left Cordisia altogether?"

"She was not spotted at the gates," he told the boy.

Waving ink-stained fingers, Kennet told him, "She arrived unnoticed as well. Little can be placed in that. But, by all accounts, the King can no longer walk or ride. One need not be able to do either aboard a ship."

"Is it possible that she headed east or south?" Willem asked.

He watched the librarian remove his wire-rimmed frames and rub at his face. Kennet, he knew, was used to finding answers, yet neither could find one now.

"If only my uncle would send word," Kennet mumbled, putting his glasses back into place.

"She has little time," Willem warned.

"Give me until tomorrow. I must think on this."

"If only Conri would have told me where to find her!" Willem roared, causing Kennet to step back from him.

Willem had found Kennet in his studies, but they had quickly left, walking to the shore. Alone, they had been able to speak on Bronwen without fear of being overheard.

"I should have never let him leave without telling me where she had gone," Willem added, still simmering with anger.

With a snort, Kennet muttered, "The Tribe is not known to be the trusting sort."

"He made mention that she might return to the Academy," Willem told him.

With another grunt, Kennet snorted, "That would be unwise. My uncle would not allow that, for he could not wait to be gone from here himself."

Willem nodded, having come to know the dark mage well. It seemed to be the only thing he knew of late with any certainty.

"Meet me here on the morrow at the midday bells. If you have learned nothing by then, I will travel to Eirrannia. And hope that I find her before my cousin does."

If he did not, both men feared what would happen, although neither spoke on it.

*****

The walk was an easy one, and the trail was clear, sandy and soft under her feet. Even with the extra weight that she now carried, Caryss preferred not to ride. Aldric kept pace next to her, allowing her silence as they walked. He had set aside his questions, Caryss realized, and she was grateful for the quiet, which allowed her to mull over her thoughts, which were many.

Within the hour, they would be upon the village where Otieno was last seen. She needed the man more than any of the others who she traveled with, even more than the dark mage. The boy needed him too, Crispin's son. She had seen it.

If he refuses to come, much will be lost.

"Aldric, how true is mage-sight?" she asked quickly, tearing apart the silence.

He slowed, but continued walking as he told her, "It is always true, yet never so."

"How can that be?" she asked him, laughing, although she knew he had not jested.

"There is what is seen, but there is also what is thought. For example, I might see a burning house, flaming and falling, yet the fire's origin could have many explanations. If I feared war, I would think invading armies responsible. If I feared thunder, I might conclude that lightning struck it. If I had many foes, I would assume that one of my enemies was to blame. Do you understand now?"

His words made much sense to her and his explanation was a fine one, yet still she asked, "And if I see this *diauxie* side by side with my daughter, instructing her and protecting her, what then? Have I concluded falsely?"

"Tell me more of the vision," he hastily told her. "What age was the girl? Where did they appear to be? You see, one must examine mage-sight with more than just the eyes."

With a creased forehead, Caryss answered, "She was young, much younger than I would have guessed to be wielding the heavy sword that she carried. Perhaps seven or so moon years. I know not where they were, but the sun was red and the ground burnt. They were in a courtyard of sorts, surrounded by wide-fronded trees."

"Yet you are certain it was not Tretoria or the Cove?"

They had both paused, although there were none around to hear them. For a moment, Caryss struggled to recall the sight, the memory of her daughter and the *diauxie*.

"It was a place that I have not yet seen," she told him finally, angry that she knew no more.

"So the girl will be with him at some point. The vision does not mean that he will come with you now."

"There is more that I have not told you," Caryss confessed, wiping at her forehead and the moisture there.

"Caryss," he moaned.

Giving little heed to his annoyance, she continued, "Remember the boy? The one I saw in the hallways of the palace. The one I said was born from fatigue."

"You believe that to be mage-sight as well?" he hurriedly asked, already knowing what she implied.

"No. More makes sense to me now, and I am certain that it was no mere vision. He traveled as the girl does, from place to place, as if a ghost. Afterward, days later, I saw him again. But that time it was the sight, and he was with Otieno."

As he listened, the mage's eyes grew sharp with interest. "You are convinced that he is Crispin's son? The prince himself acted as if you were mad to suggest such a thing."

"He later admitted to me that I was right," she told him.

Shaking his head as if in disbelief, Aldric sighed, "Caryss, why would you help the boy?"

"She will need him. There will come a time when she will need him."

Her words were crisp, as if there was no doubt to them.

"You have seen it?" the mage asked.

She knew that she was not wrong and told him so.

"Is it not strange to see so much, Bronwen?"

She smiled at his slip, but didn't correct him. "It is not I who sees. It is the babe who sees. Once she is born, I will be healer again and nothing more."

"You will always be more."

"Healer is enough," she laughed, under the bright gaze of the sun. The sound echoed around them, and, for the first time in moons, Caryss felt free, as if the gods had lost track of her.

As if she had finally outran them.

*****

He was standing beneath the swaying, feathery leaves of a palm tree when the woman appeared. There was a man with her, but the halo of light that surrounded her blinded him to all others. The sun was midway between cresting and setting, hanging with a slant toward the horizon. For a long moment, she could not see him, but he watched her from afar, unknown and undisturbed. The blaze of her hair, waving in the wind, tendrils of flame dancing across her face, gave him pause.

Beneath his dark jacket, his heart pulsed, fast and fierce, yet he knew not why.

On she walked, and, when the fog behind his eyes cleared and his pulse slowed, Otieno noticed the man beside her. Tall and thin, shadowed where she was bright. The man was not who he would have expected to be with her, and he reached for the curved sword that hung to his right, gripping it with a scarred hand, one that was etched with faded lines.

With his fingers brushing at the hilt, he waited, keeping the sword sheathed.

Again, he looked toward the tainted man, recognizing the scent of blood magic on him.

From where he stood, the *diauxie* could still not be seen. Hidden, he eyed them as they approached. The woman's pale skin glowed under the tropical sun, shimmering, tinted the color of the moon. The thin man stood just steps behind her, and Otieno slowly dropped his hand. Wearing a thick riding suit, unusual for the warm climate of the islands, the woman appeared to be without weapon. Her companion had a long sword at his hip, but Otieno wondered if he even had strength to draw it.

A cloudless sky watched them, and a salty breeze fell over them. Yet, as the pair neared, the air around him suddenly stilled. There was a ringing in his ears that he could not quiet. Bright and burning, the sun seemed to turn away from him, yet no light faded. Quickly, he dropped his eyes and backed toward the tree until he was pressed against it.

Pale and flaming, as if born of fire and star, the girl approached. About her was a light that he remembered. A light of another, one whom he longed to forget.

Behind his eyes, blood ran, reddening his vision until the sand beneath his booted feet was murky and crimson. Sticky and thick, streams of blood wrapped around his feet until he could not move.

Her voice was like a song, calling to him, gently at first, but the rhythm intensified, drumming into him with forceful and melodic thumping. Without words, the woman spoke to him. From a distance, she touched him with hands as cool as the glacial lakes of her homeland. Her fingers burned him, ice-hot. Like the *atraglacia* he long coveted. Lava rock. Black ice. Fire and flame, ice and iron.

Any other man would have fallen to his knees when she neared. Otieno did not, but his legs shook nonetheless.

When she spoke, her words were soft and light, and, with each one, the blood-haze lifted. Just steps from him, he saw her clearly now.

"I have traveled far to find you, Otieno."

He said nothing, nor did he move. Her words, both warning and song, struck as if a weapon.

"My daughter sends me to you."

He knew not who the woman was, nor her daughter. That she knew him was no surprise.

Finally, he stepped from the shadow of the tree. "Who is your daughter?" he asked, his voice gruff, as if no words had come from his full lips in moons.

"The girl is not yet born," she told him, coming to a halt, close enough for him to reach for her.

Beside her, the man stood, strange and silent, abiding and waiting, speechless. His eyes, guarded and intense, betrayed little.

Pulling his eyes from the man, Otieno asked, "How can it be so that one unborn has tasked you to find me?"

She stared at him with eyes gray, gold, and green. Her nose and cheeks were dotted with freckles, as if the gods had painted her cheeks with drops of sunlight. Her fingers, long and fine, trembled slightly where they hung at her side. Yet, in those eyes, he saw no fear.

She let him inspect her, before answering, "I am with child, Otieno, and she is no ordinary child. She speaks to me."

Otieno looked to the other man for explanation, yet his eyes were low and lidded, so he looked back to the woman, thinking her mad. As with many who were blessed with magic, her mind had become damaged, he realized as the spell of her began to fade.

"Islanders know to not play games with a *diauxie*. Be gone from here," he hissed without moving from beneath the tree's canopy of fronds.

His words were harsh ones, yet the woman smiled. A smile of madness.

"I play no game," she laughed. "I have come for your aid. And will do what I must to ensure that I have it. In truth, I was warned overmuch about seeking you. Yet I still have come."

When she looked at him, her eyes shined with desire, one that she did nothing to mask.

"Do not seek to seduce me," he warned, understanding what game she now played. "Do not try to bribe me. Nor threaten me. Many have tried. As many have failed."

The woman was quiet for several moments, her head low and eyes downcast now, hiding her want.

When she still did not back away, he told her, "Be gone now."

As if come to life again by his words, she cried, "I have come from afar to find you, and with many risks to myself and to others. Will you not hear me out? What of coin? I have much to offer."

"What need do I have for coin? I have neither home nor family. I walk with the wind and the Great Mother provides."

"What if the Great Mother wills you to help my daughter?" the woman asked, her tone serious and stern.

With a furrowed brow, Otieno growled, "*Leseda*, what right do you have to speak for the Great Mother? You are mad to even attempt such."

"Must I beg you, Otieno?" the woman pleaded, her voice high and shaky as she jumped toward him.

He nearly grabbed her by the shoulders as she threw herself at him. Pulling at his tunic, she cried, "It must be you. I have seen her with you."

"One who has not yet been born cannot speak!"

"She speaks," the woman gasped, sobbing as her fingers fell from him.

"Do not seek to woo me with tears. My path is my own, and it is one that none can follow," he chided her.

"She will walk where others cannot," the woman cried, tears shaking her body until she fell to her knees in the soft sand at his feet.

Behind her, the man moved, crouching beside her and placing an arm around her shoulders.

Into her neck, he whispered, loud enough for Otieno to hear, "Caryss, we will find another way. There are others who can teach her."

She flung the man's arm from her and scrambled to her knees, anger flushing her face. With a tear-stained face, red and wet, she looked to him.

With a gaze full of accusation, she screamed, "What of glory?"

He opened his mouth to reply, but she silenced him. "She will be like none before her."

The man pulled at her until she stood.

"Do not beg him. If he will not come willingly, then the girl will not want him at her side," he scolded her.

Stepping back from him, the woman spit, "I will not beg him, Aldric. I will show him."

Otieno watched as she turned toward the man. Her next words were spoken too low for him to hear, but the dark-clothed man released her, although his eyes blazed and his lips tightened.

Again the woman fell to her knees, but this time the man did not move. Otieno noticed how he looked about, as if on guard. His hands, yellowed and lined, rose, until they were above his head. Otieno had seen such done before, and recognized the faint hum of the air as a warding.

"You would be a fool to seek to harm me, mage," Otieno warned, reaching for his scimitar.

The man said nothing. Yet Otieno sensed the humming air and recognized mage-skill. Instead, he turned toward the woman, who reached for a pouch hanging from a braided belt. When next he looked, the woman gripped a dark-bladed dagger. Near his boots knelt a half-mad woman, with child, a child she claimed spoke to her. In hands that were unmarked and smooth was a dagger, one ancient and tainted. A blade carved of ice and smoldered in fire.

Atraglacia.

Before he could stop her, she drew a long, thin line across the palm of her left hand with the tip of the ebony ice. Blood bubbled, from edge to edge, perfectly straight, until it grew too thick and dripped down toward her wrist and over the creased sides of her hand. The blood sought the earth, falling and falling again until it reached sand and dirt.

Blood magic. The magic of his people, not hers. But with a weapon that none here would recognize.

No one talked, nor did any try to stop her, not even the man who stood white-faced and chanting. Otieno could not take his eyes from the woman, the *leseda*, as she dipped her forehead to the ground, resting it there, in submission. Except for her pale skin and black blade, she was like so many before her who sought the Great Mother's power. Knees dirtied and hands bloodied, in supplication.

Blood was blood, rich and red, all the same to the Great Mother.

Lifting her head from the ground, the woman raised the back of her right hand, the clean hand. When fingers reached forehead, she paused, marking the mother's sign there. Next, those fingers landed on lips that were red and full, swollen under the island sun. Again she traced the mother's circle.

When she moved next to above her heart, Otieno shuddered, remembering how often he too searched for the origin of the life pulse. While she sought blessing, he had sought death. Until the Great Mother had called him elsewhere. On her knees before him, the pale-faced Northern girl now called to his gods, not her own. He watched as she rested her hands over her womb, already rounded, he now noticed. Cupped and open, red with still-wet blood, her hands trembled, yet she did not rise.

They all waited.

Her blood was strong, her dagger god-touched.

The Great Mother did not make them wait long. But, it was not the goddess who came.

Steps from the mage, a woman appeared, dark-hair piled high on her head, plaited and twisted in a style that spoke of talented hands. He knew the girl to be a vision, glimmering and faded, yet still he stepped closer.

Moon-dipped fabric, nearly sheer silver and cream, wrapped her body from neck to ankle, a style of dress more suited to warm climates than the cool, Northern ones. Small jewels dotted her dark hair, glittering like stars in a sea of night. Her feet were bare, as if she had rushed off.

Drawing a deep breath, he gazed again at her face and gasped. As if she had heard his escaping breath, the girl looked to him. Just steps from him, close enough for him to reach, she watched, waiting for the questions that she could see in his startled face.

Otieno said nothing, for his mouth had gone suddenly dry and words would not form. Instead, he stared at the three black stripes, as long as his thumb, one on top of another, lining her high-boned cheek just beneath her left eye. She had been marked, her face inked in permanence.

In tribute, he knew.

When she noticed where he looked, the girl bowed, more deeply than he liked, for he was no king, nor prince, despite the stories that followed him.

"*Akkachi*," she said, the word deep and swirling, accented with a lilt he did not recognize.

The term was one of the Cove, yet hearing her speak it caused him pause.

"I am no god, nor am I his warrior," he told her with sharp words when his lips finally parted.

"And so it begins, Otieno," she stated as her image steadied.

Behind her, the healer and the mage exchanged glances, yet neither spoke.

When he realized the woman would say nothing, he hurriedly explained, "I know you not, nor your mother. What game is played here?"

"Why did she tell you that she is here?" the girl asked, pulling at the fine garment she wore, as if unaccustomed to such dress.

Beside his face hung clay-tinted braids, which shook as he called, "She seeks my help."

He stepped closer to the flickering girl. She glowed as if she had been cut from the moon, yet she wore no halo like her mother. There was a shadow upon her, even if few could see it.

"Are those the stripes of the great cat upon your cheek?" he asked, looking upon her face again.

When the girl smiled, his hands trembled, and he nearly reached for a sword.

"Newly stained, yes. You were with me, *Akkachi*, and watched as I earned them."

"You are but a girl," he grunted. "Your skills cannot be so great."

Her laughter pierced him, sharper than any sword tip, and, again, he noticed the others watching.

The girl had come closer, until her fingers, edged in soft light, pointed at his scabbard. "Drop your weapons. I will show you my womanly skills, *Akkachi*. You are a greater teacher than you even know."

"Then you should know that I would never be without weapon," he chastised her, unable to look away from the shining, spectacular girl.

Again she laughed, the sound child-like, high and without restraint, reminding him of her youth.

With twinkling eyes, she pointed toward his back, "Give me *Enyo* then."

Scowling, he retorted, "You would not be able to lift it, let alone wield it, girl."

"Let me show you," she shrugged, swirling away from him.

The girl appeared younger than the healer, yet she was taller and her arms were tight, her shoulders curved with muscle. Few could lift the Greatsword. Even fewer could swing it. Yet the girl had called for it by name. A name that none but he knew, for the blacksmith who had made it was long dead.

No longer understanding what was happening or who the girl was, he unclasped the sword and swung it around and over his head until the thick tip was buried in the sand between his boots.

"Do not name it again, child," he growled.

Bowing her head, she said, "Yes, master. Now drop it to the sand. I cannot pick it up if it is still in your possession."

Still uncertain, he did as she asked, but placed his hand on the hilt of the curved sword.

"You couldn't just go with her?" the girl called to him as she danced nearer. "You must make everything difficult, *Akkachi*, and turn all into a lesson. Now stand back," she warned, motioning to the others.

With a laugh that was honey-sweet, she teased, "As Otieno has said, I might not even be able to lift the Greatsword."

She smiled and her emerald-colored eyes shimmered in jest, but all did as she had requested.

Her right hand, shining yet solid, reached for the blade, and the girl wrapped her fingers across the hilt, placing her left hand under it. With a tight grip around the wide hilt, she lifted *Enyo* off the ground, with more ease than Otieno would have believed possible. The sword was long and heavy, but she wielded it well, swinging it from right to left, letting it cross her body with power and force, striking down at an imaginary target. The

151

girl lifted it again, this time bringing it from beside her left hip, slashing upward, across and into the air. Next, she lunged with it, a difficult move for even Otieno himself, parrying and twisting after the thrust. On and on, she flowed, swinging, slashing, spinning away then back toward them with a strike.

As the sun beamed yellow-orange rays upon her and the silver blade, she lifted it above her head, and, while her arms shook, she did not lose control, striking down in a diagonal slice that would have cut a man from neck to knee. Without speaking, she set the sword at his feet.

With a tip of her head, she said, "Let me have the scimitar."

"You have shown me enough, *leeta*," he breathed, unable to say more.

The girl walked toward him, away from her mother and the other man, who were staring wide-eyed and entranced behind her. When she was near enough to him that the others could not hear, she looked at him, sparkling and fading.

With tears in her eyes, she whispered, "My mother has never seen me fight. Let me have the scimitar please. I will show her how I dance."

Otieno looked at her, the girl, maybe sixteen or so moon years, and understood. With nothing further to say, he nodded and reached for the curved sword. Without hesitating, he dropped it to the sand, remembering her earlier words.

Her back was still facing her mother, and the sun reflected off her silvery dress until it was nearly translucent. She glowed, as if the moon stood in human form before them, fallen from the sky and with no stars as companions. Otieno noticed her body trembling, but by now he knew it was not with fatigue. Emotion swept over her, and she struggled to control it before turning to face her mother. He nearly intervened, but, as he stepped toward her, she grabbed the scimitar and turned.

What followed brought tears to his hardened eyes and a smile to his scarred face. Her mother had not lied. The girl was like none other. In her hand, the sword was not just weapon.

It was a flower, as she plucked it from the ground, bringing it so close to her face that he held his breath in fear. The curved blade tucked near her pale neck, the girl flipped through the air, landing on steady feet, the sword now in front of her, ready to strike. She brought it near her face, inhaling its delicate scent, then slashed backward so abruptly and fiercely that he scurried away.

Next, she danced as if made of water and flowed, slicing and twisting, a coiling stream of movement. A deadly rush of water. She ended with a fluid stroke, letting the blade carve a pattern into the air, whistling, like a fast-flowing river, free and furious. Her hand etched with such speed that the mist around her dissolved.

Otieno reached for his face, for suddenly he felt as if the skies had opened up and showered him in rain.

The girl continued on. Where once she streamed and swelled, now she seemed to be weightless, as if made of air. She became nearly invisible, shifting and tickling his skin with a kiss from the blade. Each time she neared, he shivered, yet he stood as if he was stone.

Otieno had never seen a sword move as quickly as it did in her hands, as if she held the wind by its hand. Again and again, she swung and struck, up and down, from left to right, faster each time, until the blade hummed, spiraling under her control. The girl kicked her feet out in front of her, without sound, and threw herself backward, rolling sideways in the air as she held the sword aloft. As she tumbled, the scimitar cut a new pattern, so close to Otieno that he did not dare breathe.

She played with him, slicing at his tunic, tearing it from neck to hip, yet the sword tip had not once touched skin.

When she backed away, he reached for his tunic, holding it closed as his eyes stayed on her. The blade now glowed gold, as if she fought inside a storm, lightning held tightly between her fingers.

Moments before she had moved delicately, swirling and dancing. Now, she was all power and force, deadly and vengeful, as she raised the scimitar above her head, striking down, over and over, until her arm grew tired. Each time the blade crashed toward the ground, he leaned into the tree, half-expecting thunder to roar overhead.

When the skies quieted, he thought her to be done as her arms burned with fatigue. Even her dress had come loose, and strands of the sheer fabric hung from her, glittering in the high sun and trailing behind her like falling stars. Dark hair, scattered waves, came free too, yet she noticed nothing, moving as if she could not stop.

Suddenly, she was ablaze. Not water, nor air, nor lightning. Now, she burned with flame, and his skin burned to be so near to her.

Frenzied and with abandon, she fought, half-crazed, leaping and cutting, with little care to whom or what was around her. Like flames, she knew no direction and had no aim. She only sought to destroy, to burn, to kill. Falling to the ground, rolling from attack, rising again, the girl fought.

Her dress dirtied and torn, she still did not stop, weaving the scimitar with the thread of fire until it burned red in her hands.

Finally, falling to her knees, she paused. Dropping her head to the ground, she rested, breathing deeply as the image flickered with each exhale.

It was enough.

Otieno stepped toward her to reclaim the weapon, but before he could, she leaned back. With one quick slash, she ran the tip of the blade across her palm, like her mother had done earlier. Blood fell heavily onto the ground.

Otieno needed to see nothing else.

"You thank the Great Mother for your life," he whispered, his words empty of artifice.

"As you have taught me," she whispered, her breath still coming in spurts.

"*Leeta*, I will be honored to call you student."

"As I always am to call you master, *Akkachi*," she sighed, the words no more than an echo.

When he looked at her again, the girl was nearly invisible, the power fading. It would not be long before she was gone altogether.

As the two talked, her mother rushed forward. The man trailed behind, with a look of pride on his face. The girl was well-loved, Otieno knew then.

Yet, he watched as the girl kept her eyes low and her back toward her mother, and heard her say, "I must go, mother. Aldric, keep her safe. You have done what you must here. It is time to head north."

Her mother nodded and would have said more, but the girl disappeared, vanishing as if she had never been. All three watched until there was nothing left of her to see.

With a deep sigh, the *diauxie* sheathed the scimitar.

"I had not thought to ever step foot onto Cordisia," he told them, knowing not what else to say.

"Eirrannia is of the North. Cordisian in name only," the mage explained.

The woman nodded, as if she could not speak. In her eyes, he saw knowledge, and he dropped his own, swallowing the words he would have said. As he walked, toward the direction where they had first come from, his eyes were wet. Under the warm watch of the sun, the tears dried on his cheeks before falling to the ground. The Great Mother's mercy, he thought, thankful.

*****

By the time the trio arrived outside of Keva and Asha's inn, the sun was nearly even with the horizon, and a dusky orange had settled across the sandy streets. The walk had been a quiet one, and the distance had spread before them as a welcome distraction. Aldric walked behind Caryss, who trailed a few steps behind Otieno, who seemed to know where they were headed. Caryss had been silent the entirety of the walk, which had not surprised Aldric, as she was often so after contact with the girl.

It had been his first time encountering the girl as she time-walked. Each time before, she had kept herself hidden, and her presence hours before had affected him more deeply than he would have once believed. She had the look of her father to her, but her eyes were Eirrannian. Her clothing, nothing he had ever seen before, had caused his mouth to gape until he had the wherewithal to close it. Yet, it was the tattooed lines across her face that had caused the most surprise.

She had the look of a barbarian about her, wild and untamed, even as striking and graceful as she was. She appeared unlike any he had met in his travels. She was, he now knew, an outsider. Aldric could not stop himself from wondering if Caryss had noticed, and what her thoughts were, yet he did not ask. He doubted that she would have heard him anyway, so lost in thought she was.

For his part, Otieno respected her silence as well, walking on fully certain in his destination. Aldric had doubted the need for the Islander, and, more than once, had tried convincing Caryss to alter her plans. Yet, once he saw the way the girl moved with the swords, he knew that he had been wrong. There was no one, not in Cordisia or elsewhere, that could teach the girl as Otieno had. Especially once they knew who she was.

There was a saying among the Lokaada people, who lived near Concordia Lake, on the southern border of Planusterra, that Aldric suddenly remembered as he thought back to the girl.

He who keeps company with wolves will learn to howl.

The girl, with the help of Otieno, and, from her brief words earlier, he as well, was learning to howl. Again, he looked toward Caryss, struggling to understand how she might feel as healer as she watched her daughter dance with weapons of death. Later, he would ask, but, for now, he walked on, grateful to see the blue-tinged roof of the inn just steps ahead of them.

*****

15

"*Leseda*, you must hurry! The babe comes!"

Caryss had been lying on the small cot, taking a break from gathering her items. On the morrow, the group planned to depart.

Asha's words had woken her and it took a moment for them to make sense. As she sat up, rubbing at her eyes, Asha cried, "There is blood in the water and Keva is sick with pain.

With still-shrouded eyes, Caryss rose, and told the woman, "Take me to her at once."

It did not take long to find Keva, at the other end of the inn, in a group of rooms that she and Asha shared. Caryss entered and found the laboring woman lying on her side, sweat-covered and moaning.

As she rushed to the girl's side, she called, "Find Sharron. And the *diauxie*."

From the door, Asha cried, "*Diauxie* men cannot put hands on women who are with child!"

She had not known such was the case and said nothing as Asha hurried away. Throwing her braided belt onto an oval table, Caryss neared Keva.

Reaching for the woman's hand, she asked softly, "Keva, can you tell me what happened?"

The woman's brow was damp and her hands and feet swollen, much larger than when last Caryss had examined her. Keva's dress was damp, too, and stained with blood at the edges, Caryss noticed as she rubbed her back.

When Keva answered, Caryss leaned closer, listening as she whispered, "I was readying the evening meal when I felt my waters dripping. By the time Asha returned from the market, the pains had come. It was not like this before."

"Moon years ago, I began giving women a tea blend that eased some of the pain and helped move things along more quickly. When Sharron arrives, I will have her set about making the tea. It is not so bad that the babe has decided to come early," Caryss told her as she again placed her hand on Keva's forehead.

"The room is dark, *leseda*," Keva mumbled, rolling onto her back, her eyes half-closed.

It was hours from nightfall and the room glowed orange. Caryss looked to the door as Sharron and Asha rushed in.

"Shhh," Caryss whispered as she nodded toward Sharron.

When the other healer neared, she stepped away from Keva. Near the window, she told Sharron, "She is too hot by far and thick with fluids. I have yet to examine her, but I'm nearly certain that we will have to speed things along. I should have all that you will need in my pouches to make the birthing tea."

"Tell me what to include, Caryss, and I will ready it."

"Equal parts sassafras and angelica, and a few drops of poppy milk."

While Sharron searched the pouches, Caryss instructed Asha to fetch boiling water and clean linens. As the two women set about their tasks, Caryss pushed a small chair toward the end of the cot where Keva moaned, rolling from side to side.

"I need you to lie still on your back while I check for the babe," Caryss told her, keeping her voice soft, yet firm.

Keva made no reply, but ceased moving for long enough for Caryss to feel for the babe. She had hoped that Keva's body was readying for birth, but was disappointed to find it not so.

Again Keva rolled onto her side, her eyes closed tightly now.

"Life pulse is weak and slow. No indication that she is opening."

The woman on the bed made no notion that she had heard or understood.

"What of a tea of wort?" Sharron asked.

Rising, Caryss answered, "I thought the same. In my large pouch, you will find mint vinegar. Add some as well. The combination of the three will circulate her blood more freely and will induce contractions. If she begins to bleed more than normal, we will need to brew a tea of yellow dock leaves and apply a poultice of fresh aloe leaves, which are abundant here, mixed with plantain oil. We can ready all while we wait for the tea to take effect."

Asha entered then, carrying a tray laden with a steaming pot and bleached towels. Sharron crossed the room for the water, while Caryss searched through two small pouches. When she had found a small container of long, lance-shaped leaves, Caryss handed them to Sharron and returned to the cot.

"Can you help me remove her dress?" she called to Asha.

As the women worked to roll the dress up, Asha quietly asked, "Have you given her something to make her sleep?"

"Not yet," Caryss told her, shaking her head. "Tell me of the last two."

Keva did little more than groan as her sweat-soaked dress was removed. Caryss watched as the woman's stomach tightened and another low moan rumbled from her lips. Asha had not been wrong to think that her sister was under the effects of poppy milk. Yet, Sharron had only just steeped the tea.

With a hand on her sister's head, pushing the woman's thickly braided hair away from her face, Asha told the healers of how her sister had labored long both times, nearing on two days. Both times, midwives had given her herbs to bring on the birth, yet little worked. And by the time the babes had arrived, it had been too late, the woman whispered, although Keva, now dosed with tea and poppy milk, was asleep and could not hear her words.

Caryss was at Keva's side, feeling again on the woman's stomach in an attempt to determine how the babe was situated. Several times over, she ran her hands along Keva's abdomen, rubbing and pushing. It was as it had been days before, with the babe's head high.

To Sharron, she called, "The babe presents with feet out. And, more, Keva is weak and her limbs loose, even though she has not yet opened. Even if we were able to dose her with the mugwort, she might not progress, as her past suggests."

In Eirrannian, Sharron asked, "Does the babe yet live?"

Hastily, Caryss told her, "Aye. But it is not the babe I fear for. Keva is too weak to be of much use."

"What of Keva?" Asha cried, hearing her sister's name mentioned, despite understanding nothing else of the Eirrannian.

Caryss was fond of both women, and it had long been her approach as healer to keep little from those she was treating. It must be no different now, she told herself.

Switching back to Common, she explained, "None of our choices are good ones, Asha. There are herbs that might bring the birth faster, but your sister fares poorly even now, and the added blood loss would only make it worse. Yet the babe cannot linger long awaiting birth, as you have witnessed with the others."

Reaching for a tall bottle, she sighed. "It is a choice that none should have to make, but I must ask nonetheless. If one is to survive, who should it be?"

Caryss uncapped the bottle and the scent of mint filled the room. On the other side of the cot, Asha sobbed. Sharron crossed, placing an arm around the weeping woman while Caryss waited, keeping her eyes downcast.

"Is it not possible for both to survive?" Asha pleaded, her words broken and stuttered, her face wet and her eyes lined in red.

Sharron glanced toward Caryss, and she knew what the other healer silently suggested. She had thought it herself, but it involved more risk than any other option. Both mother and babe could die.

Corking the bottle and placing it back among her pouches, Caryss told Asha, "In my moon years as healer, I have twice birthed a babe by cutting it from its mother."

When Asha paled, Caryss hurriedly added, "At the time, there was little other choice. It is not without risk, nor is it a guarantee that both will survive."

Asha said nothing, shaking her head repeatedly, as if to shake free from what Caryss suggested.

In another time, she might have tried to comfort the woman, but Sharron was still near enough, and her time on the Cove was growing short. But, more, Caryss knew that she had not misspoken.

"A decision must be made and since her husband is at sea, it must be you who makes it."

Caryss did not look to the woman. She was healer now, and not friend. The choice was Asha's alone.

Through tears, Asha slowly asked, "Would Keva be able to survive such an act?"

"I will do all I can to ensure that both live. But, yes, your sister would face the greater risk. I was able to feel the babe and know exactly where it lies, which is of significant importance. The babe will live, Asha."

"And Keva?" the woman gasped, leaning heavily onto Sharron.

After drawing a deep breath, Caryss told her, "She will bleed heavily. There are ways to attempt to slow it, and I will stitch her quickly after. But she is already ill, and the risk of infection will increase greatly."

"How must I choose then?" Asha cried, her eyes swollen with fear.

"I cannot tell you that. If we wait, the babe will surely die, just as the others, for your sister's womb will not open, by some defect of the bones, I fear. And, in truth, the babe is sickening her. The longer she labors, the more ill she will become."

"Asha," Caryss called, knowing how little time remained, "Any longer and both might not survive."

Around the room, lines of sunlight filtered through hand-dyed curtains, casting glimmering images of blossoms across the tiled floor. Caryss stared at the nearest, a five-petal flower whose shadow shined red as wine. Keva's room was as bright as a garden in full bloom.

None should die in such a place, Caryss thought.

Pushing fallen strands of her from her face, Caryss heard Asha utter, "It seems I have little choice then. I will not lose both."

As if she could no longer weep, Asha's words were calm ones.

With no further delay, Caryss ordered Sharron to inform the others that their departure would be delayed. Once the other healer returned, they would begin.

Caryss walked to the table near the cot where her pouches were spread out. If she were at the Academy, with the clinic nearby, the surgery would not be so fraught with risk. Her supplies here were limited to what she had packed, and, even then, she had left much back in the King's City. She had not thought of Rexterra for days, and the sudden memory caused her to think again of what could happen if they were found. Grabbing an amber-hued bottle, she hurriedly uncorked it and poured the rust-colored liquid onto her hands, rubbing them briskly together. Back at the end of the cot, she reached for Keva, feeling to see if the woman had progressed. After several moments, it was clear that she had not, and Caryss returned to the table.

From one of the pouches, she withdrew several oval and blunt plantain leaves. She had less than she would have liked and, holding one up, called to Asha, "Do you have plantain here? I have also heard it called snakeweed and waybroad."

The woman neared, examining the leaf but not taking it from Caryss's hand. Shaking her head, she told the healer, "I have not seen it."

Lifting another, multi-leafed and star-like, Caryss asked, "What of Shepherd's Purse? It is of the mustard family, and the leaves are often eaten, although they are bitter."

Reaching for the raised leaf, but not touching it, Asha exclaimed, "Yes, I have seen that one at the market!"

"Go there now and get me as much of it as you can," Caryss instructed, her voice and focus seeming distant.

Just as Asha was about to step into the hall, Caryss called, "When you return, call for Sharron. Do not enter, Asha."

The woman nodded and ran, her footsteps loud on the slate floors of the inn. Caryss busied herself readying the herbs, some dried, some sealed and pressed when freshly cut. Blood loss was her main concern and she emptied all of her pouches onto the table in search of ways to prevent Keva from bleeding overmuch. When Sharron entered, Caryss was still examining the pouch's contents.

"Aldric sits with the King."

When Caryss looked to her quickly, Sharron realized her error and put a hand to her mouth.

"Asha has gone to fetch more Shepherd's Purse and Keva is milk-heavy. You need not worry."

At times, Sharron still looked toward Caryss as Master Apprentice, and she herself a student yet. They were moons gone from the Academy, which Caryss reminded her, and titles no longer applied. Once she had taken the King, all had changed, Caryss knew. Once Master Apprentice, now she was more rogue than esteemed.

160

With a snort, she told Sharron, "We should start our own academy in the North. With regular shipments of herbs and plants from warner climes, we would need naught."

Sharron was beside her now, cleaning the small, thinly bladed knife that Caryss would soon use. Lining up the shining tools along a white sheet of linen, the younger healer nodded. "The North has need of well-trained healers. While many dabble in the healing arts, none are as skilled as the masters."

"Perhaps one day," Caryss mused, mixing more poppy milk tea.

After a moment, she added, "I should have sent for Otieno. The tea might not be enough to keep her still."

"The sisters would not have allowed it. You heard what was said about man's hands on a woman near birthing."

With another snort, Caryss shrugged off the comments. "I care little for such silly beliefs. If having him here would keep mother, babe, or both alive, they should care little as well."

"If she wakes, I will find him," Sharron agreed.

Drawing a deep breath and stretching, Caryss asked, "Do you think we have enough supplies to stop heavy blood loss? If we were at the clinic, I would not worry about what course to take, but here we are limited."

Without looking up from the steaming pot of water, Sharron replied, "The capsella applied over the incision and steeped for drinking should cause the blood to clot quickly. Peppered ale has been known to staunch blood flow as well."

"Ah, yes, I know of such an ale. Do you have supplies enough to make it?"

"I have no ale, but I can use the milk the poppy was mixed with."

"Hurry then," Caryss told her as the sleeping woman began moaning anew.

When all was prepared, and the table moved closer to the cot, Caryss asked, "Have you ever seen a babe cut from a body?"

"I have read on it, but have never seen it done."

"Were you not at the clinic either time I attempted it?"

Shaking her head, Sharron told her, "I heard of it after. Both babes survived, as well as one of the mothers."

Closing her eyes for a moment, Caryss sighed. "It is not an easy thing. If we had time to wait, I would be inclined to give her a few more days. I feel as if I should not wear the robes for admitting such."

"Before you even came upon Keva she had lost two babes. If you were not here now, she would lose a third, and Asha would most likely lose a sister as well. You have chosen well here, Caryss."

"Then let us get on with it. Keva grows more ill by the hour."

161

Hurriedly crossing the room, Caryss kicked the door closed, then walked back to stand beside Sharron. Beneath her tunic, her life pulse beat fast, thumping hard against the light garment that she had purchased at the market that morning. Her hands were steady, moon years of training had made certain of that. She thought of Willem, remembering how he had been with her on the two other occasions when surgery had been necessary.

"Mix the poppy with the dried pepper. I will open her mouth while you pour it in," she told Sharron, trying to force the thought of Willem from her mind.

"If she wakes, give her more," she warned, "And, Sharron, if need be, hold her down. She must not move."

With little more than a nod, Sharron moved quickly, and, together, they fed Keva the mix, with little response from her except throaty mumbles.

Caryss's hair was pulled back from her face, tied at her neck with haste. Eyes clear and focused, she reached for blade. Keva lay nearly naked, a thin blanket covering her face and neck.

In a voice free of emotion and history, Caryss intoned, "I will cut from side to side, just above her pelvic bones and only large enough that the babe can be pulled through. Once the babe is out, I will stitch up the skin. Then we will lay the leaves across the incision. Have enough strips of linen ready to bind her, and enough to change the dressings several times in the next quarter-moon. Asha will have to be taught what to do, for we cannot stay much longer in the Cove."

With the tip of the knife pressed into Keva, Caryss stated, "Have a needle ready."

Those would be the last words spoken.

With pale hands, long-fingered and steady, Caryss drew her knife across Keva, cutting from left to right, about a hand's length under her umbilicus. Keva moaned, twisting to her side, but she was so weak with fever that it took little effort for Sharron to hold her shoulders against the bed. Blood trailed where Caryss sliced, red and wet, bubbling before thickening into a stream.

Caryss wiped the blade on a square of white cloth before setting it aside. With no hesitation, she reached for Keva's skin, parting it with some force. Her left hand held open the skin while her right one reached back for the knife.

Again she cut, deeper this time, ripping open skin and muscle. Once the knife was placed on the table, she used her free hand to pull apart the freshly cut skin, nodding toward Sharron, who understood what was needed. Leaving Keva's side, Sharron grabbed a pile of cloths and hurried to wipe at the blood that darkened Keva's body and Caryss's hands.

162

Wasting no time, Caryss lifted her hands for Sharron to clean. Once they were again ivory and dry, she forced them into the narrow opening that lined Keva's lower abdomen. From the beginning, she knew that she would not have much time once the incision had been made. With that knowledge, she reached for where she had earlier felt the babe's feet, low and close to the birth opening. Moments later, she felt the babe's ankle, and clasped it with slippery hands.

Using her other hand, she searched, until shoulders were felt and cupped the babe's shoulder. As both hands grasped the babe, she pulled, drawing it from Keva's womb. With one final push to open the area that she had cut, Caryss lifted the babe from Keva, gently holding him as air replaced water.

He was pale, skin as white as the two *lesedas* who stood to either side of him, staring at him with wide eyes. Blue tinged his skin, but his size was fair, and Caryss quickly handed him off to Sharron, who waited with blanket in hand.

Once her hands were free, Caryss cut the cord that attached mother and son. Behind her, she knew, Sharron held the babe, rubbing on his chest in small circular motions. Caryss held linens against Keva's skin, soaking in blood.

When the babe's whimper filled the room, Caryss turned, looking at him with her gray-green eyes. As the whimpers turned to shrieks, she looked to Keva.

"Your son lives," she told the woman, who dozed, heavy with poppy milk, unaware of what had transpired.

Caryss moved her fingers to the woman's neck, feeling for her life pulse. When the slow throb vibrated against her fingers, Caryss exhaled a sharp breath. With speed, she grabbed the threaded needle, thicker than most she used when at the clinic. Over and over, she stitched, only pausing to wipe blood away from where she worked. Across the woman's body ran a trail of dark crosses, stars threaded into her light brown skin.

The room had quieted, and she called, "Sharron, what of the babe?"

In reply, the other healer walked toward the cot, lifting the swaddled babe for Caryss to see.

His eyes open, storm-cloud gray, the babe watched.

"Bigger than I would have thought. And more serious too. But his breathing came easily and his coloring is now fine. A strong boy, I think," Sharron told her with words thick and raspy.

Caryss suspected that, if she looked, she would find tears on Sharron's cheeks. Her own were dry, but her life pulse still banged heavy and loud.

Several stitches later, Caryss rinsed her hands, and then reached for the plantain and Shepherd's Purse, laying the leaves - some dried - some not, across Keva's stomach.

"If you take the babe, I will bind her," Sharron called.

But Caryss knew that she could not hold the babe.

"I will wrap her. He seems content with you."

Again she laid fingers against Keva's neck. Her life pulse was slow, but steady. Atop the poultice of leaves and tonic, Caryss wrapped the strips of clean linens, until Keva was covered from hip to breast with white cloth. A few times she had had to pause to lift the woman, but she finished quickly, sighing loudly as the last linen was tied.

"Her skin burns yet, but her life pulse is solid."

From near the window, Sharron called, "What of the bleeding?"

"I have seen worse. She will be weak for a moon or so, but it was not so bad as to cause me concern. I fear infection more than anything."

"Is it not so with most we treated at the clinic?"

As Caryss placed the blanket over Keva, she answered, "We are not in Litusia. We are at an inn in the Southern Cove Islands, which houses people from lands neither of us even know. Many enter and exit here each day, bringing with them all sorts of illness."

"Asha will do what she must for her sister. And for the babe. What of a wet nurse? Surely Asha will be too weak to provide milk for the boy."

Shaking her head as she crossed the room, Caryss told Sharron, "She will be weak, but she must try to feed him. It will aid her recovery even."

"What must come next?"

"Thrice daily, Keva will need to drink a tea spiced with pepper. I do not want her to have any more poppy milk, despite the pain she might be feeling. We have seen the problems that come of that. I have some Lavender oil that I will leave with Asha, to be applied onto the cotton wool. It does a fair job as cleanser. I have some Helenium root, as well, which can be mixed with the oil. The paste will do much to prevent infection, if applied each morning. I should have thought to bring some moss with us, but the cotton wool will have to do for dressings."

Gently rocking the babe, Sharron mused, "Asha will have no time to run the inn."

With a shrug, Caryss answered, "We have coin still. Enough to hire them some help."

Stepping away from the window, Caryss walked back to the cot, placing her hand across Keva's forehead, "By the morrow, we will have a better idea of what will come. For today, we can each sit with her."

"What of the King?" Sharron asked in between humming to the babe.

Uncertain about the question, Caryss replied, "I suppose I should turn my attentions to him. It often takes a moon or more before the poppy thirst lessens. With him, it might be longer."

"He is taking half now of what he once was," Sharron told her.

Caryss knew that she owed Sharron much, for the woman had tended to the King since their departure from the palace. Each day, Sharron would feed and wash the King, even on the boat. In truth, she was more healer to him than Caryss had been.

"You have done much for him. In the coming days, I will share the burden."

Any further discussion was interrupted by a knock at the door.

"You should show her the babe," Sharron whispered.

Shaking her head, Caryss sighed. "There is much I must still do."

She was beside Keva when Sharron reached the door, the babe asleep in her arms, still swathed in a blanket. With one hand under the babe, Sharron opened the door, stepping back to reveal Asha, frenzied and fear-soaked, her hair escaping the ribbon at her neck.

"The babe!" she gasped, falling into the wall, a hand to her mouth.

Caryss's sight grew foggy and her throat burned. It took much to stop the tears from falling onto Keva.

Sharron smiled, holding out the babe to his aunt.

"He is well. Born awake and alert and of good size."

Shaking hands reached for him, and only when she had the babe pressed against her did Asha speak.

"What of my sister?" she asked, unable to look to the cot.

It was Caryss who said, "She sleeps and has not yet seen the babe."

Asha walked to the edge of the room, half-falling into a chair and cried, "She yet lives?"

"She is young and strong," Caryss told her, "But there is much that will need to be done. For the next moon, she must rest often and move little. Few must see her, and she cannot work at all. Her dressings will need to be changed daily and poultices applied. Keva did not bleed overmuch, but she still has a large wound from where I had to cut."

Lifting her still-trembling hand to wipe away tears, Asha sobbed, "I know not how to thank you."

"The Great Mother brought you to us and Keva's son lives because of you. When she wakes, I will tell her of all that you have done."

"I am healer. I did what any would."

"No," Asha cried, "You are more. You are blood-kin. Your child will be ours and always welcome here as family. Your path leads you from the Cove, I have heard, but a home will always await you here."

Caryss bowed her head, no longer able to stay as detached as she was wont to be as a healer. Her meeting with the two sisters had been nothing short of chance, yet as Asha's words crossed the room, Caryss wondered if it had been more.

If, again, the gods watched. If the Great Mother had known her path, the one her daughter would walk.

With her head low, Caryss whispered, as if the words were weapon and dangerous, "My daughter will need warriors. For there are many who will seek to harm her. Who better to defend her than blood-kin?"

Caryss stumbled across the room and knelt at the woman's feet.

"Teach the boy to fight. With sword and air. With water and earth. And when he is ready, send him to her."

Once spoken, the words hung heavy. Caryss rose, fearing she had overstepped. But when Asha next addressed her, she knew why she had come.

"It will be done, Caryss. And not just the babe. I will find others. The inn will be home to all who will vow to defend her."

Moons before, Caryss would have wept.

Now, she simply bowed her head.

"Your Great Mother has honored me with your kinship, Asha."

The Islander's face was now dry as well. She was, Caryss suddenly realized, a woman like few others.

"The Great Mother gave me breasts and womb, *leseda*, but I wanted neither. From the time I could walk, I longed for sword and shield, so much so that my father would whip me and force me to the kitchen. Aye, I learned to cook, but when he was not looking, I would steal knife and dagger. And, then, moon years later, a bow from across the seas was left here. Once in my hand, it rarely left. You will find few who can shoot as straight or as quickly as I. This skill I will teach the boy and the others as well. What I do not know, I will learn. So the Great Mother has shown me."

Biting at her lip and with stinging eyes, Caryss whispered, "To have so much offered leaves me silent."

Asha laughed, a hardy, deep sound that made the babe bounce in her arms.

"I have waited over thirty moon years for cause to take off this skirt. You have given me reason, and none would dare object."

Even Sharron laughed now, the three women more joyous than Caryss could recall.

*****

16

"How long will it take me to get to the King's City if I leave at once?"

She rolled off of him and onto her back, laying her head on a thick pillow, much softer than any she could remember. Even with no looking glass, she could feel her hair spread out around her, wild and wavy, damp with sweat and spit. He was prettier than she, smooth-faced and youthful. Her own face was lined and sun-darkened from moon years at sea. Even though she had not asked his age, Neena knew that she was moon years older than he. It hadn't mattered, though, she thought, smiling as she pressed her body closer to his.

His full lips were sweet and his kisses fine, but lies came out of his mouth nonetheless. Even his name was false, which they both knew, even if neither had cared. He was a man she mused and expected little else.

Twisting his hair between her fingers, she purred, "By ship?"

"I am meant to travel by foot. How long by ship, though?"

"With fair weather, a fast fleet could have you at the ports in three days time."

Whistling through swollen lips, he laughed, "And if I walk I shall not be there for a moon at best!"

"Why walk then?" she teased, "Fare to the King's City would cost less than this pillow beneath my head."

"It is what is required," he sighed, rolling away from her.

Leaning on her elbows, she told him, "My lord, you do not seem one to do what is expected."

The boy's eyes twinkled as he answered, "I do what I must. But I need to get to the King's City."

"Come with me then. My ship leaves within the hour."

Shaking his head, he answered, "Not yet. I wish that I could, love, but I have not yet been given leave."

As if he had noticed the disappointment on her face, he hurriedly added, "Come back for me in a few moons. I will be ready then."

"I shall do just that. For now, I still have an hour."

His breath smelled of ale and tasted of honey, and Neena threw herself across him, keeping the knowledge of who he was from her eyes. It made little difference to her what he called himself. It made little difference at all.

*****

"Have you found him yet, mama?"

The boy had talked of little else for days, and Nicoline placed her spoon softly on the table. While Jarek refilled his bowl with more stew, she watched, knowing that she would have to answer him soon.

For the last half-moon, he had questioned her daily about finding a swordmaster. Many boys his age would have long been at arms, yet Nicoline had never permitted it. Instead, she had encouraged him to learn the ways of her kin, the ways of sky and sea. However, since his last visit to the palace, he had chattered daily on the necessity of swordplay. Of late, she relented, accepting that sky and sea would be of little help inside the palace walls of the King's City.

"I have sent word to a friend for his council," she finally told him. "Until then, you must practice until you arms grow heavy and your breathing burns."

"I shall!" the boy exclaimed, jumping up from his seat with a well-worn wooden spoon clasped tightly between his fingers.

For the next few moments, Nicoline watched as her son, lanky and excited, ran about the small kitchen, waving the spoon as if it was sword, parrying and spinning, darting from imaginary foes before jabbing hard at their stomachs. He was often trapped by his own thoughts, as most are who have the sky in their blood. Yet, with the spoon in his hand, Jarek had a clear look in his eyes, she realized. His joy was uncontained, and Nicoline laughed heartily as her son rushed about the kitchen, knocking into a pot-laden table, before spinning from the room.

When he took his battle elsewhere, she remained in the kitchen, thinking of the boy's father. One day, despite her worries, Jarek would want to leave for the King's City, the land of his father. She had spent the last ten moon years trying to keep her son hidden and unknown. If he never set foot in Rexterra, she would have rejoiced. Yet, as soon as he had mastered the skill of time-walking, there was one place he visited more often than any else.

Again and again he would tell her of his trips to the King's City. At first, she had tried to forbid him, yet having not known her own, she did not hold long to the rule. With no other way to know of Crispin, she let him continue.

Until his last visit, when he had been spotted by a woman, fire-touched and of the North, he had claimed.

He had grown strong, she knew, stronger than she and with far more mastery of the elements. For Nicoline, controlling sea and sky was more a game than anything, a toy when she grew bored or weary. For her son, it was more. It was weapon and birthright. The farm would soon grow to feel like a cage to him, she feared. And so she had written to Willem, hoping that he could aid her, as he had once done moon years prior. It had been two days since she had sent the letter, and each day she had wondered if he had received it yet. Each day she wondered if it would be her last with her son.

If not sword, then sky and sea would take him, as she had always known it would, ever since the night he was born. The boy had long been more than the son of a prince. He was born of lightning and had thunder for voice, sea for blood. He could drink the rain or draw it forth. Jarek had sky for father and sea for mother. A throne could not contain him, nor would he welcome it. He was born for more than a throne.

But, first, he had to master the sword, for he was still just a boy, she knew.

*****

When she opened the door to the adjacent room, Caryss stopped so abruptly that Sharron walked into her, causing both women to stumble. As she regained her balance, Caryss looked toward the bed, wiping at her forehead with the back of her hand, as if to clear her eyes from what she saw. Behind her, Sharron stood, composed, more so than Caryss.

With a voice tinged with fatigue and surprise, hoarse and sharp, Caryss hissed, "How long has the King been awake?"

Sharron was pale, her hair pulled tight at her neck, and her eyes wide. "I only just discovered it myself. I was on my way to find you."

Rushing back into the room, Caryss watched as Herrin, seated upright on his cot, his back against the wall, nodded toward the *diauxie*.

Barely above a whisper, she said to Sharron, who trailed behind her, "Examine him. And find out what caused him to wake. I will speak to Otieno."

Without waiting for a reply, Caryss called into the room, "Otieno, I would have a word with you."

It had been over a half-moon since last the King had been so alert, and while she wanted to speak with him, Caryss knew that she had to find out first what had occurred to make it so. Aldric was not in the room, which meant that only the *diauxie* had answers.

As he rose, Sharron passed him, hurrying to the King. Caryss turned from them both, stepping back into the hallway of the inn. Otieno followed her until they were both in her room. Closing the door with a bang, she faced him with cheeks aflame.

"What have you done?"

With a shrug of his wide shoulders, he said, "I have pledged myself to your daughter and to you as well. You have nothing to fear from me, *leseda*. When the poppy milk that you have been giving to the King faded, I did not give him more. Instead, I had him drink a blend of coca leaves, grown near where I was born. Dried and brewed, the leaves make a powerful stimulant. I did little else."

The man was calm. Too calm, she feared.

"I have used the coca myself. Even then he was only awake a short time."

He watched her with soft brown eyes. His hands did not move toward his swords and his lips curved at the edges, as if he thought her anger of little importance. Seeing him so only enraged her more.

Through clenched teeth, she asked, "How did you wake him?"

"As I said, I gave him the drink and kept the poppy milk from him."

"What more was in the drink?"

The *diauxie* pulled his hair from his face, tying it with quick hands at his neck. Caryss had never seen anyone quite like him, and she did not need to guess why most feared him. Where Conri was tall and thin, this man was thick with muscle, his skin the color of bark. His lips were full, his teeth even and fine, and when he smiled, which was not often, he had the look of kings about him, handsome and fierce.

Not many would dare to question him, but Caryss had no such fear. Moons before, she had remembered what real fear felt like. And so she stepped toward him.

Around them rays of gold filled the room, shimmering and twinkling. As the lines of light fell upon him, Otieno seemed to glow. Still, she did not care as her hands reached for his tunic.

Otieno did nothing when she pulled at him in unfeigned fury.

"I have no time for this!" she screamed, her hands gripping him.

As if addressing a child, he calmly told her, "Then perhaps your time would be better spent speaking with the King."

She pulled her fingers from his dark tunic and ran.

"Is he still awake?" Caryss asked as she reentered the King's room.

In a voice that she had heard just once before, Herrin called, "You talk of me as if I was a babe without words."

Silenced by the rebuff, she walked toward the bed, acting as if she did not hear Otieno enter behind her. When she was near enough, she reached for Herrin's hand. It was warm, more so than it had been all moon. Moving her fingers to his wrist, she felt for his life pulse, again surprised as it beat steady and strong.

After briefly glancing across his body, she noticed that his patches of rash had not disappeared and still appeared raised and crimson. He was awake, no more than that. But it was a start.

"King Herrin, do you remember who I am?" she asked, moving a hand to his forehead.

He brushed her hand away as he answered, "You're the healer girl. "We have much to discuss."

She hurriedly looked to Sharron before telling him, "Indeed, king. Can you tell me how you are feeling? You have slept much since we left Rexterra."

"How do you think one would feel after waking up in an entirely different country? The Islander tells me that you believed that I was in danger in the King's City and that I am here for my own safety."

"I had little choice," Caryss explained. "I had been there but a day, yet knew that you would never grow well if we stayed. You were over-dependent on poppy milk, so much so that we had to continue to give it to you. And, more, your skin was covered in rash and your life pulse erratic. Even without the poppy milk, you would likely sleep much, for your body has grown weak trying to heal itself. Over the last moon, Sharron and I have tended to you, and yet we cannot find what it is that had made you so ill."

She had told him as much before they had left Rexterra, but it was clear that he remembered nothing, as it often was when one needed so much poppy milk. His thoughts would not be clear for another moon, she figured.

"That you are awake now has surprised me greatly. But you are alert and talking, and I have renewed hope, my lord."

"Why have we come here?" he asked leaning back again.

Caryss waited for him to still, for it was clear that he was tiring. When his eyes looked at her again, she told him, "I needed to go where none could find us, King Herrin."

It was time he knew all.

"Your sons do not know where we have gone, nor do any at the palace. I knew not who to trust, my lord."

"I had guessed as much," he mumbled.

"Are you growing weary?" she asked.

The king nodded, and she told him, "There are those in the north who might be able to help. With your permission, it is to them that we must go."

His eyes were beginning to cloud with fatigue, yet he managed to chide, "I thought you wore the robes, my dear."

"Oh I do," she insisted, "But I can only cure what has a natural cause. There are others who know more than I."

"You speak of mages," he groaned, waving a dismissive hand.

"Not mages, my king. They call themselves *fennidi*, and they know more of poison than any, Sharron tells me. Will you permit me to take you there?"

"Poison? Is that what this is about?" he coughed.

Caryss reached for his hand, and, holding it between both of hers, told him, "From when first I examined you, I suspected so. I had hoped that by now most of it would be gone from your body, but the rash persists. We learn much at the Academy, but there are limits. Just as plant and herb and flower and tree can heal, so can they harm. Even if we were to discover what it was that you were given, I might not know how to reverse it. I believe the *fennidi* will have the knowledge we seek."

"Then you have my permission to take me to them. But I want the Islander to come as well. See that it is so."

"And your sons? Is it your wish that I send word to them?"

Shaking his head, his words low and thick, he answered "Not yet."

Dropping her hands from him, Caryss told him, "First we must make our way to Planusterra, then to Eirrannia."

"Planusterra?" Herrin muttered, through slitted eyes that watched her.

"There is something I must do there."

Caryss said no more, even though all eyes were on her. She would find the boy, and he would be given the choice to come with them and have Otieno for master or stay in Planusterra. And the King would meet his heir's first-born son.

The same boy who he had once tried to kill.

She offered no other explanation, told Sharron to feed the King, and requested that Otieno come with her to check on Keva. Neither argued.

"How fares the babe?" the *diauxie* asked as they walked toward the other end of the inn.

"Strong and healthy," she curtly answered.

"And the woman?"

"She will need a moon or more to recover, but she was awake when last I visited," Caryss told him.

"Not many would have attempted what you did. Even fewer would have succeeded."

As she pushed open the door to Keva's room, she said nothing more to him, and, when he did not follow her inside, Caryss sighed in relief.

When she noticed who sat next to Keva, holding the swaddled babe, Caryss cried aloud, "What are you doing here?"

The dark mage shrugged and called, "Asha had to help with the evening meal, for the women she hired will not be available until the morrow. There was none else to sit with Keva."

"Did you know that the King was awake?" she asked as she neared the cot.

"Sharron found me as she searched for you earlier and told me the news. How does he fare?"

As she put an ear to Keva's chest, listening to the breathing of the sleeping woman, she told him of her interactions with king and how clear his demands had been. The mage seemed surprised, as she herself had been, yet he did not argue with her or seek to change her mind. Keva was warm, but she was not burning with fever, and Caryss lifted her head. Tugging the blankets off of her, she began to unwrap the strips of cotton wool than encircled her midsection. The top layer was white, which meant the bleeding had slowed. Both good signs.

As she worked, the woman roused.

With half-opened eyes, she moaned, "Is it time for another feeding?

"The babe sleeps, as you should," Caryss whispered, peeling the final layer from her.

"It is you, *leseda*."

"Aye. But, hush. There will be time to talk after you have rested. I am here to change your dressings."

She had hoped to leave on the morrow, but they had delayed the departure by another day. Until Asha could manage the inn and look after Keva, the group would stay.

Softly, Keva mumbled, "You have done much already."

The woman was only half-awake, but her words were sincere ones, and Caryss smiled gently as she reached for clean cotton wool. The incision was still red and the skin around it puckered, but there was no sign of infection, which was victory enough. Near the bed sat a pitcher of peppered ale, and she moved to it, pouring some into a small, thin glass.

"Drink this," she instructed, slowly pouring the amber-colored ale into Keva's mouth. Some dribbled down her chin, but when the glass was empty, Caryss nodded.

After a few moments, Keva slept.

Turning toward Aldric, Caryss said, "I told Herrin of the *fennidi*. And he has agreed to let use take him there."

She reached down and took the babe from Aldric, who stood, stretching his body. It was, Caryss quickly realized, the first time she had held the infant.

"Does he know of the boy and your plans for him?" Aldric did not need to tell her of which boy he spoke.

"I told him we would take the eastern route, with a stop in Planusterra first."

"But you did not tell him why."

173

"He will know soon enough," she replied, rocking the babe.

"Have they named him?" she suddenly asked, finding it strange to know so little.

"Not that I know," the mage stated.

"Otieno is outside the doors," she told him, although her voice was lower now.

"You do not like him much," Aldric laughed.

"It matters little, I guess. The girl seemed to like him well enough."

"Caryss," Aldric interrupted, with warning behind his words. "You need allies."

"The king requested that Otieno come with us."

Walking toward her, he said, "Nothing has changed then. He was to come anyway."

"I do not need to like him then," she joked, although both knew there was little jest behind her words.

When Aldric opened the door, the *diauxie* stepped back. Caryss quickly handed him the babe, surprising all three. He nearly protested, but she would hear none of it, and walked on, leaving the two men alone.

Sharron was with the King, and Aldric would find Asha if the babe woke, so she hurried from the inn. At the Academy, Caryss often spent time alone, in thought or in study, yet it had been moons since she could recall time with none near. In another day and a half, they would be gone from Francolla. After a quarter-moon, she still had seen little of the island. Determined to change that, she rushed down the sun-bleached road, away from the town center and toward the shore. Soon, she walked along the sand, her boots leaving deep imprints near the water's edge.

It was evening and the falling sun was the color of fire, orange and red rays painting the thin clouds around it. She wore no robe or coat, but sat on the sand anyway, letting the warm, salty air pull her hair from the healer's knot. It had grown long in their travels and lighter, too, although it was still streaked with coppery flames.

Asha was alive. Her babe was as well. The king was awake and fine, more so than he had been since she had first met him, and Sharron and Aldric fared well too. All was as fine as Caryss could hope, she thought. And so she stared at the sea, thinking of the times when she had done the same in Tretoria. She was not the same girl as she had been then, yet the brush of mist that tickled her face brought her to smile again. Overhead, gulls called to her, shrieking just at the ones had done near the Academy. Lying back, she closed her eyes, letting the sun warm her freckled cheeks.

It was not until the gulls quieted and the air cooled that Caryss knew that she was no longer alone. *Even here, he finds me*, she thought, unmoving.

As she opened her eyes, her gaze fell upon thick-soled, closely fitted boots that climbed up lean legs. The man's dark jacket was no surprise, snug against broad shoulders and loose where his waist narrowed. She looked up, toward the man's face, and hurriedly scrambled back until she was half-kneeling.

Before she could cry out, a deep voice called, "My brother sends his regards, Bronwen."

Rising, she called to him, "Bronwen was little more than a child, and one who knew little. I am Caryss, as I was born and as I shall forever be."

With a bow, he told her, "Then Caryss it must be. All the same, my brother wishes to know how your travels have been and where next you intend to go. Your departure from the King's City was surprising, especially as rushed as it was."

She began to interrupt, but he raised a hand, silencing her.

"Your absence was not unnoticed. Your friend Nahla was visited by the King's Heir himself. Can you imagine that meeting?" he laughed. "A king-to-be in the Lower Streets? You seem to have a way to make men do what they normally might not, Caryss."

Even with a body's length between them, his words were sharp. When he called her name, the letters rolled from his tongue like the hiss of a snake. His smile did little to reassure her.

"You know much about me, yet I do not even know your name."

"My brother speaks so little of me then?" he teased, letting all hint of threat vanish. "I am Conall, *Rexaria*."

"Conall," Caryss murmured, letting the name roll from her tongue, "Tell me what you know of Nahla. Is she in danger?"

She had not considered fully what harm could come to the woman after she left the King's City. But, now, with Conri's brother standing just steps away, worry filled her. Nahla had done much to help them flee the city, and, if her actions had become known, the woman would be jailed, and perhaps worse. As she waited for Conall to answer, her palms grew sleek with sweat and her throat burned. Her peace had not lasted long.

She stepped nearer and pleaded in a gruff voice, "Please tell me of Nahla."

Again their eyes met. She watched as the dusky purple haze deepened, yet did not blacken. He looked less like Conri than she would have thought, but none could doubt that they were kin.

"The woman is fine," he finally conceded. "She is not without her own power, I'm learning. She was able to contact Conri, a feat that few have been able to do, and the High Lord sent me to find her. I was able to bring her north, although it was not without incident."

Gasping, Caryss whispered, "You are the boy's father."

When he smiled, she thought again of how unlike Conri he was.

"Tell me what you know of the boy," he asked, although it sounded much like an order.

"I saw him at Nahla's breast," she stuttered, "Then, later, I realized he was kin to my own child. I told her as much, although she thought me mad."

"Is she with child?" she asked, half-believing.

"You can ask her when I take you the Tribelands."

She did not think that she could speak, but, finally, she hissed, "I will not go there."

"Caryss, the Rexterran Army is at your back after what occurred in the King's City. You have few options."

When she did not answer, he asked, "Do any others know that you are here?"

"We came by sea," she told him, "And there were but a few aboard the ship."

"Why are you here?"

"In the Cove?" she uttered, stepping away from him.

When he nodded, she explained, "I came here for my own reasons and do not answer to Conri. I am safe and would not accept his protection if he offered it. Return to him and remind him of such. The path I walk is my own now."

His eyes darkened, and Conall growled, "He is High Lord, girl. You would be wise to remember it."

With eyes green and glowing, Caryss countered, "I am a healer! He would be wise to remember that. I will not break my vows, nor will I fight his battles."

Conall laughed then, the sound mocking and cruel, then said, "What weapon could you wield that we would need? Your hands are smooth and your arms weak."

"The weapon I wield is the one that many will covet. She grows strong even now, and, once born, will strengthen every day. Until none will be able to match her."

Her words silenced him, and Caryss watched as the knowledge of their truth struck him. Moons ago, she would have shook in front of the Tribesman, yet now his presence was little more than irksome. She feared little from him, which he now sensed.

"She will be a babe for many moon years yet. What then? If she is all that you say she will be, many will hunt her. Without the aid of the Wolves, the cub will not survive long. Think of her safety if you will not think of your own," he warned.

With flushed cheeks and blazing eyes, she screamed, rushing toward him, "I think of little else! We will be in Eirrannia before the moon ends. There, we will be safe from the Rexterran forces and from any else who might seek to harm her. That is all Conri needs to know."

Lowering her voice, she added, "When last Conri and I were in the North together, he killed my parents. Did you know as much, Conall?"

She did not take her eyes from him, as if willing him to answer.

Their gazes locked, Conall stated, "He was without choice."

With a laugh, she cried, "There is always choice! He has made his. And I have made mine. Tell him I will not see him. Tell him I need nothing from him."

Her voice trembled, but Caryss looked again at him, raising her voice over the increasing tides, "The girl is mine. Remind him that he promised her to me."

Conall paused, watching her, then quietly said, "As you wish. If you need aid, find me, Caryss. I will do all that I can to keep you safe."

The air around them warmed, and Caryss stood motionless as he walked from her, toward a shining spot near the water's edge. Even from a distance, she knew what it was, having seen such an animal once before, moons prior. Without turning back to her, Conall mounted the spirit animal, the *epidiuus*, and, within moments, was mid-air, astride the glowing animal, as if he rode the moon herself.

Once both were gone from her sight, Caryss retraced her steps, following her footprints in the sand, thinking of little as she walked with her eyes downcast. The gentle roll of the waves as they bubbled against the shore, now calm, and the hushed song of the wind as it flitted by her ears accompanied her as she walked, blinding and deafening. Caryss continued on, forgetting all as she moved from footprint to footprint, making her way across the beach.

Into the silence came a deep voice, crashing into her like a storm, jolting her eyes upward and her hands protectively across her midsection.

"Who was he?"

Steadying herself until her life pulse slowed, Caryss told him, "He is kin to the girl. Brother to her father."

"He is far from home, is he not?"

"No farther than I," she sighed, wanting little more than to be gone from the beach.

"Why did he come?"

Caryss dropped her hands to her side. "To make certain that I was safe. To offer me protection I suppose."

"Yet he left. And you are still here."

"Otieno, I will not take what aid he offers," she insisted. "I will not have my daughter born among the Tribe. You know nothing of them."

"I know little of your Cordisian ways."

"The sword across your back tells a different story. I have seen similar in the North."

Her words were ones that she had vowed to keep hidden, yet in her anger now, the accusation escaped through her dry lips.

"So says the healer," the *diauxie* shrugged, unbothered.

"Even a healer can recognize a Northern Greatsword. Must it always be this way between us?"

Otieno sighed, "Our paths have now crossed, yet we have always walked on opposite sides."

"Nahla warned me that you would speak in riddles if I let you. I have enough swords at my back, and I do not need to add yours. Can there be no peace between us?"

Lifting his palms to the sky, as if in tribute, he told her, "Your battles are my own. We are not enemies, nor we will ever be."

"Then tell me how you came to have the sword," she demanded.

They were near to the edge of the village and voices could be heard in the distance, which caused them both to hesitate. Caryss thought that Otieno would use the distraction to avoid her question, but when he began speaking, she turned toward him.

"Many moon years ago, a *lesedo* visited me at my mother's house. I was but a child then, and had not even entered the King's Service. I do not know how he found me, but he had urgent need of a *diauxie*. My mother told him that I was untrained, little more than a babe really, although I was perhaps ten moon years."

"Yet he would not be dissuaded," Otieno added. "I recall fearing him, although I feared little then. It was not his pale skin that I feared. It was the sword he carried across his back."

While he paused, she filled the silence, asking, "What would he want of a boy?"

"It is difficult for those who are not Island-born to understand what my people do. What one sees as dark, another sees as light. Yet, it is only the *diauxie* who can see what lives in the shadows between the two."

More riddles, she thought, making little sense of his tale.

"The man I spoke of was heavily shadowed. More so than most, much like the dark mage you travel with, yet more so. He had spent moon years away from Cordisia, trying to free himself of the taint. When he finally arrived in the Cove, he was half mad with dark rage, and willing to try anything to escape the shadows. When I explained to him that all of mage-skill would be gone if I did what he asked, he still did not waver. So I did what he requested. And, as payment, he gave me the sword, for he claimed to no longer need such a weapon."

"What is it that you do, Otieno, to wash the dark away?" she whispered.

He looked away, chestnut eyes troubled and heavy. "I take it from them."

Frustrated, she sharply replied, "Yes, but how?"

"I take it from them, no more than that, *leseda*."

Knowing she would get no more, Caryss stomped away, understanding less of the man than she had moments before and wondering anew why she had sought him.

She ran back to him suddenly, a thought heavy on her mind.

Breathing hard, she asked, "Will you be able to take her darkness from her as well?"

Otieno did not seem surprised by her words.

"Yes. But I will not do so."

"What if she asks you to? Like the man who gave you the Greatsword."

"She will not ask," he evenly stated, as if he had known the answer long before. His voice did not quake or tremble. To hear him, it sounded as if truth was all he knew.

"What if I ask you to?" she half-pleaded.

When he looked at her, his eyes were as dark as storm clouds. When he spoke, his voice boomed.

"I still will not do so. Make your peace with her father and her shadows before she is born, *leseda*. Love all of her or none of her. You do not have long to decide."

It was his turn to walk away, angrily, which is what he did, striding from her as his thick legs powered across the crushed shells of the city street.

With little regard to the Islanders around her, Caryss screamed after him, "Everything I do is for her!"

Otieno did not turn nor did he slow his pace, and Caryss could not be certain that her words had even been heard. Tears rimmed her vision, but she fought against their release, squeezing her eyes closed until they lessened. She thought of running after him, but hesitated, knowing not what she would say.

Knowing not if he had been wrong.

*****

17

Upon his return, Conall hastily found his brother, certain that he would want to hear of his trip. Conri was seated at a large desk, with quill in hand, scratching marks onto a thick piece of parchment. If he heard his approach, he made no indication.

"Should I come back later?" Conall asked, pausing a few steps from where his brother sat.

Dropping the quill and rubbing at his forehead, Conri replied, "Of course not. Tell me all that occurred. Is she safe?"

"By she, you mean Caryss."

The High Lord looked away from him then. "I was too weak to finish the mind-lock," he explained.

"Conri, she seemed well. But she is not one who seems easy to control. An odd choice, I must admit."

"It was not my choice, or have you forgotten?" Conri roared at him, rising to full height.

"I meant no harm," Conall told him calmly. "The girl refused my aid and refused to return the King. When I told her of your wish that she come to the Tribelands, she scoffed. I would have taken her by force, but she has others with her."

"The mage? Are you no match for him, Conall?" the High Lord laughed harshly.

"There was another who watched. He is of a kind I have not seen. Much stronger than the mage, I fear. And, to answer you brother, no I did not want to challenge him just then. I feared the girl would intervene."

With a nod, Conri told him, "No doubt she would have. She has changed much in the last few moons."

Walking toward the windows, the High Lord added, "Nahla tells me that Caryss is building an army of sorts."

Conall paused at the mention of Nahla, but slowly said, "A wise move. Although a few men, however powerful they might be, will be little help if the Rexterrans find her."

"Which is why they must not!" Conri howled, pounding fists against the large windows until the room shook with his anger.

Turning back toward Conall, the High Lord commanded, "Bring her here! At once."

"She will not come," Conall sighed, long used to Conri's fury and no longer threatened by it.

With a voice older than mountain and colder than river, Conri warned, "She is without choice. I will no longer abide her foolishness."

"The girl wants nothing from you. You will only make her hate you more. Think on this, I beg of you. She is safe, yet. Now is not the time to intervene," Conall pleaded.

Even accustomed to the High Lord's whims had not readied him for his brother's current wrath. Conri's eyes blackened and his lips swelled, teeth gleaming and sharp.

"Take her," he hissed, "as she took the King."

There was little to be said, and less to be argued, so Conall nodded at his brother, turned, and fled from the room. This time he would not hurry, giving the girl time to disappear.

*****

White-haired and stooped, the woman quivered in front of him as his guards held her between them. Her gaze was clear, and, even though she trembled, there was defiance behind her pale blue eyes.

"Release her," he called to his men, never taking his eyes from her.

When the woman fell to her knees, it was Crispin who walked toward her and offered her a hand, gently pulling her to her feet. After she steadied herself, he motioned for her to join him at his table. Once the two were seated, he poured her a steaming cup of tea, offering it to her as he would any other.

"My men tell me that you know the Islander who sells herself near the piers. When did you last see her?" he asked, sipping at his own tea.

Her hands were clasped tight around the small mug, obscuring the flowers painted there. The old woman did not look up as she stuttered, "Several days past. But not so much as a quarter moon."

"And where did you see her?"

"Near the piers," she answered hastily, although her words were faint.

"Did she board a ship?" he pressed, growing impatient.

After a moment, the woman told him, "Perhaps, but I was too far away to notice which."

"Is your stall open every morning?"

With a nod and clearer words, the woman answered, "Aye. Most of my sales come early with all the people about."

Beside the prince, his guards stood, having brought the woman to him after a half-day spent searching for the Islander and any who might know of her. Crispin had railed against them when he learned that Nahla had disappeared, threatening to replace them all. Each day past, the healer stepped further from his reach. And Delwin readied to strike.

Pushing the cup from him until its contents splashed across the lacy table cover, Crispin looked back to the woman. She was the only one who admitted to knowing the Islander. And his last hope.

"In recent days," he hurriedly said, "Have you seen a woman with hair the color of fire? She is of the North, but speaks Common as if from elsewhere."

He waited, without breathing, for her answer. Even though thousands of people traveled through the piers and the central square each day, Crispin suddenly realized that the woman might have seen Caryss, especially since she looked like few others.

"I cannot let you leave until you tell me what you know," he warned, eying the old woman who had grown silent.

Finally, she nodded and mumbled, "A woman like the one you describe bought ginger root from me. I only remember because she suggested adding sage to an aching-head salve I was making. I had not thought to do so, but did as she suggested. I have seen a few like her before, with pouches hanging from their belts. I believe she was a healer and took her words as sage advice."

Clenching his fist, he looked to his men.

"What more do you know of her?"

For a long time the woman paused, as if trying to remember. Or deciding if confessing was in her best interest.

"You are not so old to have forgotten," he told her, another warning clearly given.

With a sigh only one with as many moon years as she, the woman muttered, "She said something of her father being ill, and that she was taking him somewhere warm for his recovery. Many who suffer from the sea-sickness buy ginger from me, Prince. She was no different than many, although she knew much more than any."

With those words, Crispin knew where Caryss had gone. She had outplayed him once, but no longer, he vowed.

Rising from his chair, he said to his guards, "See that the lady gets home safely."

Crispin hurried to his rooms, thinking on what he must prepare before his own departure. By evening, he hoped to be aboard the swiftest ship he could find. The Southern Cove Islands called.

*****

By the time Caryss arrived back at the inn, Otieno was nowhere to be found. She thought about looking for him, but Asha found her first.

182

Since they had last spoken, just hours before, much had changed for Asha. Eying the woman, Caryss tried to keep her face free from judgment. Asha looked so different that Caryss nearly whooped upon seeing her. She had replaced her oversized dress with loose pants and a brown tunic that clung tight to her large breasts, as if it was a size too small. Her hair, once braided and dyed, had been cut short, nearly all of it removed. She looked, Caryss thought, like she should be traveling with Otieno. She looked more warrior than woman, Caryss realized, smiling at the thought.

But, more, Asha seemed at ease in the clothing.

"How fares Keva?" Caryss asked, nodding at Asha's new look.

"More alert these last few hours. She fed the babe as well. She was asking for you. I told her of your plans to leave on the morrow. Is there no way that we can convince you to stay, Caryss?"

Laughing softly, Caryss told her, "You know that I cannot. It will not be long before others come looking for me."

Graver now, Asha asked, "What of your own child? We can protect you here or at least hide you well."

"Not against the might of Rexterra, Asha. Nor do I want to make my enemies yours too. The babe must be born in the North, as I was. Of that I am certain."

"You talk little of the father," Asha commented, the words slipping from reluctant lips.

The day had been long, and Caryss stated plainly, "She will be a daughter of the wolf."

Both women stood just outside of the inn, their smiles gone.

"What occurred to make you hate him so much?" Asha quietly asked.

Her throat thick, Caryss nearly did not answer. But Asha deserved to know, she thought, and pushed the hollow words out.

"He killed my parents. Moon years ago. And made me bear witness to their murders."

Caryss heard Asha draw a long breath and almost regretted her words. It was not Asha who had done so, and the woman did not deserve her anger.

"*Leseda*," she gasped, coming close and wrapping an arm around her. "Tell me what help I can offer. If you seek vengeance, then it shall be so. If you want him dead, I will see it done. The Great Mother always balances the scales. For the life of the babe, I must offer death."

"I know not want I want," Caryss mumbled as Asha gripped her more tightly.

"But you must go back?"

Caryss nodded.

Asha released her, saying, "Will you accept the Great Mother's gift? Her kiss of death never fails."

Wiping at her face, Caryss sighed, "I would not make my daughter fatherless. I am healer still."

With a nod, Asha pulled her close and offered to walk with her to see Keva.

As they walked toward the new mother's room, Caryss again explained all that Asha would need to do to keep her sister well. In less than a day, their group would depart, and it eased her mind to know that Asha would be properly informed on how best to tend to the new mother.

When they entered the room, Keva was holding the babe; Aldric was seated near the window. Caryss looked to him questioningly, but he merely shrugged, as if he could not explain his new role as companion.

Awake and much stronger than when last she visited, Keva called, "I owe you so much, Caryss."

"Your sister has thanked me plenty, and that you can hold your babe is reward alone," Caryss told her, nearing the cot.

"Will you tell me his name now?" Caryss teased, brushing at the babe's cheek with her fingers.

Her smile wide and white, Keva chirped, "He was to be named for his father, but since he is not here to object, I have decided to name the babe for another. My sister told me of her plans, *leseda*, of how she will make the inn a place of training. It brings me much joy to see Asha so free. And even more to know that my son will be find a calling beyond the seas. And so I have chosen to give him a name fit for a warrior. He will be called Blaze. May the Great Mother allow him to burn as bright as fire!"

"The word is Common. Not many here will know it," Caryss interrupted.

"The Cove will only be his home for a short while. But his name will carry him far. And he will never forget the woman who saved him."

Caryss's hand stilled as she stroked the boy. Asleep and wrapped tightly in a multi-hued blanket, he looked as any other babe, peaceful in his slumber.

But in the moon years to come, he would be readied, with sword and shield. Another warrior for her daughter's army. On the morrow, she would sail to find the next soldier. One who was as powerful as the girl would be, for he was born of kings.

Keva talked more, but Caryss hardly listened, thinking on the battle that one day would come.

*****

18

As if sent by the Great Mother, a southern wind carried them north. The ship was a small one, but fast, and they arrived on the Eastern Cordisian coast in less than a half-moon. The captain paid them little heed, yet took their money all the same. Aldric had not trusted him overmuch and kept Caryss and the King under a humming veil anytime that the captain or his sons, who served as deckhands, neared.

It was midday when they made landfall, at a small port called Toccovo, near the border of Planusia and Planusterra. Aldric was first to depart, and still insisted on keeping the ward across Caryss and Herrin. Despite her attempts to convince him she was safe, the mage would not relent, despite his growing fatigue.

Herrin required less and less poppy milk with each day, yet his body was still covered in rash and his legs too weak to support him. Otieno was often by his side, Caryss knew, uncertain what to make of it. The king still slept most of the day, yet he would talk some of Rexterra and his sons. Once, Caryss had questioned him about who he thought responsible for his illness. And, in his temporary lucidity, the King had stated that it could have been any except Delwin and Crispin. She did not disagree with him outright, but she did not believe his words either. Few would gain from his death more than his heirs.

Pulling a long cape tight across her chest, Caryss hurried to catch up to Aldric. Behind her, Otieno pushed the King in a new cart purchased in the Cove, with Sharron walking to his side. Caryss wondered again if the *diauxie* had ever traveled to Cordisia, yet she did not ask. He would only answer her in more riddles, and she had no time for such games.

The group would head northwest from Toccovo, until they were near the Eirrannian border. Beneath the swirling cape, for it was cooler here than it had been in the Cove, Caryss shivered. It was the first time that she had been so near her homeland, and she could not warm her chilled body.

Whispering to no one but the land, she hummed, "And finally my path is my own."

Her words were hushed, but Aldric turned toward her and asked, "What is it that you called?"

"Can you not sense the rightness of what we do with each step closer to Eirrannia?"

She was beside him as he answered, "I only follow, Caryss. And trust in what you see. But I will be no fool, and, if I think you in danger, I will speak on it."

"I would expect no less," she told him. "For now, we are where we should be."

"You still think it wise to find this boy, Caryss?"

Nodding, she explained, "The girl will need him. And he longs to explore beyond the farmstead where he has lived most of his life."

"What of Crispin? Have you thought of what he will say when he learns that you have both his father and his son?"

"The boy is ten moon years old, yet the prince has not seen him since he was a babe. Nor does he speak of the boy. Prince Crispin has had enough time to name him heir, yet he will not."

"Caryss, do no act out of anger," the mage warned. "I realize the prince spoke harshly to you before we left the King's City, but do not let that trick you into believing that your actions will have no consequences. And do not forget that King Herrin once tried to kill the same boy we now seek."

His warning did not escape her notice, and Caryss quieted for a moment, dropping her eyes to the verdant grass beneath her booted feet as they made their way inland. Green and soft, the grass was unlike what she had become used to in Litusia. The air smelled faintly of the sea, but as the group distanced themselves from the coast, the salty scent faded, replaced with the stronger smells of mud and dung.

With a wave of her hand, she told him, "The king? The same one who sleeps more often than a babe at the breast? You worry much, Aldric."

Behind her, Sharron laughed.

"We have been far in the last few moons, Caryss. I had never thought to see so much. How long until we head north?" the other healer asked.

"Is the North calling you as well, Sharron? Since leaving the ship, I have felt as if my life pulse has quickened, as if my blood is raging fierce through my body. As I have never felt it do before. I, too, am ready to go home."

Her words had grown heavy, and Sharron put an arm around her, at once comforting and understanding. Caryss did not need to hear the other Eirrannian's words, but she listened anyway.

"I have been away from my homeland for half of my life. In truth, I had never thought to return. But, now, I long to see the snow-peaked mountains and sky-blue rivers as never before."

As Caryss plaited her hair, she told Sharron, "It is strange how I forget so much. I know not how to find the home I once knew, nor if any of my kin still live. Even the Faelan Mountains are but a forgotten picture to me. I recall so little of the North even now."

"You were but a child when you arrived at the Academy," Sharron reminded her.

"A child with no memory," Caryss sighed, tying a Covian scarf across her head. "Enough talk of then. We must make arrangements to get horses and more. Aldric, how far is the ride from here to where the boy is?"

"If he is near the border, then perhaps a quarter-moon. We will need a covered wagon for the King. I cannot ward him for such a long time."

"Of course. Is there coin enough to purchase all that we need?" she asked.

"Aye. But I left Asha with enough silver to buy sword and shield for the inn and its new trainees. Our purse grows lighter each day, Caryss. This will be the last of it, I would guess."

Coin mattered little to her, and she had hurriedly given all of it to Aldric as soon as they had departed from the Academy.

"Must we send word to Willem?"

Aldric's face was taut, more lined than it had been moons before. He spoke little on the toll his mage-skill enacted, yet his body, thinner now, told her enough.

"We will need lodging and supplies once we finally reach Eirrannia. There will not be enough coin for that."

Sharron was near and interjected, "My parents will help. They live near Scoutsman Road, which is not far from *fennidi* territory. It would take little time to visit, and there is room enough for us to stay."

"Aye, we can visit," Caryss agreed, "But I do not want to overburden them."

She left unsaid that she did not want to endanger them, but each who listened understood her meaning.

"Caryss, you do not know my parents," Sharron objected. "When I told them of my plans to enroll in the Academy, they quickly approved. I daresay they even expected it. They are Eirrannian-true, and once they hear of the girl, they will do all they can to help. Their home will be yours."

With little to do but nod her agreement, Caryss walked further down the well-paved road, listening as her thickly heeled boots thumped against the soft stones. The rhythm lulled her into a half-trance, until she felt as if she was in a dream. The sounds around her, voices speaking in a language she could only half make sense of - shouts, laughter - were muffled, as if a fog covered them. When Caryss looked up, she expected to find the girl.

However, when her gray-green eyes opened, the road was as it had been. Sharron walked ahead, steps in front of her, as was Otieno, his frayed braids hanging down his back, blending in with the dark tunic that he wore. As he pushed the King, the Greatsword across his back swayed, heavy and wide. As Caryss watched it, she remembered how the girl had been able to wield the sword as if it was an ordinary weapon and not half the size of a man.

To Sharron's right stood a large, three-storied inn. The style of the building was simple, unadorned except for black, wooden shutters that framed several windows. It was well tended despite its simplicity; she hurried to reach Sharron. Her hair was pulled tight against her neck, and the long scarf wrapped about it, shielding its color. Aldric had insisted upon the attempted disguise, and Caryss had cared little enough so she did not argue.

"We will stay but a night," she called to the other healer as she neared.

"Do you know where the boy is then?" Sharron asked, reaching into a purse at her waist.

"Not exactly," Caryss laughed. "There are ways to contact him if we have not seen him by the morrow."

The mood was a light one, and Sharron smiled as she entered the inn, with Caryss trailing behind. With her soft nature and gentle eyes, the healer approached a white-haired man seated behind a large, curved bar. While she negotiated rates for a night, Caryss strolled to the other side of the main room, away from the loud crowd gathered in the dining area. Her legs were still unsteady from the time spent aboard the Covian ship, so, instead of sitting in one of the upholstered chairs, she stood near a window, staring across the wide street to where Otieno and Aldric waited.

Her hands cupped together, fingers threaded through each other, across the small mound of her stomach, and Caryss closed her eyes. Suddenly, she felt a fluttering inside of her, as if one of the blue-winged butterflies that she often saw near the Academy's gardens had taken home there, gently battering the area just beneath her hands.

There was no fog, no mist, no wave or thunder. Lightning did not streak against the clear sky. The wooden planks beneath her feet did not shudder or quake. The air hummed around her, but only as it had before, smelling faintly of ale. All was as it had been.

Yet nothing was as it once was. Never before had she felt the babe move inside of her. Even when the girl visited, she had never touched or embraced Caryss. As if she could not. Now, however, for the first time, Caryss felt the girl, and knew her to be real in a way that was new and unexpected. No longer ghost or spirit or magic. She was blood and bone, skin and teeth, flesh and marrow. She was, Caryss realized, just like any other babe.

In a few moons time, the girl would be her daughter. And a child of the North.

With clear eyes painted like the Faelan Forest, she again glanced to where the men stood. Otieno, his dark face contrasting sharply next to Aldric's pale skin, caught her eye. But it was not to his face that her eyes were drawn, as the sword seemed to catch the twinkling rays of the midday sun, radiating shards of dancing light in a sparkling array of gold and red. The *diauxie* appeared to be aflame.

Yet Caryss knew that it was a trick of the light, nothing more.

Enyo, she remembered the girl calling it. Conri's gift, knowledge of language, came upon her. And she knew the name anew.

Bloodlust.

For now, the babe would be hers. But Caryss could not forget the way that the girl had wielded the Greatsword. In time she would learn to be healer. Yet she would always be Tribe.

This girl, who shined on each visit, was still a daughter of the Wolf.

Otieno's eyes found hers, and she knew that he watched her, through the thickly-paned, brightly-stained glass.

He knows more than he has admitted.

Behind her, Sharron neared, calling her name and breaking the spell that the *diauxie* had sought to weave.

*****

With him were eight of his most trusted men, although Crispin was ill at ease. Since their arrival in the Cove, he had slept fitfully, fearing that the many lies he had told to disguise the trip might soon unravel. He had nearly abandoned the idea to come so far, as he had not been able to find any record of Caryss's departure from the King's City. Yet, the old woman had sworn that Caryss had told her of plans to take her ailing father south, to warmer lands. And when the whore went missing too, Crispin realized his guess was the right one.

The Islander had help; the Prince was certain. Four dead men, two armed with swords, and several others, well-trained and well-equipped, had been fooled by the woman as she escaped.

When his men had returned and told him of the Islander's disappearance, Crispin first suspected the dark mage. With his aid, the healer had been able to escape as well, taking the King with her. He now believed that the healer had long planned the abduction, and Crispin wondered if even his cousin knew of her actions. For now, he trusted none, as he had once warned Caryss.

A half-moon past, he had wanted to save the girl and return his father to the throne. Now, he cared little of what happened to her, knowing he had been tricked once already.

It did not take long nor did it take much coin to find word of the healer. Some were reluctant to speak of her, yet a jingle of his guardsman's purse loosened lips.

"Up ahead, just there," Raoll called.

When Crispin looked to where the man pointed, he noticed an inn, unimpressive by Rexterran standards, yet clean and large, and of a style that they had seen often in the Southern Cove. Quickening his step, Crispin closed the distance to the inn, paying little heed to his men behind him. He nearly pulled the heavy door from its frame as he rushed in, wiping at his brow that had grown wet. Before the door could slam closed, his men reached him, until they all stood just inside the sun-lit entry.

For a moment, the prince did not move, looking around with haste as he searched for Caryss.

"Check the rooms," he ordered his men, who fanned out behind him, hands on their hilts.

He could hear Raoll ordering them about, dividing the guards into two groups, yet Crispin stood motionless, his life pulse racing beneath his heavily threaded tunic.

Behind him, a voice rang out, "What is the meaning of this?"

The words had been shouted in Common, and he turned on his booted heel to find a short-haired woman staring at him. She was clothed as if she was a mercenary, and, at her waist, hung a thick sword.

It was not the sword that concerned him as he looked about for his men.

She must have realized his intentions, for her next words caused him pause.

"If you call for your men, I will put this arrow through your heart, my lord."

Without taking his eyes from her, Crispin called, "My death guarantees your own. Think long on what you threaten."

"Aye," she said, showing gleaming teeth. "You think I did not expect you? Your men will find nothing. Nor will you."

Her arm did not quiver as she gripped the bow, the arrow's tip still pointed at his chest. Her eyes, round and wide, did not stray from his face, as if she dared him to move or to speak. While she watched, Crispin considered his options and nearly yelled for his men. Just before he could, another thought occurred to him.

Lifting his arms, his hands outstretched and without weapon, he called, "I seek no fight here. I have come a long way in order to find my father. If it is truly as you say and you know why I am here, then tell me of him. Tell me if he yet lives."

Only then did he notice hesitation in her, and Crispin knew that he had not been wrong. Caryss had been here.

"I know not what she told you. I have no quarrel with the healer, either," he pleaded, trying to keep his voice even. "I only wish to bring my father home."

Further down the hall voices called out, loud and deep. The sound of swords being drawn could be heard as well. When Crispin looked to the woman again, her face was severe, drawn and anxious.

"I will tell you of your father once your men have laid down their swords."

He hesitated, but finally yelled for his men to return to him. Neither he nor the woman spoke again. Heavy boots on the faded stone floors of the inn could be heard nearing them as his guards hurried back to the entrance. Crispin had to call for retreat several times before all of his men had returned, and the woman had not once taken the bow from her arm.

"Give me your word that my men will not be harmed."

"I want no blood here, my lord. It was you who came unannounced and with swords drawn. This is my home, and Covian Law gives me the right to defend it."

As the prince reached for his own, he bellowed, "Place your swords at your feet."

It did not take long for his men to acquiesce, and, within moments, the clang of sword on stone echoed through the entry. When he looked back to the woman, Crispin's eyes glossed gold and his vision darkened to a red haze.

Still the arrow was pointed at him. As he opened his mouth to complain, the woman whistled, a high-pitched sound that was soon greeted by others, calling in return.

Light footfalls closed in on them until boys not much older than his sons appeared. Each was armed with bow, like the woman's. His arms began to rise, but before he could call for fire, the woman cried to him.

"Look around you, Lord. I have twenty of my best students circling you and your men. They will not strike unless I give the order. Do not make me do such."

"You promised us safety," he hissed.

Her eyes gleaming as a smile spread across her face, the woman laughed, "You are in the Cove, Lord Crispin, where words are weapon and game. I promised no such safety."

"Would you risk war for one girl?" he spit at her, his temper firing hot.

"None spoke of war," she told him.

"Your country is a small one, with an army one-tenth the size of mine. I would have it destroyed within a moon," he screamed.

She readjusted her bow. "I don't think that likely. First, I could kill you all now, and none would know where and when the King's Heir died, for I would guess that you told none of your travel. Or I could let you all go, only to have you return with more men than we could counter. But, I would advise against that, my lord, for there are others who would strike at Rexterra in your absence, including your own brother if we hear true in the Cove."

"Gather their weapons," she called to the boys.

Crispin hurriedly raised a hand as his men shuffled behind him, ready to defend their prince.

"They are but children. Let them have the swords. If she had meant to kill us, it would have happened already. This is but a Covian game."

It was known that the Islanders were fond of game and riddle, Crispin remembered, staring again at the woman as she nodded toward a few boys as they collected the Rexterran steel.

"I will play along, but only shortly. You are guarded by children, while my men have been trained since birth to be Royal Guardsmen. I would not seek the blood of children, but do not press me."

"Ask your questions and be gone then, prince."

"Is my father still alive?" Crispin called to her, without pause.

"Aye, and improving I would say. What else would you ask?"

"Where can I find him?"

"I know where he will not be found, and that is here on Francolla. Nearly half a moon past did they depart."

"Where is she taking him?" Crispin demanded.

"I am neither her mother nor her husband, and she owes me no explanation."

His face burned and his hands ached as he clenched them, trying to keep the flames extinguished. The woman toyed with him, he knew.

"You shield a woman who has committed treason by kidnapping the ruling king. She could be put to death for her actions! Yet you would side with her!"

Her laugh rang through the room. When she brought the bow to her side, Crispin paled, wondering what game she now played.

Her voice calm and her hands steady as she strapped the bow to her back, the woman told him, "Perhaps in the Cove, laws differ, my lord, but it is not kidnapping if the King went willingly."

"He would have sent word, had it been so!" Crispin shouted. "You have seen him and know how weak he is. His silence is not consent. He sleeps overmuch and has little understanding of what occurs around him."

The woman walked near, nodding at the boys as they carried off the swords. Half of them remained, bows still taut and aimed.

"As you say, my lord. But I have been in a room with the King when he has been awake and would say that he quite enjoyed Francolla. Many come here for respite and rest, and not once did I hear him express a desire to return to Rexterra."

"Why did the healer come here?"

The Islander now stood behind a large desk, and she no longer watched him, as if she had grown bored. Crispin rushed to where she stood, caring little for the boys who still had arrows pointed at him and his men.

"Why did she come?" he screamed, slamming his hands onto the burnt wood.

With a sigh and shrug, the woman told him, "She came because the Great Mother willed it and showed her the way. She would have stayed, and your father would have recovered, had you not trailed behind her. So, tell me, my lord, which of you seeks to truly heal the King?"

Slamming his fists onto the desk again, he cried, "Where has she gone? Tell me that and we will be gone."

She shrugged again and Crispin reached for her, his hands burning.

Just as he felt her tunic beneath his fingers, he heard her call, "Hold your fire!"

To him, she whispered hotly, "The healer is not here. Nor is your father. They are a half-moon ahead of you, although I know not where they have gone. We Covians live a life of peace and seek no part in the battles that wage on Cordisia. You waste your time here, my lord."

As he released her, Crispin stepped back, spittle dripping down his chin and his eyes glowing orbs of gold fire. He could burn the inn to the ground, he knew, but struggled to control the fire that sought release. If not for the children near him, he might have let flame fly.

"Return our weapons and we will be gone."

Shaking her head, she told him, "You will understand why I am unable do that, Prince Crispin."

"Our boat awaits us at the pier. You can escort us back, if you insist, but the swords are ones that have long been carried by my men and their kin. I cannot leave without them."

When she laughed, he nearly struck her.

"We have rooms to spare if you would like to stay."

"My men could kill all of you with hands alone," he hissed.

"But you will not give that order. Half of Francolla waits outside these doors to catch a glimpse of the Rexterran prince now that my children have carried word of your arrival. You made no attempts to hide your presence and another crowd has followed. Any attack on us will be an act of war. One that Francolla will not win, but one that will force you to answer questions about your coming here. It is best for both of us if you leave without further incident, Prince Crispin."

"Where is she taking my father?" he growled.

"I do not know," she sighed, waving him off. "And if I did, I would not tell you. She is a healer, as I witnessed myself. She will not harm him, and, when he recovers, she will see him safely back to Rexterra. If you care for him, then give her time for his healing."

There was much that he wanted to say, but Crispin backed away from the desk. With a nod to his men, he strode across the room and exited the inn. The sun was bright, casting yellow streaks across the whitened buildings. For a moment, he could not see around him, blinded by the fading red fog of his fury.

When he looked up, clearer now, he noticed a large group of Islanders watching him and realized the mistake he had made in coming. While his men wore nothing to mark them as Rexterran, and he wore nothing to identify himself as King's Heir, he had been naïve to think none would recognize him. Many did, and, as word spread, the Covians had gathered to bear witness to the royal visit.

After a brief pause, he rolled his shoulders back and waved to the crowd, a large smile spreading across his flushed face. He was Prince once again, polite and respected, as he made his way through the crowd, greeting the Islanders with smiles and words of praise for their island.

It was not until much later, when he and his men were aboard the ship, that Crispin realized that his brother would hear of his visit, before he had even returned to the King's City, he guessed. By then, he knew, he would have an explanation for the visit. By then, he hoped, the girl would be found.

*****

Caryss hurried across the hallway leading from her room to the dining area, distractedly looking for the others. When she noticed that Otieno was standing near the curved wooden bar, she paused, then moved on once she realized that he was in conversation with a man near his own size, a farmer she thought. Toward the back of the room, she saw Sharron seated at a small, round table.

Dropping into the chair, she asked, "Who is Otieno talking to? Surely he knows no one here."

"He said something about finding the boy. The *diauxie* is not used to following others, Caryss. He grows impatient," Sharron told her, twirling a small mug between her hands.

Her words were spoken gently, yet Caryss heard rebuke in them, and retorted sharply, "We have no spirit animals to ride and a king who cannot walk. How quickly did he expect us to travel?"

"How do you expect to find the boy?" the other healer asked, giving little attention to Caryss's temper.

"I had hoped to ask around."

"You do not think that Herrin had already tried that in his own attempts to find him?"

With a deep sigh, Caryss replied, "I am sure that he tried, just as Otieno is doing, it seems. I had not thought on it fully perhaps. Sharron, now that we are back in Cordisia, do you think we should better disguise the King?"

"While you were still outside, Otieno told me that it was not necessary to worry about the King being recognized."

Caryss hurriedly turned to watch Otieno, who had moved further down the bar and was engaged in conversation with another blue-eyed, light-haired man. For a moment, she thought of joining him. Instead, she addressed Sharron again.

"What did he mean?"

"He is not just warrior, Caryss. And, with Aldric, they alternate who wards the King, I suspect. Then, neither tires overmuch."

"Where is Herrin now?" Caryss asked, her voice low enough that only the two of them heard.

"Sleeping. Aldric has gone to look for supplies and horses. After I have eaten, I will go back to the room. Caryss, even with the King hidden, we should not stay in one place overlong. Each night we stay brings the Rexterran Army closer."

"You think I do not know that? I think on little else," Caryss hissed. "Does he really believe it wise to ask of the boy? We need no extra attention."

Sharron's face was flushed and her hands tight on the mug as she told Caryss, "Both he and Aldric have tried to find the boy, with no luck. You have brought us here, yet still we know not where to go next. We have no time to waste searching each direction from here. On the morrow, we must choose a path."

"Then I must try to contact him," Caryss told her, pushing her low chair away from the table and rushing off.

Outside the inn, the slanting sun reminded her that it was just after midday. Several low buildings, constructed of slate and wood, stood near to the inn. The town was not as big as Litusia, and not a tenth the size of the

King's City, but it was thriving, as timber and slate had become much needed. Men lined the streets, in toil and in conversation. The women, too, were of a thick build, tall and strong, and dressed in practical grab, unlike the ladies of the King's City. Most appeared well-fed and friendly, yet, after speaking with Sharron, she realized that none would tell her of the boy. She would need to find the boy on her own, without any seeing how she did so.

After walking to the back of the inn, Caryss hid behind several wooden barrels, shielding herself despite the emptiness of the alley. The dirt beneath her feet was no longer the ground of the Great Mother, and Caryss closed her eyes, uncertain and afraid if she would be able to call the boy here. Sinking to her knees, she mouthed a silent prayer that he might hear her.

Just as she had done before, she drew forth the *atraglacian* blade. Before she could change her mind, Caryss opened her gray-green eyes and lightly cut a line across her palm, holding her breath until a thin trail of blood appeared. She cupped her hand, allowing the blood to gather in the center. When it covered most of her creased palm, she tipped her hand, letting the blood drip toward the dirt.

With her other hand, she wiped the blade clean before slipping it back into her pouch.

As her hand throbbed with stinging pain, Caryss thought of the boy, of how he looked when she last saw him. With his sun-kissed face and sky-rimmed eyes clear in her thoughts, she called for him. On her knees, in mud and shit, she begged him to hear.

Her hand continued to cascade blood onto the ground, while she gently rocked on her knees. The uninjured hand reached for the center of forehead, then chest, as she offered the Great Mother's prayer.

"Show me the way, so that you may join us," she whispered in the empty alley.

With her hand dropped low, chin resting on her chest, hands near the babe, she waited, calling for him over and over, in chant.

It did not take long, for she was still in the cradle of the Great Mother and her power strong.

"Have you really come for me, lady?" a voice called, distant and rumbling.

When she looked for him, she saw a fog-covered shape steps from her, about the size the boy would be.

"Come closer. My magic is weak compared to yours."

"Did you call for me?" he quietly asked, words louder as he neared.

"Yes, Jarek. Did it work?" Caryss asked, wrapping her hand in the ripped fabric of her tunic.

"I was seated for my lessons when I heard a voice. When I looked about, no one appeared. Then, I felt a tug at my arm, as if I was needed. It took me a while to understand what was happening, as I have never been called upon."

Breathlessly, she told him, "We need to find you soon. Do you recognize where I am?"

In a voice that was more boy than man, he called, "I have waited for you since seeing you at the palace. I knew that you would come."

Unable to hide her impatience and growing weak, Caryss cried, "Which way from here must we travel?"

The boy's eyes, a faded shade of blue now, glanced around, a faint mist trailing him each time he shook his head.

"We are in Toccovo, near the Eastern Sea," she explained, noticing his confusion.

"I have traveled little, but you must head northwest, away from the sea and toward the border with Eirrannia. The Tri-Peaks is an area where Planusterra, Planusia, and Eirrannia meet, just south of the Faelan Mountains. Several miles south the farm sits. Head west until you reach the Vollaxo River and then follow it north. A day's ride in, you will come upon a small village. Take the road west from there and you will find our farmstead, marked by a bolt of lightning across an iron gate."

"How long on horseback?" she asked, unsure if he would know the answer.

As he shook his head, bits of light scattered around them.

"A few days at most."

When Caryss nodded, he added, "My mother knows that you are coming. I told her it would be so. While it will not be easy to leave her or the farm, I know that I must."

Her eyes were tear-filled as she listened to the boy, although Caryss did not understand why.

"With me is a man who will teach you the ways of the sword. He is without rival, as you might be if you train hard. Think long on what you will do, Jarek. We are bound for Eirrannia."

The light around him shifted, as the blood she had offered seeped into the dirt beneath their boots, and she had to strain to hear his last words.

"I decided a moon ago what I would do. My bags are readied."

The flickering image of fog and light collapsed before vanishing altogether. It had been a struggle for him to stay, much harder than for the girl, Caryss thought. But he had heard her call, and had given her enough to find him.

Wiping at her muddied pants, she moved toward the front of the inn, tired and hungry. As she hobbled by several closely-spaced shops with colorful awnings, the smell of blood drew her eyes from the pebbled street.

197

Her stomach rumbled loudly, causing a deep blush to spread across her cheeks. Wiping at her burning cheeks with the back of her wrapped hand, Caryss spied a butcher across the wide street, and recognized the scent of freshly cut meat. To control the urge that had suddenly overtaken her, she bit at her knuckle, until the taste of her own blood lingered on her tongue.

As quickly as she could, Caryss made her way back to the inn, running from the temptation that she struggled to fight. Pushing through the doors of the inn, she stumbled back to where Sharron still sat. With vision edged in a shadowy red and through a bloody haze, she saw that Otieno had joined the other healer.

Falling into an empty chair, she gasped, "I must eat something."

Her hands shook when she placed them on the table, and her head was heavy. Yet, even still her vision did not clear as Otieno pushed a mug of watered wine into her hands.

"Please," she whispered to them, "I do not know what else to do to control it."

"Eat this," Sharron called to her, as if she was across the room, her voice haunting and distant.

With a spoon forced into her hand, Caryss ate. In a daze, she spooned stew into her mouth, over and over, until the bowl was empty.

When she looked up, Sharron asked, "What happened to your hand?"

Before she could answer, Otieno leaned in, and, with a voice full of disapproval, said, "She drew forth the earth magic again. And now her body is paying the price."

"Caryss," Sharron hissed, "Give me your hand."

In response, she lifted her hand, the cotton wool falling off after having been poorly tied.

But it was not the long-fingered hand of the other healer that grasped her bloody knuckles.

"I care not how many gods watch over you, *leseda*," Otieno growled as he grabbed her offered hand. "None will be able to breathe life back into your body when the earth magic claims your soul."

"I just needed to eat," she mumbled, shaking her head to free it from her ringing words.

"Only a fool thinks such! Tell me true. Can you see me?"

When she had not responded, he leaned in closer, so close that she could feel his breath on her cheek and smell the wine on his lips as he hissed, "Can you see me?"

"Yes, but not clearly," she told him. "All appears as if it has been dripped in red."

The *diauxie* released her hand, although much of it was numb, as if half of her body no longer worked.

"In the future, leave the magic to those of us who have learned to temper it," he warned.

From across the table, Sharron's words came, cutting into the battle between Otieno and Caryss and silencing them both.

"Let it be for now. There must have been a reason for her to call upon it."

Otieno pushed himself from the table, throwing his chair to the floor. The impact was enough to cause others to look. Still weak, Caryss said nothing else. In her silence, she thought on how much she disliked the *diauxie*. Yet, she needed his weapon mastery, and, now, with more understanding, she needed his knowledge of the dark magic. She needed him for the girl and for Jarek. If not, she would have left him at the inn, she thought, dizzy and nauseous.

Her voice raspy, she told Sharron, "I know where to find the boy."

She felt Sharron's fingers grip her own. "I guessed as much. But Otieno is not wrong, Caryss. You risk too much each time you use the earth magic. We are healers, not mages. Leave the magic to the others."

"There seemed no other way," she mumbled. "But I understand your concerns. Sharron, when we return to the Academy, I will tell Master Rova of all that you have done. This is not just my Healer's Journey, but yours as well. You will have long earned your robes when the moon year is up."

The woman looked at her strangely at the mention of the Academy.

"Watching you with the King reminds me of what my duties were to be. Without your help, I could not make this trip. You are kin to me, more so than any other I have know, except Sheva," Caryss added, placing a hand over Sharron's, her bloody knuckles still unwashed.

In reply, Sharron said, "Without the girl, I would have died that day when I fell from the tree. She saved me, and now you have given me a chance to balance the scales. Caryss, your path has changed, but your heart has not. I watch you struggle. I watch the doubt and fear cross through your eyes, and I wish I could ease your burden. You were meant to be more than a healer, even though you are as fine a healer as any at the Academy. You are sister to me as and will remain so until the mountains crumble and the rivers dry up."

"I do not deserve you, Sharron," Caryss whispered, looking away.

"*Roim a faidh, an taoh se eirgh.*"

The words were treasonous ones and had been for moon years. Yet, between the two women, the words were an understanding. Caryss realized now, more so than she had before, who Sharron was, and, more, why she had committed her life to both mother and child.

Eirrannia was calling them home. The rivers ran fierce and free, tempting them to sip at their cool waters. The mountains raged tall and noble, reminding them of the history written in their eyes and on their bodies. The trees swayed, rooted deep in the dark soil, mysteriously and thoughtfully, echoing the songs of their souls and the magic buried deep there.

In time, the North would rise.

Leading their charge would be a girl with hair as dark as night, like her father's, but with eyes as green as the grass of her mother's people. The eyes of her grandfather, murdered and forgotten.

The call of the North silenced anything else they might say so they sat quietly, waiting.

*****

Caryss and Sharron were still seated when Aldric arrived, flushed and unkempt, but satisfied.

He called out to them as he hurried in, "I have never seen horses as the ones that they have here. Each one I looked at seemed hardier than the one before. Beauties, nearly the whole lot. Brown or roans, grays, a few as black as night."

The women laughed as he sat down, exchanging glances, he noticed.

"You would hardly believe it. West of here, on the edges of town, there is a large paddock where horses roam. All can be bought. And for a fair price as well. I had no room to complain."

"Do you talk of horses or women?" Sharron teased.

"Alas, only horses. I was able to outfit a cart for the King as well. To be true, it is but a small wagon, pulled by a single horse, but it is covered. He should be able to rest without discomfort."

"Did you get a horse for the boy?" Caryss asked.

With a nod, he told her, "Aye, I found a nice gelding for the boy. And a mare large enough that the *diauxie* will not crush her. For you I found a silver mare with a gentle disposition and steady gait. And two even-tempered geldings for Sharron and myself."

"Well-done, Aldric," Caryss told him, although her words were low.

"Has Otieno learned aught of the boy's location?" he asked.

There was a pause, during which Aldric noticed that Caryss's hand had been freshly wrapped in linens, her palm covered in white strips. And he understood what he had missed and why she appeared pale.

"How far is he from here?"

200

Caryss did not look at him as she answered, "Two-day ride. We head west until we meet the river then follow it north. Before the Tri-Peaks, we head west again, and the boy is near there."

"Have you told Herrin of the plans yet?" Aldric asked, his eyes watching Caryss.

When she said nothing, he told her, disapprovingly, "For the boy's sake, you must tell the King. Soon, Caryss. Even though he might not be a threat now, his history with the boy is not something that we can ignore."

Getting up from the table, she said, "I will find him now and explain."

When Caryss was gone from the room, Aldric addressed Sharron. "Does Otieno know of what she did?"

"He lectured her, to be sure, and the divide between them grows deeper. I have tried to get her to understand that his concerns have merit."

"They do not have to like one another overmuch. There were men who I fought beside that, had I not been hired to defend them, I would have put a sword in their chests. She was there to see how fond the girl is of him. And, more, how well he taught her. That will be enough to keep the peace."

"Both true, Aldric, but Caryss has suffered much at the hands of men. In my time at the clinic, I came to learn how difficult it can be for many women to be at ease with men after a violent encounter. While Otieno has done nothing to her, Caryss has little ability to trust him."

"What of me? I think we all have seen how withdrawn she has become these last few moons. In truth, I feared for her. It was only in the Cove that I saw her as the woman I had first met at the Academy."

Nodding, Sharron softly explained, "You are kin to Kennett, who long provided support to her. Perhaps that is enough. But, be gentle with her, for now."

"Sharron, we cannot let her just act on whim, no matter her past. While I am vowed to serve her, I will not do so blindly."

"To be sure, none of us should," Sharron hastily agreed. "We must keep her safe, even when she might not agree with our ways."

"Aye. I am glad that we have had this talk. On the morrow, we leave then. This boy interests me deeply, I must admit."

"How long until Crispin hears of this? And what will he make of it?" Sharron asked, her voice low enough that none could hear.

Stretching his fingers wide, their tips burning, he told her, "He has cared little for the boy for ten moon years. Perhaps he meant to keep him safe, but the boy will thank him little. He is first-born, and should be prince himself one day. Mayhap Herrin will make it so, once he has come to know him."

"Do you think such could be done? If Herrin had his way moon years past, the boy would be dead."

Aldric was silent for a long moment. Across from him sat Sharron, who had only recently began offering more than just courteous words. For moons, she had followed in near silence after Caryss, as if heartsick over the other healer. If he was being truthful, Aldric knew that he too had offered little resistance to her whims and wishes. Even now, he followed, making way to the boy.

"Mayhap you're right, Sharron," he sighed, "And the King will not soften once he gets to know the boy. Since he was a babe, Jarek has been hidden, yet, with his enemies at our back, Caryss plans to ride to him."

With another sigh, he told her, "Sometimes I think myself mad. Other times a fool. Yet still I follow."

When he looked up, Sharron's face was pale, her eyes gray and serious.

"Even Caryss doubts this path we travel, Aldric. There will be times when we all want to step off, or times when we want to turn back. But we must carry on."

Rising, she whispered, "Look forward, mage, to the one still unborn. It is for her that we walk at all."

He met her eyes with his own, fading and aging. "You think I forget?"

A hand reaching for his, Sharron told him, "We all forget. Around us is peace. Even in the North the mercenaries have quieted the last few moon years. Rexterra builds and prospers, her people fed and housed. I know not what fate awaits Rexterra, but for my people, we want self-rule, as it once was. It is easy to forget the battles moon years after they have ended, but we must not. For even the unwise know that sword will be lifted again, and it is swords that Caryss covets."

Sharron pulled him toward her, and Aldric rose. Together, they walked toward the stairs, climbing them and looking for Caryss.

She must be with the King, Aldric thought.

When Sharron released his hand, he turned toward her. Their earlier words heavy on his mind, he held a hand up, and explained, "I have traveled far in my days, across the Eastern Sea and beyond. I have seen much and speak on it little. Each time I was in Eirrannia, I could not help but wonder what makes them so despised, as they were kind and welcoming. Perhaps it is because I am mage myself, but I felt at home there and look forward to visiting the North once again."

Laughing softly, her long neck exposed as her head tilted back, Sharron teased, "The North is home to muse and misfit alike. We fear none and welcome all. Yet, we are feared and unwelcomed across much of Cordisia. A strange riddle, I think."

Like this, without the light of Caryss casting a shadow across her, Sharron beamed. And he saw her anew.

His lips curved upward, Aldric said, "Those with mage-skill are often feared. And so it is with Eirrannians. Cordisia has long heard the tales of Luna and her children. Kissed by the moon are those of the North, and mad with it, some say."

"Aye, some are unable to handle the mage-taint and grow weary or wild. That is why we are not admitted to the mage-guild. Is it not, Aldric? Rexterra does not want us to grow too strong in our powers."

Sharron understood much and her mind was sharp. Aldric liked her more each day, he realized, listening to her with interest.

"I have not heard it stated so, but I do not doubt that truth. Many in the guild think on the north as untamed and untrained. We learn at an early age the rules of mage-craft. Without boundaries, the guild teaches, our magic will destroy us."

He watched as understanding crossed her face. Sharron knew little of his past, yet his clothing did not bear the patches of the Mage-Guild, nor had it for moon years. As an exile, he no longer had the right.

They stood just outside her door, where, inside, the King lay, accompanied by Caryss, Aldric guessed. He shook his head at the thought, having never imagined himself to be so near the Rexterran king, not since he had been accused of using the Dark Arts.

"And those who seek to go beyond the boundaries are forced out. Is that not so?"

His nod was answer enough.

"You will indeed be welcomed in the North, Aldric," Sharron mused.

Soft, yet insistent, her words cast a mist across the hallway, settling him and granting momentary peace.

Stepping back from her, he leaned against his own door and turned to grab the bronze handle. Before he opened it, he looked back at her.

"Why do you think the boy wants to join us?" he asked.

With a shrug of her shoulders, the movement slow and enchanting, Sharron called, "He time-walks just as the girl does. He is misfit, too, Aldric, abandoned by the man he should have called father."

"Aye," Aldric agreed, "But he is more. This boy could be king."

Rushing across the hall, and looking about as if to make certain none would hear her next words, Sharron grabbed at his tunic.

Pulling him into an embrace, she whispered into his ear, "A king in the south, just as, moon years from now, a new queen might rise in the north. Do you see the path Caryss walks now, Aldric?"

203

"Cordisia will be hers!" he gasped, lifting scarred, yellowed fingers to his gaping mouth.

"*Rexaria*," Sharron breathed into his ear.

He did not need to ask where she had heard the word. It was an old one, from a time of ancients and legends, the language lost but to page and quill. Aldric knew it still.

Kingmaker.

*****

"All I ask is for you to meet him."

"He is the son of a whore."

"His mother, from what I know of her, was no such thing. She was priestess in training when Crispin met her," Caryss countered, trying to keep her words even.

"The boy's mother was born in a brothel, a daughter of a whore," Herrin mumbled, gruff and grave. "There will be none such who carry my name."

She nearly laughed at his anger, for he was lying half-naked, his robe sweat-soaked and stained as the poppy milk withdrawal continued. Herrin was still weak, and, even now, his eyes were fog-touched and his hands trembled. The king, as it was, seemed less like a threat and more like a doddering old man, she thought.

As she wiped his chest with a soap-scented linen, she told him, "Perhaps he will not want your name, my lord."

His rash-covered, pock-marked hand struck her cheek as he waved it about in dismissal of her words. But the King was frail, and the pain was slight as Caryss continued to wash him.

"All men want the Mannacore name," Herrin told her, his hands falling wanly to his sides.

"He is a boy," she scolded, "And wants what any might. A chance to explore and learn beyond his mother's skirts."

For a moment, the King's eyes cleared and he looked at her as he said, "Your plan is for the Islander to teach him the ways of the sword."

Part-accusation, part-question, Caryss hesitated before answering. "If that is what the boy wishes."

"What interest do you have in him?" the King asked, more alert than he had been since her arrival in the King's City.

Herrin still did not know about her own babe, although nearly all else did as soon as they looked upon her. Caryss thought long on how to explain, knowing that she could not be completely truthful with Herrin, even now.

204

"It was the boy who found me, King Herrin. On the eve that I entered the Grand Palace, I spotted him."

"Impossible!" the King cried, trying to sit up.

Holding him down gently, Caryss explained, "He was not there in the flesh, but in vision, following after Crispin as a dog would to his master. Yet Crispin could not see him, nor could the others. I talked to him that night and told him I would come, if he so wanted. He has known nothing but farm life for ten moon years nearly, and the boy grows anxious and bored. That is what I have promised him, the chance to see Cordisia."

After a moment, Herrin told her, "He will not be safe once his identity becomes known."

"Then none will know him. Do you even recall his name?" she asked, pulling the soiled robe from him as she realized the King was not arguing against actually finding the boy.

With a snort, he muttered, "I cannot recall what Crispin called him, but know that it was not a Rexterran name."

Herrin shivered while she searched for a clean tunic. Caryss had crossed the room, yet heard his words all the same.

Looking through a satchel of clothing, she stated, "The boy was named for his mother's people, I believe. I will let him introduce himself to you."

Pulling a long, gray tunic from the bag, she crossed the room again, and, when she neared the cot, she paused.

"King Herrin," she started, "I must know that the boy will be safe in my keep. Give me your word that it will be so."

"You think I could harm the boy when I can no longer walk on my own legs," he retorted, his words raspy and hoarse, for he had talked more then he had in moons, she knew.

"Your word, sir," she told him, pulling him upright to slip the tunic over his silvery, thinning hair.

Once the tunic was in place, he stuttered, "I will not harm the boy, healer. Yet, I will need his word as well. In my current state, I am weaker than a child. This boy might harm me for all I know."

"Would you not deserve it?" Caryss told him, before she could stop herself from speaking.

The room grew quiet. A flush now crossed his cheeks, adding a glow that made him look hale. She knew that she should not have addressed him so, yet did not apologize. Instead, she waited.

Before long, he sighed, "You know nothing of the ways of Rexterra, and less of the ways of rule, Caryss. Crispin is heir, yet was little more than a boy when the babe was born."

"He was of an age as I am now, Herrin," she laughed, although the sound was hollow.

"But the babe was a bastard nonetheless. The girl, I believe, could not even name her own father."

"Even if I understood the ways of Rexterra, I would not support the killing of a babe. None should," she told him, making no attempt to hide the disgust she felt.

"The babe is now a boy you've told me. Alive and blessed with some mage-skill, it seems. When you told me of him earlier, I did not seek to harm him nor did I think on sending word to the palace. These last ten moon years have been unkind to me, yet perhaps I am better for it. Caryss, I will not harm this boy. Indeed, I find myself looking forward to meeting him."

After she explained to him the vows of Eirrannia, ones that she had only recently remembered, Herrin briefly told her of his kin, of the gold-eyed and flame-touched Rexterrans. He was tiring, she realized, but still she pushed for his promise.

"By all four points of the star and by the embers of the flame, I give you my word that I will not harm the boy," he told her.

With a nod, she tucked a blanket around him, and said, "I will ask the boy to make a similar pledge. On the morrow, we leave."

When she neared the door, he called out to her.

"How did you find him?"

His words were little more than a whisper now, but they both knew what more they meant. She had done what he had spent moon years trying to accomplish.

Staring at him with her eyes of the forest, Caryss answered, "He told me."

She did not wait for a reply as she turned the knob and entered the empty hallway. Walking to her room, Caryss realized that whatever poison he had been given was beginning to drain from his body. And, with less poppy milk each day, Herrin was returning to the man he once was. His body was frail, as it would be for many moons, but his mind was clearer each day. If she could find an answer to the rash and fatigue that threatened him daily, he would be nearly the same man once again. Scarred and weakened, but a king nonetheless. The healer in her rejoiced.

But she herself trembled.

*****

206

19

"What has gotten in to you today, Jarek?" his mother asked.

She was scrubbing potatoes in the large sink, occasionally glancing back at him as he jumped from the wooden chair to look out the large window to the right, one that looked out onto the main gates of the farm. Each time he looked, the scene was the same. The sun fell lower now, full and bright, glowing as it dropped. The tall grasses swayed and the dirt-packed road lay dust-free, which meant no riders had approached.

He did not doubt that she would come and moved closer to the window, standing near his mother at the sink.

She swatted at him with a linen and chided, "Run off and let me finish up."

Jarek knew that he could wait no longer to tell her of the woman. It had been two days past since she had contacted him last, and he expected her soon.

"Mama," he stuttered, dodging the snapping towel, "We have visitors coming."

He watched as his mother dropped a thickly bristled brush into the sink, heard it clang loudly, and waited, biting his lip as he did so. She slowly turned toward him, hands now emptied. With her silk-blue eyes, she looked at him, and Jarek struggled to return her gaze, knowing that he should have told her sooner.

"What do you mean?" she asked, taking her eyes from him to peer out the window.

His voice trembled, and, with a shaky shrill, he told her, "She called me, and I went to see her. She asked where to find us, and I answered. She will arrive near sunfall."

Turning back to him, she cried, "Who is coming?"

"The woman from the palace."

"Why would she come here?" his mother gasped, moving checkered curtains to again look out the window.

Jarek felt as if he could not breathe, and he knew that his fair cheeks were burning bright. In his mother's voice, he could hear anger, although she had tried to keep it hidden. There was something else in her voice that he could not place, and her eyes were shining, looking more like sea than sky.

Drawing a deep breath into tight lungs, he uttered, "To take me with her."

At over ten moon years old, he should have known what was to come, but, still, he jumped back, banging his head on the edge of the wall when the thunder struck loud and violent.

In a voice he would not have known to be hers, she asked, "Where does she seek to go, Jarek?"

Another clap of thunder pounded against the glass pane beside him, rattling loud, but this time he had expected it and did not tremble.

Instead, he rushed from the room and into the open yard, beneath the suddenly churning skies.

Closing his eyes, Jarek raised his hands above his head, spreading his fingers and stretching his arms as far as they could reach. A whistling hush of air escaped his lips as his hands traced and danced. Above him, gray clouds gathered, dark and thick, but no rain fell.

Again he pushed at the air, forcing his arms faster and faster from left to right. Around him the wind increased, pulling at his tunic and hair.

It did not take long for him to calm the storm, to clear her anger from overhead, and, when he next looked up, his mother stood watching from the wide-planked porch. The skies had lightened, but her arms hung at her sides, as if in defeat.

Jarek did not move as she walked toward him. His thin arms, long and lanky, now hung beside him, twitching only slightly. He had grown stronger, he knew, and bit his lip so his mother would not see him smile. He had moved her clouds as if they had been naught but vision. Steps from him now, she called his name.

"She will be here soon, mama," he yelled, his voice edged with air.

"You are a child!" his mother cried, "Just because the skies heeded your call once does not make you a master. You have much to learn, Jarek, and must do it on the farmstead where none can see."

"Mama, what more can I learn here? My books are falling apart with too much use and the skies here know me and offer little challenge. If I am to improve, I must visit other skies and taste other water."

"I told you that I would bring a swordmaster here. It takes time, son. Give me a half-moon yet."

Shaking his head, Jarek pleaded, "You must allow me to go with her to Eirrannia!"

He thought that she would call on the storm again, but instead she stepped near. With her arms outreached, his mother embraced him.

When she pulled back, she told him, "Your people, my people, are not found in Cordisia, Jarek. You will have to travel much farther to find our kind. Well beyond the Eastern Sea. There is nothing for you in Eirrannia."

"There are others with her. One who is called the Prince of Swords. She has promised that he will become my teacher."

"Jarek!" she yelled, grabbing him by his shoulders, "Assurances from a woman you have only seen in the fog amount to nothing! Are you such a fool as this?"

He had known for the last few moon years that the farm was no longer home to him, and although he loved his mother truly, Jarek longed to be free from the farm. At night, when he was not practicing his sky calls, he would dream of holding a sword in his hand. During the day, when he was not in lessons, he would spend hours in the fields, swinging and slashing with tree limbs for sword. When first he had started, the limbs were thinner than his arm, yet now he yielded sticks wide and heavy, moving with force and speed.

"I have been your son for ten moon years, mama. Yet, I have the blood of kings in me as well and must learn what all other Rexterran boys already know. I must be ready for when my father needs me."

When his mother threw him from her, Jarek knew what would come next. Moon years before, he had realized that thunder was simpler to call than lightning. Fog and mist were the easiest to draw forth, and he could make fog from a drop of water, mist from nothing but his breath. Thunder had come to him when he was older, nearly seven moon years, and lightning followed a full moon year later. For the last two moon years, he had used both cloud and sky as toy, yet his mother had always admonished him to keep his practice confined to the skies above the farmstead. In those two moon years, his skill sometimes surprised even himself, and, of late, he kept what he had learned from her.

With a glance to the sky, he noticed that the clouds that she had called earlier were gone, the sky a dusky blue, colors of sunfall lingering at the edges. From the clear sky came a crackle loud and threatening. Following it was a streak of lightning fiery and thick. Then another came, louder, angrier. Over and over, lightning reached her fingers to the earth, jagged and hot, circling Jarek but never coming close enough to harm him.

His mother's skill was impressive, and never before had he seen her do such magic with such control. He watched in awe, letting the sizzling around him echo through his body and heat his blood, even as he understood it to be a warning.

When his mother dropped her hands to her side, remnants of scattered lightning blinked across the sky.

In a voice full of booming rage, she called, "Your father has forgotten you, Jarek! He needs you not, nor do you need him. Death only awaits you in the King's City, or have you forgotten that your own grandfather tried to have you killed? Go North, if you must, but I will not let you enter the gates of the King's City while there is still breath in my body and lightning on my fingers."

209

She had wanted to show him that her skill was still stronger than his own, and Jarek let her believe it to be so.

Bowing his head, he told her, "As you say, mother. I will go with the Northern woman, and learn what I can from her swordmaster. If she seeks to go to the King's City, I will insist upon returning home."

Her words were jagged like ice, as if her breath was cloud, as she explained, "I have always wanted to find my father's kin. Maybe it was not my path to do so, but it could be yours. There are islands to the east of Eirrannia, many days travel aboard even the fleetest ship. Find them, if you can. There is more to learn about the sky than even I know. One day, your skill will far outshine mine."

He ran to her, wrapping his arms about her waist. His head reached just below her chin, yet, soon, he would be taller than she, he knew.

Into her ear, he whispered, "I will make your proud, mama."

They both went inside then, waiting for the woman to come. The one who would separate mother and son.

*****

"I have traveled more in the last moon than I have in nearly all of my twenty moon years, Caryss."

"Do you like it? The travel, I mean?" Caryss asked the other healer.

"Before we left the Academy, I had often wondered if the girl had spoken true, and I worried that I would not know what I was to do when the time came. So I waited. I enjoyed my time at the Academy, and learned as much as any other, but I knew that it would not always be so. It was never home."

"You are a fine healer," she told the woman.

Her words were greeted with a smile, but Sharron continued, "When I look back, my time at the Academy seems distant, yet less than three moons have passed. I do not want to return, which surprises me greatly. This life, this Healer Journey that we are on, I quite like it. How else would I have been able to see the Cove? Or the Grand Palace? And now the Twin Planes?"

"If we must leave Eirrannia at some point, will you still follow?"

Sharron's horse was nearly beside Caryss's own. When she laughed, Caryss pulled at the reins, forcing her mount to stop.

"Are you trying to rid yourself of me?" Sharron teased.

"Never," Caryss answered, her gelding circling.

"We are kin, or so I see it. My home is with you and the babe."

Caryss nodded, but the woman's words were true ones, and she loved her more for them, knowing that Sharron knew the path would not be an easy one. When the other healer rode ahead, Caryss waited, watching the two men who stood stretching their legs. Otieno looked every bit the warrior, from his broad shoulders and thick arms to his fitted boots and leather armor. Even without his swords, which she had never seen apart from his body except when the girl had asked for them, he appeared dangerous. Few would attempt to battle him without aid.

She next looked to Aldric, who remained thin and yellowed, yet there was a power to him that those who could sense it would recognize. His magic was not the clean mage-skill taught by the guild. It was raw and ancient, strong and wild. She had seen it rarely displayed, yet had heard a few tales of its use.

Her daughter's army was at three, and, with the boy and his mage-skill, whatever it might be, there would be four to serve as guard and advisor. Not nearly enough, regardless of their skill, to protect her from the Tribe. Or from whomever else would seek to harm her, Caryss knew.

In the North, she would find more, men and woman alike. She only needed to convince them to follow.

Roim a faidh, an taoh se eirgh.

She knew the words to be her daughter's battle cry. Soon, she hoped, others would too.

*****

"What more must I finish before I can be named Master Apprentice, sir?"

"Will your studies be complete in the next few moons, Pietro?" the older man asked, looking up from the bench near the Academy's gardens, where they both had been sitting for the last few moments.

"Yes, I am finishing up the last of my courses now and will need no more than three moons."

Master Rova was a quiet man, and had always been so, Pietro thought, although there was much behind his eyes, knowledge and more. Ofttimes, he would avoid the Master Healer, especially once it had become clear that Rova favored Bronwen. Yet, now, he needed the man. Without the Headmaster's approval, he would never be named Master Apprentice, and his Healer Journey would have to wait until another Headmaster was named, which would only happen if Rova fell ill, died, or relinquished his position. None looked like it would happen soon, even though Rova walked slowly and appeared to have aged quite significantly the last few moons. So Pietro had decided to change approaches, and, for the last quarter-moon, he had attempted to charm the man, showing him both his skill and passion for the healing arts.

211

Slowly, it seemed to be working. When the master began talking again, Pietro leaned forward, in attention, and listened.

"In the course of a normal moon year, we only grant Master Apprentice to less than ten students, and we prefer the journey began at the start of the moon year. It has been but a few moons since Bronwen left for her Healer Journey, Pietro. Do you not wish to await her return and hear the advice she may give before you start on your own?"

The old man's words surprised him, and Pietro hesitated before answering, "Bronwen is a fine healer, sir, and none could argue against her skill. Yet, she is not the same healer as I am, nor would we find ourselves in similar places. My skill is best used for those on the battlefield, while hers is much more useful in a clinical setting. It is no secret that I hope to one day be back in Rexterra, just as it is no secret that I hope to serve my king and his army. I do not believe that Bronwen would be able to share much with me of that, sir."

Rova nodded, reaching his hands toward one another until they were clasped together. The Headmaster did not look at Pietro as he spoke.

"We all walk our own path, even those trained here. But I would be delinquent in my duties if I did not remind you that the goal of a Healer Journey is to live and breathe the craft, with no purpose other than to help and to heal while doing no harm. I would not exclude you from traveling to Rexterra, but there are many between here and there that will be in need of your skill."

With his voice high with passion, Pietro told Rova, "My oaths bind me as any other, Master! It is only that I look forward to my Healer Journey and the chance to test my skill beyond the gates of the Academy. When you believe that I am ready, only then will I seek to leave."

"Then let us have this talk again in another moon, Pietro. Finish your courses, and I will discuss your request with the Master Council."

It was enough, thought Pietro, knowing that Master Black had assured him that he would get the votes necessary for his approval. Soon, he would be away from the Academy, and there was no other direction that he would go but east. It had been too long since he had been home, and the King's City was like no other place. With a well-practiced smile, Pietro turned to Master Rova, placing his unwrinkled and unmarked hand on the old man's, squeezing gently before he rose from the bench.

"My thanks, Master," he said, rising.

Forcing himself to walk slowly, for he still had at least a moon to go before it would be time to depart, Pietro followed the sandy trail back to his rooms.

*****

Above, the skies were gray, clouds covered the slice of Luna that remained, threatening rain. Yet, as they rode, their mounts stayed dry and the road clear. Caryss, silent and focused, rode ahead of the others, and, tethered at the rear of her horse was the mount that pulled the King's wagon.

Aldric kept his horse just behind Caryss's silver-maned gelding, following closely. A dark mood had come over the girl in the last few hours, he realized. He had only known her briefly before she was with child, but he did not doubt that the babe was who often occupied her thoughts. For a moment, Aldric thought of his nephew, wondering what the boy, who had long known Caryss, would say of the healer's behavior, especially her decisions of late, none stranger than the last she made.

A moon before, he had boarded a ship out of the King's City before the sun had fully risen, traveling to the Southern Cove Islands with few questions asked of Caryss. And, now, again, he found himself trailing behind her, watching as her unbound hair waved like a pennant, bright and red against the darkening sky. Yet, he knew that he would continue to follow, and he suspected the others would as well. Even Otieno.

Even as committed to her as he was, Aldric could not ignore her sullenness, and, riding up beside her, hurriedly asked, "What concerns you so that has slowed your pace?"

Without halting the gelding, she mumbled, "I hadn't realized that I had let the horse slow. We are nearly there and should arrive within the hour."

"Caryss, what is it that bothers you so?" he pressed, unsatisfied with her response.

With a sigh that he heard over the clomping of the hooves, she mumbled, "Herrin tried for years to kill the boy. Then he lost him and could not find him or Nicoline. What madness is it that I seek to bring the wolf to the lamb? A lamb that has been safe and unharmed for ten moon years."

"What is it that you fear from the wolf? And what could the wolf really do without teeth and legs?" he asked, with a nod toward the King's cart.

"He is recovering, Aldric. The poison leaves him more each day, and he requires much less poppy milk. Soon, he will need none at all."

"You are a fine healer from all that I have been told, but even you cannot give the wolf his legs back."

A slight smile caused the corners of her lips to twitch, and Caryss said, "A cunning wolf needs no legs at all."

Nodding, Aldric suddenly understood.

With a lowered voice, he asked, "Who matters more?"

He waited for her to answer, pulling at the reins to steady his horse. Behind him, the others neared.

She did not look to him as she answered, "The girl needs an army not a king."

A wise answer, he mused, watching her. She had learned much in the last few moons. Often, he knew, with wisdom came sadness. She was young yet to have to face such truths, but, for her, it was a necessary step.

"The king has given you his word that the boy will be unharmed, is it not so?" When she nodded, he told her, "If he breaks his word, then I will see that he pays. We do not need to speak on this again."

Kicking at his mount, Aldric called, "Now let us go meet this boy."

Nothing further was said, but her gelding trotted on, faster than before, catching up to him swiftly. Caryss stared ahead, shoulders raised and eyes clear.

As they rode, Aldric thought on the babe. Unlike her mother, she would be born with knowledge of the dark, a legacy of her father's people born into her blood.

The group was far from any town, and the sky was nearly black, no light shining across the path they that rode. Behind him, Otieno, on the largest mount that Aldric could find, which still looked small beneath the large-chested Islander, kicked hard at his horse.

With a rolling accent, he called, "Night will be upon us soon, Caryss."

Pulling on the well-worn leather reins, Caryss quickly stopped, jerking a bit forward, yet the darkness covered her near fall. Behind her, the King's cart creaked to a halt.

"It has taken longer to find the boy than you believed, and I fear the truth of his location might have been kept from you. From all that you've said, you know little about magic. Trickery is often the other side of the coin when one uses mage-skill, *leseda*," Otieno informed her.

Aldric watched with interest, knowing there was little love between the two. Otieno had long traveled a solitary path, and, now, following a young woman full of whim and emotion had been difficult for him, Aldric knew. The Islander spoke little of Caryss, yet Aldric needed no words to confirm his thoughts.

"Look to your left!" Caryss called, her voice loud and sharp as she pointed toward a twinkling orb of light. "See how the lights burn. He waits for us. Listen to the hum of the wind."

Pausing for the others to listen, Caryss added, "He calls to us."

She smiled, yet it was a smile without meaning, never touching her eyes. "You trust so little, Otieno," she warned as her gray-green eyes fell upon him.

"And, you, my lady, fear too little."

His words were not kind ones, and Aldric drew in his breath, pulling the leather reins tight against his chest as he looked toward Sharron. When the other healer gently shook her head, Aldric waited, his hands clenched, but flame-free.

Caryss's next words cracked the silence open.

"Then between us, we fear just enough I would think."

Gently kicking the side of the tall gelding, Caryss trotted off, then turned her long neck, and called, "Follow me. Around the next bend we will find the road to Jarek's farm."

In the end, she was not wrong. Before a quarter of an hour had past, the group was through the unlocked gate and upon an overgrown path that led to a small stone house. Just before the steps, Caryss halted, hastily jumping from her horse as if the house was aflame.

Silently, she hurried to the door, with no regard to those who stood surprised behind her. When she reached her hand to the door, Aldric saw that it shook. *She is afraid,* he thought, wondering if Otieno's words had affected her so. Hurrying to join her, he stood just behind as she knocked, long and heavy.

It was not the boy who opened the thick, wood door.

"You have come to take my son."

Her voice soft and smooth, Caryss told the woman, "I have heard much about you Nicoline."

"Yet I know nothing of you," the woman countered, her voice crackling and sharp.

The two women stared at each other, neither speaking nor stepping back. Aldric nearly interrupted, but, after a long moment, Nicoline asked, "Why I should let you enter my home?"

Behind her, the door was closed.

"I can offer you no reassurance," Caryss sighed, "Nor can I promise that the boy will be safe. I will not lie to you, Nicoline. I knew nothing of the boy until I met him at the palace. You, I know better, as Willem has told me of you."

Aldric watched as recognition crossed Nicoline's sun-browned face, her blue eyes like none he had seen before, glittering as if cut from the sea.

"I owe Willem much," Nicoline finally answered, "But I do not owe him my son. You have come from the Academy? The boy did not know much about you."

"Aye. I have spent half my life there and have known Willem for nearly all of it. He did not betray your location, Nicoline, and told me little of your son. I was sent from Tretoria to the King's City on orders of the King's Heir. Herrin was near death when I arrived. It was at the palace that I came upon your son, rather by chance."

"You met the boy's father then. Has he sent you here?" Nicoline asked, her words no less flinching.

Caryss hesitated, but did not take her eyes from the pale-haired woman. Finally, she spoke, but her words were hushed, although Aldric was near enough to hear.

"Crispin knows nothing of this. There is much I would tell you, Nicoline, but I fear you would be in some danger if I did so."

"You seek to take my only son from me. That alone should warrant honesty between us, healer."

Again, the words were like melting ice flowing from woman to woman. Aldric shifted, his knees cracking loud as he moved.

"As you wish then," Caryss conceded. "Over a moon ago, I arrived in the King's City, under disguise for none were to know that another healer was sought for the King. I later learned that it was Crispin who sent word requesting aid from the Master Council. My first time in the palace was a strange one, and it would not be untruthful to say that I was ill prepared for life in Rexterra. Jarek appeared to me that night, although none else saw him, not even the mage that travels with me."

Caryss paused and looked toward Aldric who confirmed her words with a nod.

Then she continued, "Much later, after I had time to examine the King, and we were settled into our rooms, Crispin appeared at my door. I thought nothing of it, but the meeting soon became tense and strained. Perhaps he was only trying to frighten me or teach me the ways of the King's Court, but it all became too much. I suspected that the King was being poisoned, most likely by someone close to him, and Crispin's visit only further concerned me. Nicoline, I fled the palace that night, under mage-ward."

With a raised hand, her palm facing Caryss, Nicoline stopped Caryss from continuing. "You need not further explain the King's Court to me, for I lived under its shadow for moon years before escaping."

Shaking her head quickly, Caryss pushed on. "There is more. Much more. Crispin would not leave my room that night, and I struck him. Not hard, but with enough force that his cheek required stitching. After I tended to him, I tricked him into drinking a tonic that put him to sleep, for a day or more, I would suspect."

Aldric watched a slow smile cross Nicoline's face. She was still a beautiful woman, pale-haired and blue-eyed, and with a power about her that made her even more intriguing. She was no whore's daughter, he knew then, thinking back on what the King had told Caryss. Yet, she was no simple mage, either. As he watched the women, he thought long on where he had seen eyes like hers.

"Nicoline," Caryss said, "I do not know what you know of the Academy, but we take vows as soon as we can, ones that we must live by or abandon the Healing Arts altogether. We had traveled long to visit the King, and I had no time to attempt a healing. And, if what I suspected had been true, it would be moons before improvement came. That night when we fled, I made a choice."

He knew what would come next, what Caryss would admit. Stepping forward, he reached for her arm, pulling her back a step. Nicoline's eyes were on him, mist-filled and ready.

Suddenly, Aldric understood who Nicoline was.

"You come from the east, past the Three Seas and the Eastern Sea, in lands north where few travel. I have met your kind once before."

"I was born in a brothel to a Planusterran mother. I know nothing of my father," Nicoline scoffed at him.

Her words were true ones, Aldric knew, but his own were true as well, and he told her, "The land is called Skavia, and the people tall and fierce, each one warrior-trained, even the women. Few are better with the spear and axe, Nicoline, than the Skavians. But it is not weapons that they are famed for."

"Watch yourself, mage," she warned.

Her eyes grayed, but still he pushed.

"Caryss," he called, pulling at her again until she was behind him, "Did Willem tell you of Nicoline's skill?"

Behind him, Caryss was silent.

"What of the boy? Does he have it as well?" Aldric asked, his words now edged and harsh.

"What is the meaning of this?" Caryss cried, trying to step around him.

Again he blocked her from moving near Nicoline.

Nicoline's eyes were darker now, shaded with the blues of midnight.

"Get to the wagon," he hissed at Caryss, pushing her back further.

His hands burned, hot and aching with a need for release. He heard Caryss stumble down the stairs, yet he did not take his eyes from Nicoline.

"This is not a game you will want to play, mage," she growled.

Before he could answer, the door behind her flung open. A cropped-hair boy appeared, sky-eyed like his mother.

Without turning, Nicoline cried, "Get back inside, Jarek!"

As if he did not hear the warning, the boy rushed around his mother, out into the yard. When Aldric turned, he saw him run toward Caryss.

"I knew that you would come!" the boy screamed to her below the dark skies, his high voice shrieking against the rumbling skies.

217

Aldric ran from the porch until he was beside the boy. Throwing an orb-light between Caryss and Jarek, Aldric stepped closer, his eyes watching the boy's gold-rimmed ones.

Her face pale and her eyes reflecting confusion, Caryss said nothing to the boy.

"Did you bring the Sword Prince?" he asked, with little regard for his mother who had neared.

The boy's words were sweet and soft, and Aldric was not surprised to hear Caryss finally answer. "He is the big man atop the even bigger horse."

As if by invitation, Otieno hopped from his horse and walked to the boy. He had been too far to hear much of the conversation, but he knew enough, Aldric concluded.

"We have traveled far to find you, Jarek," the Islander told him.

"Is it true that you mean to take me with you?" Jarek haltingly asked.

Aldric could take no more and called, "Caryss, ask the boy if he can call the storms."

"My son is no toy, mage, and this no game."

"Ask him!" Aldric screamed, grabbing Nicoline's arms, holding them to her sides so they could no longer be lifted.

With the woman pulled tight against him, Aldric again yelled for Caryss. Nicoline struggled, but he had spent moon years as a mercenary, and she was no match for him.

In a trembling voice, Caryss asked, "What does he mean, Jarek? Are you a storm-bringer?"

"Did my father tell you that? He has not seen what I can do. Not even my mother has."

"Jarek! Enough!" Nicoline yelled, her words hot against Aldric's cheek.

"He is a boy. Please, just let us be," she whispered then, as if she knew she was now unmatched.

His hands cooled, but he did not release her. "You do not understand, Nicoline. There is so much that you do not understand," he confided.

"Please," she begged, her knees collapsing.

Ignoring her, he called to Caryss. When she came forward, her cheeks flushed and her eyes flashed.

"Aldric, let her go!" she screamed at him, spittle flying onto his cheeks.

In a lowered voice, he explained, "The boy is an Elemental. I know his kind. Have you heard the term, Caryss?"

Nicoline still fought against his hold, but he would not yet release her.

When she did not answer, Aldric scolded her. "You know so little of your history, and even less of the Tribe. There are few who can challenge them, but the Elementals are one such group who can succeed where so many others fail. They have no need for *atraglacia*, for their skill is enough. There are few Elementals in Cordisia, yet there abilities are well-known across the seas. There is no peace between Tribe and Elemental, Caryss. More, they have long been enemies, before Cordisia was even born."

Caryss paled.

"You think he will harm the babe?"

In her words, Aldric heard much, and, to look upon her, he saw something akin to defeat.

With little choice, he explained, "For each Tribe, there is a counter-element, as Conri would know. For Wolf, it is storm. The Crows ride strong on the winds of their allies, Caryss, while the Wolf must take shelter or perish. Am I beginning to make sense to you?"

Looking past him, she addressed Nicoline, "Is what he says true?"

"I know little of my father and have not strayed from this place for nine moon years. I have no enemies but one. What is the meaning of this?"

To him, Caryss said, "I did not know."

Her voice broke, and the words were nearly lost. Before he could speak, the boy appeared, with Otieno trailing behind, his hand on the hilt of his sword.

"Is it necessary to restrain the woman?" the *diauxie* asked.

As way of explanation, Aldric told him, "Her kind are enemy to the babe."

"He is a no more than a child. Release the woman and let us work this through. None need to suffer here."

Caryss nodded, and Aldric relaxed his arms. "It is for you to decide how much to tell her."

"What do you want of my son?" Nicoline demanded, rubbing at her arms.

Pulling her jacket tight to her as the winds increased and the air cooled, Caryss told her, "I want what you want. What any mother would. I want him safe and protected, to teach him things that he cannot learn here. I have given you my word, and to him as well, that he will not be harmed. But I did not know of his skill."

"Willem did not mention it then," Nicoline murmured.

With a shrug, Caryss answered, "We only discussed you once, and I had too many cups of wine even before talk turned to Rexterra. And when I saw the boy at the palace, I knew nothing of his calling, only that his mage-skill was strong. Nor did Crispin tell me of him."

"You are Eirrannian, Caryss, and stories suggest that all are welcome in the North, even ones with untrained talent."

There was a long pause before Caryss responded. Aldric watched her, knowing that it was time for her to choose. The risk was great, and the High Lord would see the boy killed, Aldric feared. He offered no warning, though, as he waited.

"Our children are enemies, Nicoline, even mine who is yet unborn. Just as you must think on what is best for Jarek, I must think on what is best for my daughter."

"You are Tribe?"

Caryss pushed her flaming hair from her face as she shook her head and sighed, "The babe's father is. Nicoline, I did not know of this ancient feud."

"What feud?" Nicoline laughed. "As I've told you, I know nothing of my father. He visited my mother one night, just as others did, and never returned. His feud is not my own, nor is it my son's. All the same, though, I have never wanted him to leave. Now he has reason to stay."

"No, mama! No! You told me that I could go with them." Jarek cried.

"The healer thinks you will harm her babe," Nicoline told him angrily. "If there is nothing else, I think it best that you all leave."

Again, it was the *diauxie* who intervened.

"*Leseda*, there is a reason that you have come here. The boy is only a threat if he wants to be so. Think on this as a chance to mend old wounds. An enemy must not always be so, and the boy desires to come with us."

"Mage," Otieno called, turning to him, "The boy alone cannot be much of a threat. I know little of this land, but from what I've heard discussed here, there has been no war for generations. I see no harm in letting him come with us. And even more in letting old wounds fester."

Realizing that everyone watched him, Aldric hurriedly explained, "If the boy can harness his power, then perhaps he would be no threat. I have not witnessed an Elemental myself and know not what he can do or how well-controlled his magic is. A misplaced lightning streak would be enough to kill any of us."

"Just as if I were to swing any of my swords, you would be dead as well. And you, Aldric? What if you were to call for flame? Is your fire any less deadly than the boy's skill?" the Islander called out to him.

Caryss only listened, white-faced against a now-darkened sky. Aldric looked to her in an attempt to garner what she was thinking, but her eyes were elsewhere, as were her thoughts.

Turning back to Otieno, he argued, "A weapon can only be so if it is used. I have heard it said before. If we are attacked and you must draw your sword, Caryss would not be your target. It is not so if the boy calls a storm. We might all suffer for it, and the babe most."

"You bicker over nothing," Nicoline interrupted. "The boy will stay here."

Jarek was tugging on Caryss's arm before any of them could object, and Aldric looked to Nicoline, silently warning her to call the boy back. When she did not, he stepped toward the healer.

"We need the boy," she whispered, her words traveling no farther than his ears.

Louder then, she asked, "Nicoline, can Jarek be trusted with his mage-skill?"

"Asks the woman who carries a child of the Tribe," the light-haired woman smirked.

Across the yard, the women stared at one another, as if rivals.

Finally, Caryss called, "The babe is innocent and will remain so. She will lead one day, Nicoline, and perhaps then your kind and hers will be ally."

A blowing wind hummed around her as she continued, "What happens here today is not about us. We must consider what will come for our children and the paths that they may walk. My daughter needs friends, Nicoline, as does the boy. Who else but Otieno will teach him the ways of the sword? Who else but Aldric will teach him the ways of the court? He will learn healing, a necessary skill for any who follow the sword. If he stays here, he will be nothing more than a farm boy who plays with the skies. With us, he will learn and grow, until he is ready."

"Ready for what?" Nicoline cried.

Her words soft and floating like a feather lifted by the swirling breeze, Caryss answered, "Ask him what he dreams of just before he sleeps. Ask him why he time-walks so often to the palace. Ask him what he seeks, Nicoline. Jarek knows, even if you do not."

The boy dropped Caryss's arm as she spoke, understanding that the winds had changed again, and now she fought for him to come with them. His mother watched him, her blue eyes wide and striking, and suddenly filled with doubt. The boy stayed silent, as if he knew that Caryss spoke true.

After the airs calmed, Jarek answered, his words controlled and even, as if they had been well-practiced.

"I want the throne, mama. I am the rightful Rexterran heir, and I seek only what should have been mine by birth."

Aldric watched as Nicoline made sense of the boy's words. Her face had become a mask, betraying little. Yet, even that told him much. After nearly ten moon years, her son was no longer hers. She had lost him to a father he did not know.

"He will not be safe in Rexterra."

"Nor am I. Nicoline, I will look after him as if he is my own. And will not let him travel to Rexterra until he is better prepared. He is a child still, and will be for many moon years to come."

"The boy has never held a sword," Nicoline countered, as if she could change the outcome.

"He is late to it, as Otieno tells me, but his teacher is like none other. Most will believe he was born with a blade in his hand by the time he reaches manhood."

"I will not let him go," she hissed, having played what cards she could.

Unable to listen further to the woman's pleading, Aldric called, "We could take the boy with force, my lady, but it is not the healer's way. Your son invited her here and would just as soon leave with her. She will depart without him, if that is what you wish, but he will never forgive you. The choice is yours."

"Let it be, Aldric," Caryss told him, "She is a worried mother, as most would be. We have come here to take her son, and she knows us naught."

Her face suddenly lined and weary, Nicoline sighed, "It grows dark. Let us go inside and make arrangements."

When Caryss hesitated, Aldric knew what she would say next. Before she could speak, he was upon her, his eyes scanning her, silently warning her to say nothing more. Her fingers twitched as she held them up to him in protest, but again his eyes locked upon hers, commanding her to say nothing of the King.

A small magic, he knew, but a necessary one. As they followed Nicoline into her home, Otieno nodded. Caryss saw Jarek as he was, a child with mage-skill. But Aldric and the *diauxie* saw him as more.

They saw what he might become.

And neither would leave the farmstead without him.

Soon, they were all seated at the table, except for Sharron and the King, who waited outside, one unseen. Nicoline bustled about the room serving them tea and carving a large beef roast. The kitchen was well-tended, neat and filled with tins and plates. Aldric knew that Willem sent the woman money each moon year, and the farmstead had been purchased with moneys from Crispin. Some of the land was leased and the profits shared, but he knew that Nicoline would never suffer, for Willem would not allow it. She and the boy did not live as his father did, but he lived better than most, and much like Aldric himself had. And, just as he had once been, the boy was now of an age where a different path called.

Shaking himself free of the memory, he heard Caryss telling Nicoline, "I will require nothing of him, except a vow that he will harm none loyal to my daughter or to me. If a time comes when he wishes to leave, we will see him home safely. "

Nicoline paused, knife in hand, yet did not turn to face the healer. Jarek had gone into his bedroom, and Otieno was seated on the other side of Caryss. All waited as Nicoline considered Caryss's words.

Before she could answer, Otieno stood.

"Nicoline, if I may, I would show you what I would teach the boy." Turning to Aldric, he said, "Keep Caryss warded and away from any windows, but send the boy to me. There is something that I should have done earlier."

With that, the Islander stomped from the room, his boots heavy and his steps determined ones. Jarek rushed to the kitchen, having heard the departure and looked to Caryss as his mother followed the *diauxie* into the night.

"The Prince of Swords wishes to show you how he earned his name. Hurry now."

Caryss began to object as Jarek ran from the room, but Aldric waved her off, throwing a heavy ward over her, one that would take most of his energy to maintain. When it was in place, Aldric strode to the window.

The dance started.

No light shined above, yet, even in the darkness, the hilt of the curved sword could be seen as Otieno unsheathed it. It glimmered as if had been cut from the moon, silvery and sleek. As he swung it from hip to hip in a wide circle, Jarek gaped. Around Otieno there was a wide space, as mother and son watched from the porch. With the sword at his right hip, the *diauxie* lunged forward, flashing and fast, jerking his wrist up until the curved blade was extended above his head before slicing it across his body in a powerful downward slash.

"Bring the rain!" he screamed, loud enough that Aldric could hear the command.

When nothing happened, he again screamed, "Show me your skill, boy!"

Again the boy hesitated, for he had heard the warnings earlier.

Sheathing the curved blade at his waist, Otieno called, "She is warded and inside. I would not ask you to call the lightning if there could be harm. We are all tested, Jarek, and this is yours."

Before the boy could react, Aldric tightened the ward around Caryss until his limbs were shaking and afire. Bracing himself on the sink, he watched.

With a simple raise of his skinny arms, Jarek called the storm. As he swayed, so did the winds, coming near and brining clouds of gray. Ever increasing, the winds caused the open window near Aldric to bang against the side of the house, the glassed pane clanging each time it struck.

"Get under the table!" he screamed at Caryss.

She stuttered in protest, but soon crawled under the table. Otieno two-handed the Greatsword, holding it in front of him, readied and waiting. As Aldric watched, he thought the man a fool. He would have run to them and forced the boy to cease, but he did not dare leave Caryss unwarded. Sharron, he realized, had fled into the covered wagon, where surely the King must now be awake, he thought. Nicoline stood to the left of her son, yet her arms hung at her sides. From what Jarek had said, even his mother had not seen the full scope of his power.

When the rains came, Aldric's vision blurred. Across Caryss lay a stronger ward than he had ever weaved, and his legs threatened to collapse beneath him. Even if the boy had been trained by kin, he would not have been strong enough to break the ward, Aldric knew. Yet, still he worried, for he would not be able to maintain it long.

Outside, Otieno's black clothing clung to his body and water dripped from his chin. As the first streak of lightning cracked, the *diauxie* smiled, half-mad and teeth gleaming white. Aldric nearly threw a fireball at him, but his arms would not rise. The lightening streaked closer, and Otieno moved, parrying. Faster than the sizzling jolt, the Islander rolled onto the wet ground, his long hair trailing behind him. But he was back on his feet again before any could blink.

A jagged slash of light landed near his feet, yet he cut his sword through it, tearing the bolt in half, sending shards of crumbling light to the damp grass around him. For a brief moment, sparkling pieces of glowing light fell across his body, illuminating him as if had become a shattered, falling star.

Otieno did not speak. He moved. Over and over. With a cool rain falling on him and under a dark sky, he danced to the sky's revolt. Thunder growled at him, threatening, yet the man seemed to fear nothing. Each explosion that neared was destroyed by the Greatsword, bursting into harmless sparks that fizzled on the wet ground. The boy, even as mage-skilled as he was, could not defeat the man.

In this battle, sword trumped sky.

When the light faded and the rain ended, the boy stood with dropped arms and an open mouth. Otieno bowed. His next words crackled across the air.

"Sword over sky, boy. When wielded properly, steel can triumph over fire and water as well. What is one weapon when you can have two? Your skill is mighty, but mine is mightier, as you just saw."

Aldric dropped the ward, struggling with hazy eyes to find a chair. He saw nothing else as his head fell to the table.

When next he woke, Caryss stood behind him, cool linen pressed to the back of his neck. Jarek stood near his side as he addressed the healer.

"My mother has explained to me what you require before we depart. Under sky and star, I vow that I will defend you and your daughter as long as you wish it to be so. Under sky and star, I vow that I will devote myself to learning all that the swordmaster has to teach. Under sky and star, I vow that I will harm none that you deem friend. Under sky and star, Jarek, first son of Nicoline and first son of Prince Crispin, King's Heir, vows to be your loyal and faithful student."

"Is it your wish that the boy comes with us?" Caryss called to Nicoline.

In a whisper that sounded like rolling thunder, Nicoline replied, "Under sky and star, I vow that me and mine will always welcome your daughter into our home. Under sky and star, I vow that your daughter will be mine, as my son is yours."

"On the morrow, we leave."

Her words were the last he heard that night.

*****

20

Exile had not been unkind, and Willem had grown comfortable at the Academy. His villa was more home than the Grand Palace had ever been. Yet, since Bronwen's departure, the Academy, and the clinic, offered little for him.

He thought of her often, even more so once Crispin had sent him word of her departure from the King's City. Even with his resources, the King's Heir had not been able to locate her, although Willem found himself relieved at his cousin's latest news. Crispin had mentioned much about Caryss, as she now called herself, but he had never mentioned the babe. Either he did not know of her or something had occurred.

Punching at the door as he exited at the back of the clinic, Willem cursed his helplessness.

"I need a drink," he murmured, nearly slamming the door behind him.

A loud groan echoed behind him, and Willem turned to find a first-year student rubbing at his chin. He could not recall the boy's name, but his chin was red and swollen from where the door had struck him.

When he noticed Willem, he said, "I have letters for you, sir."

With a nod, he took the letters and instructed the boy to have his chin tended. Once the boy ran off, Willem pulled a small knife from a pouch. Hurriedly sorting from the letters, he found none from his cousin. Yet, there was an unmarked one bearing only his name. Its light wax seal, unbroken, offered no hint either. With haste, he broke the seal and pried the letter open with the tip of the knife.

It was early still, the sun only edging out of the east, but the scrolling script was a familiar one.

Sir,

It has been many moon years since last I wrote to you. I did not think to find myself in need of you once again, but I know not where else to turn. Before I go any further, let me assure you that the boy is well. He grows tall and strong, and although he is still thin, I can see the look of his father in him. He knows more than I about the sky, and I am often amazed at what he can do. Yet, I fear that even with that to amuse him, he grows bored. Of late, he has taken to traveling while he sleeps. I do not know much of what he does, for he keeps most of it from me, since I often try to dissuade him from such action. Now, he has the idea about him that he wants to train with sword. I gave him my word that I would seek a teacher for him, and that is why I am writing to you. He cannot go to Rexterra, as you and I both know. I had hoped that in a moon or two, the boy would change his mind, but he grows more insistent and more restless. Which caused me to write. Is there someone that would not recognize him who could be hired to teach him the ways of the sword until he is sufficient enough or until he grows weary of it? Someone who perhaps owes you a favor? There are men here that I could employ, but few know much of value, as we are more known for breeding horses than warriors. If you know of none, I will take no offense, as I merely promised the boy that I would try to find him a teacher, which I have now done. I hope that this letter has found you well and safe, and that you are enjoying life on the other side of Cordisia. Perhaps one day we shall meet again, and I can properly thank you for all that you have done for us. Until then, N.

With one letter, all seemed to change. With Bronwen gone from the Academy, Willem often thought of leaving. Now he had reason.

As soon as he could manage it, he would head east, yet none would know. It was time to abandon the name and face he had worn for so many moon years.

*****

Jarek proved to be an easy traveling companion and an accomplished rider, having lived among the famed Planusterran horse traders. It was nearly a half-moon into their journey north, and the boy had not once complained.

No tears had been shed, not even when they had departed from the farmhouse. Caryss had seen the way Nicoline's face caught the early morning light, reflecting water there, yet neither mother nor son had cried. The group left much as they had arrived, only with an extra horse and the boy. Each morning before the others rose, Otieno and Jarek would be at the sword. If he practiced his sky calls, Caryss did not know, for the skies had been clear over them.

On the morrow, they would enter Dallian, where Sharron had once called home. Just across the border into Eirrannia, on the eastern half, the town was a small one, Sharron had stated. Yet it was Eirrannia still.

Around her, the trees reached high to the speckled, clouded sky and the air smelled of flower and pine, unlike Tretoria which always had the scent of the sea and unlike the King's City which often smelled of sweat and mud. The babe moved more each day, as if she too knew that they were nearly home.

Home.

Looking about her, Caryss wondered how the people of the North could be so feared and hated throughout the rest of Cordisia. The trees soared and the rivers glimmered, while the still-distant hills remained calm, as if observing those who visited.

Calling out to Sharron, she asked, "Is it always so peaceful here?"

"To a Northerner, yes, it is nearly always so," Sharron told her, riding near. "But make no mistake, there are warriors here, too."

"Will they answer her call, Sharron?"

The two women rode ahead of the rest, although Jarek was near enough to hear. He still could not understand their Eirrannian words, although it would not be long before he could.

With a quick glance to the boy, who was staring ahead, lost in the daze of a day filled with riding, Sharron answered, "If she speaks in truth, they will hear her."

Caryss laughed, saying, "I see the *diauxie* is not the only one with riddles."

Sharron laughed too, for they were all much lighter so near the North. "I have been nearly as long away from here as you and was but a child when I left. Many here are blessed with mage-skill, and most accept those who are so blessed as well. The girl will not be out of place, even with her dark hair and shadowed eyes. But she will have to prove herself as well."

"I forget that you have seen her when I have not."

"It is something I hope to never forget. Her eyes are Eirrannian eyes, even with the shadows."

"What will her heart be, though? Is that not the question we all fear?"

After a silent pause, Sharron replied, "I have no fear of the girl. I would not have followed you if I had. Your fears are the same as any mother's, Caryss."

"Will she break her vows as I have broken mine?"

Again Sharron laughed, and Caryss looked to her, creasing her forehead in annoyance, until the other woman said, "You broke no vows. You acted as any Northern woman would to a man who dared to speak to you as if you were a child. You may think us all calm, but we are descendants of the first Gods. Our tongues are sharp, but our claws are sharper, when needed."

"I have never seen you speak out to anyone, Sharron. Indeed, nearly all comment on how quiet you are."

"But I am home now. And I no longer have to wear a mask."

Much had changed, and, now, even Sharron seemed altered.

With her forehead still wrinkled in thought, Caryss sighed, "I was right to come here."

"I would have let the girl be born nowhere else," Sharron told her, suddenly serious.

Caryss said nothing in reply, but a strange smile curled across her fair face as she looked in the direction of the Northern healer once again.

Both women continued to ride, as serene as the scene around them.

*****

"It has been over a moon, brother, and still you have no answer for me as to where this woman has taken father. Does he even still live?"

Tired of having the same argument with his brother, Crispin groaned, "She is a healer and is oath-bound to give aid. Delwin, I have explained to you her reasons for leaving. You must admit that there is truth in what she said. It makes little sense that he lived yet never improved while under the care of both healer and mage. He was alive, yes, but unfit to rule. Do you know who it was that kept him asleep? I was with him every day, yet still do not the answer."

With reddened cheeks, Delwin barked, "He was ill, Crispin, and little could be done for him. His healers, all Masters might I remind you, merely tried to keep him free from pain. If he slept, it was for the best."

"If he slept, he could not abdicate. And in his death, I would be king. His life was placed on hold, I believe, and with just that intention."

The two brothers were alone, without guard or friend, seated across a small table from one another in a room at the end of Delwin's quarters. Had any other been around, Crispin would have chosen his words more carefully, but little sleep and too much worry had caused him to abandon politeness.

Delwin jumped from the table and leaned in to his brother, spitting on him as he screamed, "You accuse me of poisoning our father? You go too far!"

Of a like size, neither had a physical advantage and when Crispin rose to his feet, the two men stared at one another, angry and ready to strike.

"All in Rexterra know that I am heir," Crispin countered, letting the heat in him rise.

Slamming his fist onto the table, Delwin replied in a near whisper, "And who better to dispose of the King than his heir?"

Continuing in a louder voice, he said, "Only you know where he has gone, and only you know this woman who has taken him! A moon later, and we know nothing. It is time that others know, brother. You must answer for what you have allowed to occur."

"As must you," Crispin spit, pushing his chair away from the table.

As he walked to the door, his brother's parting words followed him.

229

"We will let the King's Court decide, Crispin."

Fleeing from his brother's wing of the palace, Crispin sprinted through the palace hallways, caring little for who saw him. Delwin's words had stung, sharp and painful, especially since, in truth, he had no knowledge as to where Caryss had taken his father. His search in the Southern Cove Islands had proven that she had been there, yet little else. Even those who recalled seeing her did not know where she traveled next.

Further angering him was that the Islander from the Lower Streets had disappeared as well, taking her information regarding his father with her. His guards still searched for her, yet none had found any new information.

Tocca, whom he had sent to the Healer's Academy on the other side of Cordisia, had been ordered to send word once he found Willem. For a half-moon, his letters to his cousin had gone unanswered, causing more concern.

"Damn it all to hells!" he screamed, looking up to find himself near one of the back entrances.

It mattered little to him where the exit led, as long as he was free from the palace and free of his brother. Moon years had led to the confrontation, although it had not been their first, nor would it be their final one, he knew. Never before had Crispin voiced the accusation that it was Delwin who had kept their father ill. With no proof and his brother controlling the Rexterran Army, Crispin had few options.

Before long, he found himself in the Lower Streets, outside of a tavern with a faded sign and a wooden door that was nearly split down the middle. Few would know him there, he guessed, especially with his cheek still scarred. His clothes were well made, but free of ornament or crest, and it was dark enough that none would be able to see his gold-rimmed eyes. Yet, it mattered little to him, and Crispin pushed open the door, surprised when no eyes turned toward him.

Without hesitation, he seated himself on an uneven stool near the end of the bar. Throwing a copper coin on the bar, he waited with downcast eyes for the barkeep to fetch him ale. After the first, he had another, barely minding the sour taste.

By his third ale, he was no longer King's Heir, but still he sat silent as he cupped the large mug with his hands. As he drank, Crispin thought of the healer.

He knew it to be much his own fault that she had taken the King. His words had been harsh, and, he could now admit, intentional. Despite his promises to Delwin, he was uncertain if their father lived. Without the Arvumian guards, he could not implicate the healer without admitting to his own actions with her the night they disappeared.

His plan had come undone.

Setting the nearly empty mug on the long wooden counter, Crispin rubbed at his face, letting his fingers trail across the area where Caryss's dagger had struck. Beside him, a man brushed up against his shoulder, calling out in a heavily accented voice that sounded of years spent at sea, salty and brusque. As the man brought his heavy mug near, the contents spilled over, falling onto Crispin's arm, dampening the sleeves of his tunic where they poked out of his cape.

"Apologies, my good man," the newcomer said, smiling broadly.

In a tone that he had perfected as a young man, Crispin replied, "Nothing to worry about, my friend," pleased that he had not forgotten how to erase the palace from his words.

"Have I ruined your shirt? Allow me to buy your next drink in repayment."

"My shirt is not yet ruined, but after another ale, it might certainly be!" laughed Crispin, half-drunk.

The sailor, for Crispin knew the kind, howled heartily and motioned to the barkeep. Even though he knew that he had had enough, Crispin reached for the offered mug.

"What brings you out tonight?" he asked, lifting the ale to his lips.

After a loud gulp, the man answered, "Last night in the fair the King's City. We sail east on the morrow."

"I've just returned from the Southern Cove Islands," Crispin told him, his words lilting high.

"For hire or for pleasure?"

"For a woman," he answered, finishing half of his ale after the words spilled from his loose lips.

The man nodded, and Crispin could see laughter at the edges of his eyes. "Yet here you are, my good man, with me at your side instead of this woman. An unsuccessful trip, I fear."

With his rimmed eyes looking at the nearly empty mug, Crispin only nodded, unable to argue with the man's words.

Their conversation was interrupted when a thin man in a dirtied tunic and unlaced boots pushed up to the bar, forcing himself between them. Crispin looked away, burying his nose in his elbow and grimacing at the smell that accompanied the man. He finished his ale in a large swallow, wiping at his chin where drink had dribbled. When he pushed his stool from the bar, he looked to his side, to see the filthy man reaching for a sword that hung at his hip. The sword was plain, yet it was clean and constructed of steel.

Crispin called out, "There's no need for weapons. Take my seat as I've had enough ale for tonight."

His words had not been heard, or if they had, were ignored. Faster than he would have suspected, the man, who was smaller than both Crispin and the sailor by far, had his sword in his hand.

Before Crispin could act, the man shouted, "So I am no longer welcome on your ship because of my like for ale, but here you are with a mug in your hand! It was not me who stole the coin, Captain Azzaro! I am no thief, just as I am no drunk!"

As if unbothered, the captain laughed, "You are a thief, and a drunk. Now put that sword away before you become a dead man, Rahn."

The captain did not move from where he stood, even though Crispin noticed that he wore no sword. The man he had called Rahn still did not sheathe his sword, Crispin noticed.

With spittle flying from his mouth, Rahn pleaded, "Let me aboard the ship. I will drink no more. I am a decent seaman, Captain, and I am far from home."

Again, Azzaro showed little emotion as he told the man, "You cost me too much and work too little. I have no need for the likes of you. There are other ships that will hire you, but I will not. Be gone now."

The last word that the captain had spoken was clipped and harsh, yet still the other man had not moved.

In the silence that followed, which was no more than a long breath, Crispin reached for the dagger that was tucked inside of a small scabbard that hung from his belt. When the leather hilt was in his hand, he stepped forward, behind the drunken man.

"Be gone from here, like he said," Crispin warned hotly.

In response, Rahn raised his sword and lunged for Azzaro, who fell to his left, into a trio of bar patrons. They all turned to look at the captain, red-faced and angry as their ales spilled. The largest of the men, blonde-haired and blue-eyed, pushed Azzaro back toward Rahn. The captain was himself a large man, but he had not regained his balance and spun on his heel, exposing his back to Rahn, who, flushed and spitting, swung the sword that still was in his hand.

Crispin watched as the tip of the blade sliced at the captain, causing a streak of red to spread across his back, near his shoulder. Without thinking, Crispin pressed forward, the dagger light in his well-practiced hand. When Crispin grabbed the smaller Rahn, the man turned and faced him, unsteady on his feet. Before Rahn could swing, Crispin stepped into him further and thrust the dagger into the stinking man's stomach, twisting it until his blood-tinged sword dropped to the ground.

When the sword clanged onto the floor, Crispin twisted his dagger free, wiping it on his pants before placing it back into the scabbard, again hidden. As he looked toward Azzaro, he watched as the captain bent

232

toward the sword, grabbing it hurriedly and, with no hesitation, opening Rahn's midsection, from chest to navel, in one forceful strike.

Blood bubbled on the small man's lips as he collapsed to the planked floor.

The captain dropped the sword and nodded toward Crispin. "We should go."

With a nod, the King's Heir pushed past the other bar patrons, fleeing the tavern before Rahn's body had stopped twitching. Behind him, he heard the captain's heavy footfalls following. When they were a fair distance away, at least five blocks Crispin figured, he slowed.

"I owe you a favor, my good man, for surely you saved my life, or at least prevented another scar from adorning my body. The name is Azzaro Logetto, and I own a fleet of ships out of Mezzano. If you are ever in need of a ship or in need of a woman to replace the one you left in the Cove, ask for me. There is not a quarter-moon that goes by that one of my ships is not docked here in the King's City."

The sun was low, but the sky was tinged orange, and Crispin kept his glance low as he told the captain, "Perhaps one day I shall be in need of both. But, for now, I require neither."

"Your name, my good man?"

"Crispin."

"Just as I thought. Now you best be gone from here before the guards have been notified. My thanks, sir. And the offer stands, as it will until you claim it."

The two men parted, and, with a spinning head, Crispin made his way back to the palace, vowing once again to avoid the Lower Streets, walking as hurriedly as his unbalanced body would allow, and hoping to avoid encountering the City Guards. More of his brother's men, he thought, and quickened his pace to a near run.

It was only once he was back at the palace that he realized he had told the captain his name.

*****

After a reunion that had been nearly ten moon years in the making, Sharron listened as her mother talked of some of what she had missed while she had been at the Academy. As her mother described her brother's newly born son, Caryss moved to the door, silently. She half-expected Aldric to follow her from the house, yet when Otieno rose, Caryss hesitated. Across the room, Aldric caught her glance and shook his head, then dropped his eyes back to the etched goblet he held. His warning understood, Caryss said nothing as the door closed behind her.

233

Outside, she walked across a tall-grassed field, continuing until she was near the treeline, looking up into the high midday sun as it peaked out from a cloud-filled sky. Despite her attempts, her mind explored the possibility that she herself had once lived in a stone and thatch house tucked between grass and tree.

Yet she knew that she would never have all of her memories returned, and, from her time at the clinic, she had learned that sometimes injury or tragedy could erase one's thoughts entirely. Not even Conri could change that, and she grabbed the nearest tree as the Tribesman's face crossed through her head.

When she dropped her hand, a voice from behind startled her. Reaching for the dagger that was tied inside her pants, near her right hipbone, Caryss turned.

"You walk as if your boots never touch the ground."

"Look behind me and you will see the grass trampled from the house to here, a path that proves you wrong."

"I have been wrong enough," was her only reply to the *diauxie*, having learned that his words were never as they seemed.

"*Leseda*, you should not travel alone, especially where you have never been."

As they were most times when she spoke to him, Caryss's comments were edged and sharpened with annoyance. "I am of the North. This is not the King's City or the Cove. I know well the land here."

"Then take me to your home," he called to her, as if in song.

His words, spoken with the wind, soft and delicate, cut her more deeply than had he screamed them in her face, and Caryss growled, "Each day I wonder why I was inclined to find you."

"Because there are no others like me," he laughed, the sound twinkling with mockery.

The scowl that covered her face was answer enough, but still, she said, "Men whose words are like water, slippery and never still? Men who make coin in swordplay? Men who have no family or home? There are many like you, Otieno."

With a twitch of his hair as he threw the braids over his shoulder, he told her, "There are many men like the ones you describe, but tell me, Caryss, have those men battled the skies? Have those men swung steel through lightning and danced in beat with thunder?"

Ignoring his taunt, she asked, "What trick was it that you played to make it look as if your sword shattered that bolt the night at Jarek's house?"

"Trick? What makes you think so? Nicoline would have known had it been so."

"So I am to believe that your steel was able to break a streak of lightning into pieces? You forget yourself, Otieno, and forget that I have been healer-trained for half my life. While at the clinic, I treated many who have been lightning-struck. Few survived. And none did what you would have me believe."

"It matters little to me what you believe," he sighed. "I will teach your daughter, and Jarek as well, how to put blade to anything. And win."

He stood only a step from her, beneath a towering pine. She quieted as he mentioned the girl, as he must have known she would.

Still he lectured.

"You seek me out. You make me swear an oath to you and to the girl. You expect me to teach her as soon as she can hold a sword. Yet you do not trust me. Or even like me much. Let's talk in truths, Caryss. It is past time."

She could make no argument, so again she stayed silent.

"I am not he, Caryss. If you looked, you would see that."

Her words spilled from her lips like an avalanche, furious and icy.

"You are dark-skinned, where he was pale. You are broad where he was thin. Your eyes are soft where his are like steel. You think I do not know the difference between men? Your hands have scars and callouses and his are as smooth as Lamb's Ear. His eyes turn from purple to black, while yours are a steady shade of dampened sand. Your body is power and force, where he is sleek and fast. The swords you swing mean little to him, yet he could ring you in fire and watch you burn. When he talks, the trees still and the mountains listen. You have the wind on your words, and few can hear your true voice."

"You are nothing like Conri," she hissed, eyes flashing.

"When you look at me, *leseda*, do you see blood on my hands?"

Nearly out of breath from her outburst, she whispered, "Of course not."

"Look again," he instructed.

This time, when she looked, his hands were spread out before her, as if in offering. Thick and scarred, mottled in hue, but empty. Her forest-tinged eyes, much greener now beneath the canopy of pine and birch, fluttered.

Again, she looked. And, there, in the high grass, lush and long, she saw drops of red fall from his hands onto the green stalks, splattering upon the blades until the grass at his feet was sprinkled with blood, crimson and wet. When she looked back up to the hands of the *diauxie*, Caryss gasped. Instead of brown, they were red. Dark and damp with blood.

The blood was not his own, she knew.

"What have you done?" she cried.

235

If her feet would have moved, Caryss would have ran from him, but it was as if she was sleeping and the image of Otieno with bloodied hands no more than a dream. The Northern air was cool across her face, and she could smell the swaying pines. On her tongue, she could nearly taste the blood until she sputtered and gagged. Only then was Caryss able to move, bending in half until the midday meal that Sharron's mother had prepared for them came spilling from her trembling lips. When the heaving ceased, she stood back up, again looking to the man's hands, as if her eyes had deceived her.

They had not.

With words soft and enchanting, he addressed her.

"Only once before have I met a man who could see the blood, *leseda*. Many moon years ago, I left the Cove and traveled to a land far to our south. Lamarria, the land of sand and sun her people promise. The Lamarrians are nomadic, much like I myself have been, I suppose, although they have done it for so long that none know any differently. Among their people exists a shaman, part healer, like you, but more too. Healer, mage, leader. The Great Mother's balance to those like me. They were all of these things and well respected too. A man named Akinto, upon meeting me, asked why my hands dripped with blood. Even though he was shaman, he was unusual, often silent and alone, and his people looked at him with suspicion when his words were uttered. For no one else could see what he could, and, to them, my hands were similar to their own and clean."

"What did you tell him?" she whispered, her throat burning.

"I told him the truth."

She could take no more of his games. Wiping at her mouth, she brushed the hair from her face and pulled it into a healer's knot at her neck.

"Two masters at word play," she told him. "Both you and the shaman. I have much to do, Otieno, and no time to be your student. I have played that role half my life with teachers much finer than you. Find another to amuse you."

His smile was like fire, and her cheeks reddened and burned as he looked upon her.

"You will hear the truth, just as he did. Belief is your choice."

And then he began. With each word that he spoke, the blood faded from his hands, and, when he had reached the conclusion, his hands were dry and clear, as if they had never been red at all.

"What is one death when you have caused so many others, *diauxie*?" she asked when he had finished, surprised at how little her voice shook.

Sighing, he said, "Much like the first, the last death upon one's sword is difficult to flee from. The child should not have died, and I should

236

never have killed her. Even the Great Mother has told me so. Rarely does the Great Mother turn away from a devotion, yet when I sought to give her the blood of the child, as I had done with each death before, she would not have it. The ground stayed dry and dusty, and the blood would not wash from my hands. For days, I tried to sing her song, and for days, she would not listen. Until I was weak with hunger and nearly dead from thirst."

Caryss listened to him as she had never before.

"Then, the Great Mother appeared. And she told me that from that day on, I would no longer have a home on the Cove. She further warned me that if I caused another death, she would turn from me forever. You know little of our ways, Caryss, but without the blessing of the Great Mother, I would be but a man. A very old man, with no skill or knowledge."

"And you have abided her wishes?"

"Yes, even when my own life was at risk," he uttered.

"Yet still your hands are red?"

"Not always, but often enough to remind me of my vow."

After a moment, she asked, "After you told him the story, what did the shaman tell you?"

"That my hands would dry when I evened the scale."

Seeing her confusion, he added, "I once thought that he meant that I would need to save a child from death to do so, but I have saved more than I can count, more than I can recall to be truthful, yet, nothing has changed."

Finally, Caryss understood who he was, and why he had come so easily to Cordisia.

"My daughter will balance the scale for you."

"I believe she will."

"And then?"

Running his now brown hand through his thick braids, he replied, "I will fight at her side as I have longed to do for many moon years. I will give the Great Mother blood and dirt, and mayhap she will hear me once again."

"Will you leave her once the debt is paid?" she asked, her words tight.

"*Leseda*, I will not leave her unless she forces me to do so. If she washes the blood from my hands, it is because the Great Mother has willed it to be so. I will walk beside her always."

With her eyes on his, Caryss said, "You grow hungry for blood, yet your vows prevent you from acting."

She could see him battle the smile that edged his face and knew she spoke truly. When he answered, she also knew that between them had come an understanding.

"I am a killer, *leseda*. It is who I have been and who I will be once again. Shackled by these blood-stains, but a killer still. The Great Mother shapes us all, and I am no different. I have learned to be elsewise for many moon years now, but my hands ache for battle, and my swords scream for a fight. As punishment, she took from me what I most desired."

"I would not have my daughter be a killer, Otieno," she gasped.

As if in thought, he did not answer right away.

Finally, he breathed, "Her path is not as mine, nor would I let it become so."

"So you will serve my daughter because it is what your Great Mother wants. What if, like many gods, she becomes fickle and changes her mind?"

"You do not know her, Caryss. But, should such occur, I would still serve the girl. I am oath-bound to you and the girl and will not be named oath-breaker."

Caryss did not look away from him as she called, "If you harm the girl, I will kill you. I have no skill with sword or dagger, but there are other ways to die."

"True words, my lady, but false ones from your lips. You will not break your Healer's Oath, and you will not need to. There is much darkness in the world, Caryss, and much in me and in the dark mage. And in the girl's father as well. Stay in the light and out of the shadows, or the girl will follow. If you do not light her path, none else will. And she will lose her way."

The peace that coming home had offered vanished then, fractured and splintered like Jarek's lightning against the cut of Otieno's blade.

On the morrow, they would seek the *fennidi*. And hope to find a cleaner answer.

*****

Long after the sun had set, Jarek remained outside, sword in hand as he tried to grow accustomed to steel instead of wood. Before the others woke and after they slept, he practiced, with the Islander at his side, sleeping little.

Caryss had made him a balm to rub on his aching muscles, yet he had tried to abstain from using it, until one night when his shoulders ached with fatigue and his fingers burned with blisters. When he thought no one watched, he had rubbed his body with the minty ointment, letting the sweet and spicy smell coax him to sleep. The pain had been dulled, until the next morning when once again he picked up the sword, an average sized blade with an unremarkable hilt and an even plainer scabbard.

Days before they had stopped for a night at the home of the other healer's mother, but with the rising sun, they had departed, although none would tell him their destination. Jarek soon grew used to the silence that accompanied their riding.

When the mage came upon him, Jarek nearly fell from the saddle in surprise, even though he was the finest rider among them.

In Planusian, which surprised Jarek more than the words that were said, the dark mage asked, "What do you think of the North?"

The way he rolled his words made it seem as if he was Planusian by birth, yet he did not have the look of one about him.

"Are you a *getano*?" Jarek queried.

When Aldric made no move to acknowledge his question, he explained, "It means a fellow man. "

"I have never heard it used. Your Common is fine, but you will need it to be without fault."

"My mother insisted I learn, until I spoke it as well as any."

"And your schooling?"

"I can read and write, sir."

Smirking, Aldric answered, "No doubt. But what of the histories of Cordisia and beyond? There is much more to know than letters and numbers. What do you know of Rexterra?"

After the mage's teasing, Aldric told him, "The day that I first saw Caryss, at the palace, you were there as well. If you have been with her long, then I need not tell you that I know Rexterra well."

"You have much to learn now that you have passed the gates of the farm and come from behind your mother's skirts," the mage laughed.

"Behind my mother's skirts, I learned to control the skies," Jarek answered, keeping his words even.

"What do you make of your grandfather?" Aldric asked, unbothered by Jarek's retort.

"Does he do anything but sleep?"

Again the mage smiled. "Not really. But you would do well to understand why he is the way he is."

"Why he sleeps so much? He is old."

"It is not age that makes him sleep. Caryss believes he was being poisoned while in the King's City. Do you understand what that means?"

"He is sick, yes, I understand that. And my mother has long warned me of the dangers of the King's City."

"Jarek," the mage interrupted, "The king was poisoned. Think about that. Your grandfather is followed by mage, master, and guard nearly everywhere, yet someone tried to kill him. How do you think a child would fare in such a place, with no way to know who was friend or foe?"

"If you speak of me, sir, you would do well to realize that I have stayed away from Rexterra for just that reason. And I am no child."

"You are learning," Aldric told him. "It is time for our lessons to advance."

It was not until they had been a half-day's ride from the farmstead that he learned of the King, his grandfather. Caryss had apologized for the deceit, and the mage had explained it twice over to him. On a few occasions, he had spoken with his grandfather, but their travels left him weak and sleepy, and he spent most of his time in his covered wagon. The first time he met the King, Herrin had been alert enough to offer him a blessing of sort, although he stopped short of offering an apology.

Jarek trained while the King slept, yet hoped to show his grandfather his skills soon, and he admitted as much to Aldric.

"I never asked you what he said to you that first time in his cart."

The two rode alongside one another, which happened often when the mage wanted to instruct him.

"He told me that I looked nothing like my father and little more."

"Old men, especially sick ones, rarely guard their tongues, Jarek. Had he been well then he would have seen the rings of gold in your eyes. Nonetheless, there is much to learn from him. Herrin has long ruled Cordisia."

"When will he improve?" Jarek asked.

After a moment, Aldric told him, "He was awake more when we were in the Cove and he did not have to travel much. Perhaps when we are settled in the North, the King will once again find renewed strength."

"Will he accept me, Aldric? Will he name me prince?"

He had waited long to ask those questions, and Jarek's voice finally showed signs of distress as his words cracked and croaked.

"Mayhap," the mage sighed, "But you would have to return with him and leave the North."

So I must continue to wait, he thought, staring into the treeline that edged the path.

*****

"Perhaps you should avoid him for now," she suggested, trying to keep her voice steady and calm.

"There is nowhere that I could go, here or anywhere in the North, that he would not be able to find me."

His words were spoken slowly, as they often were, and Nahla made no reply when he had finished, as they both already knew he had spoken truly. Instead, she waited, seated in a long chair beside a small hearth burning with a small fire. Heavy curtains draped the windows, keeping the room warm. For over a moon she had stayed with Conall in the large manse that he shared with his brother. Other Tribesmen came and went at intervals, and she never knew how many called the large building home.

Thinking of the girl again, she asked, "There is no hint as to where she might have gone?"

"After the Cove? No. Are you certain that she made no mention to you of her plans?"

"Caryss wanted to find the *diauxie*," she told Conall, "And she had intentions on healing the King. She has both men with her now and is smart enough to realize that there will be many looking for her. If I were her, I would seek a place beyond the reach of my enemy's hands."

"You think she will stay gone from Cordisia?"

Shaking her head, Nahla answered, "There are reasons for her to stay. There are times, now that I am with child, that I want nothing more than to see my homeland again, to have sand beneath my feet and sun over my head, to have the sound of waves sing to the babe, and to birth this child under the gaze of the Great Mother. Caryss might not be so different."

Conall walked near to her, and for a moment, Nahla stiffened with uneasiness, but when he smiled, she relaxed, although realization came two-fold; she still feared the man, and she had told him where to find Caryss.

"The healer is here, in the North."

Silence followed his words, but the guilt was too strong, and, finally, Nahla said, "Can you not let her be until the babe is born?"

When he laughed, it was as if the trees were cracking apart around her, struck down by wind or sky. The sound filled the room, and she nervously looked around to make certain that no one else had entered the room, especially his brother.

"He will hear you," she whispered.

"Oh he probably already has. Nahla, you do not understand my role here. Or Conri's. He is not just brother to me; he is king, if you will. Yet, there is one who stands above even kings. Not all of Conri's choices are his own, which is why he has avoided calling attention to Caryss. He could have found her with ease if he had drawn on some power."

"There is much that I would rather not know, yet what I want matters little now that I am with child. My son will be of the Tribe; there is nothing that will make me forget that."

His laughter stopped, and, no longer amused, Conall told her, "Then you would do well to learn your place. Do not anger him, Nahla. While you have not seen the wolf in him that does not mean that it is not there. Conri makes the rules here, and the rest of us follow them. Do you understand?"

She glanced up at him as she said, "I understand. But do not forget that my gods are not yours, and it was not yours that brought me here."

Her eyes were dark and her cheeks flushed, and Nahla showed no fear as she looked upon him.

"What power does your Great Mother have here? My father serves no woman."

It was her turn to laugh, and the sound was musical, as if the seabirds of her homeland called out to him in mockery, "I know little of the Tribe, as you have said. Yet no man is motherless, nor any god. You will learn, Conall, as all men do."

His eyes darkened as he demanded, "Learn what?"

Nahla rose from where she had been seated and said, "From a woman, all men were born. And to a woman, all men must return. So it has been and so it always will be. In life and in death."

The Tribesman watched as she turned and walked from the room, tall and graceful, fearless and bold, as if she was not whore but goddess.

*****

"You have had enough time. On the morrow, two companies of my men head north. The girl will be taken alive if she releases father without conflict. However, if she or those with her choose to stand against my men, I cannot assure her safety."

After nearly an hour of trying to convince his brother of his folly, Crispin had given up, recognizing that there was little else he could do to aid Caryss. He wasn't certain how Delwin had managed to track her to the north when his own men had not been able to do so. But, he figured, Eirrannia was the most likely place that she would take the King, and the one place that would offer shelter from his brother's men. Now, he could only hope that the girl would do nothing rash, yet as the thought came to him, Crispin scratched at the scab beneath his eye. Caryss was healer-trained, but she was not without weapons, as he well knew.

"Delwin, we both want the same thing and that is for father to be returned to us in full health. Better than he left here for certain. The healer has no army with her, and you would do well to inform your men as much. She has oaths, ones that I believe she feels that she is abiding."

His brother snorted, the sound echoing through the small chamber that he used as his office. "It seems healing is not the only thing that is taught at the Academy these days, brother."

Ignoring the taunt, Crispin replied, "Will you be traveling with the men?"

"I do not think that nearly a hundred men will need me along to capture one girl, if what you have said is true. There is much to do around her, especially with father gone. You are not king yet, Crispin."

"How could I forget when you remind me so often?"

There would be no peace between Delwin and he, Crispin knew, and, before he could say the words that hung dangerously close to the edge of his tongue, he turned and walked from the room. If he did not mistrust his brother so strongly, he would have himself traveled with the Rexterran Guard. Yet, he would not leave the King's City to his brother's watch.

As he neared his own rooms, Crispin thought of his cousin, who had not yet found Caryss either. Hurriedly, he sat at his desk and composed a hastily written letter informing Willem that his brother's men believed the girl to be in Eirrannia. In a nearly begging plea, he asked Willem to abandon the Academy once again and head north, as he was one of the few that could convince Caryss to release the King. He hoped this missive would reach Willem, as he still had not heard from him.

Sealing the letter with crimson wax, the King's Heir shook his head, wishing he had never met the woman, even if she could heal his father. Too much had changed since her brief visit to the King's City, and none of it boded well. If the King did not return soon, even more would change. And Rexterra would never again be the same.

He left the palace and found his fastest rider, instructing him to travel to the Academy with great haste and great discretion, although Willem's exile now seemed a minor concern. If Willem could return with the King, Delwin would be forced to allow their cousin to remain in the King's City, and Crispin's greatest ally would be at his side once again, and at a time when he needed him most. Within a moon, Crispin hoped, all would be as it had been before the strange Northern woman had crossed his path near the piers. There was too much to be done for him to linger long, so Crispin returned to the palace as the rider hurried off, a gray cloak trailing behind him as his large mount galloped through the tall, iron gates that rimmed the outer boundaries of the palace.

*****

21

"Caryss, we cannot keep riding with little purpose. The king worsens, yet you pay him little mind. What is it that you seek to find in these woods?"

It was Aldric who had expressed his despair, yet Caryss had little doubt that the others felt the same. Sharron had not been wrong about how difficult it would be to find the *fennidi*, and they had searched for the elusive clan through the foothills of the Faelan Mountains for the last two days. Even Caryss was tiring of sleeping under the skies.

"Besides the *fennidi*, you mean? And a possible cure for what ails the King?" she asked, unable to hide the frustration from her words.

"Is it not clear that they do not want to be found?"

Sighing, she answered, "It is becoming clear, yes. I had hoped that it would be as easy to find them as it was to find Crispin."

"That was a stroke of luck. However, the *fennidi* live off the land, and have for centuries, changing little from the way their kin and their kin before them lived. They will not appear unless they have reason to. Do not force it if it is not the way," the mage advised.

Sharron must have told him more about the *fennidi*, Caryss realized. She had believed it would be simpler to find them and ask for their aid, yet she was near to concluding that goal was unreachable.

"Perhaps I have gotten too comfortable of late. We escaped the Grand Palace with ease, and made it to the Cove safely. Once there, we found Otieno, and, with the girl's help, convinced him to travel here with us, which now seems so foolish. Why would he agree to leave his homeland for a babe who is not yet born? And, Jarek too. He is with us, having left his mother and his home. For what? Aldric, there were times when I was at the Academy when I felt as if hands other than my own were guiding me. When we left, I felt as if I had reclaimed my life. Yet, when I think on all that has come to pass, I wonder."

The two rode side by side, and the sky was quickly becoming striped with orange as the sun sunk low behind the eastern edge of the Faelans. Caryss's hair glowed like polished copper, while Aldric's nearly black hair only seemed to darken. He was as thin as he had been when she first met him, while her belly now grew round with the babe and her face fuller, as were her breasts. The riding suit she wore clung tightly to her, and she briefly longed for the comfort of her healer's robe.

"Caryss," Aldric interjected, "As much as you would like to forget the babe's father, you cannot escape that your daughter has blood of the gods in her. Even though you have not seen him of late, do not make the mistake to think that Conri has forgotten you or the girl."

"You think he knows where I am?" she asked, tightening her grip on the reins until her hands whitened.

"I think he knows much, more than you suspect."

Pulling her horse from the trail, Caryss declared, "He will not come to me."

Jumping down, she called, "We can make camp here, but in the morning we head west. I know how to find the *fennidi*."

After several quiet moments, the others began to unpack, leading the horses away from the treeline and toward a knoll near the stream. Sharron tended to the King, who never fared well in travel. Jarek had sword in hand and was practicing alone. As Caryss moved away from the center of camp, she noticed Otieno and Aldric gathering wood. She said nothing to either as she walked on.

*****

22

It was a quarter-moon before Willem arrived at Concordia Lake, in central Cordisia, a two-day ride from the Planusian border. He was one of only a few who knew where Nicoline had taken the boy, and, as he rode, he wondered what she would make of his arrival, more so since he had sent no word of his plans.

His decision to leave had been a hasty one, yet Master Rova had not tried to change his mind. The two had even discussed Bronwen, and it seemed as if the old Master knew more than he had shared, although Rova believed her to still be in the King's City. Willem offered nothing to convince him otherwise.

In two days time he would meet the boy, the true firstborn of Crispin. In two days time, he would be Rexterran once more, even one in a different land. The thought sent a shiver across his body, and when it ceased, Willem again thought of Bronwen.

"What have you done?" he whispered, knowing there was none to hear his words.

*****

They had been following the Domahaacron River through the Faelan Mountains, and, as it was late summer, the trip was not a difficult one. The cart got stuck at least once per day, which would require the group to stop until Otieno freed it. The river flowed from the northwest corner of Eirrannia to the center, connecting the Sea of Mist with the Falk River, which then flowed into Concordia Lake. To reach the Tribelands, they would have to cross the Domahaacron, but they had not yet come upon a bridge. Even Sharron had never been as far west as they were now, so none knew if such a bridge even existed.

There was no land so beautiful, Caryss thought, staring at the high-grassed fields that flowered yellow and white.

It was in a field like this that my parents died.

The thought had come upon her quickly and she lifted a quivering hand to her lips. Overhead, the sky was clear, blue and serene, as it had been for much of their travel since finding Jarek. She turned in her saddle to look back to the others, the falling sun large and round, and so bright that her hand moved from mouth to eyes.

When she looked again, a shadow crossed, darkening the glowing orb with a streak of black. Caryss pulled at the reins, forcing her horse to stop.

As she watched, the shadow grew larger, until her vision was black and blurred from staring so near the sun. For a moment she looked away to clear the pulsing dots from her eyes, and, when she looked back, the shadow was gone. A hunting bird, she thought, remembering how near to the coast they now were. In Tretoria, the birds were gulls, smaller and greater in number as opposed to the silver-topped hawks found in Eirrannia.

Before she released her hold on the bridle, Caryss searched for Otieno, who rode just behind her, and then watched as Aldric jumped from his mount. She opened her mouth to question him, but a sudden noise silenced her as Otieno joined the mage on the ground, sword in hand. She had not seen him draw the blade, and her horse danced beneath her, tapping its feet and pulling at its bit, forcing her to pull tighter on the reins.

Finally, she, too, leaped from her horse, and, when Otieno noticed, he called out, "Caryss! Behind me. Now!"

His words were harsh and his voice was unlike anything she had heard from him, leaving her little option but to listen. She hurriedly tied her horse off to the nearest tree then rushed toward him, her vision still half-mired in darkness.

"Jarek, to my right!" she heard Otieno call. "Draw your sword!"

Aldric was positioned in front of the others, hands at his side, palms outward. In one of them, a red orb, small and flickering, burned.

Just as she was about to ask what was happening, a shriek interrupted her. A long, high-pitched cackle rang from the sky, echoing through the shallow valley until her arms prickled and her words vanished.

Again, the sound came, closer, until her ears echoed with the ringing cries.

Somehow, Caryss suddenly understood and reached for the dagger in her pouch. Still her head ached with the shrill cawing. Yet her hands steadied, despite her thumping life pulse.

From the sky came a bird, pale and silvery except for its head, which glistened black, a black so sleek and shining that it reflected the grass and sky, as if earth and air traveled with it. Its size was impressive, too large to be a hawk or even a falcon.

Crow, she thought, although she had expected it to be all black.

Before she could warn the others, Otieno moved, braids flying behind him, his longsword in hand. As the *diauxie* rushed forward, the ground beneath him shuddered, causing Caryss to sway. When she had regained her balance, she looked up to see the nearly translucent feathers, as if they had been dipped in moonlight, angling toward Otieno's side.

The bird was no longer bird.

Now, he was a man, pale-skinned with dark, midnight-stained hair, eyes black and hungry.

"No!" she screamed, looking toward Jarek, whose arm shook where he held the shortsword.

When she screamed, the birdman veered, just enough for her to lunge toward Jarek, pushing the boy behind her. Her dagger crackled in the sunlight, the dark blade as gleaming as a gem, dazzling and deadly.

Above them, the sun dimmed, and Caryss noticed two more crows flying at them. The first was near enough to see his face, bird-like once again. But his gaze was more.

Another black-headed bird dove, screeching, mouth open and unexpectedly teethed. Just as the bird dropped, it turned back to man and wings became pale arms. In one of them was a silver-tipped sword, as long and thin as the man himself. His legs were covered in black suede, as any man might wear, feathers no longer visible. His face surprised her most.

He looked nothing like Conri. Had he, Caryss might have hesitated, faltered. Instead, she slashed.

Before the Crow could swing, Otieno turned his head to where she now stood, steps away, but the Crow had been quicker than he, and her scream had drawn his attention.

The small dagger, its blade no longer than the Crow's hand, caught him across his whitened neck. Without thought, Caryss sliced, as if she held a healer's lancet. From right to left, she dragged the blade's tip, opening the Crow's neck in an even, straight line.

As he fell onto her, blood poured from his throat, red and smooth. The impact knocked Caryss to the ground, and she gasped as her back slammed against the soft grass. The man was heavy on top of her, his face pressed against her chest. He did not move.

Struggling to push the bloody body from her, Caryss choked and heaved. Feeling as if she could not breathe, she began gagging. Otieno rushed to her, kicking at the crimson-soaked Crow until the body rolled onto the ground, trailing blood. Her hands were sticky and wet as the *diauxie* reached for her, pulling her up.

He said nothing, yet his face was flushed and his eyes angry. He turned from her, in time to see the other two Crows descending.

From chest to navel, she was saturated with the Crow's blood, until she felt as if she was drowning. The smell, too, was enough to make her gag again, even though she was well accustomed to death. Healer half her life had not prepared her for what it was like to kill, and Caryss bent in half and heaved, unaware of what was happening around her as her eyes closed and her stomach churned. Vomit mixed with blood and mud, and Caryss shook with repulsion.

As she wiped her mouth on her untainted shoulder, her life pulse raced beneath her stained tunic. She wanted nothing more than to tear the shirt free, for nearly all of it was now covered in blood and filth. Yet, steps from her, the battle continued. When she next looked up, toward Aldric, she noticed how his flame had grown to cover his whole hand. Otieno had his eyes to the sky and his hand tightly held his Greatsword, the one he rarely used. She had not seen him unsheathe it, yet he stood readied, his legs thick and low.

What came next happened so quickly that Caryss had little time to react. From the sky came a screech so shrill that she thought all of Eirrannia could hear it as a silver-feathered, gray-headed bird plunged from the sky. Just as the feathers began to fade, Aldric threw the fiery orb into the air, interrupting the flight and striking the Crow heavy in the chest. Where the orb hit, fire exploded, turning the mass of feathers into screaming flames, orange and yellow, rivaling the sunset. The air was hot and smelled of singed flesh and feather. But Caryss had no time to cry out, for the last Crow was nearly upon Otieno.

She needn't have worried. The crow never made it. Before it could reach the ground, Otieno leaped up from his stance, swinging the sword as he growled, a noise that seemed to come from earth and soil instead of from man.

Caryss watched, wide-eyed and stunned, as the Greatsword struck between the man's legs, for he had at some point shape-changed. But Otieno did not stop. With bulging muscles straining at his already tight tunic, he heaved upward. As the Crow came upon him, Otieno swung, splitting the man in two. From groin to neck he was sliced, until his body crashed to the grass. The sharp, long blade had slit the man into two halves, although his head, darker than the others, was still attached to both pieces.

From his lower half seeped organ, bile, and shit, and Caryss's knees collapsed beneath her, until she kneeled where she had fallen, sitting back on her heels with her hand over eyes. When she tried to scream, no sound came nor breath either. His sword, the Greatsword with the mysterious history, was like none other, she now knew.

They were dead, all three Crows bloody and torn asunder, lying in stinking piles in an arc around her. When Caryss felt a hand on her shoulder, she did not rise or cry out.

Letting her chin fall to her chest, she whispered groggily, "Will there be more?"

"Not yet," Aldric told her, coming close and wrapping an arm around her.

As he helped her rise, he explained, "They were few, a scouting party I would guess. But there will be others when those three do not return. We must go. Can you walk?"

She nodded, looking about and searching for the others. Jarek, she realized with joy, was untouched and blood-free, sheathing his sword.

Sharron leaped from the back of the cart, pale, yet fine, and rushed toward her. Otieno was dragging the bodies into a heap, for what purpose Caryss did not know.

Into the silence, she asked Aldric, "How are two dead when no *atraglacia* touched them?"

"Mage-fire has been known to kill low-ranking Tribe, especially Crows. I know less of how Otieno killed the third. His sword is not one that I have seen elsewhere. Yet, dead is dead."

When she said nothing, he reached for her, putting his hand, still warm and faintly throbbing, on her own. "It is no small thing to take a life, Caryss. We should discuss it."

"I cannot go back to the Academy," was her only reply, her vows heavy and loud as they rang through her head.

"There are other paths to walk," he told her.

"I will never be Master Healer without returning."

"Perhaps. But you are *Rexaria* still."

"I was healer first. *Rexaria*, mother of the wolf, king-thief. All names that I was given. Healer, I earned."

Her words were quietly spoken, hushed and broken, as if she could not bear to hear them. Aldric's hand held tighter to her own, and into her ear, he whispered, "You saved the boy. *Rexaria* you have now earned."

Even though the others were distracted, she understood why his words were private, why they had not been shared aloud. The boy was Crispin's firstborn, and, by birthright, should have been named heir. If the story she heard was true, it was Herrin who would not allow such to be done. But, in truth, Jarek could be king. To speak such would be considered treason, and few would support his claim. However, he might only need a few, depending on who those few were.

With a nod, she walked away, toward the cart and Sharron, tearing the blood-soaked tunic and jacket from her still-shaking body. Halfway there, she was nearly naked, standing in blood-splattered pants and little else.

"Take this," Sharron called as she neared, holding out a clean tunic, dyed a faded yellow.

As she dressed, the other healer quizzed her on her injuries.

"He did not touch me," Caryss mumbled, walking in a daze until she came upon the King.

Herrin was awake when she climbed into the cart, although his eyes were yellow-tinged and his skin covered in rash.

"Sharron informed me of what occurred," croaked.

"You were well protected, and we are no worse for it," she explained, searching for linens to clean the blood from her face and hands.

"What of the boy?" he asked, trying to sit up.

His skin was pocked and orange, and she knew that more damage had been done from the poison than she had guessed. It had been slowly killing him, yet, without it, his body had further declined. It was nothing that she had ever witnessed, and, again, she hoped the *fennidi* could offer aid.

Wiping at her face, Caryss told him, "Jarek is well. A bit scared, but we all were, I would daresay."

"I should have never sent him away," Herrin murmured.

Caryss nearly cried aloud at his words, for he had done more than simply send Jarek from Rexterra. Yet, she stayed silent, realizing that the King was beginning to see the boy as kin.

"We must be gone from here at once, Herrin," she informed him, scrubbing hard at her neck until the bleached linen reddened.

"Caryss," he whispered, "This is only the first of many battles. You must seek shelter. We are targets on the open road."

He was not wrong, she knew, which only caused her to want to find the *fennidi* more. As she climbed out of the wagon, Otieno came upon her. He, too, was stained and stroked with blood.

"You are no fighter, *leseda*," the Islander fumed, so close to her that she could feel his warm breath across her forehead. "A blood-blade does not make it so. When next I tell you to stand aside, you will listen or you will learn to listen."

Aldric, standing steps behind them, looked away. She would have argued, but even the mage seemed to agree with Otieno, so she said nothing, brushing past him toward Jarek.

He was pale, his blue eyes wide and wild. Rushing to him, she asked, "Are you hurt, Jarek?"

"I wanted to call the storm, but you were too near," he stammered, as if in apology.

She hugged him quickly. "You did just as you should have. Now find your mount. We must leave at once."

Over her shoulder, Caryss could see her horse still tied to a swaying pine, and, on her way to own gelding, she called out, "What of the bodies?"

Aldric and Otieno glanced to one another before Aldric answered, "Get the horses from here and I will see to them."

Within minutes, they departed, all except for Aldric. She turned once to see a flame growing in his hand and did not need to ask what he planned.

*****

Throughout the night, Caryss noticed the group's fears, jumping and turning in the saddle at each sound. Jarek had even tried riding with his sword across his lap, but Otieno quickly made the boy harness it. With

251

Jarek's help, the skies cleared and between the nearly full moon and the stars, their path was bright enough to travel. Aldric rode in the front, with two small orb-lights flanking his horse allowing some additional light. The air had cooled, but Caryss was flush and warm, her cheeks red and her hands moist. They had crossed the river hours before, finding a shallow area where the horses could cross with ease. Otieno had tied Herrin to his horse, and then led the large gelding, wading in water that reached his shoulders. The covered cart had to be abandoned, so the King rode with the *diauxie* until another wagon could be secured.

Once they were on the eastern side of the river, the Tribelands were no more than half a day's ride, which Aldric insisted upon telling Caryss often. She knew that much had changed, yet the *fennidi* were still close. Too close to give up on, but she now dared not put the others at risk.

"I know how to find them, but it will wait until after we have reached safety," she announced, knowing that it was no lie.

"You are certain?" Aldric pressed.

"Yes," she swiftly answered. "Yet I know we must seek safety first."

"There is only one who can offer us shelter, Caryss. Is that what you intend?" Aldric timidly asked, as if he did not believe her words.

"We have little choice. Can you keep us shielded when we near?"

The mage paused. "All of you? Not even I can do so much."

Again, calmly, as if her mind was made up, she said, "With Otieno's aid, I'm certain that you both will be able to keep us well hidden. Just get us to the forest's edge, and I will do the rest."

*****

Once per moon, in an area of the Lower Streets of the King's City where few traveled, the Lightkeepers met. Their numbers had dwindled over the ages and many of the men were graying, their bodies thin and their faces lined. Yet, still they came each moon, even though their services were rarely needed of late.

When the men were younger, they would often be gone for moons patrolling the northern boundaries of Ageria, near the border with Eirrannia, and nearest to the Tribelands that any non-Northerner could get. But those days had long past. Now, when the group met, they would trade stories with one another, telling tales of their past glories.

As the sound of the Lighthouse Bell began to ring, the men took to their seats, and, by the eighth bell, they quieted. Lexor, a man who had become Lightkeeper when he was only twelve, stood at the front of the dusty room, bright sunlight shining on each side of him as it seeped through the low windows. He appeared to shine, but all knew that it was only trick, and no real magic was at work.

Clearing his throat, he addressed the gathered group, "May the Light be with you all on this great morning."

His greeting was met with a chorus of responses, "May the Light be with you as well."

With a nod, he continued, "We are lucky to have with us today one of our brothers who has just returned from Ageria. He even spent some time in Eirrannia, where all know that Lightkeepers are usually not welcomed. He has just arrived, and I have had but a moment to speak with him, so I wait, just as you all do, his words. Let me introduce Timmon Sagana, who many of you might not know."

A small man came forward, in dirtied linens and sandals that were held together with straps of cotton. Another chant followed him and faint applause as he neared the front of the room. His face was younger than the others, yet it was lined all the same, dirt coloring his wrinkles dark. On the edges of his head, just above his ears, and around the back, sections of hair grew, white and wiry. It was clear that he had spent hard days on the road, and, as he hobbled, acrid air followed him.

When he spoke, his voice was strained, deep and raspy, "My brothers, it is with great haste that I came here today, having departed from Eirrannia nearly two quarter-moons past. One night I spent in Ageria with kin, and then I rode directly to the King's City. You might wonder what could cause such haste to make me hurry here so. What I shall answer will surprise all."

The room had gone quiet and only the hoarse voice of the newly returned Lightkeeper could be heard. All eyes watched him, and, while they were wrinkled and weary, they were sharp, clear, and attentive.

As they leaned toward him, Timmon continued, "It seems something has changed with the Dark Ones. The Bears, as usual, are silent, but the Crows are stirring, and the Wolves have gathered. While I was in Eirrannia, which was no small feat, I heard talk of old conflicts arising between the two. Brothers, in time, there will be war."

Silence followed.

And, then, noise erupted as questions were shouted at him from all corners of the room.

"War, did you say?" someone screamed.

"What has been the catalyst?" another asked.

Lexor, who still stood nearest the man, had a gaping mouth, and, finally, when he had regained himself, called, "Silence, brothers! This man has gone without food and sleep for days to reach us. Let us call an intermission while he recovers. On the eve, at eight bells, we will meet again and more will be discussed."

253

With much grumbling, the Lightkeepers nodded their agreement, although they did not leave when Lexor and Timmon did. Instead, they gathered and discussed the implications of what their brother had reported. Not since before their time as Lightkeepers had the Tribe warred within their ranks, and the news was as unexpected as it was alarming. None knew what it would mean for the Lightkeepers, or if Tribe war would threaten the rest of Cordisia. However, what they all agreed on was that their services were going to be required soon.

As the morning sky brightened, one thought was common among all the Lightkeepers. Soon, it would be time to add to their numbers. War was coming, and they were old and few.

*****

"He might already know we are here."

"As he is stronger than all of us, I would imagine that he does," Aldric told her as the group neared the clearing.

Yet he complied with her request, weaving the pulsing magic over the group, although Otieno had insisted that he would not need it, pointing to the sword across his back. When he reached for the strands nearest Caryss, Aldric's forehead creased in concentration. At the Academy, when first he met her, before her night spent with Conri, there had been nothing but soft light around her, bright and flowing, and easy to weave. Now, the light had deepened to a grayer shade, not black like his, but no longer as pure as it once had been. He had noticed it first at Nicoline's, and now it further darkened. The babe, he thought, knowledge falling on him suddenly, and nearly undoing the work that he had already finished.

The other healer, Sharron, had been the easiest to shield, and her pulse was as bright as Caryss's had once been. The boy proved slightly more challenging as he struggled to relax enough to let the mage thread his life forces. The king had been in increasingly failing health and slept much, which made Aldric's work simple. He now lay in a small wagon, much smaller than the first. If not for him, Aldric believed that Caryss would not have sought the Tribelands.

As his hands moved around Caryss's body, he began to struggle. She had become nearly impossible to ward.

After several attempts, she hissed, "We have little time, Aldric!"

With closed eyes and his lips near her ear, he whispered, "The babe makes it difficult," then, taking a deep breath, he added, "Her power is nothing I have seen, and I know not how to contain it."

"Hells! Must I do it myself?"

As he watched, the wave around her flickered, as if she wore a long robe that she had shrugged free from her shoulders. The light dimmed, the darkness fading from it until he was once again outside the small healer's cottage in Litusia, meeting the woman he once knew as Bronwen. Aldric had to strain his eyes to see that her belly was still rounded, or he would have feared what had happened.

Before the light could darken and strengthen, he quickly worked, braiding a magic of invisibility over her, just as he had done with the others. This time, he finished in moments.

With shaking, exhausted hands, he looked to her, and asked, "What did you do?"

As he had been the one to cast the mage-spell, he could see them all still, and it was with some shock that he watched Caryss smile at his question.

"I scolded her for not cooperating."

Little made sense but he followed nonetheless as she began walking. Her steps seemed reluctant ones, like a lamb being led to the slaughter. Her tunic, dyed a faint yellow hue, only deepened the sight, until he forced himself to look away or call out for her to stop.

They arrived at the steps of the sprawling complex soon not long after, and he watched as Caryss started to climb the wide stretch of stone stairs that led to two iron-worked doors. The doors were like nothing he had ever seen before, heavy and tall, wood reinforced with swirling iron. Across both doors, starbursts had been shaped and attached to thick strands of iron. On the upper corner of the door on the right, a crescent moon had been created. Luna, he knew, and sighed, hoping the mother of the Tribe watched her children now.

Suddenly, Aldric understood why the doors seemed so unusual and he raced to intercept Caryss before she could open them.

"Caryss!" he shouted, unconcerned if he was heard.

Her pale fingers hovered just above the iron knob, but she turned to him, confusion across her sun-speckled face.

"This is no ordinary warding," he warned breathlessly, bending in half as he felt himself weaken.

Dark eyes looked upon him, no longer the color of the Northern forests.

"There is no warding that the daughter of the wolf cannot undo," she stated, as if he should have known it to be so.

His next breath did not come until they were all inside of the large building. As he exhaled, his arms raised and his fingers splayed open, dissolving the spell that had successfully covered them, allowing the group to pass by three different groups of Wolf guards. The king was lying, with limbs overflowing, in the pushcart. Sharron stood silently behind him, but in her eyes, Aldric saw worry. *She is no fool*, he thought, turning to see Otieno beside Caryss, with his large sword drawn, two hands gripping the hilt as he held it out before him. Caryss, her eyes once again her own, was pale and jittery, her courage fleeing as the girl had.

When she glanced back at him, it was as Bronwen, the same girl he had vowed himself to moons before, and he shook his head as he tried to forget the image of the black-eyed one.

"You have come as Caryss. Do not fear him. You have a weapon within reach and a weapon within womb."

His words had been spoken hurriedly and low, yet Aldric knew that their presence was now known. The air tasted of ice and snow, and, across his arms and on the back of his neck, prickled flesh sprouted.

Silence spread, thick and cold, until he shivered and shook.

The sound of boots striking the slate floors struck, hushed at first, then louder, nearing.

"My arrival was unexpected," Caryss called out, offering no bow, yet reaching for no sword.

Across from her, the man asked, "Will you see the High Lord?"

"In time. We have traveled long, Conall, and not without incident. Are there rooms where we may briefly recover?"

Nodding, he told her, "Of course. The High Lord, as it is, will likely return within the hour. And he will know that you are here, if he does not already. Have your man sheathe his sword. Even you must know what he holds."

The look that Otieno and Caryss shared was hidden from Aldric, but he watched as the *diauxie* carefully placed the large Greatsword back in its scabbard that hung heavy across his wide shoulders. When he had finished, Conall turned and beckoned for the group to follow him, and, soon, they were outside of a large room with several small cots, a well-appointed sitting area, and an attached privy in the far corner.

"You have but a few hours before Conri returns," the Tribesman told them, his voice not unkind.

He had not, Aldric realized, been surprised to see them.

Near the doorway Aldric felt a steady throbbing and understood that the room had been warded enough to only allow a few to enter, which had apparently included the High Lord's brother. Without warning, Caryss walked across the room and sat heavily on one of the cots, a luxury they all had missed over the last few moons. The Tribesman watched her, and Aldric knew that Conall had noticed Caryss's rounded belly, although nothing was said.

On his way out, Conall called across the room to Caryss, "After you speak with Conri, there is another who will want to see you."

Before Caryss could further inquire, the man was gone. As if he had not been there at all.

*****

The cot was narrow, but the feather-filled mattress was as soft as spun silk, and Caryss let her weary body collapse into it. She could not help but notice the others watching her, especially Aldric, who knew more than the rest of her hatred for Conri. It was to him that she often had turned when her fears for the girl overtook her, and it was he who had counseled and comforted her when she told him that she never wished to see the Tribesman again.

And then she had led them all to his door. Without addressing his questioning gaze, she buried her head beneath a sweet-smelling pillow. Sleep came easily, although it did not last long.

Slowly, her growing belly making it more difficult to rise from the down-filled cot, Caryss sat up until she was seated cross-legged.

He was home.

Around her, the others still dozed. Without a word, she walked to the privy, looking down at her ill-fitting tunic. It fit snugly, better suited to Sharron than to herself. Most of her clothing had remained in the King's City or had been discarded with the wagon, but in the satchel that she carried was a healer's robe that she had not yet worn.

"Sharron," whispered, noticing that the woman was awake as well, "Can you bring me my bag?"

After the two women went into the privy, Caryss closed the door. There was a large tub with a similar system to the one that she had long ago used at Willem's villa. Within moments, the basin was filling with steaming water.

"It might take half a day to wash the road from me, and the only thing clean I have to wear is a robe. Is it not strange to be so long out of our healer's garb?"

Laughing, Sharron replied, "I was never overly fond of the robes."

"It should not matter what I am wearing when I see him again," Caryss sighed as she stripped free of her clothing.

"Let it not matter then. I think it a fine thing to remind him that you are healer still."

Her boots came off next, and she tiptoed to the tub, naked for the first time in Sharron's presence in moons. When she saw the other healer watching her, she said, "Can you believe that it has already been over six moons?"

"It was easy to forget with all of our travels, but not so easy to forget now," she answered lightly.

Enjoying the moment as if they were any other women, Caryss giggled, "I have never been quite this, well, round. Do I appear as I should, do you think?"

"Yes, although perhaps it is time that we start examining you each quarter-moon. Have we both forgotten our training?"

The laughter that followed brought smiles to both women's faces and calmed Caryss more than the warm water did, but it was not enough to make her forget where they were. As she soaked in the warm water, Sharron wiped at her own face and arms, removing her soiled tunic. She was thin, Caryss realized, more so than when first they left the Academy. The last few moons had been difficult ones, and she found herself not displeased at this momentary respite.

As Sharron scrubbed herself clean, Caryss laid back, closing her eyes and thinking back on her time with Willem.

I knew so little then.

Later, after Caryss finished washing her hair and body, she rose from the tub, reaching for the towel that Sharron offered. Pulling the healer's robe over her head, Caryss was surprised at how snugly it now fit. Near a washbasin in the corner of the room, she found a hand mirror, eying herself as she hadn't done since they had left the Cove. As she pulled her damp hair into a healer's knot at the nape of her neck, she noticed lighter strands mixed in with the auburn and remembered how long in the saddle and under the sun the group had been. Her face was no longer as pale as it often was and freckles dotted her nose and cheeks, which were fuller than they had been when last she looked.

Next, Caryss loosely attached her healer's belt over her rounded stomach, and, as she did so, regretted having nothing else to wear. She looked much younger in the healer's robe, although she felt as if she had aged moon years since her time at the Academy. Having little choice, she set the mirror back down, and turned toward Sharron, who had already gotten dressed, in a robe as well, as they no longer had to hide who they were.

When both women were back in the main room, Caryss addressed the others, "He will not harm me, but I cannot promise you safety. If I have not returned by sundown, it would be best to leave as you arrived."

As she went for the door, Otieno rushed toward her. "It is not wise to go alone, *leseda*. Aldric can stay here with the rest, but I will be at your side."

Caryss only nodded, knowing that he would not accept any other answer. With one final look back at Aldric, she departed. They retraced their steps down the long hallway that Conall had shown them, but he was nowhere to be found. Once they were back in the room just off the main doors, Caryss looked to Otieno.

"He will not hurt me."

Solemnly, Otieno told her, "That is not what I fear. I have sworn my sword to the wolf cub, who will have need of both parents."

With a bitter laugh, Caryss replied, "You think I would try to kill her father?"

Dropping his gaze to her belt, he answered, "I can see the outline of the blade in your pouch, healer. And I have seen what you can do with it."

"He would kill you and think nothing of it, yet you would protect him?"

"The healer forgets herself. Or the girl is getting too strong for you to control. Either way, it no longer matters. We have company," he said, nodding his head toward the far end of the room.

Without turning, she knew who had joined them. She clung to her anger at Otieno or might have let the shaking of her legs send her to the stones beneath her bare feet. He was upon them soundlessly, as if his boots were soft-furred paws. Caryss wondered if he would be wolf or man when she next looked.

The *diauxie* took a step forward, until he stood in the middle of both Conri and her.

When the High Lord spoke, Caryss nearly reached for Otieno's arm. Instead, she called on the girl for strength.

"I knew that you would come."

It was enough to make her face him, without fear, for she had known him for half of her life.

"I had forgotten how all-knowing you are," she called, hiding nothing.

When he laughed, she remembered how much she hated him, and her hand lowered until her fingers brushed against the rough cotton pouch hanging from her belt. With her next breath, the green eyes of her father were staring up at her from where he lay in the high-grassed field. His tunic was stained red, his face pale; blood trickled from the corner of his mouth. Part of her lingered in the field beside her dead parents, despite the cool slate beneath her bared feet.

Moons before, she had done nothing when the memory came. She was not that same girl now. Before Otieno could move, her fingers dipped into her pouch.

Knowing that both men's eyes were upon her, she hesitated, adjusted her belt, and called, "Much has changed since you last saw me, Conri, and gone are the days when I was but a child's toy to you. What game you sought to play ends here."

While she talked, her hands slid back to her sides. Yet, without either man noticing, the healer had hidden the dagger in the long, wide sleeve of her robe. The blade throbbed hot against her skin, and such burning never felt so fine.

Otieno's warnings rang loudly in her ears, but she cared little for them.

"I am hundreds of moon years beyond toys, Caryss, and I do not believe I ever enjoyed them overmuch. Am I mistaken to think that you came here of your own will?"

"You do not seem surprised by my presence," she sighed, steadying her voice.

"Conall was sent to find you twice. You made his work easy by coming here, or you finally saw what danger you faced."

Her eyes were dark as she fumed, "I came at no man's bidding."

The smile that greeted her words curved Conri's lips slightly and brightened his eyes, mocking and smug, and, with laughter in his voice, he asked, "Has the girl taught you to time-walk, and you are nothing but illusion then?"

Before she could next breathe, his hands were around her waist and his lips were against her cheek, and he whispered against her ear, "Or are you here to enchant me, *Rexaria*?"

The dagger slipped into her hand as if it answered her call. Tightening her fingers around the hilt, she raised her arm, just behind Conri, and kept her eyes on his. The High Lord's eyes were a black so deep that she could see herself reflected in them, and, for a moment, she paused.

And then the *diauxie* moved, jumping forward and reaching for her hand. Just as his calloused and hardened fingers encircled her wrist, the tip of the dagger pierced through the fabric of Conri's shirt. Caryss watched as his gaze reddened, the blacks of his eyes becoming crimson and thick until streaks of blood ran through the whites of his eyes, too.

When Otieno squeezed her arm, Caryss dropped the dagger to the floor. Her eyes followed it as it clanked heavy on the gray-black stones. The bloodied blade rolled until it landed just beside Conri's boot.

"*Leseda!*" Otieno hissed, in a voice she would not have known to be his.

As he pulled her free of Conri, the Tribesman collapsed to the floor, kneeling, with his head bent low and his eyes downcast and hidden. Caryss wondered if they were still blackened mirrors as Otieno released her.

She watched, as if she was a statue, as the *diauxie* bent next to Conri, pressing the heel of his hand against the bleeding man's back, much as she would have done had the man been any other. While he worked, she retrieved the dagger, wiping it against the bleached cotton of her robe until her left sleeve was stained and striped with red. As she ran the blade over the fabric, Caryss's hand began to shake, anger fading as doubt surfaced.

"Lay him on his left side," she called, with little emotion, crouching on the floor next to Otieno.

The Islander refused to look at her, but did as she asked, never removing his hand from where her blade had penetrated Conri.

"He will not die," she told him. "Lift your hand and you will see that I barely scratched him."

Again, he did as she asked, and, together, they both watched as he lifted Conri's shirt away from his body, exposing a thumb-sized gash on the lower right side of his back. Blood still dripped from the wound, and Caryss watched with some surprise as it spilled red and wet onto the stones.

Did I think he would not bleed?

"I have never known a scratch to cause a man to sleep with death, Caryss," Otieno sputtered.

She could not argue with his words, and, truthfully, was alarmed that Conri had not yet opened his eyes. As he lay on the slate, she placed her fingers against his neck, feeling for his life pulse, as if he was man and not Tribe. When the steady beating throbbed beneath her fingers, she relaxed briefly before moving her hand from his neck to his back. His skin was warm around where the dagger had entered, yet cold elsewhere.

When he had laughed, her eyes had hazed red and her dad's eyes haunted her. The dagger had plunged into his body as if her hands were not her own.

No, she thought, *the hands that stabbed him were only mine.*

Clear-headed again, she said, "Otieno, can you bring Sharron to me? And my other pouches as well."

"And leave you with him?" he growled.

Unable to look at him, the *diauxie's* words cut her hard, stinging and cruel.

"Take the dagger with you. I should not have it while we are here," she conceded, offering up the blade.

As he rose from the floor, he grabbed the dagger and stepped to the door.

Calling out to him, she cried, "He killed my parents, Otieno!"

She watched as he paused, his back, covered by the suddenly shining Greatsword.

"Your daughter might accuse you of the same."

He left her then. Alone with the man she had tried to kill.

When he returned with Sharron, the healers worked in silence. As she cleaned the wound, Conri's eyes fluttered open, but Caryss continued to work, stitching him as she would any other. Once his back was marked with five small, black crosses, she sat back on her heels, staring at her blood-dipped fingers.

Aldric had come with Sharron and Otieno, and when Caryss saw him standing at the edge of the room, she asked, "Why does he still sleep?"

"The *atraglacia* has weakened him."

"What more can I do?"

"Nothing," he sighed, looking away from her.

"Aldric, please," she begged, rushing toward him. "There must be something."

His face gaunt and sallow, Aldric stated, "I can attempt to call him back."

"Will it harm you?" she cried.

"Not overmuch, although I will need days to recover. Is this what you want?"

Embarrassed by her tears, Caryss quickly wiped at her face with the clean sleeve of her robe and nodded.

"I should never have struck him."

The mage and the healer looked at one another, as the High Lord lay behind them, breathing and sleeping, vulnerable as his kind rarely was.

"You are wrong, Caryss. You should have struck him moons ago when you first remembered what he had done. Better late than never, I suppose."

When the dark mage smiled at her, she reached for him, hugging him tightly, causing his angled cheeks to redden.

"Perhaps when he wakes he will agree," she told him, pulling further away until the mage was alone beside Conri.

Sitting with her feet tucked under her, Caryss watched as Aldric breathed deeply and turned his attention toward the High Lord. For several moments, the dark mage ran his hands together, but each time Caryss looked, there was no fire to be seen, although she did not know why she thought that he would need it. He sought to do something different here; instead of destruction, he was working toward resurrection.

Rarely had she seen him work, except for the few spells and wardings he had weaved on their trip. The warding of Herrin's door at the Grand Palace had been quite strong, and his ability to undo it so quickly had filled her with surprise, and, again, when he had killed the Crow, she had been impressed.

When next she glanced at him, Aldric was rolling the man over onto his back. Again, the Tribesman's eyes opened briefly, but, just as quickly, closed. As they all watched and waited, Aldric began to hum, softly, and placed his fingertips over Conri's eyes, then trailed them down the man's pale face until both hands were still on his gently rising chest. Caryss watched with a creased brow and focused eyes as Aldric began repeatedly tapping on Conri's chest, over and over, in rhythm with the dull sound of his humming. The mage did not stop until Conri moaned, rolling onto his side and forcing Aldric from his body.

No one spoke. No one moved except for the High Lord. Silence spread across the room, heavy and cloying.

When Aldric collapsed, falling onto his stomach with his cheek pressed against the floor, Caryss finally moved, rushing toward him and cradling his head in her lap. Sharron was beside her before she could call out, and, together, they examined the mage. He had not been wrong, she realized. He slept, as if under heavy sedation.

With little choice, Caryss spoke, her words cracking the silence around them, "Otieno, can you carry Aldric back to the room? It will be days before he recovers."

The large man neared her, and, when he was close enough, hissed, "The dagger stays with me."

He did not look at her to see her nod, but reached for the mage, picking him up as if he was a child, and carrying him from the room, leaving only the Tribesman and the healers remaining. Conri was fully awake, his eyes purple and clouded. When they reached Caryss, she looked away, afraid to see what was written there.

She knew that he would remember what she had done.

"The dagger is no longer in my possession, if that matters," she quietly told him. "The dark mage Aldric was able to revive you. Where the dagger entered, there is a small wound, but it will heal within a half-moon."

Her words were spoken as if she had not been the one who stabbed him, emotionless and unaffected. Even her hatred for him was gone from her voice.

When he spoke, it was as if he was made of rock and granite, mountain and dirt. Harsh and coarse were his words, and Caryss shivered in their wake.

"Kill me and you kill your daughter. You think my father would let her live? You nearly played into their hands."

"Into whose hands?" she cried.

"Her enemies, and there are many."

"There are three less now," she cried, then regretted letting the words come so hastily.

He grabbed her so quickly and with such force that it seemed he had never been harmed at all.

"What do you mean?" he demanded.

"On our way here, three Crows attacked us, unprovoked. We had no choice but to kill them," she stuttered.

Caryss watched as his hands clenched.

263

"Who killed them, and how are you certain they were Crows?"

Conri's voice was still edged and rough, yet she could sense uneasiness in them.

"They dropped on us from the sky, Conri, and shifted from man to bird. What else might they be?"

Ignoring her taunt, he said, "Was it the Islander who killed them?"

"He killed one. Aldric threw fire at another. I used the dagger on the first, as he flew at me."

"Caryss!" he roared, "You would have me believe that you killed a Crow?"

Through the thunder of his words, she understood him to be whole again, and, without pity, she answered, "You must still be half-asleep, Conri. Yes, I killed a Crow, after it attacked us without cause. As he came upon me, from the sky, I opened his neck. If you don't believe me, I can show you the clothing I was wearing when it happened. What once was green is now dark with blood of the Crow."

Stepping back, he asked, "Where did this occur?"

"Half a day's ride from here."

Shaking his head, he asked, "And what of the bodies?"

"We feared another attack and departed in haste, leaving the Crows where they had fallen, but burning."

"I must take care of this, but do no think that I will ignore what occurred earlier. Just or not, you need me alive. Do not forget it. Your mage is strong, I will give him that, and, to be honest, I am pleased to know that the girl will have such an ally. But even he and the Islander will not be able to defend you from certain enemies. Until it is safe, you must stay here. I will ward this whole place to keep you here, if need be. With your mage weakened, you will not be able to leave as you came."

"The girl is stronger than any," she told him, knowing it to be true.

Her words were the only shield that she had, and Caryss used them as such, but Conri merely looked at her, with an expression that she could not read.

"She will always have admittance here, but do not think that she is stronger than me. Your word that you stay, or you and your friends will become prisoners here."

Her cards all played, Caryss said, "For now, I stay."

As he slowly limped from the room, he called back to her, "There is someone here who will be happy to see you, Caryss. I will send her to you."

His back, the same one she had thrust an *atraglacian* blade into, was all that she saw as he fled the room. And, as always, his departure left her with more questions than answers.

*****

She was as he remembered her, although there were small lines at the corners of her eyes and at the edges of her lips. Her hair was pulled away from her face, and in the midday light, her cheeks glowed red. Beneath the wide spread of a thickly-leaved tree, they sat, a blanket spread under them. For as far as Willem could see, fields of grass dried under the warm Planusian sun, fading and pale.

Beside him sat Nicoline, as lovely as she had been when he and Crispin had first encountered her. Even lovelier, he suddenly thought as her golden hair shined bright and her blue eyes fell across him. For nearly an hour, the two had discussed what had happened when Bronwen, or Caryss, as he forced himself to remember, had arrived at the farm. With each word that Nicoline spoke, he found himself more surprised, and more uncertain about what Caryss intended.

"Nicoline, why would she want the boy?"

He watched as the color disappeared from her face, and hurriedly added, "You have nothing to fear! She is healer-trained, one of the best the Academy has seen, and she has vows that she will not break. The boy is in safe hands, especially with the Islander to instruct him."

Dropping her eyes, she shook her head and whispered, "She promised me that Jarek would be safe."

Before he could reply, Nicoline's fingers grabbed his hand, squeezing him, and she cried loudly, "Have I made a mistake, Willem?"

"What choice did you have?" he told her, letting her continue to hold his hand. "It seems that the boy approached her first, the day in the palace. And she was right that Jarek was of an age where he needed to see more than just this farmstead. She will not let him be harmed, and he is with one of the best sword masters that the world has seen, or so I have heard tell. My cousin will not be pleased to hear that Caryss has him, though. And that is where she faltered."

Soon after he arrived, Willem had learned that Caryss had been there nearly two moons prior. And, he realized, she had not told Nicoline of what had occurred in the King's City. Had she, the boy would not have been permitted to go, he suspected.

"What will Crispin do? He has not seen Jarek in nearly ten moon years, Willem. Why would he care about my son now?"

"Nicoline," he pleaded, placing his hand on top of hers, "Crispin has long loved the boy, but the King's City was not the place for him. Not yet. Delwin gains more power each day, just as Herrin loses it. We all have more to fear from Delwin than from the King, as it was even when you were there. He controls the Royal Army."

265

"What are you saying?" she gasped.

"Caryss is no fool, even as sheltered as she had been at the Academy. Jarek is like a shield to her. Crispin will not strike nor will he tell his brother of her once he knows that she has the boy. She is learning how to play the game."

"And using my son as a pawn," Nicoline whispered, pulling her hand free and placing it against her open mouth.

"He is not meant for life here, Nicoline. You have known that since he was born."

Above, the skies darkened. With a voice as gray as the sky, Nicoline warned, "He is my son, and I will do all that I can to keep him safe. Even if I must search for him and steal him from her."

"You are a woman, and I would not expect you to understand," he countered. "The boy is my kin and has warrior blood in him. Better to die with a sword in hand than to die having never touched one."

"You sound like the Islander. And I will tell you what I told him. Who needs sword when you have sky?"

Smiling at her words, he answered, "He is your son, my dear, but he is Rexterran as well."

When Nicoline looked at him, there was something in her eyes that he had never seen before, as if the years had done more than aged her.

"He could be king."

Nearly breathless, Willem mumbled, "Treasonous words, Nicoline. Sheltered here, you are far enough from the crown to speak them. I would advise against repeating them, however."

She did not reply, but Willem understood well. And knew that more than ever, he needed to find Caryss. She played a deadly game and might not even know how dangerous it could be. A dark mage, a master of swords, and a child were all that she had between her and the Rexterran Royal Army. Three against tens of thousands.

"On the morrow, I will depart, Nicoline. I will find your son, and I will stay with him until I am no longer needed. For now, none will know where he is or whom he is with. Not even Crispin."

Willem had known when he left the Academy that he would not return. While Delwin still lived, he would not be able to pass through the Rexterran gates and into the city. If he managed to slip through, once discovered, he would be jailed or worse, such was his cousin's hatred for him. Not even Crispin had been able to convince Delwin to rescind the order of exile. And, now, with the King missing, Delwin would wield even more control, which meant that the gates were nearly impassable.

"Your father is from the North, is he not?" she asked, rising from the blanket.

Nodding, Willem asked, "They are in Eirrannia, you believe?"

Turning away from him, she replied, "Last night, Jarek visited me. He told me that he was well, and he looked it, even though I was unable to embrace him. The boy can do more than I even knew possible, Willem."

"Tell me all that you know."

"He did not seem worried or afraid," she sighed, waving a sun-dotted arm. "Like any boy his age, he was rather boastful about all of his new skills."

"Did he say they were in Eirrannia?"

After a moment, she told him, "No. He said they were in the home of a great High Lord. I thought it to be your kin, for I know your father has a home there."

On shaking legs, Willem rose, trying to hide his eyes. When Nicoline began walking back to the house, he followed, and, with each step, his legs shook less.

He knew where she had gone, and did not speak again until they were seated at the table, both holding goblets of wine.

"There is a peace to you that I had not expected, Nicoline."

Sipping at the light-colored wine, she said, "My son has become more than I hoped. His path is one that even I dared not imagine for him."

"Do you trust the healer, Willem?" she asked suddenly.

His gold-rimmed eyes met hers, and, for a moment, he did not mask himself. He did not doubt that his answer would affect what it was that Nicoline might do next. Even though he doubted that she would be able to find Caryss, he dared not risk it. Nor did he want to stoke her motherly fires.

With thought, he told her, "Jarek will be safe, and she will see to it. Otherwise, she would not have let him go. I have met none like her, Nicoline. Under different circumstances, you two would be fast friends, I think."

"You are in love with her."

His silence was not a denial, which both he and Nicoline understood, yet both knew how little it mattered.

*****

With nothing else to do, Caryss explored the quiet hallways that seemed without end. Into each empty room, her gaze fell, searching for the woman whom Conri mentioned.

Conri's home was much larger than she had first suspected, and, soon, she was near the kitchen, a large area that seemed unusual in the home of a Tribesman. The room itself was unoccupied, yet, as she looked about, Caryss noticed that it was as well-equipped as the one at the

Academy. As she neared the large sink, she saw several plates and two large cooking pots, and pushed at them with her hand, laughing aloud as she realized that even Tribesmen must eat.

"What last did I eat?" she murmured into the emptiness.

A quick search turned up a wheel of cheese twice the size of her hand and, in a large basket, she found a rounded loaf of bread. She squeezed at the bread, and although it was not as fresh as what Sheva would serve at the Academy, it still made her stomach rumble with hunger. Grabbing at the bread and with the cheese tucked under her arm, Caryss turned to leave the kitchen, hoping to be able to find her way back to the room she was sharing with the others.

Forgetting to grab a knife for the cheese, she hurriedly stepped back into the kitchen, setting both bread and cheese onto a wooden shelf. As she flitted about the room, opening and closing drawers and doors, Caryss did not hear anyone enter. Yet, as she turned, a woman appeared.

Full lips parted in surprise and her soft brown eyes shining, the woman called to her, words dancing as if in song.

"I would recognize that hair anywhere."

Startled for a moment, Caryss knocked a large plate to the ground, where it clanged and shattered, sending pieces of lightly painted clay across the stone floor. Neither woman moved, the broken plate between them.

"Nahla!" she cried, rushing to the woman and embracing her quickly.

As they separated, the Islander told her, "I am with child. I thought you a fool, but it seems as if I am more the fool than you."

Caryss laughed, although it seemed as if she had not done so for moons and the sound was strained.

"You are thick with the babe, Caryss!" Nahla teased as she eyed her.

Looking down at the too-snug robe, Caryss answered, "And I have nothing that fits because of it."

"Is that why you have come?" Nahla asked.

There was no easy reply, and Caryss shook her head as she walked back to where she had stored the bread and cheese. After she tore a chunk of bread loose, she faced Nahla again.

"I had not planned on coming here, but there seemed little other haven after what happened," she explained between bites.

With concern growing, Nahla asked, "Is the Rexterran Army near? It was only so long before the princes learned about the King."

"I know not where they are. We sailed for the Cove with ease, found the *diauxie*, and made our way back to Cordisia. Yet we stayed far removed from Rexterra. It was on our way through Eirrannia that death found us."

"What do you mean?" Nahla gasped, her hand resting on her neck.

When Caryss looked to her, she noticed Nahla's newly rounded face and swollen breasts.

"We were attacked by a band of Crows. Although we were able to be rid of them, it became clear that a new foe had been roused."

"What of Otieno?"

"None of us was injured. Not even the boy, although I think it was his first time witnessing death."

Again Nahla's softened face showed concern and confusion.

Before she could ask, Caryss explained, "Jarek is nearly ten moon years old, although he has seen little of Cordisia. His mother comes from a line of mages far from here. His father is King's Heir."

Her words trailed off, but Caryss noticed Nahla's eyes sharpen with unasked questions.

After a moment, Nahla told her, "Crispin visited me the day after you departed. I told him little, but he is no fool. He set men to watch me, although Conall was able to help me escape. His cheek will scar, no doubt."

A curved smile crossed Nahla's face.

"How long before the King's Heir learns that you have his son?"

"He abandoned the boy long ago," Caryss laughed, although there was no joy in her words.

She would have said more, but voices could be heard approaching. Neither moved, but, within moments, Conall and two other Tribesmen entered the room. When he saw both women, he dismissed the men and joined them.

When he looked at her, his eyes were dark with threat.

"A lesser man than my brother would have you killed for what you did," he harshly scolded, his lips pulled tight over sharp, straight teeth.

The last time she saw Conall, it had been pleasant enough, yet, now, her life pulse raced fast and her throat tightened at his words.

Trying to recover her breath, she cried, "He still lives, while both my parents lie dead! Do not try to scare me, Conall. If he kills me, he kills this Tribe. You think I do not know what the girl will mean for all of you?"

He was upon faster than she could blink.

So close that she could feel his life pulse against her cheek, he growled, "The babe will be here in a few moons. You might not, Caryss. What then? The babe will be Tribe, and you will be gone. Have you thought on that?"

She was shaking now and backed away from him, looking to Nahla for aid. The Islander gazed at the floor, as if she did not want to play sides.

Bumping hard into a shelf, Caryss half-yelled, "I no longer have the dagger!"

"Think on what the High Lord's death would mean for your daughter," he warned without repenting. "She will have one less ally. And from what I hear, you are adept at making enemies."

When she said nothing, he continued, "You think Eirrannia will shelter her? You have twice-over committed acts of treason. And you seek to bring war to the door of Eirrannia when she is ill-equipped to fight it. There is nowhere safe for you to go now, without one of your foes finding you. Make peace with him, Caryss, or perish with your vengeance."

"And so I am trapped?"

"By your own doing, yes, it seems that you are."

A reddish haze flickered behind her eyes, and, closing the distance between them, Caryss hissed into Conall's face, "I will be no prisoner, to god or man."

His eyes were nearly black, but his words were calm. "Then leave now while the High Lord is recovering. I will escort you as far as our scouts think it safe, and let Conri know that you chose to leave. Your friends' deaths will be on your watch."

Her cheeks burned and her lips parted to answer. Strong hands pulled at her, until she was steps from the Tribesman. Nahla stood just behind Conall, across the room. Otieno's braids tickled at her neck as he held her tightly. In her fury, she had not seen the Islander enter.

Trying to shake him off, she screamed, "I will not raise my daughter among Tribesmen! If I must stay here until she is born, then such it will be. After, I will run from here. Far and fast, and with the babe."

When she felt Otieno's hands loosen, she twisted herself free. He followed her from the room, silent and accusing, his boots strangely quiet against the hard, slate floors.

*****

23

Within a quarter-moon Aldric had recovered enough to walk about the complex that housed a number of the Wolf Tribe. For two days, he had slept without waking, much like the King, and their cots lay next to one another, with Caryss and Sharron tending to both. Knowing that she had little choice but to stay, Caryss had reminded herself of why she had left the Academy, and, to that end, she focused her attention on Herrin.

"At times I feel as if I have forgotten much since I left Litusia," she mentioned to Sharron.

Otieno and Jarek spent most of their time in the central courtyard, while Aldric alternated between watching them and exploring the complex. The women were often left alone, and not even Conri entered when they were with the King.

Herrin's hand, the skin nearly translucent and marked with pocked scars, rested beneath Caryss's as she gently rubbed her fingers against it. Without looking up, she called, "I had hoped that it was the poppy milk causing much of his sleepiness, but he has been without it for long enough that it cannot be so. And still he spends most of the day abed. The poison should long be from him by now, yet his skin is colored as if his bowels are not working. We must start over, as if he were at the clinic."

Sharron neared, standing just behind. "It would do us both good to forget where we are and remember where we once were. We must think on what could cause harm long after it has gone, just as we must start mixing tonics, trying the standard ones first. As long as we can continue to get him to drink goat milk, we should have at least a moon to work."

Dropping the King's hand, Caryss sighed. Without Sharron to remind her of the Academy, Caryss feared that she would forget the girl Bronwen once was.

"You are right of course," she agreed readily.

Sharron had offered advice and kindness after she had learned of the attack on Conri. Aldric, too, understood, but Otieno and Nahla had not. None spoke of it, and Caryss herself tried to forget what she had done. Yet she knew from the wary glances that she received that the peace that now existed was unstable, which only caused her to want to depart sooner. It was Sharron who had finally convinced her to stay until the babe was born.

"Once healed, you hope the King will grant you protection?" the other healer asked, as Caryss rose.

"It seems impossible to think that Herrin would shelter a child of the Tribe, but I cannot stay here," Caryss answered, withholding nothing from Sharron. "The Tribe is quickly becoming divided, and, by killing the

Crows that attacked us, I have chosen a side. Or one has been chosen for me. I still know not how they found us that day."

"The North will shelter us," Sharron hummed, the words Eirrannian.

Shaking her head, Caryss told her, "I will not bring this fight to their doors. In peace they have lived for more moon years than we can count, and in peace they should stay."

"Silent and dormant. Until it is time."

Again the other woman's words were spoken in the chimes of the North.

A half-smile swept across Caryss's freckled face, but she said nothing. Sharron was like a sister to her, kin where she had none, friend where she had few. It was not until they had departed from the Academy that the two had become close, yet Sharron had come to be just what Caryss needed.

Working together, they undressed the King until only a light blanket covered his skin. Despite Sharron's care, his legs were still too weak to support him, even if he did wake.

After several moments, Caryss said, "We must start a small garden. Nothing like we had at the Academy of course. Our supplies will not last many more moons if we stay here. I have become spoiled by the clime of the south, Sharron, and will rely on you to teach me the plants that thrive in the North."

"Would it not be easier to ask Conri or his kin for what we need?"

"They have little need for healing as we use it," Caryss explained.

Once she had finished prodding the bottom of Herrin's feet with a thin knife, Caryss walked across the room to where her riding bags had been placed. Over her shoulder, she called, "I had thought to start with thrice daily administrations of licorice root and cayenne, which I hope will cleanse anything else left in his stomach and will also improve his circulation, which is poor, as evident from the lines that mark his lower legs."

With a small bottle in her hand, Caryss turned and stopped. Her face was drawn, as if in thought, and one of her hands went to her mouth to rub at her lower lip.

"Will the *fennidi* come here? Into the Tribelands?"

Mixing a mug of goat's milk, Sharron stilled.

"None know what they will or will not do," she explained. "When I was a child, before the Academy, my mother told me a tale of how the *fennidi* came to be. Whether there is truth to it or not, I never knew, but it is said that they are the kin to the Tribe. There are many here who would know the answer better than I."

"Find Conall, if you can, Sharron."

There were questions written on the other healer's face, even though she did not voice them, but, as way of explanation, Caryss added, "Neither mage nor healer has found what is wrong with the King. But he is no normal man. And yet we all have sought to treat him as such. The *fennidi*, from the little I know, are neither mage nor man."

Sharron did not question why it was she that needed to find the Tribesman and not Caryss. All knew of their conflict.

He is not his brother, she thought, hoping to find peace with him as she waited for Sharron to return.

*****

After having spent so many moon years at the Academy, Willem felt uncertain in the saddle, and, after a few days, his body ached and his mind drifted. To distract himself, he would often talk aloud, although the large, curly-maned mount beneath him was his only companion. In less than a moon, he had traveled from the southwestern corner of Cordisia across the heart of the land, and now he was heading north, to a land he had not seen since just after his exile.

When he had been forced to leave Rexterra, it was assumed that he would settle in Eirrannia, with his father's kin, yet his banishment had marked him as traitor, and he had decided he would not bring that shame to his father's door. His mother, own sister to the King, had begged her brother to reconsider, but Herrin had told her that the only other option was for Willem to be hanged for his treason. Under the threat, his mother quieted, and he departed, choosing the Academy, and its distant location when little else seemed tolerable.

His time at the Academy had taught him much, and running the clinic had become rewarding to him. Yet, in the moons since Bronwen had been gone, it no longer seemed like the Academy offered him enough reason to stay. If he could not find her, little choice remained to him but to return to Eirrannia.

"I will not go until she tells me so," he murmured, prodding the gelding along.

He had crossed through much of Planusterra, where the land was flat, and the high grass was beginning to brown under the early autumnal sun. In a day's ride, he would be at the base of the Faelan Mountains, and in Eirrannian land.

"She is near, Lucky," he said, smoothing the gelding's course mane with his free hand.

Willem traveled on, thinking of the girl he had last seen moons before when he helped her leave the Academy, reminding himself that she no longer called herself Bronwen.

No matter, he thought, *I will find her all the same.*

*****

"He will not let you go, Caryss," Conall explained, for the third time, no longer able to contain the anger that edged his words.

"I will not be gone for long, and, if you go with me, he would never know that we were gone at all."

"There is little that escapes my brother's watch, even when he is engaged elsewhere. You will have to find another way."

Louder than before, Caryss exclaimed, "There is no other way! If you will not go with me, then I shall go alone. I am not Tribe and have oaths of my own. I have taken the King from his homeland, and, as you have explained, I now have the most powerful army in Cordisia after me. For all involved, the King must be healed. And to do that, I believe I need the *fennidi.*"

Sighing as he ran his fingers through his long hair, Conall replied, "I do not know a way to safely reach their lands."

"What about the spirit animals?"

"The *epidii*? They are a fickle bunch and would not permit one such as you to ride."

"One such as me?" she huffed.

"A mortal. They have long served our kind, although serve is a strange and not at all fitting way to describe it."

"Did Nahla not ride one from Rexterra?" Caryss asked, already knowing the answer.

"She was with me."

"Then we are at a cross-battle it seems. I must seek them out or try to call them here."

"What do you mean?" Conall asked, although Caryss noticed that much of his sharpness had disappeared.

Knowing she needed him, Caryss softened her words. "The babe's mage-skill is strong, enough so that with help from the Great Mother, I have been able to summon her for help when necessary."

"Caryss," he warned, "You cannot call on a foreign god here! Not within the Tribelands. Promise me that you will not try it."

"Then call for an *epidiuus*. Surely you know where to find them."

The Tribesman said nothing. When he turned and walked from the room, she followed, continuing until they were at the back of the large building. Sharron parted from them as Caryss and Conall strode through a field, still in silence. The sky was darkening, and the air had cooled, causing Caryss to pull the sleeves of her cloak down and wrap it tight across her chest.

"Where is the dagger?" he asked without turning to look at her.

"With the *diauxie*," came her muttered reply.

"Conri has better control than I. Had it been me that you struck, your death would have come swiftly. You will do as I say and ask no questions, and, if you cannot abide by such, I will have the *epidiuus* bring you back here."

Caryss nodded, although she knew much of his words were bluff. The last few days had shown her much, including that Conall was far less threatening than the High Lord. The younger Tribesman was quite likeable, and she regretted that she had made an enemy of him when she had attacked the High Lord.

She watched as he lifted a small, aged horn from a strip of leather that hung from an iron gate. The horn appeared as old as the gate itself, tarnished and dull, the metal no longer shining. When he pressed it to his lips and blew the air from his cheeks, she heard nothing, and reached for him, tapping him on the arm.

Again he blew the horn, and again she heard nothing.

After a third, and final, blow, Conall tied the horn back on the gate, looked to Caryss, and said, "What you cannot hear, they will. Now we wait."

It was not until the sun was nearly hidden beyond the horizon that Conall said, "You are in luck, healer. She comes."

Hurriedly looking about her, Caryss saw nothing against the black sky, wondering if all the spirit animals were white like the only one she had seen, moons ago on the beach with Conri. For several moments she scanned the dusky sky, listening and watching.

Noticing her movement, Conall laughed and said, "I am so unused to mortals that I forget your ears and eyes are not what mine are. Look, just there," he pointed. "She arrives from the west, from their home close to the sea."

And then Caryss saw her, a glistening streak moving fast and angling downward, part lightning, part falling star. As she got closer, the outline of wings could be seen feathered against the sky, silver and fine, fluttering like a butterfly. Yet, she knew that, when it came aground, the *epidiuus* would stand nearly twice her height, and it would look more mirage-like than real.

Stealing a quick glance at Conall, who was far less impressed than she herself was, Caryss wondered how the Tribe had gained the use of the spirit animals, who many had long believed were myth. Before she could

275

look back to the sky, the animal was nearly at her feet. Falling backward, Caryss stumbled until she regained her footing. Her hair flew across her face as the creature shook out her wings. Once recovered, Caryss bowed her head, not knowing why she did so, but awed at the animal before her.

"Being astride her will be similar to sitting a horse," Conall explained. "However, we must sit far enough back to be out of the way of her wings. As you can see, there is no saddle, but the hair across her body is thick enough for you to grasp, which you must make sure to do. I will sit behind to prevent you from falling. Laysa will do the rest."

"Her name is Laysa?" she asked, as Conall stroked the beautiful, glowing animal's neck.

"My brother has served you poorly, Caryss, and, as a result, you know little of our ways, even though you have the pup inside of you. Already Nahla knows much more of the Tribe than you. If you would so like, upon our return, I would teach you some of the ways of my people."

His words were kind, and she did not doubt that he meant them to be such. He offered her a new beginning, one that she wanted to accept.

Yet she told him, "I am only in the Tribelands out of necessity, Conall, and, when I can leave, I will. My daughter will be my own, as I have told Conri. When she is of an age to know her father's people, I will not stop her. Until then, she is no more Tribe than I am."

The laughter that came from him startled her, although she noticed that Laysa was as silent and still as ever. Conall continued to laugh as he reached for Caryss, grabbing her gently and lifting her with ease until she was atop the *epidiuus*. Just as quickly, he mounted, settling himself in behind her and folding his hands together just above her rounded stomach.

Into her ear, he whispered, "The babe was Tribe before she was even created. Our father willed it so. There is nothing that you can do to change that, and nowhere you can go that will make it less true."

Louder, he called, "Laysa, to the sky!"

Caryss said nothing to him, nor could she speak at all as the creature jutted forward and leapt into the air. All she could so was hold tightly to Laysa's thick mane, until her hands were white and her arms taut with effort. As they flew over a darkening sky carved with the light flickers of early stars, Caryss closed her eyes, forcing herself to breathe deeply despite the sensation that her lungs were heavy and failing. Conall's hands had not moved, and, behind her, his body pressed against her back. Yet he seemed as relaxed as she was scared. He has done this many times, she reminded herself, but still her eyes remained closed and her throat tight.

Nearly an hour they rode, away from the setting sun that was no longer visible. The moon was clouded over, and the sky was gray, and, when Caryss peeked out from half-opened eyes, she could see little. Bile stung her throat and, a few times, tears fell onto her lips. Only through breathing and will was she able to stop herself from vomiting all over the shining white coat of Laysa. When she thought that she could no longer fight the retching, Laysa slowed, gently descending, unlike how she had raced to the ground earlier.

When Laysa's hooves struck ground, Caryss leaned across her arched back and heaved the contents of her stomach onto mud and grass, gasping and panting until she was sobbing.

"I should have warned you that the ride would not be an easy one. Fear not, healer, many react as you have. Gather yourself as quickly as you can, for we are near *fennidi* land, and, soon they will know that we have arrived."

In a voice raw and raspy, she asked, "Can you help me dismount?"

Conall hurried to her side and again effortlessly lifted her from Laysa and set her shaking legs on the ground, keeping a steady hand at her back. If it had been Conri who had ridden so close behind her and who comforted her now, Caryss did not believe she would have tolerated it half as well.

The thought was enough to rouse her from the queasiness that had seeped into her whole body, and she shook slightly, yet Conall did not remove his hand.

"And so we wait?" she murmured, wiping at her mouth with the back of her sleeve.

"I see no need to do so if you feel as if you can walk. I know where to find them."

"I had been told that they are only found if they allow it."

Again his laughter came as he told her, "For most that might be true, but none can hide from me, Caryss. Conri has his own skills, and I have mine. Many of my kin call me *le faegal*. Do you know the word?"

"No," she answered as she pulled her hair, which was now thick and messy into a healer's knot at the base of her neck.

"I am called the hunter."

His words hit her like an arrow to the back, and she nearly staggered, and might have had his hand not steadied her.

"You are the dog then, and your brother the master. But it was not you who killed my parents."

There was no more laughter after her words, sharp and bitter, fell upon him.

Solemnly, he sighed. His hands dropped from the arch of her back, then reached up to brush his graying hair away from his face. His eyes, amber and smooth, gazed upon her. In his gaze, she saw something akin to sadness.

"I warned him that you would never forgive that act. Nor would he be able to make you forget it. Caryss, I offered to do it for him, often in fact. Yet he would not allow it, even though I have made many kills for him in the past. Because, as you mentioned, I am his to command. Perhaps you will never understand why it was done or why it had to be so, but you must realize why Conri insisted that none but he strike."

Her eyes were still wet as she uttered, "My parents are dead, and he is the reason why. I need to know nothing more."

"When we return, there is something I need to show you. Until then, we have other things to concern ourselves with. The *fennidi* have found us, it seems."

Frantically, she looked around, back and forth along the path, each side lined with thick, heavily leaved trees that, in the darkness, looked like they were reaching for her as they swayed and creaked. Caryss saw nothing, and heard little, except for Laysa chewing on a patch of soft grass. Dry, withered leaves fell to the ground, crackling and crunching.

Without thinking, she moved until she was beside Conall, their legs touching, and whispered, "Will they help me?"

"Not without cost. Such is the way of the *fennidi*."

His words were hushed, spoken near to her ear, and Caryss twitched as warm air tickled her cheek. Under the cover of a darkened sky, the blush that spread across her cheeks wasn't visible, but where their legs stills rubbed, Caryss knew that Conall had felt her recoil. Without much memory of the North, the mysterious and elusive *fennidi* scared her, even with a Tribesman by her side, yet she knew that she needed them, just at much as Herrin did.

"Do you mean coin? I did not think to bring any with me," she mumbled.

She knew that he smiled, and knew that he wanted to laugh. Instead, Conall whispered, "Some pay in coin, when they have nothing else the *fennidi* want, but your coin will buy no answers. From you, they will demand more. Have you thought this through, Caryss? You will leave here unharmed, but you will leave with ropes tied about your wrists, so fine and soft that you will not even know they are there. Until a time comes when the *fennidi* tug at them. No matter where you are, your wrists will sting and your thoughts will fade, as if you know nothing but what it is they want you to know."

Caryss scratched at her arms with pale fingers.

Conall placed two fingers lightly on her lips and murmured, "Nothing more. They come."

He was not wrong. Where once only large-trunked trees edged the path, five *fennidi* now stood, four men, dark-skinned and small, and one woman, hair as silver as the *epidiuus* and hanging well past her tiny waist. They were all of a similar height, and none taller than Caryss's chest. Their bodies were covered in leather, fine and soft, yet close-fitting on their small frames. When first she looked, it seemed that the leather had been painted green, to match the abundant leaves, yet, looking again, she realized that it was dark, of a shade more similar to the trunk than to its leaves.

Yet it was their skin that shocked her most.

In the Southern Cove Islands, she had seen skin of various shades of brown, tan and dark. At the Academy, the Tretorians, including her foster mother, had nut-colored skin. At the clinic, she often saw skin reddened from the sun or fever or nearly white with sickness. Yet, never had she seen skin like that of the five *fennidi* that circled them. Where leather didn't cover, green skin glimmered, the color of faded grass, she suddenly thought.

Strapped to the backs of each of them hung a crescent-shaped sword, unsheathed and shining in the darkness.

"Ohdra, I had not thought to see you here," she heard Conall call, his words lilting and sweet. "Blessings, friend. You honor us with your presence."

When he bowed to her, Caryss did the same, although not nearly as gracefully, for her stomach would not allow it to be so. However, through her half-lidded eyes, she could see that it mattered little as the small woman whom Conall addressed had her glistening, opal eyes on the Tribesman and seemed to hardly notice or care about all else.

"And you surprise me with yours, old friend. Who is the child? I had not heard that the Tribe keeps Northern pets now."

As the words slipped from the tiny woman's mouth, Caryss began to understand. Moments later she realized that they were spoken in the language that she had heard Conri use moons before, the night the babe had been created. The language of the Old Ones, she thought, uncomfortably, knowing she had little right to the words. A gift from Conri, one that, while useful, felt strange and undeserved.

In a voice she hardly knew as her own, she addressed the woman. "Which child do you speak of? I am a woman grown, and, soon, a mother myself. Nor am I leashed and chained as if I was no more than a hound."

Next to her, Conall paled, his skin even whiter than usual. With a slight movement of his hand, his icy fingers wrapped tightly around her own in warning.

Ohdra's words sliced through the air, cold and sharp, as if carved from the trees around them.

"I see your pup can bark."

When Caryss laughed, half-mad, she knew, Conall's grip tightened until she pulled her hand free.

279

"A strange song that the caged bird sings. Tell me, Ohdra, when did you last see land outside of these trees? Tell me, when did you last hear the sea kiss the shore? You are no more than a half-day's ride from both the Sea of Mist and the Great Sea, yet I would guess you have forgotten them both. I know little of your people, but I know enough to remember that there once was a time when you lived in peace with Eirrannia. And the land was yours to roam."

Caryss knew her words were truth, yet she could not decide if they were from her memory or Conri's, especially since, moments before, she had known none of it. The mind-lock she had lived with for moon years, nearly half her life, was unraveling, as he had promised it would. Yet, this was something more. The knowledge of the *fennidi* did not seem to be memory; however the flush across the faces of those around was proof enough. Two of the males had their hands over their shoulders and clenched around the hilts of the curved swords.

She was not the only one who had noticed.

"Ohdra, we are unarmed, and came in good faith. Check your men," Conall called, his voice deeper now.

"Good faith, you say, yet beside you stands a stronger weapon than any my men have. Do you think we have not heard the tales, Conall? Do you think we know nothing that happens outside of these hills and trees? You Wolves think us nothing but lesser kin. The Crows see us as more."

"The Crows seek to use you for their own gains!" he hissed, "Once so used, you will be nothing to them and all promises forgotten."

"Tell me why you are here then," she answered, nodding toward her men as she talked.

Once the men's hands were back at their sides and swords untouched, Conall said, "Beside me stands my brother's *orla*, mother to his heir. We had hoped that the babe would remain unknown, and Conri will be ill-pleased to hear differently upon my return. We are not masterless, as you know, and my brother was without choice. It will be up to him to tell you fully what has occurred and what might occur, but you are aware that there has been a split among the Tribe. The Crows grow hungry and crave what the Wolves have long held. The Bears, for now, have little concern for the fight, but will ultimately have to choose sides."

Pausing, he added, "As will the *fennidi*."

None but Conall spoke, and he continued, "A battle will come. And if it is anything like the last one, it will be long and deadly. Caryss is no warrior, although the babe will be Tribe, and even half-blood, will be like none we have seen. I will let her explain to you why we are here, but I will remind you that the Wolves have long aided you and yours. When the lines are drawn, we would want you on our side. But that is a discussion for another day."

"We have not been known for aiding mortals, Conall, but I will hear out the so-named *orla*."

The look that Conall gave Caryss was akin to a threat, and she drew a deep breath, understanding more how dangerous and complex the situation within the Tribe was becoming.

Simply, she said, "A few moons ago, I was sent to Rexterra to heal the King, yet I have been unable to do so despite my moon years training as a healer. But I believe that you can help."

"Usually when one seeks assistance, she will do so with a defter and more polite hand," Ohdra murmured.

"With apologies. This is not a game I am used to playing. I do, however, think that we can help each other."

A half-smile lined Ohdra's face. "What do you have that my people need, healer?"

Again, she knew, not through memory, but deeper. With eyes clear and unmasked, Caryss let her answer fly like across the forest as if carried by the winds.

"Freedom."

Silence came. Even Conall did not move.

"Others have promised the same," the *fennidi* queen finally told her.

In that moment, Caryss understood how much she needed the fabled forest-folk, and, without their aid, Herrin would never recover. And she would never be able to leave Conri's compound.

"None have promised you what my daughter can," Caryss called.

"She will be of the North, but not as I am. She will be kin, Ohdra to all who call the North home. She will be the bridge between Tribe and Eirrannia, just as she can be the bridge for the *fennidi*. I know not of the war between you and my own people, but my daughter will not be a weapon. She will learn as I did the oaths of a healer."

"A babe? One not yet born will free us from these woods? The same babe that the Crows will kill once they know of her?"

Caryss cheeks blazed red, but it was Conall who cried, "Any attempt on the girl's life will be seen as war! Nox knows of the girl, and, if the Crows attempt such, he would intervene, which none want. In this game, we all must choose carefully."

"They will find others to do it for them."

Ohdra's words silenced them all until Caryss realized what had to be done. She stepped forward, out of the reach of Conall, and fell to her knees. When she felt him move behind her, she raised a hand and shook him off, preparing herself for what next had to be done.

"I have no knife," she whispered, suddenly remembering that the dagger was now in Otieno's possession.

"Ohdra, can one of your men assist me?"

Without looking up, Caryss waited until one of the leather-clad men knelt beside her, then said, "Draw your sword."

When he had done so, she continued, loud enough for all to hear, "Run the blade over the palm of my hand, enough so to make me bleed."

She thought that Conall would intervene, but when he did not, she lifted her hand to the green-skinned man beside her, and dropped her eyes to the ground. The strike was quick and crisp, and as she felt the blood bubble from the slice, she brought her hand toward her, cradling her left hand beneath it. Next, she spilled the warm blood onto the cool ground, where minutes before her boots had left marks in the dirt. Then, with more ease now, she recited the words of the Great Mother, touching fingers to forehead, to chest, to her rounded stomach, before letting them rest, bloodied and black, on the ground.

Beside her, the man still stood, and through slitted eyes, she could see silver light reflecting off the curve of his blade, even though the moon was slight and faint clouds covered the stars. Leaning back on her heels, Caryss looked up and waited, knowing what would happen next and watching for reactions from Ohdra and Conall, who had yet to meet his niece, the one that the Wolves long awaited. As the darkness faded around her, shadows appeared in an arc around her, a black outline of the *fennidi* warriors.

Ohdra's face whitened as the light reflected off of it and her silver hair glowed, as if the strands were shards of ice. Conall's face was blank, expressionless, but his hands were clenched at his sides.

Let them all watch, she thought, *and let them see their weapon.*

The girl did not disappoint. Out of a burst of white flame, she came, more solid than she had ever appeared, as if she was blood and bone. Caryss longed to embrace her, but the girl was not as she had been when last she saw her, in the Cove, where she had been dressed as Luna herself. Now the gown was gone, and in its place was leather and armor.

Warrior. Weapon.

Caryss did not know whether to weep or rejoice.

Her arms were bare and a sweat and blood-stained vest was all that covered her upper body, tight pants tucked into high leather boots. Her hair, dark and sleek, was pulled back from her face, hanging long down her back. The black waves that marked her cheek were matched by black streaks that ran down her right arm from shoulder to elbow, scratched and painted black. In her hand hung the scimitar, similar to what had called her here.

The girl's face, older than before, but still younger than Caryss herself, was serious and stern, as it had never been before.

As if she had come expecting a battle. Or had just escaped one.

While the others stared, awed and intrigued at the girl, Caryss rose from the ground, wiping her hands on her now dirtied pants, and, breaking the spell that her daughter had created, called out, "Your freedom, Ohdra."

In Ohdra's eyes, Caryss saw desire. Deeper than memory. Deeper than belief. Deeper than vows.

Silently, the small woman walked toward the girl and dropped to her knees, placing her forehead against the ground. For a long moment, she did not move.

When she looked up, Ohdra vowed, "The *fennidi* are yours to command."

The girl seemed distracted and waved at the bowing woman. "Rise, Ohdra, I have no time for such formality."

To Caryss, the girl called, "Mother, tend to your hand. The soil is poisoned here, as Ohdra should have warned."

When Caryss reached for her healer's pouch, the girl turned, settling her gaze on Conall, who looked more unsettled than Caryss had ever seen him. His face was pulled tight, his teeth sharp, his eyes rimmed in shadows.

"Uncle," she said, bowing her head slightly, "Your son sends his greetings, although he troubles me much, and I would send him to you if I could."

In a voice rich with emotion, Conall called to her, "Your markings prove your courage, pup. Your father would be proud."

With a half laugh, she replied, "The High Lord is rarely pleased with me."

The corners of his lips turned slightly inward as he fought a smile, but Caryss found herself enjoying the interaction between her daughter and Conall, a man she was beginning to enjoy as well. As she poured a distilled, bitter-smelling liquid over her hand, pain seared through the gash, but still she listened quietly as her daughter continued.

"What has brought you to *fennidi* land, uncle?"

"It was your mother's choice. She needs their help with the Rexterran king."

With a furrowed look across her ash-smudged face, the girl said, "I had forgotten that he yet lives. Perhaps it would be best to send him back to the King's City, mother."

Her words were strained, as if she had difficulty speaking them, and when Caryss looked at her, the girl was staring at the ground. Her image was still solid, a gift of the magic-stained soil perhaps. Dark magic.

"What of my vows?" she asked.

"Not all can be healed."

"One of his sons wants me dead and the other wants me captured," Caryss explained. "Herrin is the only shield I have between the Royal Army and myself. I do not know how your time-walking works, but much has changed since last I saw you. Three Crows attacked us last moon, and all three are now dead. I have little choice but to remain in the Tribelands until Herrin can call off Delwin's men."

Shaking her head and rubbing at her cheek with dirt-tipped fingers, the girl mumbled, "Ofttimes I forget what I have seen and heard when I travel back. I have been warned that it will get worse the more often I do so. Mother, if Herrin dies under your watch, you will have all of Cordisia against you. If he cannot be healed by you or by the *fennidi*, hire mercenaries to see him home. Let him die there."

"You forget the vows of a healer!" Caryss gasped.

"All of that matters little," the girl said, looking toward the silver-haired woman who, even standing, reached just past the girl's waist, "And will matter less if Herrin dies. Ohdra, will you give assistance to my mother in exchange for my help when the time is right for the North to rise?"

Before Ohdra could answer, Conall stepped toward his niece with raised hands, and called, loudly, "What madness is this, girl? You are Tribe and need not beg for help. The *fennidi* are few, and fewer still in your own time. Ohdra has no choice but to help. You should know not to bargain with them."

With a shrug that caused her hair to catch in the wind, the girl told him, "My way is not the way of the Wolf."

Coldly, her uncle asked, "What are your markings then?"

"Hard fought and earned. That is my way, as my allies know."

Taking a step closer and dropping his hands to his side, he asked, "Not yet born, you were branded an enemy. The *fennidi* are friend to that foe, so what does that make them to you?"

Smiling broadly, which surprised Caryss, the girl answered, "I shall never understand how Blaidd lacks much of your wisdom, uncle. Yet, his charm far surpasses your own. When his smile can't get him out of trouble, he calls for me. But he has long been more than kin, and I owe him much. It is the same with the *fennidi*. I have a debt to pay and forgiveness to seek."

She seemed older now, just not in looks, but in the way that she spoke and carried herself. Not just older, but harder too, Caryss had to admit. The girl seemed lost for a moment, her image flickering. When it steadied, she turned toward the *fennidi* queen.

"Ohdra," she said, softer, and, as Caryss looked again, she noticed the edges of the girl were beginning to ripple, "What does my uncle speak of? Have you drawn sides with the Crows?"

284

"We chose no side for we had no reason to until now."

"And now?"

"My swords are yours."

Reaching into a small pouch that Caryss had not noticed, the girl pulled out a leather cord, and from it hung a small metal rune. Unable to see what was engraved into the metal, she looked to Conall, who stared at the girl with focused eyes, smoky purple now and glazed. He appeared surprised, and again she remembered that he had never before encountered his time-walking niece. Caryss herself had seen the girl enough times that she had believed that little could surprise her. What happened next proved her wrong.

Throwing the rune onto the ground quickly, she called, "Ohdra, take the necklace. All who see it will know it for what it is. You are Wolf-vowed now, and, unless it harms my mother or her kin, you will answer to Conri. Where the two conflict, you will be my mother's first. In exchange, I offer you peace. But, more, I will offer you the North to roam and hunt once again as your own did many moon years ago. Have we a deal?"

All standing in the clearing knew of what the girl spoke. For generations, the *fennidi* had been isolated and imprisoned in a small section of land, caught between Tribe and Eirrannia, friend and foe to both. Caryss did not know what had caused it to be so, but she knew enough to understand the significance of the girl's promise.

"As the trees watch and the mountains listen, as the sea surges and the sun rises, the *fennidi* are yours," Ohdra proclaimed, her words echoing off the trees and spreading through the dense forest, for all her kin to hear.

Ohdra bowed her head, as did her men behind her and reached for the necklace, examining it under fading light. Conall quietly watched, steps from both of them, until the girl addressed him.

"Uncle, remind my father of his promise."

"Which?" Conall asked.

"He will know. There has only been one," was all she answered before turning to Caryss.

The girl was nearly invisible in the darkness, more shadowed and less glowing than the other times that she had visited. Caryss gazed at her with a mother's pride, nearly weeping at what the girl was becoming.

In a distant voice, as she trailed off, her daughter whispered, "Stay safe, mother."

The small man near to Caryss shivered, which caused his long hair to catch the wind, tickling Caryss's cheek. When she reached a hand to brush the silvery strands away, Caryss noticed the girl watching the man. Her daughter's emerald eyes appeared troubled. When Caryss gazed back at the man, she noticed him shake his head, yet she knew not what it meant.

Looking away, her brandings stark against her pale skin, the girl proclaimed, "Tell Jarek to work harder on his parry if he hopes to best me."

The laughter that followed sparkled and twinkled, as if the stars had fallen and landed softly around them. When the sound faded, they all knew that she was gone. For a long moment, none spoke. For Caryss, the girl had offered something more than peace. More than freedom.

She had offered hope.

It was Conall who cracked the silence of the forest clearing. "She is unlike any other, Caryss."

Her voice shaky and low, Caryss asked, "What will the Tribe think of her?"

With a shrug, he replied, "She will lead them one day, and it will matter little what they think as long as they follow."

"How will she lead if they do not accept her?" Caryss pressed.

"By destroying all of those who don't."

For a moment, she nearly questioned his words. Instead, she welcomed them, knowing how little she understood the Tribe.

To Ohdra, she asked, "What have you decided about the King?"

Motioning to the man who had knelt beside Caryss, Ohdra said, "Gregorr is one of our finest healers, although we do not call them so among the *fennidi*. He has long served our people, and, if you would permit it, he will return to the Tribelands with you. He will see to your needs and those of this king."

When the man stepped forward into the light of the moon, Caryss noticed that he appeared older than the rest. Deep lines cut across his forehead and at the corners of his eyes. His skin, like the others, was green-tinged, but he was darker than Ohdra, the color of pine. As all of the *fennidi* were, Gregorr was covered in leather, but, unlike them, across his back hung a large satchel. The sight made her smile.

To Ohdra, she said, "My thanks, lady. And my apologies for earlier."

The blush that crossed her face remained unseen, and she walked to where Conall now stood. Without comment, Gregorr followed. Nothing further was said, except by Conall who called for Laysa.

When all three were on the back of the *epidiuus*, Conall whistled, and the animal lunged and leapt, just as she had done earlier. Caryss sat between Gregorr and Conall, who again rode behind her with his arms wrapped about her waist. As before, Caryss kept her eyes tightly closed, and tried to ignore the churning in her stomach. Drifting in and out of sleep, Caryss opened her eyes a final time and realized that Laysa was descending.

With clenched hands, she watched as the animal slowly curved her way to the ground, gliding from side to side until she hovered just above the soft grass where she had first found them waiting. Caryss half-feared that Conri would be waiting for them, and when Laysa's hooves touched ground, Caryss exhaled, relief taking the place of nausea.

Wanting to waste little time, she jumped down, only to be interrupted by Conall as he said, "Conri must be told what has occurred."

She was already steps from him when she called back, "Do what you must. I need to find Sharron and the King."

Turning once to make sure that Gregorr followed, Caryss once again felt like the healer that she had been for half of her life.

A gift from the girl, she mused, and wondered why Gregorr had come without complaint. Or without surprise.

*****

There was little left for him to do before his Healer Journey was to begin, and Pietro walked with a light step and a half-smile on his face from Master Black's cottage to his own. For moons, he had planned the trip, and, with the Master's aid, he was a quarter-moon away from leaving the Academy. On the morrow, he would meet with the Master Council, who, Black had assured him, would approve his Healer Journey, leaving him free to begin the final step before becoming a Master Healer himself. After a moon year spent traveling and healing, he would return to the Academy, and, after a final meeting with the council, Pietro would no longer be a student.

He could return home.

Rexterra. He could still recall much of his homeland, despite having not seen it in over ten moon years. The Grand Palace, where he had often visited, was unlike any building in all of Cordisia, larger and more ornate than any he would find as he walked throughout the land. When he was young, his father, a cousin of the King, had moved from the palace and into a large complex nearer to the coast, where most of his ships were docked. His brothers too, who each had their own merchant fleet, now lived a day's ride from the King's City. Pietro had decided that he would visit the coast before the King's City, even though it would add days to his journey. The thought of impressing his brothers when they would see him in his healer's robe was enough to make the decision an easy one.

Arriving back at his rooms, Pietro hurriedly touched his hand to the door, releasing the warding that was there, and rushed inside. As the door swung closed behind him, his skin prickled.

Shivering, despite the midday Tretorian heat, Pietro realized that he was not alone.

"I thought that you had forgotten me," he shakily said, balling his hands into fists.

A cackling sound, which Pietro imagined was laughter, seeped from the man and caused him to tremor, until he remembered that the man needed him still. It would not serve to harm him.

With a shrug of thin shoulders, the man told him, "On the morrow, you must depart. And so I am here."

Stumbling over his words, Pietro replied, "I cannot yet leave the Academy. In a quarter-moon's time, I will be free to go."

Stepping toward him, the Tribesman explained, "On the morrow, you will head to the King's City, as quickly as you can. Once there, you will meet with Delwin, who is cousin to you from what I hear. You will remind him that the healer has his father, unrightfully so, and that he is in danger each moment he is with her. The king will die if he is not tended to, or so you will tell his son. Now that you are healer-trained, you will offer your services and your skill to Prince Delwin. You will also convince him that the Northern healer must be killed."

Pietro's mouth fell open, but the man continued.

"You will find the girl in the Tribelands, with the High Lord of the Wolf Clan. The Royal Army will no doubt be reluctant to enter the lands, and with just reason. However, when you are within a day's ride, you will contact me, and I will make sure that most of the Tribesmen are gone, leaving the girl and the few she has with her open to attack."

"How will I contact you?" he whispered, as if they were not alone.

Reaching into a small pocket on the inside of his jacket, the man said, "With this," and threw a small token at Pietro, who barely managed to catch it.

Turning the wooden disc coin over in his hand, he saw an image of a crow, long-beaked and sharp-eyed, glaring at him. With another shiver, Pietro quickly turned it over until the unmarked side shone.

"When next we meet, which will be within a moon or two, you will learn more. For now, your plans are simple. Travel to the King's City and convince Delwin that the girl is a threat to Rexterra and to his father. He has been looking for her for a moon already, and your news will be welcome and rewarded."

Backing to the door, the man added, "You will not tell your cousin of me, not until you are just outside the Tribelands."

"What if he does not believe me?" Pietro murmured.

"Did you hear nothing I said, boy? He has been looking for the healer for a moon! When he finds her, he will need a reason to strike."

"To strike whom?"

"Are you a fool? Have you forgotten so much about your homeland? Who has long been the enemy of Rexterra? The one they cannot tame as they have the others?"

With a hand on his chest and shaking his head, Pietro exclaimed, "Eirrannia?"

In the darkened room, the sharp, pointed teeth of the man glowed white, as if he smiled.

"Just so. The healer woman has played her part nicely. And, now, with her soon to leave the Tribelands, she has given us just the chance we needed. I want the girl, and Rexterra wants the North."

"What you speak of will be war!"

"Perhaps."

The man was at the door before Pietro could close his gaping mouth.

"Cast the token into a fire, and I will find you when it is time."

The door gently closed behind the man, as if the soft, warm Tretorian breeze blew it shut. As if the man had not been there at all.

Looking down at the wooden token in his hand, Pietro closed his fingers around it. Soon, his hand began to burn, and he dropped the disc to the floor.

"Damn you Bronwen," he spit, reaching for a cotton strip to wrap around the token.

When he had cloaked the coin and placed it into a pouch, Pietro began to sort through his belongings, organizing and packing for a journey that no longer was his own.

*****

He woke to the sound of howling, and when his golden-rimmed eyes were fully open, he scanned his surroundings, reaching for the longsword that lay near his leg. Clouds covered much of the night sky, obscuring both moon and star. The night had been cool, especially so near the north, and a small fire still burned near, casting crackling rays of orange over his darkly-clothed body.

Again, howling moans surrounded him, yet with the sword now clutched tightly in his hand, Willem feared little and looked around with clear eyes. The Tribelands were a short ride from where he had camped, and had it been bellow or caw, he might have worried. Howling meant wolves, and wolves meant Conri.

And where Conri was, Bronwen would be as well, if Nicoline had been truthful.

Into the darkness, he scrambled to his feet and yelled, "Where is he? Send me the High Lord!"

Under the smoky black sky, silence answered his plea. The wolves quieted, but he knew that they had not yet departed, and several pairs of yellow eyes glowed from the distance. Man or wolf, he could not tell, and, in truth, Willem had never seen Conri as anything but man, and did not know if it was lore or truth that a Tribesman could do so.

But he was too near the Tribelands for doubt to come now. His golden-rimmed eyes could see more than most, and when the sky lightened, he noticed.

When none approached, he waited, adding wood to the fire and boiling water to brew tea from leaves he had brought from the Academy. With a steaming cup in hand, Willem sat at the edge of the fire, poking at it with the tip of his sword, still heavy in his strong hand. When next he looked, there were less eyes on him.

When Conri arrived, it was no surprise, and Willem rose to greet him.

"Are you alone?"

The words were sharp, yet spoken just above a whisper.

Shrugging, Willem replied, "Does it look like any others are with me? I have little doubt your sentries have watched me for days, Conri. Surely they have seen no one else."

The High Lord was just steps from where Willem sat and made no attempt to come closer as he said, "Why are you here?"

"To correct a mistake I made moons ago. I should never have permitted Bronwen to travel so far on her own."

"She is not alone. There are four who travel with her, and two who have been with her since she first left the Academy."

Four, he wondered, but asked, "Is she well?"

"How did you know where to find her?"

"After all that she has done, where else could she find safety?"

With dark eyes, Conri stepped toward Willem and hissed, "I have no time for games! Why are you here?"

Gold met black as Willem returned the High Lord's stare.

"For Bronwen."

When Conri laughed, the wolves howled, and Willem felt his eyes get hot and his hands begin to burn. For more moon years than he could count, he had been able to control the fire that burned inside, just as it did in his kin, yet he could not recall a time when it threatened to burn so hot and wild, as it did now.

"Would you really keep me from her, Conri?" Willem asked, without fear.

"Did she send for you?"

"My cousin's men have no doubt started searching for her, and they know enough to first begin in Eirrannia. I am here to help her and to keep her alive. Let her decide if I stay or not."

"What do you know of the Rexterran Army? Are they on the move?" the High Lord sharply demanded.

"I know little of their whereabouts, nor have I heard from Crispin."

Stepping back, Conri called, "The boy could one day sit the throne of Rexterra."

Shaking his head, Willem countered, "It would be unlikely. While he is Crispin's first-born son, he has not been recognized as so. His grandfather and uncle would never allow it, and even Crispin himself would never try to make it so."

Again Conri laughed, quieter this time, as he said, "I had thought you wiser, Willem. When has the path to a throne ever been clear? It matters little right now, however. The boy is an interesting lad, and his powers have impressed me. His kin have long been gone from Cordisia."

"Do you know of the Elementals?"

After pausing at the query, Willem stated, "When last I saw him he was but a babe, toddling about. But I know his mother had mage-skill, although I did not know it was so strong in him. Bronwen was less a fool than I had thought to find him."

Conri's eyes darkened and his brows rose as he explained, "You do not know the history of the Elementals then. They have long been foe to Tribe, although many generations ago, they chose to leave Cordisia."

With a laugh, Willem chided, "They chose? Or were they forced to leave?"

Smoother still, as if undisturbed by Willem's laughter, Conri answered, "It was war, and although our kind took many losses, theirs did as well. It would have continued if they had stayed. It benefited all for them to seek a home elsewhere. The boy's grandfather broke vows in his return."

"You would not seek to harm the boy, would you Conri? Caryss has granted him safety."

"Jarek understands the danger his powers bring. With control, he could be less of a risk. She has told me that he will not draw from his power while they are in the Tribelands."

"And after?" he asked.

When Conri looked to him it was not as man, but as High Lord. His eyes were fierce, darkening by the moment. His face, finely angled and defiant, turned toward Willem with haste and aggression. It was enough to make the Rexterran wish that he had not pushed further.

"There is safety here, and she will not leave."

He does not know her, Willem thought, but did not say.

"Is it still your wish to come with me?" Conri asked.

With a nod, Willem told him, "There is no place else for me."

And so Willem would join Bronwen and Aldric once again, moons later. The Academy seemed long past, and Willem feared none of them would see it again.

*****

For nearly half the day, Caryss, Sharron, and Gregorr sat at the bedside of King Herrin and discussed their healing options. The *fennidi* spoke in a thickly accented, but still Eirannian, voice, although both women struggled at times to understand what he was saying. Gregorr's words rolled from his mouth as if his tongue was thick and his lips cracked. Several times the two Northern healers looked at one another over the small man's silver-haired head, hoping the other had understood his words. What should have taken little time had now occupied much of their day, and still they had no plan to heal the King.

Both had learned much about which plants and herbs the *fennidi* used, and, with Conall's help, a plan was made to build a glasshouse for growing and cultivating what they did not have in their stores. Already, several Tribesmen had begun building, and Caryss rose from where she had been sitting to look out the window, watching the men as they quickly worked. At the Academy, they had little use for glasshouses, as the airs rarely cooled. But here in the North, glasshouses were often used, and she wondered if the men had prior experience in the construction, as they seemed to nearly be complete, only needing to add the heavy glass panels.

When Conall entered the room moments later, she called, "Your men will be finished before the sun sets. This must not be the first glasshouse that they have built."

She had come to enjoy her time with the Tribesman, although she rarely visited the High Lord.

"There are a few that the cooks use, but this one will be for your use only. Caryss, is it possible that you know so little of the Tribe? What use would we have of plants that heal?"

Her smile faded, although his did not, and, even as she realized his jest, she asked, "Do you require no healing, then?"

"Not as you do. We live or we die. There is little to prevent either. Although I have heard of what the mage did for the High Lord."

As if in explanation, she called, "I did not strike him deeply."

A raised eyebrow was his only response.

"What of the Elementals?" she asked, looking about for Jarek.

When she did not spot him, Caryss knew that he must be at practice with Otieno, as they often were. The boy was learning quickly, or so she thought after her last observation of his swordplay.

"Elementals are mages, of a sort, but unlike Aldric or his kind. The mage-guild that most know in Cordisia is but a small piece of magic compared to what else has been seen elsewhere. Here, mages learn a bit of all the elements, yet true Elementals are masters at only one, and their skills far surpass what any Cordisian mage would have. Many generations ago," he explained, "a great war broke out between Tribe and Elemental, for their kind had been created to keep us in check. Or so our tales tell it."

"I know all of that," she huffed," before adding, "Aldric used fire on the Crow."

Waving a hand at her, he said, "If you would let me finish, you would understand more and interrupt less. Yes, he was able to kill with his fire, but he is no ordinary mage, I would bet. There had to have been a touch of Elemental in him. And the same must be said for the sword that the Islander used. You must know that neither man you travel with is of the light, Caryss."

"They are both sworn to me and to the girl, and I trust them. Nothing else matters."

"I do not know how you came to have both vowed to you, but, if you are correct and they can be trusted, you have two men at your side that even my brother would not dismiss. What of the boy?"

Her cheeks flamed hot, and Caryss looked away from Conall, and tried to keep her voice free from quivering as she said, "He's a child and presents no harm."

"Has he been mage-trained?" Conall asked.

"Aside from having a king for a father, he is little more than a farmboy."

While she no longer smiled, Conall beamed, and, even though Caryss still did not look at him, she sensed that as he grinned, he watched her for a reaction. Biting the inside of her lip, she struggled to keep her face free and her mind clear, as if he could know her thoughts.

"A farmboy, perhaps, but he smells of rain."

His words resounded loud against the slate floors, and Caryss could do nothing but wait as he continued.

"As fire can kill Crow and earth can kill Bear, sky can kill Wolf. The mage told me that you knew of this before allowing the boy to join you."

Conall's words were accusation, she knew, and Caryss struggled to reply. He was not the first to warn him about Jarek. A moon before, she had been forced to explain to Conri why the boy had come. In the end, he had let Jarek stay, although he warned her of the danger that could arise. But given the choice, she would find him again, she knew. And with that knowledge, she faced Conall.

"You and your brother like to remind me of how little I know of the Tribe. And while that might be true, I know enough to know the enemies my daughter will have. The boy will be an ally, a very powerful one. I am not the fool you think I am, Conall."

"You arm your enemy and teach him skills he did not have moons ago."

Gregorr and Sharron still stood by the King, while she and Conall had moved nearer to the door. Stepping into the hallway, she pulled the door closed behind her and leaned against it. Conall stood just steps away, having followed her.

"His kin might have once been foe, but Jarek is not. From what I hear, the Wolves have more to worry about than an Elemental boy. When the Crows strike, does it not seem wiser to have the boy on your side than theirs? Think of his power in their hands, Conall. What would that mean for your kin?"

By the way his eyes shifted, Caryss knew that she had convinced him.

"Do you not see what I have done?" she half-cried. "I have brought the *fennidi* to your side, where once they swore allegiance to none. A boy whose strike could kill you is now vowed to your High Lord's daughter. Perhaps instead of this interrogation, I should be getting praise."

His smile lightened his eyes, and Caryss sighed with relief.

"You are wiser than I had guessed, but I still must speak to the boy before Conri returns."

"Let us go now," she told him.

He said nothing, but trailed behind her as she walked to the inner courtyard where she knew that she would find Jarek and Otieno. Conri had wanted to send Jarek away, yet knew that doing so would cause her to flee as well. Now, he would use Conall, she knew.

When they entered the courtyard, Caryss noticed that Jarek had grown taller, and his arms had grown thicker, although he still was much a boy. He was wearing fitted leggings and a pale tunic that fell just past his elbows. As he swung a curved sword, his tunic rose, nearly tearing with the pull.

We must find him some better-fitting clothes, she thought.

As she got closer, Caryss could see streams of sweat flowing down Otieno's dark face. Jarek's pale hair was stuck to his forehead, wet and messy. When she was just steps away from the pair, Otieno paused, just long enough to allow Jarek an opening. With no hesitation, the boy cut through the air, slicing from right to left until the tip of his blade rested in the center of the large Islander's chest. Jarek held the tip there until Otieno looked back to him, nodding. Both sheathed their swords and wiped at their faces before turning their attention to Caryss and Conall.

Speaking Common, Otieno called, "Is there something you need, *leseda*?"

With a shrug and a forced smile, she told him, "Conall needs to speak with Jarek."

When Otieno tipped his head, Jarek stepped forward, his blue eyes bright and shining under the clear sky.

After a long moment of silence, Caryss glanced toward Conall, who watched the boy, and, with no attempt to hide her annoyance, she asked, "Jarek, what has your mother told you of your skills?"

Before he could reply, Otieno asked, "What is the meaning of this? The High Lord has asked him as much already."

"Conall is interested to know how your blade was able to slay a Crow, Otieno."

Half-smiling, the Islander replied, "*Enyo* was a gift to me many moon years ago, but since then, I have learned that she is no ordinary sword, and may be cursed, as you say. She has killed many, and that day with the Crow was no different than anytime before."

"Who gave you the sword?" Conall asked, his eyes darkening.

"A blacksmith."

Caryss could see Conall stiffening beside her, but before she could intervene, he threatened, "I will play no games with you. Why my brother has permitted you to stay here makes no sense to me, but you have guest-right, and I must abide by his choice. Make no mistake, though, I know your kind and will not be as easily fooled as the child and the healer seem to be."

With a shrug, Otieno told him, "I seek to fool none."

More calmly, Conall asked, "Did you know the boy was an Elemental?"

Nearly black eyes met deep brown ones as the two men stared at one another, silently, until, after a long pause, Otieno answered, "No more than he himself did."

When she next looked at Conall, Caryss paled. His eyes were black and glistening, as if they were *atraglacia*. Knowing not what else to do, she quickly stepped in between the two men, placing her hands on Otieno's chest until he stepped back a few steps. Her eyes met the Islander's, and she let him see all that was written there, until he dropped his own to the ground.

It had been nearly a moon since they have arrived in the Tribelands, and now the uneasy peace began to unravel.

Turning, she faced Conall and scolded, "Jarek is a child. What madness is this that you fear him?"

"A child? He is a weapon. A Rexterran weapon."

"Boy," Conall called, "What do you know of your power?"

Jarek's voice trilled and squeaked, caught between childhood and adulthood, like the rest of him. Caryss wanted to run to his side, but she let him speak, as she knew she must.

"My eyes might be gold-rimmed like my father's, but I have never been his son. I am my mother's child, and it is her blood that runs through me. Blood older than the King's, older still than Cordisia. Our gods are not your gods, Lord Conall, but neither are they your foes, as they once might have been. I have come with no intentions of harm, and have slept and eaten under your roof."

Caryss nearly wept at the boy's words, realizing that he was more than even she had thought. Still, she held her tears, waiting for him to finish.

"My mother did not know her own father, either, and we never had a name for what it was that we could do. I first learned of the Elementals when Caryss visited. We do not call ourselves such, but it is clear that is who my grandfather was although I know nothing of him. But I do know the skies, and I know them better than most. Well enough even to have no fear that I would harm any without intent."

With his eyes fading, Conall asked, "You time-walk as well?"

"When necessary, yes."

"What exactly do you know of the past between Tribe and Elemental?"

Jarek kept his hands at his side as he answered, "That we were created by our gods as shields against those who threatened us. That after a great war, my kin fled from here. Lord Conall, I do not even know if any else like me can be found in Cordisia."

"Can you understand my concerns, Jarek?"

His voice high, Jarek called, "I am not your enemy, sir, nor will I be the enemy of Caryss's babe."

Shaking his head, Conall replied, "If you draw forth lightning and we are too near, we could die. Enemy or not, that is not a risk my kin or I would take."

Conall's words silenced the others, but, finally, Caryss said, "He will stay, or we all will go. Just as I told the High Lord."

To Jarek, she asked, "Will you promise to not draw forth lightning when any Tribe is present?"

After a moment, he replied, "If I am in danger, I must use my weapons, Caryss, but if the Tribe means me no harm, then I will promise to control the call of the sky."

"Conall?" she asked, looking to him for acceptance.

With a shrug, he answered, "It will be for Conri to decide."

"He has already," Otieno added, his face etched and angry.

"I must speak to him myself," Conall told the *diauxie*.

"Jarek, gather your things and mine as well. We are done for today," Otieno added.

Once Jarek was far enough from them to hear, Otieno said to Caryss, "For over a moon, we have supped and slept here. I know not why the boy is no longer welcome. Why bring him here? Why have me teach him? Caryss, I had thought it was your goal to make your daughter's enemies into friends, and I thought it a wise choice."

"I have not had a change of heart," she sighed, pointing to Conall. "He is concerned for his kin and wanted to question the boy himself."

Conall interrupted.

"It is one thing to have the boy here now, but in a moon's time, when the babe is born, all will change. I need not have to explain how vulnerable the pup will be."

"Nothing has changed," Otieno cried in a rare display of emotion. "I would argue that it is even more important now that he stays with us. Treat him as a son and let him be raised as kin to your daughter. It will be one less enemy she will have to face, and he will be a more powerful ally than any she could find. Even me."

"How can he be ally without the sky?" Conall interrupted, coming near with speed that caused both Otieno and Caryss to pause.

Smiling broadly, Otieno answered, "I will teach the girl how to fight the sky, as I have done, and to win."

Suddenly, Caryss remembered the night at Nicoline's farm when he had broken her lightning into pieces, and she exclaimed, "You can teach her to fight as you did that night?"

"I will teach her that and more. She will become even more than me. The Great Mother has willed it so."

With his final words, Otieno bowed, offering up his hands to the Great Mother, as Caryss had seen him do once before.

Turning toward Conall, she said, "Is that enough? The boy will be well-trained enough to pose no threat."

With an elegant shrug, Conall answered, "It is for the High Lord to decide."

*****

When it came time to leave, Pietro was alone, which was just as well, since only he knew that his Healer Journey would not be what the Masters had expected. Before the sun had fully risen, Pietro had woken and washed. At the eighth bell, he had met with the Master Council, and, after a short discussion, he had been dismissed and allowed to begin his journey.

He knew not why it had gone so smoothly, but he suspected that Master Black, disliked yet powerful, had aided him in even this.

He knew enough to not complain and departed from the room with a smile and a bow.

Across his back was a large bag, heavy with extra clothing and blankets. Attached to his waist was his healer's belt with several pouches hanging full. Until he reached Rexterra, Pietro intended on honoring his Healer Journey, if only for a moon or so. He had spent over ten moons years at the Academy, and without the title of Master, he would have little to show for his time. With or without the dark man's interference, his journey would not be wasted, and, in a moon year's time, Pietro planned to return to the Academy to account for his time spent in travel.

Just past midday he walked out of the gates of the Academy, his robe clean and pressed and his smile wide. His sandaled feet poked out of the bottom of his wide-legged pants and left soft tracks in the sandy path as he moved. Through the center of town, he walked, smiling at those who glanced his way, and nodding in greeting to those who shouted out encouragement or waved goodbye. For a moment, he paused outside the doors of The Gull House, where he had spent many nights, often meeting Talia just after her shift ended.

For nearly a moon he had not spoken with her, and so he kept walking, remembering when last he saw her, and what accusations she had thrown at him. Some were true, he thought, yet he cared little enough for her to try to make amends. Louissia, too, no longer spoke to him, confirming to him that she had told her cousin of their time together.

It no longer mattered, he knew, as he walked on, past the clinic where he had spent a moon year in practice for his journey. Near the end of the Litusian Square, he heard his name being called, and turned to look. Even from a distance, he knew who it was from the tall, thin frame and the unkempt hair. Slowing down, Pietro waited for Kennet to reach him, surprised that he had remembered that today was his departure day, yet even more surprised that it mattered that the librarian had remembered.

"Pietro!"

Holding up a hand, he waved, and then smiled as Kennet nearly stumbled into him.

"I had thought I missed you," the lanky man called, nearly out of breath.

"Nearly so. My final Master Council meeting was this morning. Now that I am beyond the gates, I suppose my journey has begun."

With a long sigh, Kennet told him, "It will be strange to have both you and Bronwen gone from the Academy."

Pietro could not believe that he had forgotten to inquire about when last Kennet had heard from Bronwen, and nearly yelped with excitement that he now had another chance.

"Have you received word from her of late? How fares her journey?" he asked, trying to keep his voice steady.

Before he answered, Kennet's face flushed red, and his lip trembled, yet he managed to reply, "Nearly a moon ago, I had word from her. She is well and seeing places that she had never thought to. More than that I do not know, as her letter was quite brief."

Pietro suspected that Kennet was lying, and asked, "Did she travel to the North, as most suspected that she would? Or did she head east, knowing that it is where most healing can be found?"

When Kennet did not answer, Pietro's suspicion was confirmed, and he said, "I mean her no harm, Kennet. We are both soon to be Masters, and our time at the Academy will be only fond memories. Perhaps I will even encounter her along my own journey. It would be a welcome sight to see her, no doubt."

Kennet only nodded, and Pietro knew that he would get no more information from him.

Bowing his head slightly and offering Kennet a wide smile, Pietro stepped forward and hugged the librarian, who wrapped his long arms around him in return. Just as quickly, Pietro stepped back from him, nodded again, and continued walking. Without looking back, he knew that Kennet watched him. He would watch many healers come and go from the Academy, yet he would never be one of them. If Kennet had not lied to him about Bronwen, he might have felt bad for him, yet now he cared little. No longer a use to him, Kennet was no longer a friend, even if he had been the only one to tell him goodbye.

*****

"Have you received word from the men you sent north?"

"Would it surprise you if I told you that they are finding it difficult to gather information from the Eirrannians?"

"They have learned nothing then?"

Walking through the central courtyard of the Grand Palace, Delwin and Crispin make a striking pair, dark-haired and golden-eyed, both wearing fine clothing and neatly polished boots. Delwin, as usual, donned the silver and blue uniform of the Royal Army, while Crispin wore mostly black, except for a small silver crest sewn across his left chest. Neither had crown or guard, as if they were no more than just brothers.

Adjusting the sword that hung at his hip, Delwin replied, "It is as if she was not there, Crispin, but there is nowhere else in Cordisia that would offer her safety. I have ordered them to keep searching for the next moon, and I opened their purses, which should assist their questioning."

With a snort, Crispin said, "You think to buy knowledge of the girl? Surely you know the Northerners better than that."

Shrugging, Delwin answered, "There are always those whose tongues wag for coin. You are fond of the Lower Streets, Cris, and must know that for truth."

Not wanting to argue, Crispin sighed, "True words, if unfortunate ones."

"I had thought my men would have found her by now. It has been moons since father was last seen, and word spreads that he is unwell. Soon, we will need to address the rumors, and one of us must be ready to take the crown."

Finally, he speaks aloud the words, Crispin thought, unsurprised. Even before Caryss had taken Herrin, his brother had wanted their father to relinquish his rule. Though Crispin was the elder of the two, Delwin had never accepted that the throne should go to him next, and, since Herrin had fallen ill, conflict had risen. Without Herrin to formally crown him, Crispin would have less backing from the Circle of Council.

All that Crispin mulled over as he walked next to his brother, yet he only said, "Give your men their time, and, if nothing has been discovered by the end of the moon, then we will talk again."

"I have heard those same words too often, Crispin. If the Northerners do not give up the girl by then, my men will strike. The time for talk has ceased."

"Strike?" Crispin grunted, grabbing his brother's arm, and forcing him to stop marching.

"Eirrannia is sheltering the woman who kidnapped our father!" Delwin barked. "How else are we to see that but as an act of war."

They had neared the Central Wing, and, around them, guards listened, with eyes downcast. Delwin had shaken free from his grasp and stood gaping at him, eyes aflame with fury.

After a long moment, Crispin said through barely parted lips, "I will have Uncle Derry send word to his kin in the North. Perhaps when they hear of what will come of sheltering the girl, they will reconsider. Until I hear back, do not act, Delwin. This it no time for war, nor the right enemy. Rexterra is not strong nor rich enough to strike so foolishly."

His last sentence hung heavy with threat. Over the last moon years of Herrin's reign, gold had become scarce, and the coffers were nearly empty. Rexterra had little resources to wage war, yet his brother cared little for coin, and would offer his men other reward for their risks, an offer that Crispin knew few would turn down. Many would die, and those who survived would be wealthier for it. Yet, the coffers of Rexterra would suffer most.

And there would be those who would seek to use the Crown's poverty for their own gain. Like the Mage-Guild, Crispin thought.

"One chance," Delwin finally conceded. "Either Derry can convince the North to release her or we find her ourselves. If they refuse, I will head North myself to lead the assault."

Crispin did not reply as he hurried back to his rooms. There was little time. Too little.

*****

Seated cross-legged on the tiled floor, Caryss looked up at Nahla, who was weaving colorful yarn into a blanket. The woman's fingers moved swiftly and gracefully, humming as they brushed against the small loom.

Sharron and Gregorr were with the King, who had been given a tonic that the *fennidi* had brewed, a mixture of powdered pumpkin seed and crushed walnut hulls. She had not thought to try the two together, but Gregorr had insisted that both worked well to expel what often could not be seen. Poison, she thought, as she knew he did, too, but neither said it.

Within the day, the King's bowels would loosen, and for days to follow, he would have to be given water and his underclothes changed often, Gregorr had warned. Caryss had not objected, and Sharron had agreed to sit with him for the first half of the day, releasing Caryss to her room, where Nahla had found her.

Both women had sat silently for most of the morning until Caryss, glancing toward the closed door, said, "Conri has returned."

With her fingers still moving, Nahla asked, "How can you be certain?"

Rising from the floor, she answered, "I have never been wrong."

Her words were clipped and short, and she nearly apologized, but Nahla did not seem bothered, so she slipped from the room without further explanation. Her feet were bare, and Caryss wore a healer's robe that fit tightly across her chest and belly. Beneath it were soft and well-worn cotton pants, tied just below her rounded stomach. As she walked down the hallway, she quickly braided her hair, letting it hang across her left shoulder, appearing as if she was still at the Academy.

Soon, she was opening the glass door to the inner courtyard, where she knew that she would find Otieno, Aldric, and Jarek. Jarek and Otieno were sparring with wooden staffs, while Aldric watched, calling out suggestions to the boy, and causing Caryss to remember that he had spent many years as a soldier after he was exiled from the Mage-Guild. The three were still a strange sight to see, despite the time that they had spent together.

301

As she neared them, Aldric spotted her first and called out her name, causing Otieno and Jarek to drop their weapons.

"He has arrived."

Otieno bowed his head slightly, and asked, "Has he sent you for the boy?"

Without taking her eyes from the *diauxie*, she answered, "I have not seen him yet. I see no reason why Jarek should miss a lesson. Continue, and let Conri come to us."

"Caryss," Aldric warned, walking toward her.

The sun was high and bright, and she could not remember when last she sat beneath its rays, like she used to do often in Litusia. Ignoring Aldric, she walked past him to an iron-wrought bench, and, once there, she lay upon it, throwing her arm across her eyes. There she stayed, listening as the wooden practice swords of Otieno and Jarek banged off one another. She did not hear Aldric, but knew he was there still, as he would not leave her side now, not while they waited for the High Lord. It was cooler in the North than anywhere else she had been, especially so compared to Tretoria and the Southern Cove Islands, but the sun was strong and warmed her bare skin, no doubt causing more freckles to appear across her nose. A few times she found herself dozing, but each time shouts from Otieno would rouse her.

When next she woke, Conri was above her, looking down at her as if she was a stranger.

In a hoarse voice, she whispered, "Did you think me dead?"

From half-closed eyes, she watched his gaze darken. Fighting against the half-smile that threatened to overtake her, Caryss rolled to her side, then slowly sat up, keeping her own eyes on the High Lord. Behind her vision was a blackened haze, and much around her was filtered through a soft fog, except for Conri, whom she would know anywhere.

After blinking several times, her eyes cleared, and, noticing that he watched her, she said, "You have spoken to Conall."

His words, when they came, were as cold as any she had heard him say, and, for a moment, she knew fear.

"My brother is not yours to command just as my orders are not to be ignored. You should have never left the Tribelands, Caryss."

Ignoring her pulsing heart, Caryss told him, "Nothing amiss came of it, and the King might fare better because of the *fennidi*. And let us not forget that I secured you an ally, Conri."

His eyes blazed and his smooth forehead wrinkled in thought, and Caryss realized that Conall had not yet told him of all that happened with Ohdra.

"You have not yet heard," she half-taunted. "Ohdra has vowed to defend the Wolf. She stands at your side, now and against what it is to come."

His expression was unreadable as he stated, "The *fennidi* offer nothing up without payment. What did you promise her?"

With her eyes on him, to gauge his reaction, she called, "Freedom."

"How is that yours to give?" he growled.

"It was not me who offered it. Our daughter is of the North, and it is she who can promise what you and I cannot."

"She risks too much," he hissed. "Caryss, it is not safe for her to time-walk so often."

With a shrug, she told him, "It will be much less once she is born. As Aldric explained, it is easier to travel to a place where you once were, yet nearly impossible to go where you have never been. For now, she is always with me, and when I call, it is never difficult for her to come."

"Conall was with you for all of this?" he asked, pushing his hands through his dark hair.

When she nodded, he said, "Then we will discuss it at length later. Now, we must talk about the boy."

With an exaggerated sigh, she told him, "It has been discussed already between us."

"Call for him."

Knowing that he would not back down, she rose from the bench, and directed Otieno to bring Jarek to her. She could feel Conri's gaze and knew that he did not like that she had included the Islander. He had not forgotten that Otieno had been able to kill the Crow, and he must know, too, that the longsword was still across his back. With no words, Caryss wanted it known that she would not allow Jarek to be hurt.

Aldric joined them as well, and, for a moment, Caryss looked toward Conri, his dark eyes greeting her gray-green ones.

Without lightening his eyes, he warned, "I could kill them all, Caryss, and only you would remain. I tire of this petulance. If the Islander reaches for his sword or the mage for his fire, they will die. And the boy with them."

Her lips trembled and her tongue thickened, and, when words would not come, Caryss dropped her head, squeezing her eyes closed until the throbbing in her neck and the burning at the back of her throat lessened. Too often she forgot that he was Tribe, just as the girl would be, she reminded herself. Before she had fully recovered from his words, Conri was speaking, and she forced her eyes open, staring just past him as he talked.

"Jarek," the High Lord called, "Have you confessed all that you know of your kin?"

With a shaky voice but clear and focused eyes, Jarek answered, "Each day I learn more of them. Am I to update you each night?"

Caryss hastily looked away, raising an arm to hide her pleasure at the boy's words.

With her eyes to the ground, she heard Conri step nearer, his boots nearly silent in the thick grass.

"There are few of you in Cordisia, Jarek. You might be better served to travel across the Eastern Sea to seek the others."

Shaking his head, Jarek told him, "Cordisia is my home, and I do not need to tell you that by birth-right, Rexterra should one day be mine."

"A boy's dream," Conri uttered.

"I do not think the dream will die as I age, my lord."

In a few moons, Jarek had bloomed under the tutelage of Aldric and Otieno, and he faced the Tribesman with his chin high and his cheeks flushed. *As if he was a king's son*, Caryss thought.

"If one day you sit the throne, what will the Tribe be to you? Friend or foe?"

Conri's question rang loud through the courtyard, each present listening and awaiting the boy's reply.

When it came, Caryss nearly embraced him.

"I am friend, and will be, unless given a reason to become foe."

"Easy words for a child to proclaim," Conri laughed, "But harder ones for a man grown to keep."

"I have given you my word," Jarek sputtered, frustration growing.

As if teasing, Conri mockingly called, "I would be a fool to risk the safety of my people on the crackling vows of a boy who sounds and looks child-like."

"Do you name me oath-breaker?" Jarek cried.

With another laugh, this one biting and sharp, the High Lord told him, "Perhaps."

Jarek's narrow wooden sword swung across the space that separated him from Conri faster than any could move to stop it. Across the High Lord's chin, a red welt began to form.

Caryss rushed forward, hoping to shield Jarek, but felt a hand on her arm, and turned to find Otieno pulling her back as he hissed, "This is his fight, not yours."

When Jarek pulled the sword back to his shoulder and began to swing again, Conri reached for it, grabbing it quickly, as he should have done the first time, Caryss knew, remembering the speed with which he could move. With little effort, the sword was in his hand. Before she could blink, he threw the sword at Jarek's feet and waved his other hand. As they all watched, wood turned to flame, orange and crackling until there was nothing left of the sword and blackened ash floated around them all.

His blue eyes shining as she had never seen them, round and sparkling, as if the sea had frozen, Jarek screamed, "I will not be named oath-breaker!"

With no weapon and his arms at his sides, he rushed to the where Conri now stood. He stood near the High Lord's chest and quivered.

"When my word is given, it will be so until I die."

The ice in his eyes had reached his words, and Jarek did not look away from the Tribesman.

Rubbing at his chin, Conri said, "I will ask them again in another ten moon years."

"Ask them as often as you like. They will not change."

Conri's smile vanished as again he questioned the boy. "Will you vow to never harm my daughter or those who aid her?"

With a hand to his chest and his bright eyes on the High Lord, Jarek crisply answered, "Just as I have given Caryss my word, I will give it to you High Lord Conri. I vow to protect the girl and her kin as if they were my own, to fight for her and at her side. I offer my sword, and I offer the sky."

"And you will never bring the sky upon her?"

"Nor will I bring it on you or your kin, my lord."

After a moment, Conri stepped toward Jarek, and, with his hands raised, palms up, as if in peace, said, "What is it that you want in exchange?"

None moved, not even to draw breath.

"You will help me win the throne."

It was Conri who moved first, stepping closer to Jarek. As Caryss, Aldric, and Otieno watched, he reached out his hand, paused, then clasped the offered hand of Jarek.

"The crown will be yours, Jarek."

Suddenly, Caryss understood the game that had long been played. More, she knew how little her part mattered. And why he had allowed the boy to enter the Tribelands at all. Her eyes filled with tears, her throat thickened and dried. Her hands shook, and her vision blurred. *I have given him what he wanted all along. Rexaria.*

Across the field, leaning against the glass-paneled door stood Willem. Caryss, even through the mist of knowledge, recognized him from afar. He had come, just when she needed him most, and she rushed across the courtyard until she collapsed into his embrace. She did not need to turn back to know that they watched.

*****

305

24

"Not too long now," she mumbled, looking down at her expanding belly as she paced across the hallway.

It had been nearly a moon since Willem had arrived, and, in that time, they had learned of his correspondence with his cousin, who still did not know that Jarek was with them. Both Caryss and Jarek had begged Willem to keep it so, and, finally, fearing for the boy's safety, Willem agreed.

When she arrived in the small courtyard to the east of the complex, Willem was already there, seated on a bench of stone, with a thick parchment in his hand. Her life pulse quickened as she hurried to him.

Nearing, she called, "What do you have?"

The letter dropped into his lap, and his face darkened as he told her, "Word from the North."

With a voice full of doubt, she asked, "Who knows you are here?"

"My father."

"Does he not live in the King's City?"

Rubbing his hand over his face, he mumbled, "It seems that he has been in Eirrannia for a half-moon, on orders from Crispin."

"What?" she shrieked, trying to reach for the letter.

He did not release it, but pointed to the scrolling words and explained, "As we have long suspected, Delwin has sent an army to track you and bring the King back to Rexterra. For the last two moons, his men have been in Eirrannia, with coin and sword, looking for you or information that could lead to you."

"And now Crispin hunts me too," she whispered.

Shaking his head, Willem sighed. "Crispin and my father have sought to put an end to this madness. Yet it has been moons, Caryss, and Crispin can no longer buy you time. Delwin means to strike."

Falling heavily onto the bench beside Willem, she asked, "Delwin plans to attack Eirrannia if he does not find me?"

"Just so," Willem agreed.

His words were not unexpected, yet Caryss felt as if she could no longer breathe.

Nearly choking for air, she cried, "The king needs more time."

After a moment, her throbbing chest slowed, and Caryss added, "Herrin fares better each day, and, with Gregorr's help, his poisoned stomach is healing. Just yesterday he was able to walk the length of the outer courtyard. He is weak, but his mind is regaining its sharpness, although he remembers nothing of our journey here. Do you think he is fit to rule?"

Without looking up at her, Willem answered, "Caryss, I no longer think my uncle will ever regain his throne. Too much time has passed, and Delwin has tasted the sweet juices of the crown. Crispin is too powerless to stop what his brother plans. Delwin has the Royal Army behind him, while Crispin has nothing. Even the merchants now fear to go against Delwin. Crispin is many things, but he has never been cunning enough to rule, and his heart is too soft."

"I had thought you to be Crispin's ally."

"Caryss, I know that you learned little but healing at the Academy, so let me try to explain. With Herrin gone, the throne has been open. Word has spread, with help from Delwin I would guess, that Crispin is responsible for the King's disappearance. So while Delwin valiantly leads a search for him, Crispin waits in the palace and appears to do nothing. Delwin is deft and moved with swiftness to turn Herrin's absence into his own gain."

Folding her hand in between his, Willem continued, "Think on this. Delwin's men will wage war if Eirrannia does not tell him where to find the King. Yet, as you have told me, none but the *fennidi* know. There is no outcome but one."

Slowly, she was beginning to understand. She was not what was sought. Nor was the King.

"Delwin will strike. In the name of the King. As prize, with or without Herrin found, the throne will be his."

Aching and spinning, Caryss mumbled, "I will not let Eirrannia suffer for my crimes."

His gold-rimmed eyes looked at her with kindness, yet his words cut.

"It is too late."

She had brought war to her people. To the people her daughter hoped to rule. All for vows to a king that cared little for the North.

"There is little else to do but return the King and let him defend our cause. Send word to Crispin," she told him, her words cropped and shallow, as if defeated.

"Will he recall enough to be of use?" Willem asked.

Shrugging, she answered, "He has had no poppy milk for nearly two moons, and most of the poison is gone from his body. Yet, his thoughts are fog-touched at times. In truth, I know not what he will tell them."

"Caryss," he cried, "You will be sending a half-mad man who remembers little back to Rexterra! Does he remember giving his word to keep Jarek unharmed? Or does he forget that you even have the boy?"

Closing her eyes, Caryss confessed, "He forgets much, a result of henbane that we had given him to ease him off the poppy milk, I believe.

He does not think himself a captive, Willem, nor does he think we are trying to harm him. There is no pattern to what he remembers and what he does not."

"As he is now Herrin is little more than a child's toy, and Delwin will use him as such."

"What choice do we have but to risk the King's return?"

His voice deeper than before, Willem growled, "Eirrannia will face war. If not now, then soon."

"We have played into Delwin's hand," he continued, "Perhaps without knowing we did so. With or without his father, the throne is his, even though all knew that Crispin was heir. Caryss, despite your attempts, you were not unseen while in the King's City. It was Crispin who sent for you, which, by now, I believe Delwin must suspect. What followed was treason, or near enough to look as if it was. If Herrin is returned, he will be questioned. And you are unsure what he will answer."

In a whisper, Caryss mumbled, "Nothing has turned out as I had thought it to."

When he said nothing, she asked, "What would you have me do now, Willem?"

"Choose. Which matters more to you, delaying war against Eirrannia or giving the Rexterran throne to Delwin?"

"I care little for Rexterra," she snorted. "Is there a way to prevent both from happening?"

Rising from the bench, Willem answered, softly, "Go with Herrin to the King's City and meet with Delwin, who, if I know him at all, will no doubt have you in chains before the meeting ends. If you are not in Eirrannia, he has less cause to strike."

"Conri will not allow it."

"Nor should he."

"Willem, if Rexterra attacks Eirrannia because of me, would the Tribe not become involved as well? What then?"

"Now you begin to see, Caryss. From what I have learned since I've been here, there is war brewing between the Crows and Wolves. Conri would be a fool to send his men to defend Eirrannia when a stronger enemy is at his own door."

Shaking her head back and forth, Caryss gasped, "Have I caused all of this?"

Willem placed an arm around her and wrapped her in a tight embrace, as he had done in her final moons at the Academy. Into her ear, he whispered, "My dear, Cordisia has long been a sought after prize. Man, mage, and Tribe all have battled for her heart and her rule. It has been lifetimes since a great war has been fought, but the winds have changed."

"My daughter will be a weapon," she sobbed, clinging to him, making sense of all that had occurred over the last half-moon year.

He pulled himself from her, and gently said, "The girl is not yet born, and, even then, she will not be of age for many moon years to come. Perhaps by then, the winds will have changed once again and Cordisia will be at peace."

With tears on her cheeks and eyes red and swollen, Caryss cried, "I have always known there was much wanted of her, yet Conri told me little. She will be his sword, Willem, and shield between Cordisia and Tribe."

"Or she will be queen."

"Queen! Of where?" Caryss cried, spittle flying and snot running from her nose.

"Eirrannia. Rexterra. All of Cordisia. She will have her pick."

"You might think me a fool, Willem, but I have long known that she would need an army. What else have I been doing these moons but finding her ally and soldier?"

With a smile, he replied, "I once told you that you were not the lamb you pretended to be, Caryss, and, again, I am reminded of that. While the girl grows and learns, Cordisia will battle. But when she is ready, she will return, with army and power. No one's weapon but her own."

"And the North will rise," Caryss whispered, clear-eyed.

"Just so," Willem answered.

Not for the first time, Caryss wished that she could love him.

"We must leave Cordisia."

Her words were the truest ones that she had ever spoken.

He nodded, "Yes. The fight coming is not hers."

"Where will we go?" she asked, the Northern breeze carrying her words across the courtyard for any to hear.

"To lands that offer safety and swords," he told her.

Sighing, Caryss said, "I feel as if I am running from a mess that I helped create."

Shaking his head, he told her, "You are but a player, Caryss, in a game that started long before you were born."

Rising from the bench, she nearly complained that she had not wanted to play. But she knew that mattered little.

When they reached the door, she asked, "What of the North? Am I not abandoning them in their time of need?"

Laughing, he said, "You are a healer, Caryss, not a fighter. What you might not know is that Eirrannia has long known this battle was coming, and they are prepared. It is not you whom they need."

"They will wait for her."

"Indeed," he answered, as she pushed open the door.

*****

For nearly a moon Pietro had traveled, all by foot, as was required for a Healer Journey. Often tempted to barter for a horse, he continued with a nearly empty purse and boots that had worn thin. There had only been two nights when he had not had a roof to sleep under, and even those had not been as bad as he had feared. The land was now familiar to him, and he knew that within a day he would arrive at the gates of the King's City.

Pietro lived as if he was a Master in training, healing and tending to small injuries as he made his way east, although he did not hurry as the Tribesman had commanded. Despite his worry over what would happen once in the King's City, Pietro found himself enjoying his Healer Journey, and tried to commit much of it to memory, knowing that he would have to report to the Master Council at the end of the moon year.

Some moments he would omit, such as the time spent with the golden-haired Planusian beauty. The next morning, as she lay blushed and sleeping, he had quietly departed. After two hours of walking, he had collapsed, sleeping beneath an orange-leaved tree, only waking when a small child found him. It had been too long since the fire had taken him, and he had forgotten how exhausted he always felt after its departure.

A light rain had been falling all morning, but as the skies darkened and the rain came harder, Pietro hurried to find shelter. There were several buildings around him, and, after a moment of searching, he discovered an inn, running to it as water dripped from his hair and down his face. Just after he entered the crowded room, a man came up to him, half-bowing.

"Are those healers' robes, sir?" the man called in a voice heavy from the hills, the words thick and clipped.

Wiping at his face with the back of his sleeve and adjusting his eyes to the dimly-lit room, Pietro answered, "Soon to be Master's robes, once I finish out my Healer Journey."

Upon closer look, Pietro noticed the man appeared pale, as if he was unwell, and his hands were trembling.

"Are you unwell?" Pietro asked.

"No, not me, sir, but my son. A few days ago, he was helping me in the kitchen and he sliced his finger. It did not appear to be so bad, but he has been abed all day. I am the innkeeper here, and my son is a good lad. If you would be so kind as to tend to him, you can stay the night and have as much food and drink as would suit you."

With a nod, Pietro called, "Show me to the boy."

Following as the man led him past tables and through other dusky rooms, Pietro nearly ran into the innkeeper when he stopped in a small

310

room. It was dotted with tapering candles, and soft light revealed a small cot and two wooden chairs. When the man pointed, Pietro hurried to the cot, finding a shivering, gray-skinned boy tucked beneath several blankets.

Pietro pulled a chair toward the bed, untying several pouches from his belt and setting them within his reach. Without even touching the boy, he knew that the cut, which he had not yet seen, had become diseased and was affecting the rest of his body. It was not uncommon, although in one so young, it was less so.

Reaching for the boy's hand, which was wrapped in clean linen, Pietro asked, "What was he cutting?"

"Chicken, sir, which he has done many times. I do not know what made the knife slip."

Neither talked further as Pietro cut the cloth from the boy's hand, unraveling it and revealing a nearly severed finger. It had not blackened, as he thought it might. As quickly as he could, Pietro emptied out the pouch that carried several medium-sized bottles, grabbing one filled with a clear liquid. With steady hands, he poured the liquid over the split finger, and as it bubbled, the boy woke with a scream.

"Hold him down," Pietro called to the man, leaning further onto the boy to keep him still.

After the man stood at the top of the cot and reached for the boy's uninjured arm, placing it between his much larger hands before half-sitting on the boy's chest, Pietro reached for a long, thin needle and thread. As quickly as he could, he reattached the finger, weaving the dark, thick thread until a nearly complete arc of black crosses circled it. The boy had settled, although he still had not fully wakened.

As he wrapped the finger in fresh linen, Pietro said, "The wound will need to be cleaned every other day and fresh dressings applied. After a moon, the stitching must be taken out with the tip of a knife that has been cleaned and fired. It might be moons before the boy has full use of his hand, if he survives the infection that has spread throughout his body."

The man paled. "Is there nothing more you can do for him? I have coin to pay."

"I can take no coin, but food and a room will gladly be accepted. The boy will need to take a spoonful of a tonic that I will leave with you each morning and night. The bottle will last a quarter-moon, and does much to heal infection. If he has not recovered by then, nothing more can be done for him."

Rising from the bed, the man half-sobbed, "Your arrival was well-timed, healer, and whatever you need will be yours, as well as my thanks."

The man's face was red-splotched now, causing Pietro to look away as he followed him from the room. After climbing a wide staircase, the innkeeper stopped, reaching for the keys hanging from his belt. His hand

311

shook, and the metal clanged, echoing through the empty hall. When the door was finally opened, Pietro hurried in, wanting little more than to replace his wet and muddy robe.

Before the man could leave, he told him, "After some food and ale, I will check on your son again."

With a nod, the innkeeper closed the door, and Pietro tore the robe from his body. There was no mirror in the room, and little more than a feathered cot and table, but he knew that he had grown thinner since leaving the Academy. Without the monthly stipend from his father, he was living like the other healers who had journeyed. As Bronwen did too, he guessed.

Sitting naked on the cot, he thought of her, of where she could be, and of the Tribesman who had taken an interest in her. His hatred for her had lessened, he realized, wondering anew what she had done to attract notice. Over the last moon, he thought much on Bronwen, especially of her babe. The Tribesman planned to kill her, although he hoped that he would be able to convince his cousin of the folly of such an action.

Pulling the cleanest robe he had from his satchel, Pietro dressed.

As he neared the door, he muttered, "If only he could forget us both."

Later, seated at a brick-paved bar, Pietro thought more on his options. His golden fingers combed through his hair, which had grown longer, dipped in sunlight and shining. With a mug cupped between his hands, Pietro thought of leaving, heading north or west instead of east to the King's City. Yet, the man's face, white and ashen, his teeth sharp and his eyes nearly black, appeared behind his own eyes.

He was a healer, having had no skill during his singular moon year spent training in the King's City, before he entered the Academy. Pietro knew that he would be no match for the Tribesman, nor could he count on any to offer him assistance.

*****

25

Securing an audience with Prince Delwin was not as easy as Pietro had expected it to be, and few remembered who he was after his long absence. In the end, he had used his father's name to finally gain entrance to the Grand Palace, which still stung as he tapped his sandaled foot against the marble floor, waiting for Delwin to join him. For most of the afternoon, he had been waiting, with little to do and afraid to leave the room for fear of missing the prince. Several times he had emptied his healer's pouches, writing an inventory of what he would need to replace.

In just over a moon's time, he had gone through more supplies than he had planned, and, if the Tribesman had been correct, he would need much more before trying to heal King Herrin. There had been rumors, even when he was a small child, of the King being in poor health, but, now, he realized something must have changed, especially if Bronwen had become involved. He still could not make sense of why neither she nor any other of the established Masters had traveled to the King, but it was a question that he hoped to ask his cousin, if he ever showed up.

As the room started to darken and the sun vanished, the door behind him swung open. Swiftly, Pietro rose.

Accompanied by several guards, Delwin entered, looking much the same as he had many moons years before, when Pietro had left for the Academy.

With no introduction, the Prince called, "One of my men informed me that you requested an urgent meeting. Make it quick, for I have little time."

There were three guards behind the Prince, all with sword and shield, and, Pietro noticed, Delwin wore two swords as well. His hands were moist and, for a moment, he could not speak.

He had been long gone from Rexterra, and stuttered, "My Lord Prince, I have come from the Academy, a moon into my Healer Journey. At the end of the moon year, I will be a Master Healer full and full and prepared to return to the King's City to serve the realm if she will have me."

There was more he needed to say, but Delwin interrupted, "Yes, I see the robes, boy, and I am no fool to as to what they mean."

When he would have responded, Delwin leapt toward him, cheeks ablaze and eyes gold and shining, and said, "Do you know the healer, Caryss?"

"I know none by that name, my lord," he replied, shaking his head and backing away from the Prince.

Slamming his hands onto the table, Delwin screamed, "I knew her to be a lying whore! My brother is more fool than I had even thought to believe her to be healer-trained. When I find the fire-haired witch, she will burn for all Rexterra to see!"

"Wait!" Pietro cried, "There was a healer who set out for her own Healer Journey moons before I did, my lord, and, it might be the same one you spoke of, but I knew her by a different name. However, I have heard her called fire-haired."

Delwin turned and stared at him so deeply that Pietro's knees nearly buckled. He waited as Delwin watched him, as if trying to decide if his words were truth or not.

Finally, Delwin demanded, "Was she from the North, this girl you know?"

When Pietro nodded, Delwin smiled, although it did nothing to ease his fears. He swallowed hard as Delwin loudly dropped into a chair, uncertain if he should sit as well. His doubt lasted just moments as the Prince pulled another chair from the table and told him to use it.

After they were both seated and facing each other, Delwin asked, "Tell me all you know of this healer, and forget nothing, even if you think it matters little."

There was no more time for hesitation, and, despite his reluctance, he haltingly said, "My lord, Bronwen, whom you know as Caryss it seems, is the reason why I am in the King's City and why it was necessary that I speak with you. Before I left Tretoria, I was visited by a man that wanted me to deliver a message to you."

"What man?" Delwin interjected, laying a hand on his sword.

"A Tribesman," Pietro barely managed to reply.

He waited for the prince to react to his words, yet none came. As if he expected them, Pietro feared.

"Tell me all that he said."

And so Pietro told his cousin all that the Tribesman had said, pausing often to add details that he remembered or to answer Delwin's questions. He explained how the man had first found him, how each visit concerned Bronwen, and how he seemed to know much of what was occurring in the King's City, including the King's illness, which Delwin still had not confirmed. What interested Delwin the most was the idea that Bronwen was in the Tribelands, and he made Pietro explain twice what the man had told him. When he had finished, the night sky was dark and the room was lit softly with orb-lights. And Prince Delwin was quiet.

"Is it true about the King?" Pietro finally mumbled, uneasy in the silence.

"That he is with the girl? Yes, although I had no part of it, nor would I have allowed it. This healer has committed high treason, and, when I find her, she will face trial. My men are within a day's ride of the Tribelands, as I was until I hurried back here to attend other matters. Before the moon is out, she will be located."

"What of your father?" Pietro asked, dropping his gaze.

"You have told me more than my own men. If what the Tribesman said is true, then he is still alive. When he is found, my men will bring him back here, and the Masters will tend to him."

Delwin rose, but before he could leave, Pietro called, "My lord, the girl is a healer and has taken an oath to do no harm to any she might come across. I do not believe she would seek to harm the King."

Slamming the chair into the heavy, wooden table, Delwin spit, "Healer-trained or not, she committed high treason. She could have killed him when she took him from the palace and from the care of the Masters here!"

"My lord," Pietro stuttered, "Bronwen is one of the best healers the Academy has ever known. Your father could find none better."

Thrusting a finger into Pietro's reddening face, Delwin roared, "Hold your tongue, boy, or you might be joining her in a cell!"

Pietro did not move, nor did he answer as he waited for Delwin to back away from him. Beads of spittle covered his face, yet he held his hands in his lap, afraid to further upset the Prince. When Delwin moved toward the door, Pietro slowly lifted his chin, watching as he raised his hand to remove the warding.

Just as he was about to exit the room, Delwin addressed his men, "See the healer to a room and keep a guard outside. When I leave for the North, he will be accompanying me."

As the door closed, Pietro dropped his head into his hands, realizing that the Tribesman had not been wrong. He would be going north, yet it was not as he had thought. For a moon, he had traveled freely, living and healing as the Master Council required. Now, his travel would no longer be his own.

I will be more prisoner than healer, he thought, as he rose and followed the uniformed guards from the room.

As he trailed the Prince's men, he searched for the anger he often had for the healer, only to find that it was no longer there.

*****

"How does he fare, Gregorr?"

"Improved," the *fennidi* chimed. "And much stronger than when I first arrived. His body is healing and he has been able to walk across the courtyard on several occasions."

Caryss had learned much from the man, surprised each time he suggested an herb or a tonic that she had not thought to use. He reminded her much of Kennet, and she doubted there was much that he did not know or seek to understand. Like Kennet, too, he had become quite talkative, although he joked and laughed more often than her old friend. Jarek was already taller than the man, and, once, when the boy asked how old he was, Gregorr had said only that he was older than the grass but younger than the trees. Caryss smiled as she remembered Jarek's reply.

The sky is older than both.

She and the *fennidi* stood just outside the large glasshouse under an angled sun and cloudless sky, and the brightness made the man's skin glow a lustrous green, as if he was kin to grass and tree. Heavy with child and knowing the girl's birth was near, Caryss paused for a moment to reflect on the odd army that she was assembling: a king's bastard child, a promising mage who had turned to the Dark Arts because of a lost love, a gentle healer who mothered them all, a warrior unmatched in skill but without desire to fight, and, now, a tiny wood sprite. Five people, one a child still, against the might of Rexterra.

The smile quickly faded as she asked, "What of his mind? This morning he seemed to forget who I was."

Shielding his eyes as he looked up at her, Gregorr answered, "At times he remembers all, including you. But there are times when it is as if no time has passed and he is still on the throne. Other times he refers to his sons as boys. As you well know, Caryss, what we try to heal ofttimes becomes more damaged. Such is with the King, I fear."

"It took a moon to wean him from the poppy milk, and I feared then that it was too late. Answer me this, Gregorr. Which is worse: a confused mind or an empty one?"

"Worse for whom?" he asked, twinkling still.

With a sigh, she told him, "For the woman who stole him from slumber. There is an army searching for us, and if Herrin cannot tell his sons that he came willingly, if he cannot remember coming with me on his own accord, then we will have no respite from that army."

"And if he has no memory at all?"

"The boy will at least be safe," she hurriedly answered.

A look of understanding crossed Gregorr's face as he said, "You want Conri to mind-lock him."

When she nodded, he asked, "What then?"

"We leave Cordisia until it is safe to return."

"Giving Jarek time to learn the dance of swords," Gregorr whispered, letting his hand fall away from his face and running his fingers through the long, silver hair that hung past his narrow waist.

After a few moments, he said, "You will pit brother against brother, Caryss, and the one that you want to win has no army."

"There has been no peace between Crispin and Delwin for moon years," she huffed, "And, besides, it is not our battle to fight. We are five, Gregorr, and need time to build an army that can hope to defend the girl."

He said nothing, but his nod was agreement enough.

For a moment, her life pulse raced, and Caryss reached for her stomach. Beneath her fingers, she could feel her body tighten.

With a leap toward her, he placed an arm around her back, asking, "Does the babe come?"

"Soon," she mumbled, bracing herself again.

"Is it time yet?" he asked, still holding her.

With a shudder, Caryss mumbled, "Near enough. Can you help me find Sharron?"

The small *fennidi* was only as tall as her chest, but he looped a thin, green arm around her and helped her as she slowly walked across the fading field and into the home of the Wolf Tribe. They encountered no one until they neared the kitchens, where Nahla nearly ran into them. In the moon since Gregorr had been there, the woman's belly had grown, too, and it was near the size of Caryss's, even though her own babe was nearly four moons from being born. As she looked upon Caryss, her eyes widened with surprise.

"The babe comes!" she cried, reaching for the pale-skinned healer.

Together, they helped Caryss until she was seated on her bed, more clear-eyed as the pain lessened.

With a steady voice, she told them, "I will need motherwort and skullcap, and ginger as well. Sharron should have most of it readied. Nahla, will you find me some linens?"

When the woman rushed out, Gregorr asked, "What of the High Lord? He will need to be told."

Caryss paid him little heed, only realizing he was gone moments later when her eyes opened.

Alone, she nearly sobbed.

*****

Sharron was with the King, as he suspected, and he wasted no time telling her of the babe. Before he left, he noticed that she ran across the room, grabbed two large pouches, and made her way down the long hallway to Caryss's room. As she rushed off, the glass jars housed in the pouches banged into one another, sending twinkling sounds through the hallway, as if in song. With each step that Sharron took, the jars clanged and chimed until Gregorr was too far to hear them anymore.

In the far corner of the complex, Conri had a section of rooms, ones that few were permitted to enter. With little choice, Gregorr quickly found the rooms, hearing voices as he neared. The doors around him were all closed, and heavily warded, he guessed. Unsure what would happen if he touched the warded door, Gregorr stopped steps outside the room where he heard Conri's voice, his arms hanging at his side.

From a pocket sewn into his loose, brown pants, he withdrew a stone. It was no bigger than a coin, dull and round. As Gregorr turned it over in his hand, he eyed the small engraving on it.

Three interlocking circles.

With little time to waste, he opened his mouth, placed the stone on his tongue, and walked closer to the door. Drawing a deep breath, he placed his hands on the door, murmured, and closed his eyes.

When next he opened them, he was inside the room, and Conri's eyes were large and dark as they gazed upon him.

Rising from a chair, he growled, "You dare to cross my ward!"

The *fennidi* and the Tribe had a long history, one that had been fraught with battle and peace, and Gregorr had lived too long to fear the High Lord. After removing the rune from his mouth, he calmly explained, "Your daughter comes, Wolf Lord."

Shock crossed the man's face, his eyes nearly purple, as he cried, "Caryss is not yet in her ninth moon!"

Gregorr repeated, "She comes. Swiftly. Sharron is with Caryss now."

Conri disappeared before Gregorr's mouth closed, and the *fennidi* looked toward Conall, who shrugged, but smiled.

"And so we finally meet this Wolf Queen," Conall called out, rising slowly from his chair.

When Gregorr said nothing, Conall further explained, "It will be strange to have a babe about this place. You must excuse my brother, Gregorr. This is his first child, and I need not tell you how long he has waited for this one."

Conall walked toward the door and gently placed his hand on it, opening it, and both men walked the same path that Gregorr had just run.

Halfway back to Caryss's room, Conall laughed, "What a sight it will be to see the girl as a crying, suckling babe!"

With a smile in return, Gregorr replied, "Careful what you say, or she might hear you."

Laughing louder, Conall said, "A time-walking half-breed who can kill or heal, live in shadow or bask in light. Who will have the *fennidi* on her side and the Wolf Tribe to guard her back. And, if Caryss has guessed true, the sky overhead to keep her safe. What will Eirrannia think of her, Gregorr?"

His silver hair flowed behind him and his eyes twinkled, gray, green, and gold.

"Some will fear her and some will hate her. Most will worship her. All will serve her if she frees them."

"And Rexterra and her allies? What of them?"

"They will want her dead."

Frowning now, Conall sighed, "As I feared. The Tribelands will be her only home then."

"War comes, as we both know, Conall. Perhaps not now, or for moon years yet. But, still, she will not be safe here, not until she is of an age to control her power."

Grabbing the *fennidi's* arm, Conall asked, "What are you saying?"

"What you already fear. We must take her from Cordisia. Until she is ready to return."

"My brother will not allow it."

With a snort, Gregorr replied, "It will not be his choice. But, he, too, must know it is the only way. If he doesn't, you must convince him."

Conall slammed him into the wall and hissed, "What is in it for the *fennidi*? I know your kind and know that nothing comes without cost."

Gregorr could see purple rimming the outer edges of the Tribesman's eyes, but he looked at him openly and answered, "We have been promised freedom, and you were there to witness it. To that end, we will do what we must to keep the girl alive."

When Conall released him, Gregorr shrugged. The men walked on, reluctant allies, awaiting the birth of the babe who could save them both.

*****

As she sipped on a warm glass of raspberry leaf tea, Caryss closed her eyes. The skullcap that Sharron had mixed with a ginger tonic was helping to ease some of the pain. The tea would prepare her for when it came time to push, she knew. The motherwort would become necessary as her birthing cramps increased, and Sharron had readied it, too. A tincture of yarrow, cayenne, and crampbark was nearby in case of excessive bleeding, Sharron explained, reminding Caryss of their preparation. All the others had gone from the room and it was only the two women who remained, although Caryss did not doubt that Conri, Willem, and Aldric were nearby, and perhaps the others, as well.

319

As she lay on her side on the large, down-filled mattress, Caryss called, "I am still in my eighth moon. The babe will be small and perhaps come out quickly."

"Maybe. Do not worry, Caryss, she will be strong and healthy. You have seen what she becomes."

Sharron's words were spoken softly, as most were, but there was a depth to them that Caryss heard as well. When last they had all seen the girl, she was only a few moon years younger than Caryss herself, and to next see her as a blood-covered babe would be odd. Yet, for Caryss, nothing had been normal since Conri had unlocked her memories, and this was no different, even if it was much more painful.

The room was dark, except for several small candles, and Caryss asked, "Has the sun set for the night?"

Looking out the window nearest to her, Sharron answered, "Yes, but the moon has not yet risen."

It was not the first time that Caryss had asked, and both knew why she did so. She wanted the babe born under the watch of Luna, mother to the Tribe and mother to Eirrannia. Under her watch, the girl would be safe in the darkness, and safe from the god that she would not name. None spoke of him, but he was known and feared, and Caryss had long wondered what he would do with the babe. Once, she nearly asked Conri, but he had silenced her, making her promise to never speak of him. It was one of the few times that she had listened, and she laughed aloud at the memory.

Her thoughts were interrupted with another painful burst, and she gasped, wrapping her hands in the blankets that covered the bed.

Through gritted teeth, she moaned, "Sharron, it will not be long now. There is little time between the birthing cramps. Now is the time to leave."

"Leave?" Sharron cried.

In between bursts of pain, Caryss rose, wrapping a crimson-hued blanket around her as she walked across the room. "I will not have her born in his house. There is little time to go anywhere but the courtyard. At least there she will be in full view of star and moon."

"It will grow dark soon, Caryss."

"Are there not many here who can strike fire or orb-light?" Caryss laughed.

Sharron smiled, shaking her head, and sighed, "Willem will not approve."

Both women laughed as Sharron pushed open the door. Several chairs had been brought outside the room and placed in the hallway, and from each chair heads snapped up until several pairs of eyes stared at the women. She had expected Aldric, Conri, and Willem to be there, but she had not thought to see Otieno, Jarek, Conall, and Nahla. Further down the hall and lying on the floor was Gregorr. He hurriedly jumped up and ran to join them.

"Have the birthing cramps ceased?" he asked, walking beside her.

Caryss paused, reaching for Sharron's arm, and when it became clear that she was again cramping, the other healer told him, "She wishes to birth under the night sky, as the priestesses of Luna do in Eirrannia."

From the corner of her eye, Caryss watched the High Lord rise from his chair and walk toward them. Silence remained, but it did not stop him from picking up Caryss.

"Where shall I take her?"

Through clenched teeth, Caryss cried, "Release me at once!"

When he did not move, Sharron looked at him and said, "It will help with the pain if she walks."

Caryss watched as Sharron stared at Conri, as if daring him to challenge her words. When he gently placed her on the ground, she reached for Gregorr, balancing herself as she made her way to the courtyard.

The pain was strong now, and she longed for the calming tea. As she panted and moaned, someone embraced her, wrapping an arm around her shoulders. Only when she opened her eyes did she realize that it was Conri.

"How long until the moon rises?" she nearly wept, her words a whispery plea.

Without taking his arm from her, he answered, "Nightfall has come."

Forcing her eyes to open, Caryss looked to the sky, casting her eyes about until she saw the shining, silver orb, a sliver missing as Luna hung low and heavy. Uncertain why, Caryss felt tears slip from her eyes, wetting her cheeks and landing bitter and salty on her lips. With one hand on the ground to hold her weight, she brought the other to her face, wiping with shaking fingertips.

When next she looked to Conri, she saw much, their darkness unable to hide what she had come to learn of him.

She had not expected to see his fear, and she hurriedly looked away, knowing not which to believe.

The babe was coming, rushing into the night, impatient and fiery, Caryss mused, her mind wandering as another cramp gripped her.

"Sharron," she whispered, her voice low and rumbling as she fell to her knees.

As the woman knelt down beside her, Caryss, feeling Conri's arm still across her back, said, loud enough for both to hear, "The babe is coming."

Crawling to where someone had placed blankets, Caryss looked about, searching for Gregorr and Sharron. Even Conri stood apart now as the other two neared.

"What of the tea?" she pleaded, reaching for Sharron's hand.

Her words were hardly spoken before the healer offered up the mug, warm and sweet. As she sipped at it, she whispered, "Sharron, if something happens to me, I want you to promise me that you will take her from here. Take her away from Cordisia until she is strong enough to return."

"Please," Caryss begged, "Promise me that you will teach her of the North."

Still on hands and knees, Sharron embraced her and murmured, "She will know of the North and more. She will know of plant and tree, of sea and sky, of fire and earth. She will know the words of her people and the songs of the land. Caryss, she will be what we have both seen and more. You have my word, with the mother of us all as witness, that the girl will be safe."

In a sterner voice, Sharron told her, "Let me help you rise. The night is fine, and it will do you well to walk for a bit."

Gregorr was still beside her and helped lift her from the ground, taking the mug from her as she slowly strolled beneath the star-speckled sky.

Willem and Aldric stood at the edge of the courtyard, as if they could not decide where to be. Sharron busied herself next with neatly arranging clean linens and lining up several large bottles, some clear and some tinted brown. Caryss watched as Nahla joined Conri, coaxing him a few steps from them.

The *fennidi* walked with her, shimmering in the light from the moon, and sung, "*A sheonn, chonnair cheo, asla salah, tua la faine, tua la faine, tua la faine.*"

Five times he repeated the words before switching to the Common tongue as he sang, "Oh child, come home, through the mist and to the light. To the light. To the light."

His voice was airy, as if the wind carried it to her, yet it throbbed, pulsing and fast, dipped in the waters of the Northern rivers.

As an intense burning tore through her stomach, Caryss howled, digging the heels of her feet into the cool grass. She could not recall when her shoes had been removed, but beneath her toes, the ground was comforting, soft, and soothing. Unlike the other cramps before, this one did not end, and the pain spread deeper until it felt as if her midsection was ablaze, bone and veins crackling in the flames. Her skin, lighter now that she had been gone so long from the Tretorian sun, smoked and smoldered. To her eyes, she saw red and orange leaping, as if her skin was afire.

322

When Gregorr put a hand to her own, she cried, "Do not touch me!"

He hurriedly pulled it from her, and, when she looked at him, his eyes were a dark shade of green, and she shook herself free from the flames.

"I feel as if I am burning," she whispered, in apology.

"I am here, Caryss, and shall be. I will burn with you."

With a choked cry, she told him, "Just before you reached for me, I thought I saw flames of gold shooting from my skin. I know not what it means, but I feared you would be set ablaze as well."

With a smile that made his pointed ears curve high, Gregorr laughed, "Do you know the tale of the juniper?"

Breathing quickly through open lips, Caryss murmured, "We have long used juniper at the Academy."

Sharron joined them, listening as Gregorr explained, "For healing no doubt. But my people have long used berry and bark. Will you let me show you, my lady?"

When she nodded, he reached into a small, leather satchel tied to a braided rope about his waist. After a moment, his hand reemerged, several small blue berries clutched in his green-hued fingers. Caryss watched as he crushed one of the larger berries between his fingers until they were stained and wet.

Once the color of the trees, his fingers were now tinted like nightfall, blue-black and shining.

"Can you kneel?" he asked softly.

Nodding, she dropped to her knees as he lifted his stained fingers to her forehead.

As if she was parchment, one of his thin fingers trailed across her forehead, painting on pale skin that glowed ivory under Luna's kiss.

Caryss could not see what was written there, but she could feel him trace two intersecting lines.

Loud enough that only she and Sharron could hear, he told them, "First, I mark you as loved."

He removed his hand and crushed another berry. Again, he lifted his finger to her forehead and chanted, "Now, I fill you with strength."

His fingers drew a square, each edge meeting in union.

With the next berry, his finger traced a straight line, from one side of her face to the other, just beneath her hairline. "With this comes peace."

Continuing, he crushed another berry, dampened his fingers and drew a line down the middle of her forehead, from the edge of her forehead to the tip of her nose.

"Memory will always be yours," he told her.

The next mark connected two slanted lines with the long one that divided her face in two. In his eyes, she watched him write, the reflection clear and shimmering.

"No evil will touch you here," he whispered.

As he worked, her pain lessened until it seemed to not exist at all. After the fourth rune was drawn, she thought him to be finished.

But, again, he crushed a juniper berry.

On each of her cheeks, she watched as he painted a triangle, a trinity of lines of equal lengths. When he was done, his lips lightly touched her own.

"For you, I call for balance," he sung.

When his hand, stained and sweet-smelling, fell to his lap, his eyes joined hers, and, without words, she thanked him, bowing her head. Across her body, the fires cooled.

And she knew it was time.

Sharron had sensed it as well and reached for a large roll of bleached linen. "Would you be more at ease lying down?" she asked.

Caryss felt as if she could no longer speak, her body flowing and swaying to a song she could not hear, only feel. With a nod, she let them lower her to the ground.

A blanket was draped over her and the healer's pants removed. Around her, the courtyard was quiet, the light faded except for a dancing orb-light across the field.

"No magic," she breathed to Gregorr, who was seated beside her.

Just as quickly as she had muttered the words, Gregorr was gone, and, when she looked up again, the orb-light had disappeared.

The birthing cramps still came, one after another, but the pain had lessened, from Gregorr's runes or from the herbs, she knew not. As she shifted her body, leaning onto her elbows, Caryss felt dampness spread across the blanket where she lay. It was too dark to see if it was blood-tinged or not, but she had birthed enough babes to know that her own time was near. For the last moon, Caryss had known that the babe was facing downward, unlike Asha, whose own babe would have died if Caryss had not cut him from her. For a moment she thought of the woman, hoping that both mother and child were thriving.

Sharron whispered to her, and a wave of consciousness fell over her, bringing her back to the courtyard. "Are you ready to push?"

More times than she could remember, Caryss had been, like Sharron now, kneeling with her sleeves rolled high, at the feet of a woman ready to meet her babe. With her mind again clouded with pain, Caryss thought of the clinic, a life long past, and stared into the silver-edged darkness.

Again, Sharron was speaking, and Caryss had to shake herself back to understanding.

"Open your eyes!" the other healer called.

With effort, she followed Sharron's command, struggling but finally managing to keep her heavy eyes raised. When she looked to her, Caryss noticed concern.

For a moment her lips would not move, yet, after a few tries, she asked, still in a daze, "Is something amiss?"

"It seems as if you are sleeping, Caryss, and the babe is ready. You must begin pushing."

"I feel as if I am on boat, Sharron, sailing across the sea on gentle waves," she mumbled, as way of explanation.

"You are on no boat," Sharron chided. "You are lying on the ground outside the home of the High Lord. Gregorr's blessing calmed you too much perhaps. I need you to keep your eyes on me. Do not look away from me, Caryss. I want you to breathe in deeply, and push both breath and babe from you."

Like a child chastised, Caryss could only nod and obey, keeping her eyes on Sharron as she sucked the misty night air into her. As she exhaled, Caryss squeezed her hands closed and pushed, never looking away from the other healer.

"Good," Sharron called, "But not quite strong enough. Again."

So again she pushed, this time groaning as a fiery pain tore through her, bursting and crackling. No longer sailing gently as her thighs grew sleek and her lower half ripped open.

In the air, cool and foggy, she tasted blood.

"Have Gregorr prepare some cayenne and chamomile tea," Caryss moaned as she readied herself to push again.

Without moving, Sharron turned her head, and called for Gregorr. When he joined them, she hurriedly explained what was needed, pointing to a bag of dried leaves mixed with a fine, red powder. Carefully, he built a small fire, without the aid of magic, and reached for the small pot, setting it into the growing flames.

As he waited for the water to heat, Gregorr lay beside her, humming as his hands reached for her own.

"I can hear her song, Caryss," he whispered.

Between her legs burned a fire hotter than any she had ever known, and Caryss screamed in pain, the noise echoing through the yard, as if all of Eirrannia could hear and silencing the *fennidi's* singing. With the searing ache came a sudden thought, and Caryss grabbed Gregorr's hand, clasping it tightly as she forced her eyes to open.

Through clenched teeth, she hissed, "Are your runes strong enough to keep the gods away?"

His eyes, almond-shaped and forest-stained, shifted, as if he did not understand her concern.

"The night the babe was made, it was as if someone else was there, too. I will not speak his name, but I do not want him here tonight. Will your spell protect her even from one such as him?"

Twinkling as if his voice was a bell, Gregorr answered, "My lady, Ohdra has long known of the girl, although none of us knew what she would mean for the *fennidi*. She is Tribe, as is her father, and his father, who is more. I am here for you and for your daughter, as are all my people now so vowed. We are not here for the men who came before her or the gods who are kin. Tonight, her story will begin."

With his hand still in her own, he told her, "Tonight is yours alone."

Gregorr placed his black-tipped fingers into his mouth, and reached for Caryss once again. Across her rounded stomach, he painted Luna, slivered and hanging.

The tears that fell from Caryss's forest-colored eyes glowed as bright as Luna herself. When she wept, the gods watched, absent, yet knowing.

There was only a small fire burning, a naturally made one, and the woman at her feet was no mage or god; she was only Sharron. Beside her sat the *fennidi*, who despite his green skin and silver hair, was like her, and would die as he had lived. All present were man and not god, light and not dark, and, for that, Caryss cried anew, loving the *fennidi* deeply for giving her this night with the girl.

Both Sharron and Gregorr sensed the change, as Gregorr prepared the tea and Sharron opened Caryss's legs gently, her pale and slender hands steady and bright against the darkness.

Exhaling, Caryss pushed again, panting and moaning.

"Her head is nearly out!" Sharron exclaimed, reaching closer.

With shaking legs, Caryss pushed, biting at her lip to prevent herself from screaming. Tasting the blood there only made her push harder, until Sharron started weeping, her shoulders shaking as her hair fell from the healer's knot that she had tied earlier.

"Sharron?" Caryss cried, still watching the girl.

When Sharron lifted her face, her eyes were like the sea and her cheeks were wet, but she was smiling, and Caryss watched, breathlessly, as her hands rose.

Into the silence came a squalling cry as Sharron placed the babe onto Caryss's chest.

Nearly purple, her tiny face trembled as she cried.

Under the soft light of the small fire, Caryss examined the babe, reaching for the linen that Sharron had readied, and wiping away the birth fluids as she gazed upon her. Her hair was dark, although Caryss knew that, in time, flames of red would join the black, and covered all of her head. Her eyes, still mostly closed, were dark too, although Caryss knew that they would lighten, until, like her grandfather's, they would shine as green as a gemstone. The babe had been born early, but her size was fine and her breathing steady.

Once wiped clean, she was wrapped in a finely woven blanket made of golden thread, and Caryss looked down, imagining that the babe glowed. But it was only the blanket, bright and shining against the dark sky.

Without looking up, Caryss whispered, "It is as if I hold the sun in my hands, yet they do not burn."

To Gregorr, she called, "It was she who was aflame."

Sharron, her face red and still tear-soaked, sobbed, "All my days at the Academy were for this moment. Just this."

"Will you mark her, Gregorr?" Caryss suddenly asked, gently rocking the babe who lay quiet in her arms.

Handing a mug of steaming tea to Sharron, he answered, "There is only one rune needed for her, Caryss. With your permission, I would give her it now."

When she nodded, he picked up a juniper berry near him, rolled it between his thumb and forefinger, and crushed it, as he had done with Caryss. With darkened fingers, he leaned close, his silver hair falling across both mother and babe. Yet, when his hand was ready to begin, the babe's eyes opened, dark and clear.

As if she watched.

With a laugh that sounded like song, he continued, placing his stained fingertip over her reddened forehead. Caryss watched as he slowly painted a small, blue streak, as if it was a bolt of lightning, down the center.

When he was done, he lifted his fingers and sang, "Let this be the first step along your path, both doorway and guide. And remember how many wait for your return. Seek knowledge, child, with each step that you take."

He had not been wrong, Caryss thought; only one rune had been needed.

Before he rose, he told Caryss, "Call for the boy."

She nearly questioned him, but nodded toward Sharron who hurried to find Jarek.

All three had been so focused on the babe that none had heard Conri approach until he, kneeling beside Caryss, whimpered, "Ask anything of me and you will have it."

Caryss struggled to sit up, wincing in pain as she shifted her lower half. As she felt a gush between her legs, she reached for the mug, knowing that she still bled. Sipping the tea, she looked at him, with eyes newly opened.

There was so much to be said between them, and so much ruin behind.

She loved him, she realized then, although it was impure and damaged, beyond repair, even to her healer's touch. The High Lord had taken more from her than her parents, more than her memories. He had taken her life, using it for his own gain.

For that, she would never forgive him. Even with the babe as gift. He would not apologize, she knew, nor did she have need for it.

Without taking her gaze from him, Caryss said, "I want what I have always wanted and nothing more. Keep her safe, Conri. No matter the cost."

"May I hold her?" he asked, his voice low and rumbling.

Wrapping the babe tightly, she lifted her to him. But before he could reach for her, Gregorr yelled out, stopping her.

As he neared, with Jarek trailing behind, Gregorr called, "There is one more rune to be written, Caryss. It might be the most necessary of all."

She knew not what he meant, nor why Jarek was needed, but she cradled the babe as they kneeled beside her. The boy looked scared, his hair messy and his hands clenched into fists, but he did not object when Gregorr handed him the juniper berries. With the *fennidi's* instructions, he crushed the berries, allowing the juice to color his fingertips dark.

Nodding, Gregorr told Jarek, "Before either of you were born, your kin were enemies, and our lands were torn apart as you battled. A new day has come. If you mark her now, Jarek, you offer her protection. Your protection."

Reaching for the boy's shoulder, he asked, "Do you understand what is at stake here?"

Caryss listened, as did Conri, whose dark eyes watched, veiled but filled with unspoken warning. She thought he might interrupt, but he waited for Jarek to answer as they all did, in silence.

"If I mark her, sky and storm can cause her no harm," Jarek quietly answered, holding his berry-stained fingers in front of him.

"Is it your desire to offer her such protection?"

"Yes," he told them all, his words clear despite his shaking.

Had she not been holding the babe, Caryss would have reached for him. In her arms, the babe stretched, trying to open tired eyes.

"On her brow is the mark of wisdom. Atop it, you must place three lines, drawn from west to east. The first shelters her from storm, and the second from sea. The last marks her as yours."

"What is the meaning of this?" Conri hissed.

Caryss, too, was surprised by Gregorr's words and asked what he intended.

"It is an old rune, one of the oldest known to my people. What the rune offers, it also asks in return. If he marks her, she will be safe. But she will owe him that in return."

"She is but a babe!" Caryss cried.

"Caryss," Gregorr called, "The choice will be hers. I doubt the boy will hold her to a birth-night vow."

"Did I not tell you such were the ways of the *fennidi?*" Conri growled.

It was Jarek who answered.

"I offer her my protection. What choices she makes will be her own, High Lord. I desire nothing more."

When she had first met the boy, she did not know the history between Elemental and Tribe. Now, she knew that the girl would need Jarek, more than most perhaps.

"Make the mark, Jarek," she called. "She will honor the vow just as you will."

The boy looked to the High Lord, who, with a quick nod, gave his assent.

Without waking her, Jarek brushed his fingers across her forehead, each line steadier than the last. When all three were complete, he held out his hands to Gregorr, who wiped at them with a cloth threaded with runes, some that she had not yet seen. The boy's hands would likely remain stained for days to come, but he did not seem to mind.

"Jarek," Gregorr said, "Let's go tell the others the news of the babe."

Sharron followed them, leaving Conri and Caryss alone. Knowing that Sharron would return soon to tend to her, Caryss glanced down at the babe, lightly traced the juniper stains, and quickly handed her to Conri, before she could change her mind.

The babe woke, her gray eyes blinking slowly at the High Lord. Caryss watched, wondering if the girl's eyes would darken in recognition. As he looked down, the babe's eyes shifted, turning from gray to gold to green. They were murky yet, not the shimmering hue they would one day become, but Caryss could see her own father in them still.

She is mine, Caryss thought, *and of the North.*

In his large hands, the golden-wrapped babe looked tiny. When his finger brushed gently along her cheek, Caryss half-gasped.

Where just moments before green eyes stared out, now the babe's eyes were as black as night, the eyes of her father.

Around them, unseen and hidden, rumbling howls erupted, deepening and loudening as Conri stared at the babe. Beneath Caryss, the ground trembled as the drumming of the wolf calls echoed through the Tribelands.

Over and over, they called to her, in greeting, their howls welcoming the new daughter of the wolf.

Smiling, Conri took his hand away, and, again, her eyes faded. The howling ceased. Wordlessly, Caryss sipped the tea before reaching for her daughter. Let them rejoice, she thought.

After he had given her back, Conri stood, and asked, "Have you given her a name?"

Each time the girl had visited, Caryss had never called her by name, not by intention. She had never known it, she realized as Conri waited for her to answer. As Conall often reminded her, she had learned little of the Tribe and did not understand their naming rites. But the babe was more than Tribe. She would always be. To name her for her father alone would never be right.

The girl would be more than Tribe. And more than Eirrannian, if Caryss had her way. And she must have a name to match it.

A name that many would follow.

She was asleep in Caryss's arms when the healer looked toward the High Lord.

"Syrsha."

Freedom.

*****

With Gregorr beside her, Caryss stood, leaning on the small man while keeping a woolen blanket wrapped around her lower half. For a long moment, the night darkened further and haze covered her eyes, her head heavy and spinning, as if the ground shifted beneath her bared feet. Without Gregorr's aid, she would have fallen, weak with blood loss from the birth. Sharron held the babe, who was neatly wrapped in a blanket, fine and soft, more so than any Caryss had seen.

"It is too soon, yet, Caryss. Rest here until your strength is restored, or let the High Lord carry you inside," Sharron scolded her.

Her words were spoken softly, as if in hesitation, yet Sharron was not wrong. Caryss held tightly to the small *fennidi*, her fingers cutting into his earth-dyed skin. With each step they took, Caryss felt her thighs growing slick with blood. The night sky masked the wet trail that followed her, but she knew that both Sharron and Gregorr sensed her weakening.

"It isn't much farther," she told them. "There is little else I want than a bath and a bed."

"Aye," Gregorr agreed. "Let us see her to her bed and tend her there if necessary."

He offered again to call for the High Lord, but Caryss refused. As she did when he nearly called for Otieno.

With none but Gregorr beside her, Caryss stumbled her way across the courtyard. When she entered, the slate floor was cool beneath her feet, yet soon the stone shined, glistening with blood.

Soft orb-lights glimmered around her, and Caryss noticed how stained the blanket she carried had become. Steps away, a large tub sat, steaming and fragrant as a mint-scented fog encircled it. Without thinking, Caryss dropped the blanket and peeled the ripped healer's robe from her tired body. Again Gregorr was near, leading her to the tub, while Sharron stood just behind them both, the babe asleep in her arms.

For how long she rested, Caryss did not know, but when her eyes opened, the water had cooled and was tinted with blood. Sensing someone beside her, Caryss rolled her head to the right. Through slitted eyes, she saw Conri standing over the tub, with the babe in his arms. It was not whom she had expected.

Clearing his throat, he told her, "The babe grows hungry."

Moving slowly, she climbed out of the tub. Sharron had laid towels nearby, and Caryss reached for one, pulling it around her cape-like. Conri did not watch as she dressed, and only neared once she was seated on the cot. For the second time since the birth, the babe took to the breast, and Caryss paused, reveling in a peace that had become rare since her departure from the Academy.

It was not long before the silence was broken.

"Is it still your desire to leave the Tribelands?"

Sighing heavy with pain and fatigue, she murmured, "In a half-moon, I should be strong enough to travel."

"Will you return to Eirrannia?"

"I seek safety, Conri, for me and the babe. Where can I find shelter from both Tribe and crown?"

Running a hand through his dark hair, he replied, "They might not think it so, but Eirrannia is still under the rule of Rexterra. You travel with several who are unforgettable, and some from the North might sympathize with the crown."

Before she could answer, he stepped toward the bed, sat beside her, and said, "Worse, though, is the danger you will face from my kin. Crow and Bear will be interested once word spreads of the babe, although they have been commanded to stay their hands."

"Commanded?" she asked, still staring at the babe.

"My father knows of her birth, Caryss. He is, I believe, interested to look upon her."

His words were accompanied by a smirk, as if he knew that the statement was a foolish one. Even as High Lord, he could not stand against his father.

"What of the men we killed?" she asked, uncertainly.

The edges of his lips dropped as he told her, "None know. Yet. For the last half-moon year, several have been killed, my men included, yet my father has done little. He lets us squabble for now. Syrsha will not be touched, Caryss. He has promised me so."

Giving voice to what she had not yet been able to, Caryss whispered over the babe's tiny, dark-haired head, "Even now, you do his bidding, Conri. When will it end? What else of mine will he make you take? His word means nothing to me."

In his arms, the babe still dozed, in peace. Yet, as Caryss stared upon them both, she knew that she must soon go. When Conri next spoke, she understood that he now agreed.

"Moon years ago, I vowed to keep you from harm. You might not believe it so, but much of what I have done is for you and the babe. What power he has is beyond me, Caryss, and even with allies, I can't yet wage war. When you are recovered, I will provide you with provisions to leave. But you must go beyond Eirrannia, beyond Cordisia, to be far enough from his reach. If you must go, then I will not allow you to stay in Cordisia."

"The North is her home," Caryss whispered.

Over the babe's covered head, he hissed, "As it will be moon years from now when she is strong enough to claim it. Her enemies are many and her powers are weak. Let her learn and grow, and, when she is ready, she will return."

"I had not thought you to wish us gone," she sighed, unable to argue further.

His eyes downcast, Conri answered, hoarsely, "I had not thought to feel for the babe as I do."

The sadness that followed his words surprised her, and, without shame, she wept, tears washing the babe, as if in blessing.

*****

A quarter-moon into the journey north with Delwin's men, Pietro thought of fleeing more times than he could count. Days before they had entered into Planusia and began heading west, leaving the Vollaxo River, which they had followed since their departure from the King's City. He had been given an old gelding, and often rode near the rear, where the two other healers rode in a coach, for both were too old to sit a horse. At night, he shared a tent with the wizened men, listening to their snores, coughs, and grunts and thinking of ways to escape.

He wore no chains, yet Pietro realized that he had few options. The Prince knew of his interactions with the Tribesman, and with Bronwen, which had marked him as useful. And so he said little, and did little, except tending to the small injuries and illnesses that often affected the Royal Guardsmen.

Jassen, the older of the two Master Healers, loudly groaned and rolled over, until his bony knees pushed into Pietro's back. The fire behind his eyes burned hot, warming him against the coolness of the night. Only with considerable effort was he able to calm the pulsing, yet sleep was no longer possible. Grabbing a cloak to throw over his healer's robe, Pietro walked from the small tent, toward the center of camp, where a large fire still burned.

Joining the Guardsmen who were seated around the fire, Pietro glanced around the camp looking for Delwin, yet he did not see the Prince. From the way the other Guardsmen watched him, Pietro knew without doubt that he would not be allowed to leave. Not until Bronwen was found, he guessed.

Shaking himself free from the thought, Pietro walked back to his tent, trying to forget the fire-haired girl and wishing he had never gone to Rexterra.

*****

26

His brother had returned, although briefly, to the King's City, but now was gone again. Crispin believed him to be in Eirrannia, despite the Eirrannian Council's declaration that they knew nothing of the healer.

Even those loyal to Crispin had no knowledge of his brother's plans, although a few had sent word that Delwin neared the Tribelands. Not many dared to travel to the northwest corner of Cordisia, and his brother's actions were both foolish and dangerous. For the last moon, Crispin had sent word to any who might offer him aid, including his cousin Willem and the Master Council at the Healer's Academy, hoping that his pleas would be answered. From Willem, he had heard nothing, and the Master Council had only replied that the last they had seen the healer was when she had departed over a half-moon year before. To tell them more, he would have had to expose much about Caryss, yet he had not.

It seemed as if none knew of her whereabouts, he fumed, squeezing his hands into fists as he sat behind his large desk.

As if she had been little more than a time-walker. Like she had once claimed about his son.

The thought caused him to stumble back from his desk, the large wooden chair thrown against the wall. Books fell to the floor, crashing one after another with a thunderous roll.

"I must go to Nicoline," he mumbled, rushing from the room with no regard for the mess.

Before the sun reached its peak, he was astride his stallion, with little more than traveling clothes and coin. The ride would be a long one, perhaps a quarter-moon, he figured, yet he had told none of his leaving, except for his two longtime guards and his wife. Even then, he told them little.

If his suspicions were true, then Caryss might have sought the boy. Or the boy might have sought her. It was a desperate guess, he knew, but with no other choices, he hurried north. And with Delwin gone, none would follow him.

For hours, he followed the Vollaxo River, stopping infrequently and only to let the stallion rest. As night fell and the skies above him darkened, he slowed Jellani, letting the horse lead him to the western bank of the river. After dismounting, he reached into the large satchels attached to the thick leather saddle and found his water pouch and several strips of dried, salted meat. After tying the mount to a nearby tree, Crispin walked, chewing the dried meat as he stretched out his legs.

Sipping watered wine, he sat down, leaning against a thick tree. With a full belly and a weary body, Crispin dropped the pouch to the ground and slept.

Hours later, he woke to a star-dotted sky and bubbling water. Pulling his cloak tighter around him to stave off the cooled air, he rose, shaking out muscles that had grown stiff. After he relieved himself, he walked to the river, kneeling low in the soft grass and leaning over the swiftly running water. With cupped hands, he splashed his face, shivering as the water dripped down his neck. Awake once again, he walked toward Jellani, untied him, and jumped into the saddle.

As he rode north, Crispin looked to the dark sky, with no hint of light. It was hours before the sun rose, and he had had little sleep. Yet, somewhere in Cordisia, possibly Eirrannia, his brother rode, too. Red stained his view, mixing with the dark night, until tree and sky, grass and dirt, river and air were all dusk-colored, dusted red with his fury. Faster he rode, pounding his heels into the sides of the stallion.

*****

"He told you that it would be wise to leave Cordisia altogether?"

The babe was with Nahla, leaving Willem, Aldric, and Caryss alone in her room. Willem stood near the door while Aldric was seated on the bed. Caryss busied herself examining clothing Conall had given her, packing what would be useful into a satchel as the two men addressed her.

It had been less than a quarter-moon since the birth, but Caryss knew that she was recovering well, although the bleeding still occurred. Soon, though, she would be well enough to travel, she figured, tidying the old clothing into piles. The birth had been as easy one, even Sharron had admitted such, and the babe fared well, sleeping and taking to the breast often.

Without turning to face Willem, she sighed, "He mentioned that our enemies are many and their reach extends through all of Cordisia. Of course he wishes that we would stay here, but he is uncertain what his father has planned."

It was as much as any of them would say of the dark god, and Aldric hurriedly asked, "Is it still your plan to return Herrin?"

Throwing a torn riding jacket onto the floor, Caryss called out, "I seem to have little choice." In a softer voice, she added, "We have cleared the poison from his body, and he is better than he has been in moon years, although his memory cannot be fixed."

Pacing the room, his Rexterran boots thumping loud against the stones, Willem told them, "Delwin will have little cause to strike once his father has been returned. Admittedly, you will not be permitted in Rexterra,

335

but I see no reason why the North will not have us. My kin will welcome us. All of us."

All in the room knew that Willem spoke of Aldric, who stayed silent despite the mention.

"Even without Rexterra against us, our enemies are many. It will not be long before word of the Crow deaths spread. And while none saw what happened, I will not risk what could happen if those deaths are discovered."

His face growing flushed, Willem cried, "Crow has always been inferior to Wolf! Why must we run scared?"

Shaking her head, Caryss explained, "There is one whom they all must bow to, Willem."

Her words had done what she thought that they would, causing Willem to pale and Aldric's hands to clench.

"He would not harm you," Willem hissed.

"I not know what he would do to me. But he wants the babe. I will run as far and as fast as I must to prevent him from even gazing upon her. Conri knows it as well, which is why he told me that we must go."

"You have only just given birth," Willem muttered.

When Caryss smiled, her eyes sparkled, older eyes, with tiny lines at their edges and hints of sadness etched into the gleaming gray-green. Both Aldric and Willem watched her, knowing she was not the same girl she had once been.

Feeling their stares on her, Caryss mumbled, "I will have Sharron and Gregorr to tend to the babe and me. Sharron is as fine a healer as I am, while Gregorr has more knowledge than any of us."

"What of the boy?" Aldric asked, his words crossing the room, as if they were breath.

She heard him though, and replied, "He still has much to learn, and I will have need of Otieno. And so he will come with us as well."

"Your plans have changed much from what they once were," Willem interrupted. "What of the North? What of your people and mine? I thought you wished the girl to be raised in Eirrannia."

Willem's words, true ones, stung, biting at her skin and reddening her cheeks, but, with a shrug only, she answered, "The North will wait for her. As will the *fennidi*. In time, she will return, with power and hope. And an army. Until then, she must disappear. It is the safest way."

"And the King?"

After a pause, she sat on the bed, pulling at her robe. Caryss had thought long on Herrin and her vows to him. Yet, it had been nearly a half-moon year since she had found him near death in the King's City, and his health had improved as much as it could. While some days, he seemed well and clear-minded, there were others when he would spend the day abed. Keeping him with them, even after they left Cordisia, made little sense and would only slow them down. And give Delwin more reason to strike.

Before she could explain her thoughts to the men, Willem walked to the edge of the room and leaned against the door. His gold-rimmed eyes flittered as he said, "If you would allow me to offer suggestion, I would tell you of what I think might work best here."

When she did not object, he continued, "Bring the King to my father's kin. Mihal, who is uncle to me, still lives on the western edge of the Faelan Lake. He is half a day's ride from Edanburg, and more often than not beside a hearth with several books at his feet. Many moon years ago, he left the city, resigning his position on the Eirrannian Council. Since then, he cares little of what occurs outside of his home. Herrin knows him well enough, Caryss, and it would be of no great shock to find the King with him. And it would be also of little surprise that Mihal did not know the King was being searched for, such is his isolation."

"How far of a ride is your uncle from the Tribelands?" Caryss asked, growing interested in his idea.

"No more than a quarter-moon."

"What if we used the *epidii*?"

Willem's forehead wrinkled in thought, and, after a long pause, he said, "A few hours at most, although I know little of them. Caryss, would not it bring attention upon us that we do not need?"

"The sooner we are gone from Cordisia, the better, I think."

He crossed the room and reached for her hand. For nearly a moon year, he had begged her to go to Eirrannia with him. Even now he did so, she thought.

"Let the North see the girl first, Caryss. Let them know she has come."

Gently removing her hand, Caryss turned to Aldric, who had been mostly silent, and asked, "What would you have me do?"

When he looked at her, she knew that he would answer with truth. "Eirrannia has not seen war in many, many moon years, but she has not been free either. If war comes soon to the Tribe, Eirrannia will have lost her shield. What then? For as long as I can remember, Rexterra has been sword-readied for that day. A swaddled and powerless babe can do nothing."

Her eyes grew mist-filled, but Aldric lifted a hand.

"Caryss, she is not ready. Not for moon years to come. But she will be. Let them know her. Let them hear of her birth. Let her story grow. If Syrsha is to be their queen, let them learn of her now. Let her be seen and known. And then we take her far from her. Until she is ready to rise."

"And after we deliver the King? Where must we go, Aldric?" she asked, her words edged with fog and haze.

"We head further east. Until we are at the coast. From there, we hire a boat to take us across the Eastern Sea."

"Do you know the lands beyond the Eastern Sea?" she pressed.

With a nod he told her, "I was gone from Cordisia for nearly ten moon years, and, most of that time, I was in the East. I know the lands well and the people, too. The lands are vast, the people friendly but hardened. To the southeast, even further still, there is a port city where you will find faces from unheard-of lands. Words spoken in tongues you have never known. We will not be so odd there, with the *fennidi* and myself."

From across the room, Willem called, "Do you speak of Cossima? I have heard tales of that great city, but know none who have gone."

"There are few cities like it, Willem," the mage told him. "All are welcome, and the laws are just ones. There are many learned men there, yet blacksmiths too. You will find farmer and mage, singer and swordmaster. It could be home for many moon years, I think."

Laughing, for Aldric was rarely so animated and joyful, Caryss asked, "When were you going to tell me of this?"

The corners of his lips rose slightly as he replied, "When you asked."

Throwing the folded clothing into the nearby satchel, Caryss told them both, "Ready your things. If possible, we will leave on the morrow. First we must find Willem's kin and make certain that the King will be safe. Then we will head east until we can find a ship to take us to Cossima."

When the room emptied, she sat back on the bed. "Cossima," she whispered, wondering what the fabled city would bring.

*****

Sharron was holding the babe, pink-faced and sleeping, when Caryss finished tying her last bag to the side of the gelding. With a final pat on the gray's side, Caryss turned, and, with her hood pulled over her hair, walked back to where the others stood. As she neared, she looked over the group.

Otieno was the first she noticed, and the first that most would as well. He was taller than the rest, mahogany-skinned and darkly clothed. His hair, braided and thick, was pulled back from his face, tied and hanging across his shoulders, like snakes curling about the swords that hung there. In the moons that they had been in the Tribelands, he had grown larger, Caryss thought, although she had seen little of him since the babe had been born and doubted that it could have been so. But, still, his arms were heavy with muscle and his legs thicker than any she knew.

Next, she looked to Willem, who was ever the Rexterran, hair newly cropped short and fitted in expensive garb, his eyes sparkling with anticipation. He, too, looked as a warrior should, despite his age, which Caryss knew was nearly twice her own. She had been surprised when he offered to join them, leaving Cordisia, the second exile of his life. But she would not turn down able hands, nor one who was as learned as Willem. Where they planned to travel, his knowledge could ease their way.

Aldric looked as he always did, aged and ragged, although his thinning hair was longer now. The tunic he wore had been a gift from Conall, edged in gray and woven with fine, dark thread. His pants were new as well, although his boots were his own. His face was always unreadable and today was no different, she knew. Perhaps even more so, the dark mage kept his thoughts his own. Yet, of all the men, he was the one she trusted most, for he had no ties to Cordisia or to the crown.

Jarek was less boy than ever, she thought, as she walked by him. His height was nearly equal to hers now. Although he was thin, as most boys his age were, he was growing tight with muscle, no doubt from the hours he spent training. His hands were no longer the soft hands of a schoolboy, but were now calloused, often bloodied and bruised, like the rest of him. Otieno was no easy master, nor was Willem, who had begun work with Jarek as well, teaching him the ways of Rexterra. In his blue eyes, Caryss saw fear, but he knew little of their plans, which she now knew had been a mistake.

Pausing beside him, she whispered with a smile, "I saw you knock Willem to the ground last night."

His shoulders dropped as he relaxed, fighting a smile that she could read in his sky-colored eyes. Next to him stood Sharron and Gregorr, both clad in new clothing as well. They were all in dark, unmarked clothing, with little to identify from where they came. Gregorr's long, silver hair was braided and knotted at his neck, hidden by the hood of his cape. His skin, unmistakably green, was nearly all covered, and his hands were gloved. Only his face was visible, yet, beneath the hood, most would think him a child, slight and shy as he was.

Taking the babe from Sharron, who had replaced her healer's robes with well-fitting pants and a thick tunic, Caryss hardly recognized the other Northerner. But, she herself must have looked similar, as they had both dressed in clothes that Conall had given to them. Except for the babe, they appeared as a hunting party, not unlike any other that they might encounter as they traveled east.

With Syrsha in her arms, Caryss dropped her gaze, knowing who stood just beyond the others. As if he wore a skin of night itself, shining and sleek, reflecting the early morning sun, Conri waited. His face was pale, his hair falling about it, a black frame around a nearly perfect face.

Unable to call out, she approached him, forgetting the others, forgetting all else. Nearly forgetting that the babe was in her arms.

Had she been watching, Caryss would have noticed the others turn away as she came upon the High Lord. As they busied themselves with their own packs, she closed her eyes and sighed, letting the air escape her body as if it had been caged. In her arms, the babe kicked at the blanket that had been wrapped tightly about her. Perhaps she knows, Caryss thought.

When she next looked up, Conri's eyes were on her. Dark eyes, thick with blood, yet still his own.

Her own eyes burned as her vision blurred, until tears dripped from the bottoms. With one hand tightly holding Syrsha, Caryss wiped at her cheeks with the other, angry that she had allowed the tears.

In a shaking voice, she told him, "She will find a way to visit you."

For a moment, Caryss hesitated, then, quickly, before she could change her mind, handed the sleeping infant to the High Lord.

As he held his daughter, for what they all knew would be the last time, Caryss looked away. Near the others, whom she finally remembered, stood Nahla, heavy with her own child, a son of the Wolf.

"Will Nahla be safe here?" Caryss asked with downcast eyes, uncertain why the Islander had decided against going with the rest of them.

Gregorr had sent word to the *fennidi* for help when it came time for Nahla's babe to be born and had assured Caryss that his kin would arrive soon. With Conri's permission, a few would stay with her for a moon or more. Yet, Caryss still felt as if she was abandoning the woman who had done so much to help her. Without Nahla, they would have never made it out of the King's City.

When Conri still had not answered, she pressed him again, asking in a louder voice, "What will come of Nahla and the boy?"

"You have seen the boy, have you not? They will be fine."

His words were short and sharp.

"Blaidd will be a child of the Wolf, just as my own is. And Nahla has done much for me. Keep them safe, Conri."

In a voice softer than she thought him capable, he told her, "Conall's son will be Tribe, but he will be half-breed and not god-touched. It will not be an easy life for him here."

"He will be kin and ally to our own daughter," she retorted.

"He is Wolf, but his path is his own to walk, and none know what his powers might be."

"Your father will not want him?" she whispered, knowing how he did not like to speak of Nox.

"The boy will be accepted and welcomed," Conri shrugged. "Conall already speaks of his plans for him, and he will raise him as his only son. But, no, he will not be marked as the girl has been."

Still unsatisfied, she asked, "What of the other Tribes?"

"None know of him, Caryss. He is no threat."

With a sigh, Caryss finally understood and said, "Keep it that way then, Conri."

Standing in silence, the High Lord gently rocked the small babe swaddled and sleeping in his arms as Caryss watched. Unlike Syrsha, Conri could not time-walk with ease. Each time he had visited her, it had been in flesh.

"Will you be able to visit us as the girl does?"

Shaking his head but not taking his eyes from the babe, he answered, "If necessary, I could. However it is best that I do not know where you have gone. He will ask. Caryss, there is much you must teach *faela*, and she must understand the danger she faces when she time-walks. And she must learn of her enemies."

"*Faela?*"

"Wolf-pup. She is not queen yet. She will need to earn her name."

He was not wrong, and Caryss said nothing in reply. The sun was fully visible now, and the others had finished readying their supplies. The time had come to depart. Conall, she knew, had argued with Conri about letting her leave unaccompanied, yet they all were aware of how it would appear for their group to be traveling with the High Lord, or any other Tribesman. Their only safety was in anonymity, without affiliation to Tribe or crown.

It was best if none found her, Conri had repeated often, demanding that Aldric keep them well warded.

Her arms, heavy and paralyzed at her sides, began to tingle as she struggled to lift them. Across her chest hung a blanket that Nahla had woven into a sling to hold the babe as she rode. Beneath it, her life pulse struck against her chest, insistent and hurried. Her hands, glowing red under the morning sun, trembled as she reached for the babe. Caryss half-expected the babe to cry as Conri gently handed her off, yet she slept still, as if nothing had changed.

Quickly, she cradled her against her chest, tucking her into the sling, and wondering if the wolf-pup could feel how her life pulse quaked.

For a long moment, Caryss waited, unsure what to say. There was much between Conri and her, yet words would not come. Unbidden memories, lost to her for so long clouded her thoughts.

Images of her parents, dead at his hands. The fog across her eyes shifted, faded as her heart slowed.

"What were my parents' names?"

Her words were faint, unexpected and sudden.

"Your father was called Iain and your mother Morra."

Caryss turned then, dry-faced and steady, and walked to where the others waited. Nahla rushed to her, hugging her and the babe, as they were still one, and whispering words of her own tongue into Caryss's ear.

Words of prayer, from the Great Mother. Lullaby and blessing both.

Wanting to assure Nahla that the *fennidi* would be arriving soon, Caryss opened her mouth. Yet no words came. When she freed herself from Nahla's embrace, she just nodded, knowing that the Islander would understand.

As she carefully climbed atop the gelding, Caryss realized that the last moon year had been spent in travel, with more departures and farewells than she could recall. And soon, she would leave Cordisia for the second time, knowing not when she would return.

Kicking at the sides of the gelding, she grabbed the well-worn leather reins and turned the mount, kicking harder until he trotted free.

Not once did she look back.

*****

"It took me a quarter-moon to find you."

For a moment, he wanted to lie, to tell the man nothing. Yet he was dressed in healer's robes, trapped with the Prince's army. The Tribesman shined as he stood in Pietro's tent; his black cape moving as if it had been weaved from water. The man's eyes were dark, too, although there was little light to see them clearly. In his hands pulsed a small orb-light, although Pietro had not needed it to know who had stolen into his tent without notice.

The lie was on his tongue, but, before he could answer, the man crossed the tent and grabbed him by the throat.

Hissing as if his voice was smoke, the Tribesman seethed, "Have you found the girl?"

With a stutter, Pietro chokingly cried, "You think Prince Delwin informs me of his plans? I am nothing to him, only here to nod my head once he does find her."

"If you do not tell me what you know, you will not even be able to do that, fool!" the Tribesman half-screamed, throwing Pietro onto his small sleeping mat.

Rubbing at his neck, he mumbled, "Our course changed yesterday evening after scouts showed up at camp. We rode through most of the night, and, even now, we have only been given three hours to sleep. Soon, we will be astride again. Something must have happened, but, like I mentioned, I am not privy to Delwin's plans."

"You should have used the rune to call me. Take me to him."

Breathlessly, Pietro said, "He will kill you."

With a laugh that seemed to rip through the sides of Pietro's small tent, the Tribesman spit, "If he is fool enough to try, I would welcome the fight."

"What of the mages?" Pietro moaned.

"Had they any skill at all, they would have already known I was here."

With no other choice, Pietro exited his tent, his fingers near his burning throat. The sky was gray-black, although there were hints of orange on the horizon. Around them, others were preparing for the day's travels, although, much to Pietro's amazement, none noticed as he and the Tribesman walked toward Delwin's tent. Even when they were just outside the Prince's large enclosure, the two men were not stopped, or even acknowledged, Pietro suddenly realized.

When the Tribesman pushed the hanging door open and entered without comment, Pietro followed, as if he walked in his sleep. Through foggy eyes, he could see Delwin, wearing only his underclothes. Beside him was a squire, a boy moon years still from adulthood. Neither looked toward them, despite being just steps away. He knew not what the Tribesman had done, but his presence was not yet known.

Until, in a voice high and shrill, the Tribesman cawed, "Has the girl been found?"

The squire shrieked, dropping the blue and gold jacket that he held. Delwin turned, with speed, and looked straight at Pietro. Then, as he looked to the healer's right, saw the Tribesman. With eyes wide, Delwin scrambled for his sword, which was leaning against a nearby chair.

"Your weapons will have no effect on me, Prince."

Giving little heed to the words, Delwin lunged for the sword and held it in front of him as he asked, "How did you get in here? What have you done to my guards?"

With a wave of his hand, the Tribesman replied, "They are where you left them, just outside the tent. Let us not waste time, Delwin. I know the boy here told you of me. We share a common goal and can be considered allies. I am not here to harm you, or you would have been dead before your fingers curled around the hilt of your sword. I am here for the girl, and no more than that. You have been long searching for her. Too long, although I have heard that you are finally near."

Pietro's legs were shaking as the prince looked at him, as if seeking an explanation. When the healer opened his mouth to speak, the

Tribesman's gaze silenced anything he would have said. Instead, he waited, until Delwin answered.

With feigned confidence, Delwin explained, "Days ago, my men located a small party traveling through the western Faelan Mountains. There is a particularly tough spot to pass, and my men have been camped there for nearly a moon. Just south of Arranwain, there is but one trail fit for human travel. It was here that my men saw who they believe is the healer. They reported seeing a woman with hair the color of fire and a man near my father's age being pulled in small wagon. From there, they tracked her heading east."

"They are still following her?"

"At a distance, yes. But, even if they lose her, I now know where it is that she goes."

The two now spoke as if they had forgotten whom the other was, and Pietro's mouth dried and his heart pounded. Against Tribe and Rexterra, Bronwen had no chance.

Do no harm, he thought, silently cursing himself and swallowing the bile that was thick in his mouth.

"And where would that be?" the Tribesman asked, his voice growing louder.

Grabbing his coat from the pale-faced squire, Delwin said, more calmly than Pietro thought possible, "With her travels a man I once knew well. He is cousin to me, but on his father's side there is Northern blood. One of my guards recognized him and sent word. I believe they will seek shelter with his father's kin, who live less than a day's ride from here."

Pietro watched as what could pass for a smile crossed the Tribesman's face, raising his arched cheeks high. Trembling, Pietro hurriedly looked away.

With the same strange smile, the Tribesman said, "What nice timing. I will accompany you, Prince Delwin, and once the girl is found, I will see that she is punished for her treason."

Half-collapsing, Pietro reached for a wooden table that had been set up near the center of the tent, steadying himself as the two stared across the tent.

"The girl will be brought back to the King's City and jailed for her crimes!" Delwin roared, as if he no longer feared the Tribesman.

"She is with child," the Tribesman told him. "While I care little for the healer, her child is Tribe and belongs to my people. What you do with the girl once the babe is born is little concern to me, and you have my word that I will deliver you the girl after the babe is born."

Delwin's cheeks flushed red and, through gritted teeth, he hissed, "This girl kidnapped the rightful king and had her own guards murdered, as if they were animals and not men. I do not know what you want with this healer, but she must return to Rexterra for trial."

Calmly, the Tribesman smirked, "I did not know that the Tribe was known for mercy."

When Delwin did not reply, the man added, "I could kill you now, Prince, and find the girl on my own. You have told me enough to know where she is. Yet, I will not if you assure me that the babe is mine."

"The babe has been born already. My men reported seeing the healer riding with an infant strapped across her chest."

The words were half-whispered, part anger and part fear, Pietro realized.

With a cackle that again crashed around the tent, the Tribesman laughed, "Even better. Promise me the babe, and the girl is yours."

Delwin's gold-rimmed eyes stared across the tent, and Pietro knew that a red haze was burning hot behind them, but he coldly replied, "The babe is yours. Now let us ride."

He had said nothing while the two men talked, nor could he speak once they had finished. Pushing himself from the desk, he followed as Delwin and the Tribesman walked from the tent, keeping stride with the young squire. As they crossed the camp, men gasped, yet none spoke.

Among them was a Crow.

*****

27

"When I was a child, I would visit Eirrannia for the summer, doing little more than riding and exploring. Sometimes, I would leave just after the sun rose and would not return until midday. These fields were home to me, and, with a few of the local boys, we would stay gone all day. On a morn like this, Caryss, we would ride under the clear sky, as if we had no troubles or concerns."

"I'm not certain that we have no troubles, Willem," she said, but a small smile covered her face. "How much longer until we reach your father's brother?"

Looking around, Willem hesitated, before finally saying, "A few hours perhaps. If I am correct, we will come upon a small stream soon, and, following that will lead us to his house."

"It was with this uncle that you spent your summers?"

"Yes, Mihal is a fine man and taught me much of the North."

"Does your father ever return to Eirrannia?"

His large stallion was next to her gelding, and when she turned to face him, the smile had faded.

"He is Rexterran now and to return would displease my mother."

With a sigh, Caryss asked, "Were we not too isolated at the Academy? To know nothing or so little about the rest of Cordisia seems so strange now. I knew not even of how Eirrannia is viewed in the south."

Nodding, he told her, "The Academy is like no other place and welcomes all whom seek learning. I do not think it should be any other way."

Caryss agreed with him and added, "It is an easy place to miss."

"What of your foster mother? Have you sent word of late?" Willem asked.

She dropped her eyes, and, quietly, answered, "I should have never left her there. What if something has happened to her since you departed? The Prince must have sent men to Litusia. What if she was questioned, or worse?"

When Willem's brow wrinkled in thought, Caryss knew that she was not wrong to be concerned. For moons, she had not written to her foster mother, nor did she ever make mention of the babe. Before arriving in the King's City so many moons before, Caryss had written occasionally to Sheva, mostly of matters of little importance. Yet since she had taken the King, she no longer wrote, fearing what would happen if Crispin or Delwin found the woman.

"I must find knowledge of how she fared this last moon," she pleaded, thinking on Willem's assurances to her when he first arrived.

After a few moments, Willem told her, "There are but two options. Either you contact Conri for help, or you wait until we are free of Cordisia and hire a courier."

"Send a Tribesman to her door?" she gasped. "Then she will not only have Rexterra on her heels, but Crow as well."

"Then we wait until we reach Cossima."

Knowing she had little choice, Caryss kicked at her horse, urging the beast to canter faster.

Otieno and Jarek rode at the front of their small pack, silently pacing the group. When Caryss's horse galloped up to them, it slowed, unaccustomed to being the lead.

With a curt nod to Otieno, she asked, "Can we quicken the pace? I am ready to be gone from Cordisia. The sooner we are without the King, the sooner we can make for the coast."

"What does Willem say? Are we close?"

Each time the Islander spoke, Caryss heard salt and sea at the edge of his lilting words. The words, like a song, were rough, although not unpleasant, she thought.

"No more than two hours, he thinks."

Otieno said nothing, but gently tightened the leather straps that he held in his wide, calloused hands.

"What do you know of Cossima?" she asked suddenly, thinking on how often the Islander knew more than he let tell.

"Would the mage not know it better after his moon years spent in mercenary work?"

Shrugging, Caryss replied, "I suppose. But tell me what you have heard. Will a group as odd as ours stand out?"

"Not so much, I would think. I knew of several Islanders to visit the city-state, and none complained after returning. What are your plans once there, *leseda*?"

"To let Willem handle it all," she laughed, the sound crisply ringing across the empty valley.

The babe, whom Gregorr had been carrying, cried aloud, in tune with her laughter. For one who wailed so rarely, the noise disturbed Caryss, and she turned in her saddle to see where the *fennidi* rode. She spotted the slight man, the infant strapped to his small chest, nearing.

Pulling at her gelding, Caryss noticed a stream ahead, dotted with rocks and running fast.

Jumping from the horse, she threw the reins to Otieno. "The babe grows hungry."

He and Jarek trotted toward the stream, and, when she turned back to the others, Gregorr was beside her, holding the now-quiet infant in his arms.

Reaching for Syrsha, she softly said, "If I did not see the tears on her cheeks, I would not have thought I heard her crying. You calm her better than I, Gregorr."

With a pleasant snort, he told her, "Among the *fennidi*, children are passed from one hand to another."

"Is it true that ofttimes the babe's father is unknown?"

He had dropped his hood and his long fingers, lighter than when she had first met him it, combed through his silver hair, which hung down his back. Watching him, Caryss suddenly realized how beautiful he was, like a sliver of moonlight reflected on wet leaves.

Before he could answer, she added, "I never asked if you had to abandon those you love to follow me."

Dropping his hand to his side, he chimed, "I have no child of my own, although you are correct that we do not view parentage in a way that others might. The *fennidi* lay with whom they please, Caryss, and when children come, they are welcomed by all."

"How do you know that you have none, then?"

With a deep laugh, he exclaimed, "I do not lay with women."

She joined him in laughter, and, shaking her head, told him, "I have been too long at the Academy. We learn little there beyond healing. Cossima might seem like another world entirely to me."

The two of them walked toward the others, who were enjoying a respite from the riding near the stream. Sitting down, Caryss brought the babe to breast, no longer hurrying. Days of travel had left her weary and, as she nursed the babe, her eyes closed.

So she stayed until a shiver ran through her. When she opened her eyes, mist clouded her vision, dropping a soft haze on her surroundings. Looking down at the babe, Caryss shook her head.

"How can it be?" she whispered aloud, scanning for the girl.

But when she did not appear, Caryss grew frantic, hurriedly unwrapping the blanket and putting her ear to Syrsha's chest. With a heavy sigh, she felt the babe's life pulse beating hard beneath her ear. Awake now, Syrsha gazed up at her.

With dark eyes.

Bundling the babe up with twitching fingers, Caryss jumped from the ground and ran toward the others.

"Something is not right!" she screamed, her words echoing, shrill and frightened.

Sharron was nearest to her, tending to the King who was awake as well. Handing the babe to the other healer, Caryss rushed toward Willem.

When she stumbled into him, she grabbed at his tunic and cried, "The babe's eyes are black!"

"What are you saying?" he gasped, pulling her toward him.

"Give me your dagger," she begged.

Roughly, Willem grabbed at her hands, holding them in his larger, stronger ones, and called, "Caryss, what is the meaning of this?"

Unable to free herself, she sobbed, "Her eyes were green when we stopped, and now they have darkened. Willem, we must leave this place! Something is amiss."

Dropping her hands, he turned to the others.

"We ride!" he yelled, the order thunder-filled and echoing as his words trumpeted across the valley, commanding and forceful.

Jarek and Aldric raced to their mounts, while Sharron quickly handed the babe to Gregorr so that she could see to the King. Gregorr, the babe cradled against him, hurried toward Caryss. The *fennidi* said nothing, but his eyes told her much.

With shaking fingers, she pointed to the babe, and, with tears on her cheeks, dripping into her mouth and down her chin, she begged, "Do what you must to keep her safe."

Nodding, he backed away from the healer, then turned and headed for the wagon. Caryss watched as he climbed in, disappearing beneath the large leather cover.

In a pouch at her waist, the dagger burned, and, with fingers like ice, she grabbed it.

The others, except for Otieno who stood near the stream, gathered their horses. None spoke as they readied to ride.

*****

"Why are you here, *faela*?"

When the child did not answer, he said, "Nothing will change. You must go."

The girl was younger than when he last saw her by several moon years, her body that of a child still, small and thin. She was dressed in what looked to be nightclothes, her hair, dark and full, scattered about her face in tangles, as if she was a child who had just stumbled from bed, her cotton gown hanging to her naked feet. Her cheeks were red, flushed with emotion, even though her eyes were clear when he had expected to see tears.

Green eyes. But he knew that she would have darkened them if she could have.

He thought her to be fading, yet when she spoke, her voice high and accented, her image appeared solid.

"I couldn't sleep," she mumbled, as if in explanation.

"She cannot see you this time?" he half-asked, realizing that Caryss was still with the others.

When the girl did not answer, Otieno tried to reach for her, yet his fingers passed through the air as if he was alone.

"How many times have you come back here?" he finally asked, knowing that he could not embrace her, nor could he force her to flee.

Lifting her shoulders and without taking her eyes from where her mother stood, the girl told him, "Too many, or so Aldric tells me."

Her words, much like the child herself, were distant, and Otieno understood why she still came.

"Why come to me?"

Without pause, she answered, "To watch you fight."

The scimitar was in his hand before she continued, "I have been having trouble mastering the repartee, and you suggested that I pay closer attention to how you block. There are few who challenge you, and so, when I couldn't sleep, I came here."

He did not need to tell her of Caryss's warning. The girl knew, as she always had, what would happen here, Otieno realized.

Flickering under the rising sun, the girl began walking toward the wagon, slowly, as if she was made of stone, not air or mist.

Over her shoulder, she called, "They will be here soon."

The girl with the messy hair and the sparkling eyes slowed and stopped at the edge of the wagon, waiting, and Otieno rushed to join the others. He did not look back toward her, but he knew where she had gone.

*****

When she looked again, Otieno had his curved sword in hand and he was rushing toward her. The meadow was empty, yet Caryss did not doubt that his sword would be needed. In her own hand, she held the *atraglacia* dagger, its black blade etched with star and sky. To her right stood Aldric, fire burning in his palms. Jarek was just behind Otieno, who now stood to the right of Willem, who also had sword in hand. His face was cold, no longer the Master that she had long known.

Had they not had the wagon, Caryss thought that Willem would have suggested that they ride from the meadow. But, with it, and the King and babe inside, they would not get far.

Standing near Otieno and Willem was Jarek.

Caryss called, "The boy should not be here."

With the wind, Otieno's voice carried as he cried, "For half a moon year and more he has trained with me! He will fight."

"With sword or sky?" Aldric asked.

"Both," the *diauxie* told them all.

Lowering her voice to an almost whisper, Caryss gasped, "I was a fool to forgo Conri's help."

"Can you call for the *epidii*?" Willem asked, having heard her words.

With a stutter, she said, "I would not know how."

Pointing to her trembling fingers, he told her, "Your blade."

Around her, the meadow was clear. For how long it would remain so, she did not know. Biting her lip, she lifted the dagger and brought it to her outstretched palm. Dragging it across, like she had done each time before, Caryss called upon the blood magic. With closed eyes, she begged for help, her hand stinging with pain. Falling to her knees, she watched as her bloody palm dripped red, splattering the tall green grass with shining droplets.

Aloud, she whispered, "Come to us, please."

Her words sounded as if someone else had spoken them, yet her throat ached as if she had screamed. Looking up at Willem, Caryss cradled her bleeding hand to her chest.

With a nod, he said, "When they arrive, take the babe and the boy and go."

"And what of the rest of you?" she cried.

"Take Sharron and Gregorr too, if there is room. I will see the King safely returned. Otieno and Aldric will find you in Cossima."

He had spoken in haste, yet she did not argue.

Cutting a strip of fabric from her tunic, she wrapped it around her hand, tying it clumsily. Before she could finish, Caryss heard pounding. Even the soft grass could not dull the unmistakable sound of hoof on ground.

Each time she had ridden an *epidiuus*, she had been awed by their silence. Her life pulse heavy and fast, Caryss looked across the narrow stream, fearing what she would see there.

With a longing glance to the empty sky, she stood, just behind Willem. If Crispin came, no blood would be shed, she thought. If it was not he, Caryss knew not what would happen. The babe's eyes had darkened, she remembered, giving her the answer.

*****

The Crow and the Prince rode at the head of the group, a smaller one, after Delwin had decided to leave many of his men at the camp in order to make haste. Pietro counted twenty men, armed with sword, shield,

351

and bow, along with the two robed healers. Unlike them, he was in riding clothes, having given up the robes in a pique of anger at his captivity.

As he followed, he thought of his time at the Healer's Academy, remembering most of it fondly, despite his battles with Bronwen. For moon years, he had hated the girl, yet now even that had faded as his anger shifted elsewhere. She had never been as experimental as he, yet she was more skilled than most, he could admit. Perhaps between them, they would have learned much about the healing arts, he thought. Instead, he was aiding Delwin, who would never use her well-learned skill, and, instead, would imprison her.

Behind Pietro's eyes, the red fog spread, until he fought against it. With little choice, he rode on, trailing the others and hoping that Delwin's men would never reach her.

*****

As the army neared, and the sound of riders loudened, Willem called, "Circle the wagon! We will fight from there, if necessary."

Aldric and Otieno, both well-tested warriors, nodded, and repositioned themselves until they formed a small circle about the wagon. Caryss stood in between Otieno and himself, while Jarek was between the mage and the Islander. A brief glance to the now cloudy sky showed no sign of the *epidii*. Without them, he knew not how the battle would end. Herrin was their only weapon now, he thought, hoping to use the King as both protection and safety.

Between glances toward the sky overhead, Willem stood without moving or speaking, as did the others, and waited, swords readied, for Delwin and his men to approach.

Perhaps he has only come for his father and will depart once Herrin is handed over.

When the blue and gold banners of the Royal Army became visible, Willem hastily looked about for Delwin. Atop a large, silver horse sat the Prince. He looked no different than when Willem last saw him, many moon years before.

As he opened his mouth to call out to his cousin, Willem realized that Delwin's eyes were already upon him. He had known he would find him here.

"Have your men back down, cousin!" Willem cried, his hand tight on his sword. "Your father fares well."

With a laugh that Willem remembered well, Delwin spit, "Your word means nothing. Sheathe your sword and stand aside."

Behind the Prince were his men, all of them more heavily armed and guarded than Willem, Otieno, Aldric, and Jarek.

"No one needs to get hurt here, Delwin," he pleaded. "Let the others pass, and I will return with you to the King's City, with the King as well."

"You are not welcome in the King's City!" Delwin fumed. "If you return, it will be as a dead man."

Anger growing as he recalled who Delwin was and all that he had caused him to suffer, Willem shrieked, "Would you kill your own father? What next? You will kill your brother as well? This woman tried to help heal the King and has done him no harm."

Spittle dripped down his chin and, when he reached his hand to wipe at it, Willem's gazed turned to his left. Behind the army, too high for them to notice, soared three *epidii*, nearly indistinguishable from the clouds. They were far enough away still that none else saw them, he realized. For a moment he thought of informing Otieno, but he would not yet risk having them seen.

Looking back to the prince, Willem saw doubt, and he turned to Caryss and hurriedly said, "Wake the King."

He would have said more, but he could see understanding in her eyes alongside fear.

As she turned slowly toward the wagon, Willem called, "Your father yet lives, and improves each day. Delwin, I daresay he is better now than he has been in moon years."

While Willem spoke, Caryss had climbed into the wagon. Her back was toward him, but he knew that she was rousing the King, although he was not certain how. The babe was quiet, which, although strange, was a blessing. When he heard Herrin coughing, Willem turned and saw the King sitting up, with Caryss beside him. The king's eyes, even from a distance, seemed clouded with confusion. But, he needed more time, for the spirit animals had done yet come close.

Herrin had forgotten much during their stay in the Tribelands, and while his health had improved, his memories had not. He sometimes did not recall Willem, forgetting too how he had come to be with Caryss. Yet, he remembered often that he was king, and Willem wondered if he would know his own son. While his mind had not cleared, his body had gained strength during their stay, and each day he had walked more, regaining use of his weakened legs. No longer dependent on milk of the poppy, the King was faring better, and he would improve, although perhaps not in the King's City.

Behind him, Willem could hear Caryss whispering, coaxing Herrin awake. The wagon was still half-covered, yet he listened as Caryss pulled the

King toward the edge. Sharron was beside her before he could move, and, together, the two healers held the ailing king between them.

After a few moments, they walked him toward the front of the wagon, and into full view of Delwin.

Herrin's eyes were shaded with fog, the gold rims no longer visible, yet he hoarsely cried out, "Delwin, what is the meaning of this?"

Willem had not thought that the King's words had been heard, but when next he looked, Delwin had jumped from his horse and was running toward them.

When the Prince was within arm's reach of Willem, he spit, "My father rides as if he is swine! Has your exile made you forget who is king here?"

"I forget nothing, cousin," Willem hissed, keeping his eyes on the prince. "The King has had a long recovery, and he is still not able to ride. It was a mercy to let him rest as we traveled. Your father is well, better even than when last you saw him."

He did not look around at the others as he addressed the Prince, but Willem knew all watched and listened, even the King, although he would understand little, Willem feared.

As if he had not heard Willem's words, Delwin strode past him, toward Herrin. Willem followed, listening as Delwin called out to his father.

"I have long searched for you, father, and shall see you returned to Rexterra within a moon. Can you walk or should I call for my men?"

When Herrin said nothing, Willem interjected, "He has only recently regained some movement, and he can't yet sit a horse. Once we ride free, the cart is yours, as is the King."

With a snort that might have been a laugh, Delwin spewed, "Your men are two against twenty. On my word, my men will strike. You have nothing to negotiate here, cousin."

Anger began to heat Willem, his hands burning and his eyes aflame.

Before he could control the red haze from spreading, he saw Caryss, hued in colors of the sunset. She was just steps from Delwin.

Sharron, having heard the exchange, rose from the back and embraced Herrin, whispering into his ear, which caused a wan smile to cross the frail man's face.

As Delwin's men neared, the Prince called toward Caryss, "The others will be allowed to leave, but you must come back with me to the King's City and answer for you crimes."

Addressing him for the first time, Caryss stated, "I have been to the King's City once, and I have no need to see it again. I notice that you travel with healers, Prince Delwin, and I would speak to them on how best to care for your father before your departure."

"You are not even full Master, I hear," he taunted, his face reddening. "Your advice is not needed. I have seen that my father is well, and, because of that, I will allow the babe to stay with your men. But you will be coming with me. Either willingly or not. If you choose to fight, my men will spare no one."

For a moment, Caryss paused, weighing the prince's threats. Before she could answer, Willem stepped near, pushing her behind him.

"You dare to threaten a healer, Delwin?" he bellowed, "Caryss has said vows and has done naught but act upon them. No crime has been committed here."

"Let her be, Delwin," Herrin croaked.

Silence spread throughout the meadow following the King's words. Finally, Delwin waved his hand. "So be it."

When he turned on his heel and walked back to his men, Willem sighed heavily. Looking to the sky, he searched for the *epidii* that he had spotted earlier. After several moments, he saw that they were just west of the clearing.

"We must hurry," he whispered to Caryss. "The *epidii* come, and we must leave at once. The prince should not be trusted."

No one spoke, yet all kept looking toward the sky.

*****

He could not remember a time when they had both been out of their healer's robes, if ever. Even with no healer's robe to identify her, Pietro recognized Bronwen as soon as his horse neared the stream. Hooded and with her hair pulled away from her face, he had still known her, although she had not seen him. In simple riding clothes, Pietro supposed that he looked as any other Rexterran might, although he was not uniformed like the others. Only he and the Crow, aside from the two elderly healers, were not in the blue and gold of the Rexterran Army. Yet, they had both been too far for her to see.

His life pulse thickened beneath his tunic, beating so loudly that he feared the Crow would hear.

It had been agreed that the Tribesman would not make himself known, but Pietro knew little else of what had been planned. Nor did he know what would happen now that he had done what the Crow had asked and was no longer needed by the Prince or Tribesman. Delwin had suggested that he could join the palace healers, yet Pietro no longer wanted to stay in the King's City. Too much had changed, and he himself, he knew, could no longer abide behind the city gates.

After hearing Delwin call for his men to see to the King, Pietro nearly fell from his horse in relief. Beside him, the Crow shifted in his saddle, yet he still did not make himself known, for none called out in warning. Once the wagon was with the Royal Army, Delwin stomped away from Bronwen, without a sword having been raised. Yet, Pietro felt ill at ease.

As Delwin's men were attaching the covered wagon to their own horses, Delwin walked to where he and the Crow still sat atop their mounts. Delwin paid him little notice and approached the Crow.

Once he was close enough, Pietro listened as Delwin hissed, "Let them think they are free. On my call, we attack."

Had he not been holding leather reins in hand, Pietro would have fallen from the gelding.

He means to kill them all, he thought, swallowing hard as his stomach churned. When he looked across the field, all he could see was Bronwen, her hood now around her shoulders and her hair ablaze, sun-touched.

The king lives, her vow has not been broken. We are healers, both the same.

With fire behind his eyes, Pietro kicked at his horse, as if trying to outrun a rapidly spreading fire.

*****

"Look! Just there," Caryss told them, pointing to the west.

When Willem followed her finger, he saw the *epidii*, circling, and coming lower each time.

"Hurry!" he mouthed. "Grab the others."

Sharron, who held the babe, reached for her leather satchel, and threw it across her shoulder, then allowed Aldric to help with the wrap that Nahla had sewn for the infant. Otieno and Jarek stood near the horses, both adjusting their swords, although not sheathing them, Caryss noticed. Gregorr had his pouches already attached to the leather rope at his waist and waited for the others.

Confident that there was little else to be done, Caryss stepped toward her mount, reaching for her own bag, and looking to the sky once again. The *epidii* would soon land, she figured, watching them circle. As she was untying it, the sound of thumping hooves caused her to reach for the dagger, as she scanned across the field.

On a dusty gray horse, a lone rider came rushing toward her. His tunic was brown and finely made, his hair cropped short. With no helm and no uniform, Caryss did not think him to be one of Delwin's men, nor did he appear to be Tribe. She had not noticed him before, and looked to Otieno, who rushed beside her.

When his gelding halted just steps from her, she choked and reached for Otieno. "I know him. We were together at the Academy."

"Stand behind me, *leseda*," he warned, lunging in front of her.

Without letting go of his thick arm, she sharply whispered, "Look closely. He has no sword."

Shaking his head, the Islander told her, "He travels with the Prince. He is no friend, Caryss."

Nodding, she released his arm, but kept her eyes on Pietro. It had been nearly a moon year since she had last seen him, and suddenly she realized that he must be on his own Healer Journey. Yet she could not make sense of why he was with Prince Delwin, although she did remember that he was rumored to be kin to the royal line of Rexterra.

Breathing hard, Pietro threw himself from the saddle and rushed toward her. Before he could reach her, Otieno grabbed him, despite Pietro's struggles.

"Please!" Pietro cried, "Bronwen, you must go. Delwin plans to attack!"

His words were half-sobbed, torn and broken, as he himself suddenly appeared to be.

"Why are you here, Pietro?" she cried, forcing the words from lips that seemed to be made of clay.

"There is no time to explain," he pleaded, nearly collapsing in the Islander's arm. "Listen to me! He has a Tribesman with him. A Crow who has warded himself to near invisibility. They know of your babe, and Delwin has promised the Tribesman that he can have her."

His words were clear, yet her vision whitened. Swaying as if ale-heavy, Caryss began to shake, clutching at the dagger as she looked to the sky.

Uttering a small cry, she drew her dagger across her hand, just below where the bandage was still tied. She could not see through the veil of fog that clouded her eyes, yet she felt the blood bubble up on her hand. Without falling to her knees, she let the blood rain onto the ground, mixing with the tears that now fell. Around her, she could see nothing, blind and nearly paralyzed.

"Please," she sobbed, rocking back and forth, calling for Conri.

Over and over she rocked, unaware of what was happening around her, as if she was under a mage-spell. It was only when Otieno embraced her that Caryss's eyes cleared and the haze settled.

Only then did she see the *epidii*.

There was noise around her, the sound of galloping horses, voices calling out orders. Sword on steel. Yet, Caryss heard little, as her eyes focused on the shimmering spirit animals, just steps away, kneeling and gleaming white against the high grass, sprinkled with small, yellow flowers. Wobbling, she let Otieno push her toward the animals. Half-blind, she searched for the Sharron and Gregorr, suddenly forgetting who had the babe.

And then she saw them rushing toward her, with Jarek, too.

As if she had done it hundreds of times before, Caryss steadied herself on the *epidiuus* and swung her leg over the animal's smooth back. Behind her, Jarek threw himself across the animal's back, his sword hanging from his waist, unused.

Her head was spinning and her vision darkened, and Caryss looked down to see blood covering her hand.

"The babe," she mumbled, swaying, until she realized that it was her own blood, from the calling.

Clumsily, she attempted to wrap her hand again, tightening the stained cotton that had slipped free. Blinking away the darkening fog, Caryss hurriedly glanced around until she saw Sharron, with the babe tightly bound to her. She and Gregorr had climbed atop an *epidiuus*.

She still could not recall giving Sharron the babe, yet she screamed, "Go!"

Her words echoed through her ears, but still she knew not if she had uttered them. Weak with blood loss, she fell forward, spinning and sick. Behind her, Jarek held onto her, and, for a moment, Caryss opened her eyes enough to see Sharron and Gregorr soaring above them.

Around her, Caryss thought she heard screaming, but her head was heavy and her senses dulled. The field was awash in gray mist, thick and blinding.

Willem, with a blood-soaked sword, was between two men wearing the blue and gold of the Royal Army and appeared as a shadow, dark and soft.

As his blade arced, she kicked at the sides of the sparkling mount. With soldiers to her right, and only Willem to keep them from attacking, Caryss kicked harder until the animal darted forward. When she felt the beast's wings flapping behind her, her body heaved, yet her eyes cleared, lightening.

And she watched as, below her, Willem struggled. One man lay unmoving, his jacket dark with blood. Climbing higher, she could still see Willem swinging and parrying. Clinging to her, she could feel Jarek trembling, yet he did not cry out.

Just behind them came the third *epidiuus*, carrying Aldric and Otieno.

"We are free," she whispered to him. "We will be gone from Cordisia before the sun next rises."

His voice hoarse and high, he asked, "What of Master Willem? How will he find us?"

"He knows we are bound for Cossima," she reassured him. "He will meet us there, Jarek."

Her words were hollow, and her smile hid nothing.

*****

His right shoulder stung with pain, as if small needles pierced him. Again, he cursed himself for not having a shield, yet Willem's cheeks were flushed and his eyes, liquid gold, dazzled bright. He was no longer Ammon the healer; he was Willem once again, the man who had, before his exile, worn the same colors as those he now fought. Across the field, his cousin stood somewhere, as did his king.

His King.

No, Willem, thought, as he back-stepped to avoid a clumsy strike, *he is not my King. I serve another now.*

Briefly, when he realized that the *epidiuus* that Caryss rode had flown off, Willem wondered if Delwin would call off his men. But memories of his time in the King's City surfaced, reminding him of Delwin's history. Murder and exile committed in his name. Even Crispin's son had nearly become one of his victims. Willem knew, as he continued to slash, backing up more each time, that his only hope for aid would be if Herrin intervened, yet the old king was much too ill to stand up to his son. Even in his stronger days, Delwin had held sway with him.

With a downward strike against the gold-sashed soldier, Willem sliced at the man's chest. While he stumbled back, Willem lifted his sword again, slashing near the man's exposed neck until blood erupted, wetting him and splattering his face. Another soldier jumped toward him as the first fell to the ground. Willem noticed how the newcomer's well-muscled arms strained tight against his finely stitched jacket. Where the other man had been young, this one was older, experienced and lethal, strong and thick with moon years spent in swordplay.

And patient, Willem soon realized.

When one man jumped forward, the other parried, as if they danced, moving together and then apart, spinning and ducking. The Rexterran soldier was the first to draw blood as he jabbed Willem, who turned away too late and felt the sharp tip of the man's sword rip across his cheek. Having forgotten the sting of an open wound, Willem stumbled backward, until he came hard against the wagon. Blood, hot and wet as it ran down his face, tasted sour when it reached his lips. Using the side of a large oak tree as support, Willem righted himself and waited for the man to near.

He had a moment to quickly look across the field, to where Delwin was in conversation with a man dressed in dark clothes. The Crow, he realized. Neither had raised sword, yet both scanned the field, as if searching.

The pain in his shoulder lessened as he watched, and Willem quickly wiped the back of his hand across a cheek. With clear eyes and a scowl across his nearly ageless face, Willem readied his sword as the man came within reach. His timing was exact as his sword knocked away the man's shield, sending it banging into the tree. Knowing that he had little time, Willem struck again, drawing his sword back down and across the man's chest, which was covered in light, leather armor. As he had expected, the leather protected the man, yet Willem had hit him with enough force to make the man stagger. As the man struggled to regain footing, Willem dove at him, tackling him to the ground and kicking away the sword the soldier still clung to.

Without hesitation, Willem drove the tip of a dagger into the man's neck and pushed, until the Rexterran stopped moving, except for the involuntary spasms that often accompanied death. Rising to his knees, Willem reclaimed his sword and looked back across the field, to see who next dared to challenge him.

What he saw made him scream in rage, fire burning hot behind his eyes.

The Crow soared above him, and when Willem rose, ready to strike, the Tribesman flew on, higher and higher. Willem finally understood why Delwin had only sent two of his men to challenge him. They had been sacrificed and used as a distraction so that the real threat could escape unharmed.

One who could fly, untouched and beyond reach.

There was little that he could do except look to the sky, watching as a gleaming black bird streaked fast and sleek after the *epidiuus*. Where there were once three of the glowing creatures, now, Willem could only see one.

"No!" he screamed, as the Crow chased Caryss's mount.

Again and again he cried out, until his throat burned and his voice cracked, until no other sound could come from him.

"Stop him," he sobbed. "Delwin, call him back!"

His pleas were unheard or ignored, forcing Willem to rush toward his cousin. With his blood-splattered sword held high, he closed upon the Prince, who stood alone across the field.

Before he could take another step, four men rushed at him, with shields and swords raised. When he looked up, four more men had bows pointed at him from where they sat atop their horses, unnoticed until now.

Yet they did not shoot.

He wants *me alive.*

The men descended upon him and Willem tried to resist, but against four trained soldiers, he could do little. As Delwin watched, three men held him while the fourth stripped him of his sword and tied his hands behind his back. Another uniformed man then did the same with his feet.

With a laugh that sounded half-mad, Delwin hissed, "I will return to the King's City a victor, cousin. I have not only found my father, but I return with my exiled cousin in chains! You will be imprisoned for the crime of kidnapping and treason. Enjoy the sun on your face now, Willem, for you will not live to feel it again."

"A father whom you tried to kill!" Willem fumed, spitting in the direction of Delwin and struggling against the man who held the long rope at his back.

"King Herrin!" Willem yelled, searching for his uncle in hopes of pleading with him to call of his son's men.

No reply came, and the Crow grew closer to Caryss.

"You think that you will recover under Delwin's watch?" he cried aloud, hoping the half-witted man would hear him. "Your son ordered you to be poisoned, and will see you returned not to the throne, but to your sick-bed!"

Across the meadow, the King was seated in the wagon, as he had been for days, but the cover had been pulled back. Even awake, he did not seem to listen.

Willem knew that he did not have a moon or more to wait for Herrin's mind to sharpen. Delwin would see him hanged before then.

Sensing defeat, Willem again struggled against his captors. Noticing that his feet were loosely tied, he dove forward and rushed at Delwin.

"You will destroy Rexterra just as you have destroyed your father!"

"Gag him!" Delwin raged, his face reddening.

It took three men to subdue him and force a thick cloth around his face and mouth.

"Uncover his eyes," Delwin called.

With the cloth still tight across his mouth, but his vision clear, Willem was able to look upon Delwin as he smiled and said, "Look to the sky, just there, to your left." Pointing, he added, "The Crow has found its prey."

When he refused to look, Delwin stomped to where his men had Willem, and grabbed his chin. Unbound, the Prince would have been no match for the larger, stronger Willem, yet even struggling did little to stop Delwin from jerking his head to the side, forcing Willem to watch as the streaking black Crow dove to where the *epidii* glided.

The cry that came from the spirit animal shattered the sky, high and shrill, as if in pain. The *epidiuus* flew lower, trying to get clear of the Crow's grasp.

Just above them, the two soared, diving and circling. The Crow was black and sleek, his wings stretched out, shining and vast. The *epidiuus* was larger, glowing white against a blue sky. Atop the spirit animal, Caryss and Jarek hunched low in an attempt to avoid the talons of the Crow.

In Caryss's hands, Willem could see the *atraglacia* dagger reflect the rays of the morning sun.

Another shriek came from the sky, to their west.

Willem threw his body madly around, trying to dislodge the gag.

"*Use the dagger,*" he tried to scream, but words would not come.

If the men had not been holding him, he would have fallen to the ground. His knees buckled beneath him as the shrieks continued.

The dagger, he silently pleaded, even though Willem knew that she could not hear him.

Kill him or he will find the babe, he begged wordlessly.

When the clouds appeared, thickening, darkening the sky, Willem stood straight, forcing his quivering muscles to steady. By the time the thunder roared, his eyes were clear. As lightning quaked and crackled, he smiled, as if madness had overtaken him.

Kill them all, Jarek.

The light rain that fell across his face never felt so soft or tasted so sweet.

*****

Master Ammon, wearing leather armor, looked nothing like he had remembered. More warrior than healer, the man fought to free himself as Pietro watched. For a moment, he considered kicking at the sides of his horse, yet he knew that he would be no match against Delwin's men.

Above, another battle flared, loud cackles and roars causing prickles to erupt across his skin. The night-feathered bird chased the lone spirit animal, closing ground as Pietro watched Caryss and the boy cling to the animal's back.

Much had changed for her since she had left the Academy, he had learned over the last few moons. Pietro could not help but wonder if the woman herself had changed, as well. It had been nearly a moon year since they had last spoken, and even her appearance had changed. Her hair was still as streaked and colored as a setting sun, yet her eyes, even in just the brief glance he had gotten, were unlike what he remembered, as if she had seen much since she left. She was of an age to him, yet appeared older, and, now, he knew, she was a mother.

Suddenly, the sky darkened, and Pietro looked about wildly for the spirit animal, losing it in the heavy clouds. The storm that flashed

362

unexpectedly felt unnatural, and Pietro wondered if the warrior-mage that Delwin traveled with had the mage-skill to control the skies. Yet, as he looked across the field, the Prince appeared just as surprised as the others when heavy rain fell upon them.

With the rain came clanging thunder, pounding and shaking the ground beneath his trembling horse. It began to kick and spin, and Pietro jumped to the ground, nearly thrown from the mount, as it ran away from him. Stumbling, he hurried after the horse, knowing it was his only way to escape, but slipping on the sleek grass. His hair, newly cropped short for the journey, dripped warm rain onto his face. With an unsteady scramble, he listened to hear if anyone gave chase.

Out of the gray sky came hot, glowing lightning that cracked and screamed, falling so closely to him that he stumbled. Once recovered, Pietro threw his hands over his head, as shield. Up ahead, he could see the horse standing, with its head shaking about, at the edge of the treeline. The storm continued to strengthen, until lightning came all around him and his ears drummed with the heavy thunderous beats.

On he ran, occasionally looking back. Pietro tried to look for Caryss, yet he could see nothing through the rain. Shards of lightning smashed from sky to ground, and he could hear screaming, but little else, as he hovered beneath the towering pines.

The horse was just steps from him when a sudden shriek filled his ears. Looking to the sky once again, he saw the spirit animal, shining white against the dark clouds, falling fast. Against the blackened sky, the creature plummeted, near enough to him that he could see patches of red staining its silver-tipped feathers.

Not far from him, the animal slowed, landing with a thud against the high grass.

Just behind it came the Crow, diving toward where the creature had fallen. His mount, twitching and nervous, was steps away, but Pietro hesitated, his gaze on Caryss, who lay unmoving beside the bleeding animal.

His hands clenched and taut with indecision, Pietro ran to her, unaware that the lightning had ceased. The skies had quieted, although a steady rain still fell and the ground was slick and soft, running now with mud. His legs had never moved so quickly, and Pietro was upon her before the others had even moved.

"Bronwen," he gasped, shaking her shoulders gently before placing an ear to her chest.

"Open your eyes!" he begged, nearly sobbing with relief as her life pulse thumped against his cheek.

When he lifted his head, he stared upon her face, freckled and fair, as he had remembered it. Yet, across her left cheek were four gashes, as if she had been clawed, the skin sliced open and bleeding heavily. Her jacket, too, was blood-stained. Pulling it from her, he searched for its cause, yet her chest was unscathed, rising slowly under his gaze.

Beside her, the *epidiuus* languished, moaning and still. Then he noticed the boy, who was kneeling, spitting blood from his mouth.

With his hands under Bronwen's shoulders, Pietro called to him, "Help me carry her to the horse!"

Nodding, the boy crawled to him, and, together, they lifted the healer, who had not woken. The boy was only slightly smaller than Pietro and strong, making it easy work to carry her to the panting horse. In the distance, he could hear screaming, and, above, the Crow circled, unsteady, as if he too was injured.

"They're coming!" Pietro cried, urging the boy to hurry.

By the time they reached his horse, Bronwen's eyes flitted open, and she haltingly choked, "Jarek, call the lightning."

As they lifted her to the back of the horse, the boy whispered, half-crying, "I can't control it!"

Her breathing was shallow, no doubt from the impact, Pietro realized.

Yet, she told the boy, "We have no other way out, and we will die here."

Bronwen's words were harsh, yet he did not think she was wrong.

Breathing slowly, she sobbed, "Jarek, if we are taken, they will torture us until they learn of the babe. You must never tell them where she is, or who you are. Do you understand me?"

There were tears on the boy's face, but he nodded. His eyes shimmered like glass, and Pietro noticed the rims of gold around them.

When she turned toward Pietro, his throat was thick and his eyes burned with sight, yet he did not look away. Neither of them spoke, but understanding came.

"Go!" he yelled, slapping at the horse.

The gelding began to run, but Bronwen grabbed the reins, and turned it back to where Pietro and the boy stood. As the horse bucked and reared, she clung to its back, wrapping her legs tightly about its sides. When the mount settled, she jumped from its back, holding onto the leather straps.

"I cannot leave the boy," she said, simply. Then, raising her voice, she called to him, "Now, Jarek. Call the storm."

Pietro watched as the boy lifted his arms, his eyes bluer than the sea, the rims of gold now streaking with fire.

"His eyes," he mumbled, reaching for Bronwen.

She said nothing, but shook her head, as if to quiet him.

Thunder beat heavy and dense around them as the storm formed. Next, the dark skies lit up with flashes of light. This time, the streaks seemed nearer, jagged and aflame as they stretched from sky to ground. Across the field, Delwin's men came, some on horseback, some on foot, but all aglow under the halo of lightning.

"Let sky be sword!" Pietro heard Bronwen call.

Pietro watched with a gaping mouth as a streak of lightning angled out of the sky and struck one of the Rexterran men, dropping him to the ground. When he did not rise, Pietro knew him to be dead. As the second man fell, the others hesitated, trying to avoid the storm. Fear paled their faces, yet, behind them, Delwin hurried, barking orders for them to seize the healer.

When the third man fell, Pietro jumped back, feeling the ground shake beneath his feet, vibrations causing his teeth to slice through his tongue. With his mouth filling with blood, he watched Bronwen struggle to control the horse, as she jerked at the reins in her hand. Kicking and throwing its head, the gelding tore the reins from her and ran off, yet none offered chase.

"We will find other horses," Pietro said weakly.

His words were interrupted by a scream, high-pitched and pained. He and Bronwen looked at the same time as the boy fell to the ground, clutching at his arm. She was beside him before he had even moved, her face still bloody, half of it covered in talon gashes.

From the boy's right upper arm hung an arrow, its point buried deep. As Bronwen fell to her knees, Pietro stepped toward them, watching as she broke off the shaft of the arrow.

With a black-bladed dagger she cut through his sleeve, exposing the arrowhead. "Pietro, hold him while I work."

She needed to say no more, as he knew what she intended to do, yet as he grabbed the boy in a tight embrace, Pietro looked across the field to see several bows pointed at them and the rest of Delwin's men rushing toward them, swords raised. When the boy had fallen, the storm had faded. Only mist remained.

Anew, the Rexterrans attacked.

"It is too late," he told her, his voice unrecognizable as his own.

When she looked up, it was as if the skies had darkened again. Her gray-green eyes fell upon the Prince and his men.

In a booming voice, Delwin called, "If you continue to fight, my men will shoot!"

Beside him stood the Crow, his left arm hanging limply at his side. Just past him stood Willem, bound and gagged, forced to watch.

Whispering, Bronwen begged, "Pietro, please take him and run for the forest. It is me who he wants."

"What do you mean to do?" he asked hurriedly.

"I will go with them," she replied flatly, before reaching for the boy. "Jarek, if you escape, find the others. If the Prince's men take you, tell him you are an Elemental, but do not tell him any more than that. He will want you alive, and will keep you so until we can return for you."

The boy nodded, and she hurriedly added, "Do not despair. I will send Conri for you. Give this to him or to Otieno. Hide it from all others, Jarek."

Again he nodded as she handed him the black-bladed dagger. The boy tucked it beneath his boot, a spot that none would think to look, Pietro guessed.

Rising and shielding the boy as she did so, Bronwen mumbled, "Now, Pietro. Take him and run."

As he grabbed the boy, he looked upon Bronwen, the dark cape around her shoulders, the hood hanging at her back, blazing hair afire and free. If he had time, he would have apologized, yet the words were many and the time too short, so he nodded. And ran.

If he had looked back, he would have noticed her walking toward Delwin, arms raised and hands empty.

In surrender.

*****

Had his legs not been chained, he would have gone to her, despite the guard at his side. Instead, he watched as she walked across the field, thinking her never more enchanting than she was now, with a blood-covered face and mud-covered clothing.

She walked as if she was a queen.

None could take eyes from her, and Willem wondered if she had been mage-touched. If, with all the other gifts that Conri had given to her, he had blessed her with mage-skill as well. He knew not what she had planned, but Caryss walked alone, and Willem knew not where Jarek had gone. When he looked around the field, pulling his eyes from her with difficulty, he saw none but Delwin's men, who all stood as he, awed and unmoving. With urgency, he looked around again, searching for the boy. Without Jarek, escape would be impossible as the skies cleared.

Caryss and he would be returning to the King's City with the Royal Army, he realized, his body quaking with anger at his failure.

There was so much he wanted to say to her, to call out, yet his mouth was still tightly bound and, even distracted, the guards at his sides kept a hold on him. When he looked toward Herrin, the old king was lying still in the wagon, nearly asleep. Willem's only hope was that Herrin would soon remember Caryss and all that she and Sharron had done for him. Only Herrin could offer them safety, he knew.

If he could have begged Delwin for mercy, he would have, yet the Prince's eyes had not strayed from where Caryss walked.

When she was in the center of the field, Delwin called out, "Find the boy!"

Willem watched as two uniformed men kicked at their horses and rode toward the wood, and, looking at Caryss, knew that she had heard Delwin's command as well. Her face, half of it blood-covered and slashed, was not the same face of the girl he had known at the Academy. He almost wept for her then.

And, now, the babe was gone. Nearly all was lost. Her eyes, empty and dark, showed him the truth.

Yet, she did not slow as Delwin and one of his men approached her, nor did she struggle as the soldier grabbed her, clumsily pulling at her arms. Just steps from him, Caryss finally lifted her eyes. Tearlessly, she smiled, and all breath escaped from him.

Through a reddened haze, he listened as she whispered, "*Roim a faidh, an taoh se eirgh.*"

The words, Northern ones, echoed through the valley as if riding on the wind and skipped across the bubbling stream.

Again, Caryss called, louder this time, "*Roim a faidh, an taoh se eirgh.*"

Her words, her last weapon, again rang through the air, "*Roim a faidh, an taoh se eirgh.*"

Willem beamed, his legs straightening beneath him until he stood tall. Overhead, the sky remained gray and light rain dampened them, yet his face glowed as if warmed by the Tretorian sun he had known for so long. For a moment he thought of his time with Caryss under that warm sun, seated in his courtyard with little worries.

He listened for the gentle flapping of wings, but heard nothing. He searched for the glowing eyes of wolf kin, yet saw no one. They were but two, he and Caryss. Willem could not think of another moment when he had loved her more. She stood, as she had always been, just out of his reach. Had she not walked with her head high and her eyes clear, he would have given up. Instead, he did not take his glance from her, memorizing the way her gray-green eyes angled at their corners. The way her fire-kissed hair hung in waves, clinging to her sun-dotted, blood-streaked cheeks. The way her tunic fell, half-opened, beneath her dirtied cape. Her hands, one wrapped in bloodied linen, rose, wiping the rainwater from her face.

That, too, Willem watched, wanting to forget nothing.

For a moment, Caryss was all that he saw.

Until Delwin rushed toward her, his face reddened with rage and his lips pursed open. The Prince grabbed Caryss by the hair, and, yanking her head back, screamed, "You think to entrance me with your spell, foolish girl? Your words are no more than the barking of a bitch!"

With her head angled back, her pale neck spattered with blood, Caryss told him, "It is no spell, Prince Delwin. But it is a warning, one that you would do well to remember."

Her words were loud enough for all who remained in the field to hear.

Pulling her head closer to him with a forceful jerk, he hissed, "The words of the North mean nothing to me. Am I to fear you, healer?"

The prince's laughter crossed the meadow, striking at all who watched; his hand still laced through Caryss's blood-streaked hair.

Willem listened as, once again, she chanted, "*Roim a faidh, an taoh se eirgh.*"

Before she had finished, Delwin pushed her to the ground, her hair still clasped in his hand. Having fallen to her knees, Caryss whimpered, yet did not cry out. Willem stepped toward her then, but was quickly restrained by the two guards beside him. Just as Caryss had been, he was thrown to his knees, with two booted feet pressed to his backs of his legs. Unable to rise, Willem could do nothing but watch.

Under the stormy sky, gray and thick with clouds, Delwin pulled his sword from his scabbard and thrust the tip of it against Caryss's pale neck.

"If you seek to live, you will tell me of your words!"

Her mouth hanging open, as if she could not breathe, Caryss cried out, "In time, the North will rise!"

The soft hush of falling rain blanketed the field. Willem's hands, tied at his back, clenched into tight fists, his knuckles white and large. His eyes, no longer shaded in red, were orbs of gold, yet he could not move. Not even when Delwin's arm lowered and the blade fell from her neck to hang innocently at his side. Not even when Caryss's head dropped, her chin falling to her chest, trembling.

As if a statue of marble and not blood and bone, Willem watched, unmoving and breathless, as the black-clothed Crow leapt forward, grabbing the sword from Delwin. Before any could move or shout, the Crow lifted the sword, swiftly, soundlessly.

Caryss, he realized, had closed her eyes.

When metal met neck, Willem's world darkened.

*****

28

Hands slick and shaking, Jarek struggled to control the panicking horse as it reared in fear. Behind him sat the healer, who was noisily clicking and trying to calm the mount. The two had run into the woods, just as Caryss had instructed. When they had found the horse, he had nearly cried aloud, but the other man's presence stopped him from doing so.

It had taken several tries to settle the gelding, even once the lightning had stopped. His experience helped, but controlling it was proving to be difficult for Jarek as he jerked hard at the leather straps.

Behind him, the healer called, "We must hurry! I hear riders."

Kicking at the mount, Jarek gathered the reins in his hand and pulled, his arms tightening and burning as he yelled, "Hiya!"

Again he kicked, over and over until the horse had stopped circling. Without loosening his grip, Jarek leaned forward until his cheek was beside the gelding's white muzzle. He could feel the healer pressed into his back and knew that the man had copied his stance. Nearly bent in half, they rode, wincing as branches struck them and the horse galloped blindly.

The arm that had taken the arrow hung limply in front of it, unusable and throbbing. The healer had hurriedly wrapped it for him, yet they had no time to do aught else. Caryss had removed what she could, but she too had had little time.

Thinking of the woman made Jarek's eyes sting, and he kicked harder at the horse.

Without turning, he asked in a quaking voice, "What will happen to Caryss and Willem?"

In a voice as unsteady as his own, the man answered, "They will be jailed most likely. If it is true that the King went with her willingly and he is well enough to take back the throne, they will be freed."

Shaking his head to clear his eyes, Jarek told him, "The king does not remember much. Most days, he knows nothing of how he came to be with us."

The crunch of leaves beneath the horses thumping hooves nearly drowned out his words, yet the healer must have heard because he sighed, "She is a healer, boy. They will not harm one who has vowed to do no harm herself."

Both quieted, although neither was comforted.

Nor did either believe that Caryss would escape harm.

*****

"Where am I?" he asked the child.

Her eyes glowed green, and, despite her youth, she seemed wise. He had thought to ask who she was, but, before the words could be uttered, knowledge came. There was only one with such eyes, he remembered.

She was young, yet in her jewel-like gaze he saw that she would never truly be so. Without looking away from her, Willem twisted his body until he was kneeling, his hands still bound behind him. His head ached from where the guard had struck him, and the cloth that had been used to gag him hung loosely around his neck, freeing him to speak.

With effort he tore his eyes from her and looked around hastily, searching for the girl's mother.

Many of Delwin's men were gone, yet the prince and the Tribesman stood where he had last seen them. Two guards, the same men who had previously held him, were near Delwin.

Next to them lay the body of Caryss.

Turning back to the girl, he dropped his head and whispered, "I could do nothing to help her."

His confession sounded hollow and distant, as if he called to the child from across the meadow.

Chiming like the bells at the Academy, the girl told him, "None could save her. I often tried."

"Why are you here, Syrsha?" he uttered, awed by the child, yet sickened with despair.

"I couldn't sleep," she told him, with a shrug of her thin shoulders.

The child, younger than many of the first-years at the Academy, did not weep.

"Am I to die, too?" he asked, looking up at the girl who stood just taller than where he still kneeled.

"Will that answer bring you some comfort?" she asked steadily, as if she knew he would ask.

"Not as much comfort as seeing a blade through my cousin's heart," he hissed, forgetting for a moment that she was much a child.

In her voice of bells, she hummed, "Rest easy, sir. The Prince will pay for what has happened here."

Nodding, Willem again asked, "Will I die here?"

With another sigh, she kneeled next to him, her white sleeping gown folded over her skinny legs, and her pale hands clutched in her lap. Positioned so, she looked like a marble statue, delicate and eternal, gleaming ivory skin and midnight-dyed hair under the rising sun. Willem longed to embrace her, yet his hands burned behind him, the shackles clawing at his wrists.

"You can die a free man here or die an imprisoned one in the King's City. I have seen both happen."

Her dark, thick lashes fluttered over her gemstone eyes, and Willem noticed gaps in her mouth from missing teeth. A child, still, yet her words were ones spoken as if from a woman battle-weary and cold.

"I would die a free man, with a blade in my hand if I have choice. I would die with the blood of my kin on that blade if I have luck."

"Fall to your side, as if asleep," she hurriedly instructed.

When Willem complied, she leaned near to him and said, "Feign sleep until Jarek returns. The Prince's death is mine, but the blood of the Crow is yours if you want it."

"What of my hands?" he mumbled, keeping his cheek pressed to the wet grass.

"Jarek has something that I can use," she told him, looking toward the treeline.

He knew then that the boy would not escape and nearly wept at the thought.

"Can you not help him be gone from here?" he begged the child.

"I have tried," she stated, sitting back on her heels and turning her gaze back to the treeline.

Without moving, he asked, "Are you in danger?"

The girl only shook her head, keeping her face turned toward the wood. Except for her eyes, she had the look of her father, fair and raven-haired, with long, thin limbs. Her eyes were her own, not like her mother's, yet not unseen in the North, either. She would be a girl of beauty, but most would fear her, Willem thought, staring at her through nearly closed eyes. In Cordisia, she would most often be seen as Tribe, although few would know her as such in Cossima and beyond.

"I will die easier knowing that you escaped, Syrsha. Can you tell me as much?" he whispered.

Through slitted eyes, he watched her shrug again as she answered, "Cossima was home to me for many moon years."

When he would have asked more, she raised her hand, pointing across the field. "They have been found. Jarek and the healer."

"Free my hands. I must protect the boy!"

Syrsha rose and explained, "He has my dagger. I can do nothing without it."

At times she sounded young, her words high-pitched and strained, half-whining. Yet he knew that she was no ordinary child. Before he could respond, she walked across the field, glimmering, although none could see her. Syrsha's magic was strong and her image steady, surprising him greatly, for she could not be more than seven moon years past.

He did not need to look up to hear the sound of horses nearing, as the ground beneath him trembled, the grass tickling his cheek. Saying a silent prayer to the gods of his youth, he begged them to spare the boy, true heir to the Rexterran throne. If Delwin learned of the boy's identity, he surely would have him killed, as he had tried moon years before, unsuccessfully. The boy's eyes were gold-rimmed, yet few noticed, and Willem could only pray that his cousin was not one of those who did.

When he caught sight of the boy, Willem nearly cried out to him. Thrown across and tied to one of the Rexterran soldier's horses, Jarek had been stripped naked, except for his dirtied pants, his hands tied at the wrists. Willem knew that the Prince was no fool and had seen the furious power that dwelt in the boy's hands.

Across the field, he listened as Delwin screamed, "Bring me the healer!"

Pietro, clothed but bloodied, was pulled from a horse and marched to where Delwin stood scowling. From where he lay, he could not hear what was discussed, and turned his attention to where the girl lingered. Still unseen, she was able to walk up to where Jarek hung.

Again, he could hear nothing. Yet when the boy lifted his eyes, streaked red and puffy, to where she stood, Willem knew that he, too, had seen her.

Syrsha's hands moved closer, and he understood what she sought, although she moved so quickly that no one could have seen the ice-black dagger emerge from the bottom of the boy's boot. When she began walking toward him, Willem let his head fall back to the ground, once again feigning sleep.

His life, one that had begun in riches before turning to exile, was nearing its end. Yet, as he had told the girl, he believed it would be far better to die with the blood of his enemy on a blade than die imprisoned in his former city. He was still thinking of a life spent in riches, both in the King's City and in Litusia, when Syrsha bent beside him and brought the dagger close, cutting his chains as if they were made of cloth.

Whispering and fading, she told him, "If Delwin dies, Jarek will as well for the Crow has no reason to keep the boy. It is the only reason the Prince yet lives. I have little time left, and I must bring the dagger back with me when I go. If you want the blood of the Crow, it is yours."

When he looked at her, Syrsha's small hands reached for him and his skin prickled, as if a sudden chill had overtaken him.

She placed the hilt of the dagger on his palm, where it burned and blistered, as if the blade itself was made of flame. He had not expected the pain to be so sudden, and Willem jumped to his feet, no longer bound. Before any could stop him, he ran to where his cousin stood alongside the

Tribesman. For a moment he thought of ignoring Syrsha's warning and sliding the sleek dagger across the neck of the Prince, something he had wanted to do for over half his life.

But the child knew something that he could not. She had watched this scene many times before and knew that Jarek would live only if Delwin survived. It had to be enough, he told himself.

With a cry that tore through the meadow, pained and dull, yet drumming and thumping, Willem plunged the dagger into the Crow's chest. The Tribesman had turned to face him a moment too late. The dagger, no bigger than his forearm, was heavy in his hand, hinting at its unnatural origin. With another cry, he turned it, curving it into the Crow as blood seeped onto his fingers and flowed across his arm.

From the Tribesman came a shriek that cut across the field, as if an arrow that pierced Willem's ears until he could hear nothing else. Still he drove the dagger in deeper as the Crow continued to scream.

When the Tribesman fell to his knees, Willem collapsed too, nearly falling on top of him. Only then did he pull the dagger free.

Half-blind with anger, Willem swung a leg over the Crow, and, sitting on him, dragged the black blade over the Tribesman's pale neck. Across his hand, blood poured onto him, thick and red, covering both men until the hilt nearly slipped from him.

The Crow's eyes, darker than anything Willem had ever seen before, stared up at him.

Dead eyes, Willem thought, pleased.

From behind him came yelling. Hands pulled at him, yanking him off the Crow.

Too late, he smiled.

"What have you done?" screamed Delwin.

Most of his cousin's words were lost to him, as the shrieks of the Crow still sounded in his ears. Not until the child came to him did his eyes clear and his hearing return.

Red and wet with blood, he looked at her, imagining the child to be his own.

"I'm sorry that I could do no more," she mumbled.

In her eyes, he saw his death.

Wiping the dagger clean, he told her, "Be not only queen, but healer, too, Syrsha. It was what your mother would want."

Tears filled the girl's eyes. She was only a shadow now, but Willem could see how her green eyes shimmered with sadness at the mention of her mother. Before he handed her the dagger, he raised it, staring at the plain handle, one as usual as thousands in the King's City. His cousin was still calling orders behind him, as two of his men knelt beside the fallen Crow.

Death was on his lips, his tongue thick with the taste of it.

With his eyes on the girl and his thoughts on her mother, he plunged the blade into his heart.

*****

When the Prince's men had come into sight, Pietro had jumped from the horse, yelling for the boy to ride hard. Yet, he had been unable to stop the Guardsmen, who rode past him, falling upon the boy with swords drawn.

Jarek, he recalled Bronwen calling him, wore a longsword at his waist, yet the boy had no time to ready it as Delwin's men circled him. Within moments, Jarek had been stripped of his clothing and sword and tied to the back of one of the Rexterran mounts. Unable to lift his arm, the boy could do little, and a calm resignation had fallen upon him. Pietro, too, was now listless, for he had been unable see Jarek to safety and felt as if he had failed.

Caryss lay dead, and, now, so did Master Ammon.

Moments before, Pietro had watched as the master had murdered the Crow. It had happened so quickly that none of Delwin's men had moved, not even as the Tribesman's body sunk to the grass. Without delay, Willem had fallen upon the dagger himself, causing Delwin to scream at his men to intervene. It was too late, Pietro knew, as he witnessed Ammon collapse.

I have caused this, he thought, barely able to stand as his vision darkened and the ground rippled beneath his feet. Yet, still, he knew that it was he who had led the Prince to Bronwen, just as it was he who had told him of the babe and of the Crow. He was not sorry to see the Tribesman dead, although Pietro wished it had been he who had done so.

Standing before the Prince, half-aware of what was being yelled around him as soldiers dashed about, Pietro thought of how the Academy now seemed a lifetime ago, as if he had never been there at all. He recalled how his hatred for Bronwen had begun, yet she was dead and his hatred long faded. His healer's oath was long broken, his Healer Journey ruined and his life forfeit, as he waited for the Prince to order his death. It was with surprise, but with little care, that Pietro listened when Delwin called to him.

"You are kin, Pietro, which makes your crime worse. I should kill you here, along with the rest, but instead you will be brought to the King's City and tried for your treason and accessory to murder. All will learn of how you tricked me into this trap. Yet, for all your plotting, your plan did not work, and many have died as a result."

374

With spittle flying from his reddened face, Delwin screamed, "Chain him!"

For a moment, he thought of protesting, yet he knew it mattered little. For the second time in a moon, he would be returning to the King's City, the place he had so often longed for during his time at the Academy.

Smiling wanly, Pietro offered no struggle as two soldiers bound his hands and feet, all the while thinking on the blue skies of Litusia. Of Louissia and Shana, even Kennet. As he was led away and placed alongside the King in the back of the wagon, Pietro thought of all he would do differently. His face sticky with blood, he laid it on a crumpled cape, breathing deeply.

The cape smelled sweet, and his head ached less.

Mother's milk, he knew, remembering the smell from his time at the clinic.

Tears mixing with the blood on his cheek, Pietro silently wept for Bronwen and for her babe.

*****

She told him what to say, and though she was moon years younger than he, Jarek did as she instructed. Her eyes, the same ones he had seen for the last two moons, were kind, just as her mother's had been. And when the prince had asked for his name, he did not hesitate, answering quickly with the name the girl had provided.

Tomasz. The name tasted sour on his tongue, like a tart berry, yet he had held the Prince's gaze as he answered, steady and calm.

Again, the Prince addressed him, with gold-rimmed eyes that hid little, making the Prince easy to read.

"How did you come to be with the healer?"

The girl, flickering beside him, still unseen, whispered, "Tell him you come from across the Great Sea, and that my mother found you in the North, in a temple where you have been for moon years."

Again he obeyed the child as he answered, in Common, "A moon or so ago, she and the others showed up at the temple where I had been living. I have no kin, and she offered to take me with her. Moon years before, my parents had died in our voyage to Cordisia from lands east of here. It was either stay in the North, or go with Caryss."

Scowling, the prince demanded, "Was it at the temple where you learned your mage-skill?"

Shaking his head, and with no prompting from the girl, he told him, "I remember little of my parents, Prince, but I have long known how to make the skies rain. The other skills have come as I have gotten older."

"How is it that you know Common?"

375

For a moment, Jarek paused. The girl was still near, just behind him, and he could feel her shadow across his naked back.

"The temple was home to many, from vast and distant lands, my lord. Common was our shared language."

"You must know Eirrannian as well, then, boy, if what you say is true. Tell me what the healer was chanting."

Beside him now, the girl reached for his hand. Her delicate fingers prickled his skin, yet warmed him as she whispered, "In time, the North will rise."

With his blue eyes on the Prince's gold-rimmed ones, his uncle, he knew, Jarek replied, "She sent you warning, my lord."

Spitting onto the grass, Delwin hissed, "What should I fear from one such as her?"

When he did not answer, his uncle continued, "What warning did she give?"

"That one day the North will rise," he told him without hesitation.

He sensed the girl fading as her shadows darkened. Her small fingers gripped his own as she promised, "Jarek, I will visit as often as I can."

When Jarek nodded, he noticed the Prince watching him and struggled to remain still as Syrsha continued whispering.

"Never let them know who you are. Give the prince no reason to fear you or to harm you. Pretend to know nothing of me or of my mother. In time, you will know how to find me."

Around him, the air hummed, and Jarek knew that she had disappeared.

His thoughts were quickly interrupted by the prince who stepped nearer to him and, staring hard, said, "There are ways that my mages can tell if you speak truth or lie. For now, you will return with me to the King's City. Once there, you will be questioned further. If I learn that what you have said is false, you will be imprisoned or worse. Boy, if between here and the King's City any storm of unnatural origin falls upon us, you will be killed. If you want to live, you will pledge yourself to me and to Rexterra."

With a frantic nod and an unbalanced bow, Jarek called, "I give you my word that I will be a loyal and true soldier for Rexterra, my lord."

The Prince turned, nodded toward his men, and ordered his men to bound his hands anew.

To him, Delwin said, "I am not without mercy, Tomasz. If you prove yourself to fight for and defend Rexterra, then I will see you rewarded and ranked within my army."

It would be enough. For now, Jarek knew. Looking around, he realized that Syrsha was gone, just as were all the others.

He was alone.

*****

"I keep hoping that you'll arrive sooner, yet you never do."

Her words were like shards of ice, sharp and jagged, even as sweet as they sounded. Shiny and clear, they cut as if made of steel, slicing at him where little else could.

She was young, and, for a moment he nearly smiled at the strength of her. To time-walk so soon suggested that she was even more than he had hoped. Yet there was danger in that thought, too, and he knew that many would covet her skill.

Despite her eyes, ones that he remembered seeing many moon years before, she looked like kin, dark-haired and pale-skinned. His own eyes altered, blackening in greeting.

"Take me to her," he finally told the child.

His words, simple ones, needed no further explanation as she led him through the trees and into a cleared meadow, near a stream that flowed fast. The sound of water breaking on rock echoed across the field, heavy and pounding. Slowly, the girl, wearing only her nightclothes and without shoes, walked across the field. Her head down, long, black hair falling in waves down the white cotton of her gown, she walked as if she had done so many times already.

Conri followed, silently.

And then he saw her.

He cried out then, for Luna, for none else could understand his wrath. But the sky was light yet, and she offered no solace.

In his rage, his eyes blackened further, hot and burning, as if fire lived there. His hands shook, and his back arched forward. Conri fell to his knees, collapsing onto the still-wet grass. Half-kneeling, he howled, as if the sound could wake her.

Over and over, he howled, as mountain and sky looked on. In the distance, his call was answered with pleading whelps, yet none neared. But for the girl, his daughter, Conri mourned alone.

As he his legs shook and his face contorted, Conri struggled against himself. Fed by his anger, his body began transforming, something he long ago had learned to control with ease. Yet, here, with his daughter beside him, he weakened. The High Lord could see nothing but a thickening haze, dark and blood-tinged. Without recourse, he thought of Caryss, of how she had never seen him except as man.

The thought gave him renewed strength, enough so that he breathed hard, panting and drooling, and fought further. Soon, he stood, unchanged. Man once more.

The child had been watching.

"I would not see her last as wolf."

Syrsha nodded, and he found himself forgetting that she was but a child. Her mother lay dead, steps from them both.

"Why did you come, *faela*?" he finally asked, his eyes shrouded.

Lifting her bony shoulders in a shrug, she told him, "So I can remember."

Caryss, her face bloody and her hair spread around her like coppery flames, lay unmoving. Across her neck was a gash that spread from ear to ear, her once-ivory neck stained crimson, until no white remained. Her eyes were closed, sparing them both. Yet he knew that his daughter had watched her mother die.

"Tell me what happened," he whispered.

Softly, as if she would soon be gone, the child told him, "The prince attacked while they rested. She called the *epidii*, and they came, but the Crow took to the sky and attacked. Two were able to escape, one was not. The *epidiuus* that mother and Jarek rode was struck and fell. They might have escaped when Jarek opened the sky, but an arrow hit his arm. The other healer, the one mother knew well, tried to help. He and Jarek rode for the wood, but they were soon caught."

With a bowed head, he asked, "Whose sword slayed her, *faela*?"

Standing beside her mother, her nightdress falling past her bared feet, the child answered, "It was the Prince's sword, but the Crow took it from him. She was killed by kin, father."

She must have noticed his gaze, because Syrsha hurriedly added, "Willem killed the Crow. You will find his body just there."

Across the field, where the girl pointed, lay a black-robed body. And another nearby.

Unmoving, he asked, "Willem is dead, too, then?"

When she nodded, he asked, "How was Willem able to kill the Crow? I see no trace of fire around the body."

"With my dagger," she whispered, as if reluctant to admit such.

"*Faela*," he began, but as he glanced to the girl, who was now sobbing, her image flickered with the wind, as if made from flame.

When she next looked up, her eyes wet and gleaming; she stared at him with eyes of the wolf. He knew then, his blood hot and his eyes sharp, that Syrsha was Tribe.

"They will all die," she vowed. "Not just the Prince and his men. The Crows, too. I will kill them all."

Reaching for her, his hand found only air, and, pulling back, he told her, "You are but a child. I will do what must be done."

With a furious shake of her head, she stated, "Her death is mine to avenge, father, as you have promised. Have the Wolves ready for my return."

Her voice did not waver in fear.

"*Faela*, this cannot be so, even as much as I may want it. War is coming, no doubt, but we cannot go against his wishes."

With a laugh, the girl stood.

For the first time, he noticed her gap-toothed smile and winced.

"I am not afraid of him as you are," she hissed. "I owe him nothing, for he allowed my mother to be killed."

Her eyes, so much like those of her grandfather, revealed nothing, as if she was without weakness. She had much to learn, he knew, just as he knew that he would not be the one to teach her.

The High Lord would have chastised her, but, for a moment, he saw her as she was. The image steadied, and she shined.

"Your word, father."

Looking once more at Caryss, he sighed, lifting his dark eyes until they found the girl's.

"Her death is yours to avenge. As the Wolves are yours to lead when you are ready."

With a nod, she rose.

"Jarek is with the Prince. He knows where the others have gone, and I think the Delwin's mages will try to find out. Help him, father, whenever he may have need of it."

"I will find him," he told her, without rising. "Go, child, you have been gone too long already."

Despite himself, Conri smiled. The girl was unlike anything he had expected.

*****

29

After several hours of riding, the Prince called for camp to be set. Jarek watched as the remaining men, fewer than before, dismounted and began briskly constructing a high-peaked, thickly-clothed tent. Soon, their job was completed and Prince Delwin jumped from his saddle, threw his reins to his squire, and made for the tent.

For a moment, Jarek sat unwatched, but it did not last long as a large, light-haired guard made his way to him, pulled him from the horse, and guided him to sit by a hastily built fire. The healer, who had been confined to the cart with the King, was nowhere to be seen, and Jarek figured they were to be kept apart. He would have no friends here, he knew, nor many in the King's City.

His shoulder burned where the arrow had scorched him, yet he frequently moved it, making certain that the area did not tighten up. As he sat, his hands still tied at his back and his feet, bound too, Jarek watched the yellow and orange flames leap from the charred logs, as if trying to escape. Feeling envy, he looked about, yet his hopes were dashed as two more guards joined him near the fire.

The prince had told him little, leaving Jarek to worry what would become of him once they arrived in the King's City. The healer was to be jailed, and Jarek wondered if he would, too, having killed two Royal Guardsmen. Once in Rexterra, he thought of time-walking to find his father, yet each time he had tried to do so in the past, Crispin had never been able to see him. He was not as skilled as the girl, and could not risk being seen by others, he figured, nor could he be gone from his body long without suspicion raised.

He would wait, he figured, knowing not what else to do. If Delwin was to be believed, he could join the Royal Army, where his mage-skill would be rewarded.

None talked to him, and only the light-haired one looked his way. A few of the men began heating water, and Jarek's stomach rumbled, having not eaten for most of the day. His feet were dirty and marked with blood, his hands as well. Dried and cracking blood lined his shoulder, yet with no hands free, he could not clean the wound. His sword had been taken from him, as had his teacher. Without Otieno, Jarek would never become the swordmaster he had hoped. Only then did he drop his head to his chest, tears stinging at his eyes.

Dirty and cold, he cried quietly under the blanket of night, longing for the farm and for his mother. His hunched shoulders shook and tears dripped onto his knees, dampening the only clothing that he had been allowed.

The fire jumped and parried, crackling and smoking, and soldiers came and went, talking among themselves but never to Jarek. He was nearly asleep when he was grabbed from behind and lifted into the air. Moments later, he was roughly placed on shaking legs.

"Prince Delwin wants to see you," the light-haired guard said, half-dragging him across the field and into the Prince's tent.

Once inside the tent, it took his eyes several moments to adjust to the orb-lights that floated about, and another long moment to realize that the prince was addressing him. When the guard struck him in the back with his elbow, Jarek looked to his uncle, forcing himself not to tremble.

"My advisors would have me kill you for what you did to my men, Tomasz. Yet, I am not in the habit of killing children. Or I could have you imprisoned alongside the healer, where you would live out your days. Which would you prefer?"

Syrsha's words came to him as he stood half-naked before the prince. *Make him think you mean him no harm*, he reminded himself, knowing that he would have to convince the prince as much for his life to be spared.

His words unsteady and cracking, Jarek told him, "I would prefer neither, sir."

"And what of the men you killed?"

With his eyes shielded by sky, Jarek answered, "There are few who can do what I can, my lord. Perhaps none in all of Cordisia. I am young yet, with none to teach me, and, at times, I have been misguided."

"What would you have me do with you?" the Prince asked from across the tent, seated behind a small table with a plate of food before him.

Jarek needed no further prompting and knew that his answer was his only chance to live outside of a prison, having thought of little else as they rode.

"Let me replace the men that I have taken from you. With training, I can be as good with a sword as they were, and more, too, once the skies are mine to command. There are none like me, my lord, as you yourself must admit. I have no kin and am far from my homeland. Let me fight for Rexterra and at your side."

The prince's eyes were mostly gold and across them flashed interest, but Jarek sensed that there was more.

"What of the Northern healer?"

Keeping his eyes on Delwin, Jarek evenly replied, "She lies dead. As I have said, I know little of her. No one else wanted me, sir, and when she told me that she could take me from the temple, I gladly went. If you prefer, send me back to the temple. Or let me fight at your side."

The golden eyes watched him, as he had never been watched before, and Jarek nearly dropped his gaze. Yet, he stood taller, keeping his sky-tainted eyes on his kin, and keeping the golden rims vacant from his own face.

Let him judge me, he thought, having learned from Otieno how to keep the lie from his face.

"Tell me of the others. The ones who were with you," Delwin called, reaching for his fork.

With ease, Jarek explained, "There is another woman, also from the North, who is healer, too. A dark mage, a man of the forest, and a swordmaster from the south."

"And the babe? What of it?"

Nodding, Jarek replied, "Yes, a girl not yet two moons."

Putting the fork down and chewing slowly, Delwin again brought his gaze to Jarek, then asked, "What was their plan?"

With the lie, he blended in truth, as he answered, "The king was to be delivered to kin of Willem, the man who killed the Tribesman, somewhere in Eirrannia. That is where we were headed when you found us. Caryss had tried to heal your father, my lord, but she feared there was little more she could do. After he was safe, we were to travel to the Southern Cove Islands, to the home of the swordmaster. He promised to instruct me, and said that I showed talent."

"Why would the healer go there?" Delwin demanded.

"To protect the babe. From what I overheard, the babe is Tribe and would be unwelcome in Cordisia."

The prince was silent, as if considering what Jarek had said. While he waited, Jarek struggled to appear calmer than he felt. With little clothing, he felt as if he had little to hide behind, except the lessons that Otieno had drilled with him over the last several moons.

"You think they will head south?" Delwin mused, as if he did not quite believe Jarek.

"I do not know Cordisia as you do, sir, and I have never been out of the North, so I do not know how the babe would be seen. Otieno, the Islander, often talked of his homeland and promised safety was to be found there."

"You would not lie to the man who will one day be your king, would you, Tomasz?"

With his words, Jarek could hear his men reach for sword.

Again he thought of the *diauxie*.

"Did you not mention that your mages would know truth, my lord? If you would bring them in, I could prove myself further."

Again, the Prince sat, in judgment.

After a moment, he called, "Izzo, find the boy some clothing and something to eat. Untie him as well. You will stay at his side, and, if he calls for lightning, you will put your sword through him."

Jarek struggled to keep the emotion from his face, and listened as Delwin continued, "Tomasz, if I find that anything you have said is lie, you will not be spared. Keep your hands at your side and attempt no escape, nor any storm. You have heard my instructions. My men will not hesitate to kill you."

"It will be as you say, my lord," Jarek mumbled, feigning fear.

Dismissed, he followed Izzo from the tent, who said nothing as he led him to another tent, where piles of clothing were laid, as well as bits of armor and uniform. First, the guard cut his feet free, then his hands. Once done, he pointed him to the clothing.

"You will need boots, too, boy, and will have to beg a pair as I see none here," Izzo gruffly said.

As quickly as he could, Jarek dressed, looking nearly identical, except for the coat, to the Royal Guardsman. The clothes hung from him, but he had grown much in the last half-moon year, and would catch the man soon, and surpass him, too, he guessed. When he was finished, they left the tent and went back to the fire, where Izzo fetched him a steaming bowl of soup. The sky was still thick with clouds, and the flames of the fire were the only light to be had, so both men sat fireside and ate.

I am a soldier now, he thought, *a Rexterran one*, looking at the men around him, huddled and quiet around the fire.

Someday, I will be their king.

*****

It was not hard to find the boy. The mages that the Prince traveled with were novice ones, unable to notice when Conri walked through the campsite. The boy had surprised him during his stay in the Tribelands, and his powers were old ones, and rare, even if he still had not fully mastered them. Although, Conri had to admit, Jarek did possess some control over them, evident by the charred bodies that he had found in the meadow.

The High Lord had lost much, yet having the boy with him would offer some solace, he thought, nearing Jarek, who lay curled up beside a dying fire. Wearing a light mask of fog, he approached.

None had seen him, although he cared little as they posed no threat. Each of them he could kill easily, even the Prince.

Gently, he kicked at the boy, rousing him. Blue eyes opened and settled on him, in fear, until recognition came. The boy looked much as he had when he had last seen him in the Tribelands. Yet, nearly all had changed since then.

383

In a whisper that fanned the fire, Conri told him, "Come with me Jarek."

Jarek sat up and shook his head.

"Did you not hear me? I am here to see you safe."

Quietly, as if he was afraid the others would hear him, Jarek mumbled, "If I am to be king, I must learn of the men I will lead, as Otieno once said."

Nothing the boy could have said would have surprised Conri more.

"You wish to stay here? With the Rexterrans?"

"Can I speak freely?" the boy asked.

With a nod, Conri told him, "We are cloaked. None can see me or hear us."

"Then heed me, High Lord. And know that I will never be Delwin's. He thinks me a boy, and that I will nod and listen and obey. And I will. Until I have learned all that I have need to. I am heir, not he, and not my father. Rexterra is mine."

"Syrsha feared for your safety."

"I have sword and sky," Jarek hissed.

"Yet you are here, and Caryss is dead," Conri answered, growing impatient.

Sadness crossed the boy's face, and he dropped his eyes, yet said, "Was it not you who warned me not to call the sky if the babe was near? I had to wait until she was gone. By then, it was too late."

His words, true ones, hung between them, before Conri spoke. "I can do little to help you in Rexterra. Think on this hard, Jarek."

"I have. None will know me for who I am. Not even my own father. I will be Delwin's pet until I am ready."

"You still think to take the throne? A boy's foolish thoughts," Conri warned.

"No more foolish than Syrsha's," Jarek quickly retorted.

The glow of the fire cast its shadow on them both until Conri's pale skin shone, and Jarek's face reddened.

"You know too much, Jarek, and Delwin's mages will question you. Have you thought on that and what it means?"

"I owe much to Caryss and to the others. They are kin to me now."

"You know nothing of what will come."

Conri's words cut through the air, loud and crackling, yet none heard, and the fog around him thickened.

Suddenly, he knew what he must do.

"If I cannot convince you to come with me, then you leave me little choice, Jarek."

The boy paled, looking around hastily.

Conri kneeled beside him as he lay on the ground, and raised his arms, "I must make sure that none know of the babe. Nor of her plans."

In a voice filled with panic, the boy asked, "What do you mean to do?"

"You will not be harmed. But you must forget what you know."

"Lord Conri, please," he begged, reaching for the Tribesman, "I will tell them nothing!"

"You might not want to, but you are not yet strong enough to fight the mages. This is the only way."

The boy sobbed, "You will make me forget all those who I have loved, including those who lie dead."

Jarek's cries were muffled by a growing haze as Conri hummed and placed his hands on the boy's forehead. With little time to work, he hurriedly searched Jarek's thoughts, until he found the boy's first memory of Caryss, when he first saw her in the Grand Palace in the King's City. From there, he mind-locked everything, erasing the boy's memories until nothing remained. Jarek struggled against him, but he was young and his powers too raw to stand against Conri's.

Within moments, the mind-lock was complete.

When he dropped his hands, the boy looked at him with renewed fear, then glanced around blankly. With little time, Corni hurried to explain what had occurred.

"Jarek, you are with Prince Delwin and his men. He is no friend to you, but you will pretend that he is. Let none know of your true identity, for you will not long survive in the King's City if it becomes known. Learn what you can, all that you can, and strengthen both sword and sky. I mean you no harm, nor will I, if you see me again. If you have need of me, seek out a dark mage. Any will know how to find me. Learn and grow, Jarek, until the time comes."

"What time?" the boy grumbled, his words thick and his eyes wide, as if he had just woken.

With a smile that showed sharpened teeth, Conri answered, "To take the throne."

Before the boy could speak, Conri was gone, drifting away from the fire and toward the edge of the camp. To his left was a tent, larger than the others that dotted the camp, and he knew it must be Delwin's. His eyes darkened, yet he kept walking, thinking of his promise to the child.

When he saw the wagon, the same one that Caryss had brought to his compound, Conri stopped.

Then walked toward it, deliberate and slow.

As he neared, his hands, pale and white, the hands of his moon mother, grayed.

He did not struggle. Not this time. Not here. Soon, his long fingers were covered in fur, soft and silent. His dark hair shortened, edging a silver-white face, fur-covered now too. His nose lengthened, his teeth sharpened further. Arms became legs, and he dropped to the ground, dirt beneath his paws.

Behind him trailed a tail, a sliver of moon, arched and dipped in night.

When he leaped into the wagon, he made no sound. When his teeth seized the King's neck, he made no sound.

As he bit into the frail man's skin, blood spilled from Herrin's neck, silently. The king's eyes never opened nor did he cry out. His face, scarred and lined, was splattered with blood, his lips red, his cheeks dotted.

The tunic he wore, once a faded blue, was nearly black with blood, sticky and smelling of steel and salt. Herrin had not once moved, peaceful in sleep. He, too, made no sound.

Dropping the King from his grasp, Conri jumped back. His jaw wide, his long tongue licked the blood from his lips. His dark eyes began to lighten, his paws, tipped in red, shed their fur. Four legs became two again as his tail disappeared.

His face, man once more, remained blood-streaked, smeared and stained with the blood of the King.

Conri lunged from the wagon and fled.

War had come.

*****

EPILOGUE

"Can't you see how she is struggling? Have pity, Otieno, and take the sword from her."

The mage's words were true ones, yet Otieno scowled. "While she rests, her enemies gather."

With a laugh, Aldric told him, "She has not yet seen her fifth moon year, *diauxie*, yet everywhere she goes, she must drag that sword with her."

"The more she carries it, the sooner she will be able to raise it," the man dryly answered, undeterred.

Aldric looked to Gregorr for help, but the *fennidi* offered none, nor did Sharron, who was more mother to the girl than any of them.

With a sigh, Aldric groused, "When Syrsha rules, I will be beside her while you three will be in the kitchens."

The child laughed, smiling broadly, her tanned cheeks high and her green eyes bright under the Cossiman sun.

"None of them can cook, Aldric!" she squealed. "But I will find jobs for them. Otieno can clean my sword, and Gregorr can tend to my gardens. And Sharron, well, she can take care of the *epidii*."

"The *epidii*?" Aldric asked.

"Gregorr told me that I shall have as many as I want when I am queen."

Her voice was high, song-like, and even Otieno smiled.

"To be queen, you must first learn to lift that sword, little one," he told her, hiding his amusement.

"I want my other sword back," she huffed, her lips full and pouty.

"The other was the blade of a babe. You are nearly five now, *faela*, and five moon year-olds must not use toys for swords."

Aldric had heard Otieno say similar words many times, and he knew the sense in them, yet still it pained him to watch Syrsha walking from the square with the large broadsword being pulled behind her, arms too weak to lift it back into its sheathe.

They had been in Cossima for nearly five moon years, and the city had become home. On three sides was sea, yet to the west was land. A great wall had been built, and few arrived but through the ports, as they had, moon years prior. Their coin had allowed them to purchase a home several blocks from the city square, one with a large courtyard where Otieno and Syrsha could often be found. Gregorr and Sharron had quickly established a reputation for healing the town's sick and injured, and a room had to be set up near the front of the house to accommodate all their visitors.

Aldric spent his time in study, or teaching the girl the ways of the mages, which early on she showed talent for. When she began to talk, she was well-versed in several languages, and all of them came to her with ease. Cordisia seemed far, yet she spoke Common and Eirrannian as if she had never left. None could teach her the language of her father, yet she knew it nonetheless. None asked her how.

Cossima itself was a unique town, and their group fit in well, despite Otieno's dark skin and Gregorr's green. There was talk that soon they must depart, yet none was in a hurry, as Syrsha thrived.

When they arrived back at the house, sun-bleached and gleaming, Syrsha's cries interrupted his musings.

"Can I drop it now, Akkachi?"

"One must never drop her sword," he chastised.

With a huff and a whimper, she continued to drag the sword behind her, over the painted tiles, and into the house.

"Do not look at me like that, mage," Otieno told him. "You have spent too many moon years for hire to not know better."

"Ofttimes, you forget she is a child," Aldric countered.

With his soft brown eyes on the mage, Otieno warned, "I forget nothing. She is a child. A child of the wolf."

*****

Queen of Stars and Shadows, Book Three, Coming December 2016

Not for the first time, he found her dozing with a sword in her lap. Reaching for his own curved blade, Otieno neared, surprisingly silent as his thick boots crushed the half-browned grass that separated student from master. Across her face, waves of black tresses hung, tinted red by the midday sun, serving as mask and helm and obscuring her gaze.

Her chest rose softly, he watched, as her sky-colored tunic flitted near her pale neck.

Beside her lay the faded leather armor she had worn for the last moon year. Speckled with blood and streaked with dirt, it appeared well-used, as he knew it to be. Yet, piled in a heap just outside of her reach, the armor was now useless.

And her neck unguarded.

He did not pause as he pulled his sword from its sheathe, without sound, gently, as if it was no more than a feather.

The girl leaned against a long-branched tree, its ferny leaves offering a shaded veil against the cloudless sky. Dank air wetted his skin and his long braids stuck to his damp face, but Otieno's fingers did not move from the hilt of the sword.

Steps from the girl now, he smiled. With a lunge forward, he thrust the tip of the scimitar toward her ivory neck.

He missed, as she rolled away from him, already on her feet behind him, as graceful and fast as the desert cats they had seen the moon year before on a rare trip outside the city.

Laughing, the sound young and high, she called to him, "You smell of roses and sage. As you often do after an evening spent in the bathhouse. Even in slumber, I knew that you had come."

With a shrug, he pointed toward her armor and asked, "What good is it unworn?"

"It slows me down," she explained. "I only wear it because you insist that I must."

Her own sword, larger than his in length and width, was cupped between slender fingers, its sharp point resting on the grass. Long before, she had learned to keep it near. When she had not, the punishment was severe. He had been a difficult teacher, as for the last fifteen moon years, had trained her without much respite. There were others to offer the girl instruction on mage-craft and the healing arts – Sharron, Gregorr, and Aldric. But, it was he alone who would keep her alive.

"*Faela*, you will one day face an enemy who is even quicker than you.

Just as there will be many who are stronger. Do I need to explain again how the well-balanced fighter is the enduring one?"

She did not reach for the armor as she answered, "I mastered the spear moon years ago, Akkachi. And the scimitar as well. Even you must admit to being impressed with my skills with the Greatsword. Few can wield it as I do."

The girl was more than student to him, and had been since her birth, moon years before, across the seas in Cordisia. He had watched her mother die, along with the girl, although he had been too far to offer aid. From the back of an *epidiuus*, he had witnessed the Crow slice open Caryss's throat. His screams that followed had caused his voice to fall silent for nearly a quarter-moon after, and it was not until they had reached Cossima that he once again spoke.

Shaking his head to free himself from the memory, he asked her, "What is it that you are seeking? I know you well enough to understand this game, *faela*."

Her mother had named the babe Syrsha, an Eirrannian name, yet none here called her so. They had long sought to keep her hidden, and most knew her in Cossima as Kali, a name out of the East, aptly given because of the child's midnight-hued hair. But even then, Aldric, Gregorr, and he rarely called her anything but *faela*, for they all recognized her to be a child of the wolf.

It was only Sharron who spoke to her of Cordisia and in the language of the North. Just as it was only the Northern healer who whispered the girl's true name as she told tales of Caryss. Sharron had known the girl's mother the longest, yet even she could not tell Syrsha much of her mother's story. Aldric, the mage, perhaps knew the most of the girl, for he understood more than any of them about the Tribe and Conri, the High Lord of the Wolves and the girl's father.

Fifteen years removed from Caryss's murder, the story was still a painful one and difficult to discuss. Even less did they speak of the High Lord or Syrsha's god-tainted blood.

Any news from Cordisia came from what Aldric could learn on his morning trips to the market, and most of it of late was dire.

And the girl knew as much.

Before she could answer, he stepped close and chastised, "I know how weary you grow of Cossima, but it is not yet time to return to Cordisia. With Crispin's death, Delwin became king, and, with that, war will come."

He did not need to explain how much had changed with Crispin's death. Since their exit from Cordisia, he had ruled as king, following the murder of his father as the hands of Syrsha's. A tenuous peace followed, despite Delwin's insistence that the Tribe be destroyed. Word had come that while Crispin sat the throne, Delwin built his army even stronger, offering rank to mage-trained soldiers. He also expanded the Lightkeepers, tripling their numbers and opening the royal coffers for their use. With mage and Lightkeeper at his side, Delwin grew anxious, Aldric believed.

Within a moon year, war between Rexterra and Tribe would come, he reminded her again.

"It is not to Cordisia that I want to go," she countered. "There is little more for me here, Akkachi, even you must recognize that. I have thought long on this and know where it is that we must visit."

Pulling his hair from his mahogany face, he scowled at her. "You have convinced the others that it is time to depart."

He watched as she forced her own pale face to reveal nothing.

"The others agree that we must soon leave. Even Aldric, who warned me that Delwin has renewed his interest in finding me. The reward for my capture would give a man a small kingdom, Otieno. We have stayed too long here, and many suspect that I am not Kali."

Syrsha's eyes, unforgettable and gem-like, stared at him, and he knew the game that she now played. Even aging and without practice, Aldric had taught her well. There would be few who could fool the girl, even those mage-trained.

"You waste my time, girl. Be out with it," he finally insisted.

She was little more than a child, yet of late she thought herself more. In their safety, she would become reckless, he suddenly realized. Even now, the girl found herself to be undefeatable. When she looked away, swinging the heavy sword until it lay across her back, where she sheathed it, Otieno's cheeks burned.

In his anger, he nearly reached for his Greatsword, yet soon she was speaking and his clenched fists hung at his side.

"I have heard tales of the Sythians and of their skills with the bow. I have learned much here, but the courtyard offers little room for archery. Aldric has told me much about them, and they are but a half-moon ride north from here."

A long hiss escaped his full lips. "The bow is the coward's weapon."

"You are wrong. It is the woman's weapon. The Sythians need no men to lead their armies, for their aim is rarely off and their horses swift and strong."

"All women need men, child."

Her laugh echoed off clay bricks and faded grass as her teeth, straight and shining, gleamed bright. Otieno could not stay his hand as the bells of her laughter rang around him. Without armor, Syrsha was no match for the Greatsword, so he grabbed the short broadsword from near his hip and raised it. Just as quickly, the girl had daggers in each hand.

The courtyard quieted, but her emerald eyes dazzled with amusement. She would let him strike first, he knew, stepping toward her slowly as he watched the leather-hilted daggers crossed in front of her. As the broadsword came toward her, Syrsha would attack, dodging his charge with a roll until her daggers were near enough to press into his skin.

Instead of circling the sword above her for a downward slash, the *diauxie* ducked low, throwing his shoulder to the ground and spinning, until his hands were near enough to her legs to pull her down. In her surprise, she offered no counter.

Before she could recover, he pinned her hands above her head, the daggers sharp but unthreatening. The girl was strong, more so than most men. She was god-kin and no easy fight. Yet he was no ordinary man, either.

With the broadsword in his strong hand, he brought the hilt toward her, striking her hard across the cheek.

Syrsha cried out and struggled to free herself. The right side of her face was red and puffy, but Otieno cared little.

Rising on his own, he told her, "You have grown lazy and predictable in your insolence. Have Sharron tend to your cheek."

She began to argue, but he again lifted the sword, as if he would strike her anew where she still lay.

"We will make way to Sythia within the moon. Tell the others."

As he walked away from her, Otieno could hear her shouting at him.

"You are not my father, akkachi!" she screamed, her voice edged in shadow.

He did not turn around, nor did he call out to her.

I am not your father, he thought. *The High Lord would have left you bloody and silent.*

****